JOHN DAVID'S calling

Book one,
1967 - 1970
  The Revivalist Trilogy

Praying my story gives God glory!

A companion book...

JOHN DAVID'S CALLING, book one of **The Revivalist Trilogy** may also be considered a '**Companion Book**' to the **Texas Romance Family Saga** as David is by blood, a Nightingale, son of Buddy and Sandy (CHIEF OF SINNERS), grandson of Nathaniel and Evelyn (MIGHTY TO SAVE), and great-grandson of Charley and Lacey Rose (HEARTS STOLEN and JUST KIN). Rosaleen Fogelsong Nightingale Baylor is his great-great-grandmother, and the famous Texas Ranger Levi Baylor, his step great-great-grandfather.

David was the baby on Sandy's hip at the end of CHIEF OF SINNERS, book nine and the last installment of Caryl's Texas Romance Family Saga series.

So, if you've enjoyed that series, you will undoubtedly love this trilogy. Yet, each story totally stands alone, so if it's your first to read, and you find yourself loving these characters . . . you have many novels in store!

Do go back to the prequel VOW UNBROKEN—published by Simon and Schuster—then enjoy the whole series—nine more titles—covering five generations and over a century of love and struggles, faith, and overcoming, and characters you're sure to consider friends or wish they were family!

You'll enjoy another companion story, THE BEDWARMER'S SON in which Nathaniel and Buddy Nightingale make an appearance. In it, you'll also meet the Harris family ancestors. (CHIEF's heroine Sandra Louise and her father Mister John Harris)

More Companion books are coming in 2019 with HANNAH'S WILDERNESS and KING DAVID'S TABERNACLE.

All of Caryl's Books

Historical Christian
Texas Romance Family Saga *Vow Unbroken* 1832 / *Hearts Stolen* 1839-44 / *Hope Reborn* 1850-51 / *Sins of the Mothers* 1851-53 / *Daughters of the Heart* 1853-54 / *Just Kin* 1861-65 / *At Liberty to Love* 1865-66 / *Covering Love* 1885-86 / *Mighty to Save* 1918-24 / *Chief of Sinners* 1826-1951
Companion Books *The Bedwarmer's Son* 1859 & 1926 / *Son of Promise* 1950 / *John David's Calling* 1967-70
Others *Silent Harmony* 1867 /

Contemporary Christian
Red River Romances *The Preacher's Faith* / *Sing a New Song* / *One and Done*
Apple Orchard Romances *Lady Luck's a Loser*

Biblical Fiction
The Generations *A Little Lower Than the Angels* / *Then the Deluge Comes* / *Replenish the Earth* / *Children of Eber*
Others *I AM My Beloved* /

Mid-Grade / Young Adult
River Bottom Ranch Stories *The Adventures of Sergeant Socks: The Journey Home, bk 1* / *The Bravest Heart, bk 2* / *Amazing Graci, Guardian of the River Bottom Goats, bk 3*
Days of Dread Trilogy *The King's Highway, bk 1*

Miscellaneous Novels
The Thief of Dreams ~ **not written for the Christian market!** / *The Price Paid (based on WWII true story)* / *Absolute Pi* (audio; mystery) / *Apple Orchard B&B* (re-released as Lady Luck's a Loser)
Non-fiction
Great Firehouse Cooks of Texas / *Antiquing in North Texas* / *Story & Style, The Craft of Writing Creative Fiction*

Five Star Review!

This book is about revival and Pentecostal healing ministries as David is called from the staunch, sedate church of the grandfather who raised him to the Spirit-led ministry style of his father who wasn't in his life much as a child. He's torn between obeying God and devotion to his grandfather. In the mix is a school girl he has his heart set on marrying. There are moments of crying, both for praising the Lord and the suffering of someone, as well as several laugh-out-loud situations. A wonderful story of obeying God.

~ Cindy Nipper, an Oregon reader

John David's Calling is the beginning for a whole new exciting series, The Revivalist, by Caryl McAdoo. I was so excited when I found out she was coming out with a new series. After reading this one, I was not disappointed. I have always enjoyed her other historical fiction books, and this one was no exception.

John David Nightingale was likable from the start. His struggles and turmoil were relatable for me. I believe other readers will think so, too. I enjoy watching him as a character and had no problem turning the pages to see where he was going to be lead to next.

I give John David's Calling a well-deserved 5-plus Stars, and I highly recommend it. I will be eagerly waiting for book two from The Revivalist series. I cannot wait to see what Caryl McAdoo comes up with next.
A fabulous read that is full of faith and inspiration.

~ Amy Campbell, a Virginia reader

Dedication

My dedication of this story is to all those who God has called that answered, "Yes, Lord." We are His hands and feet in the earth. Who would go if not me? If not you? He knew us from our mother's womb and had a plan for us even then.

And to my dearest husband and best friend since we were sixteen in 1966, I dedicate Son of Promise.

And to my second son, Gregory William McAdoo who also has God's call on his life; a mother so loves her sons and prays for God's very best. Greg and his wife Melissa have a purpose to fulfill in this world for the Kingdom, and this mother's heart prays they will choose to answer and obey.

I love you, Son. I love you, too, Melissa—one with him.

It is a good thing to give thanks unto the LORD, and to sing praises unto thy name, O Most High!

To shew forth thy lovingkindness in the morning, and thy faithfulness every night, Upon an instrument of ten strings, and upon the psaltery; upon the harp with a solemn sound.

For thou, LORD, hast made me glad through thy work: I will triumph in the works of thy hands.

Psalm 92:1-4

Acknowledgement

    First acknowledgement always goes to God Who faithfully guides me. My Heavenly Father is due all the glory.

    And to my 'golden' husband Ron—fifty years wedded in June 2018—who harbors such patience and kindness—my sweetest heart and beloved who loves me more today than yesterday, but less than tomorrow. An awesome man God blessed with wisdom and for some unknown reason to me, created in his mother's womb to be my husband.

    And to a bevy of lovely ladies who deserve acknowledgement for catching my errors and reading my novels and reviewing them for me: Lenda Selph my proof reader, Louise Koiner, Judy Schexnayder, Cindy Nipper, Cass Wessel, and more. I never mean to leave anyone out! I love you and thank you all and thank you profusely!

    And for my cover, I have Carpe Librum and Evelyne LaBelle to thank! I'm blessed that God crossed our paths and thank Him! Thank you, sweet Evelyne!

For I know the thoughts that I think toward you, saith the LORD, thoughts of peace, and not of evil, to give you an expected end. Then shall ye call upon me, and ye shall go and pray unto me, and I will hearken unto you.

And ye shall seek me, and find me, when ye shall search for me with all your heart. And I will be found of you, saith the LORD: and I will turn away your captivity, and I will gather you from all the nations, and from all the places whither I have driven you, saith the LORD.

And I will bring you again into the place whence I caused you to be carried away captive. Because ye have said, The LORD hath raised us up prophets in Babylon;

Jeremiah 29:11-15

JOHN DAVID'S *calling*

*Book one,
1967 - 1970
The Revivalist Trilogy*

CARYL McADOO

Praying my story gives God glory!

This book is a work of fiction. Any references to historical events, real people, or real places are used fictitiously. Other names, places, characters, and events are products of the author's imaginations, and any resemblance to actual events or places or persons, living or dead, is entirely coincidental.

© 2018 by Caryl McAdoo

All rights reserved including the right to reproduce this book or portions thereof in any form whatsoever- except short passages for reviews – without express permission. For information, address Post Office Box 622, Clarksville, Texas, 75426.

First Edition May 5, 2018

Printed and bound in the United States of America

ISBN-13 : 978-198-6217-682
ISBN-10 : 198-6217-68X
AISN : B07B6WJNZ3 (ebook)

For contact with the author or speaking engagements, please visit www.CarylMcAdoo.com
or write Post Office Box 622, Clarksville, Texas 75426

Chapter One

He'd about made up his mind; been thinking on it a while though he hadn't asked anyone's counsel. David eased the truck to a stop right at the edge of Aunt Iva's property then faced his cousin. Good as any to try it out on.

"Sonny, my man, I've made up my mind. Want you to be the first to know."

"Hey! What are we talking? You finally given up grape for Coca-Cola? Because I know you ain't decided to enlist."

His favorite cousin could always put things in perspective. He grinned. "Nah, nothing as dramatic as that. I've decided to change my name. I'm going to court and make it official. But from now on, I'm John David Nightingale."

"Oh man! You can't do that. Everyone will think you're copying John David Crow! Plus, why whip up all the tongue-waggers? Reminding everyone about your mama and daddy can't be any good for her."

"I know, but—"

"Hey, she ain't going to like it any more than Uncle John. What? You wanting to give them all a good reason to call you a bast—"

"Don't you dare, Sonny Harris." David held up a warning finger then waved him off. Of all people!

"Just like you said. I know who my father is, and it's for sure I don't want to carry Harry Prescott's name. I like John David way more than David John. Sounds better; don't you think?"

"Oh yeah. Just rolls off your tongue. But I never heard of anyone changing their name. Don't you have to be eighteen or something?" Sonny pulled out a smoke and flicked the match to life with his thumbnail. " 'Sides, ain't Jay's first name John?"

"Yeah, but so what? I'm still going by David. I'll sign J. David Nightingale."

"Uncle John's going to flip, and you know it."

"I'm hoping me putting his name ahead of David might soften the blow, you know?" He pinched the cigarette from his cousin's mouth, took a drag, then replaced it and blew smoke rings out the truck window.

"I love my grandfather—both of them—and think each one will know I'm trying to honor him. PawPaw for putting John first and Gramps . . . He's going to love me finally being a Nightingale."

"Whatever." Sonny turned sideways in the seat, facing him. "Hey, before we kill us a mess of coons, there's something I need to tell you."

"Shoot. I'm all ears."

"You know how Dad thinks I'm going to Mama's for a month?"

"Yeah, what about it?"

"Well, I'm not. I wrote her last week and told her I'm staying here to work with you, hauling hay and hunting coons and ringtails." He laughed. "Me and Sissy Kellogg are headed to San Francisco, man. Don't you know it's the summer of love?"

"Now that's the craziest scheme I've ever heard."

"Not as crazy as changing your name, nitwit."

"You're going to California. With Sissy." David shook his head. "How you going to get there? Where are you going to stay?"

"Who knows? First things first though. Here's the deal. I need you to front me the money I've got coming for our skins."

"I thought we decided you were going to stay away from Sissy."

"Well . . . We did talk about that, but . . ."

The silence hung heavy for a minute.

"But what?"

"Hey, she's a hard lady to say no to. Aren't you even a little interested in the hippies and all their free love and—"

"Drugs and booze and no telling what else those idiots are doing."

"What are you talking about? You telling me that doesn't all sound grand?"

"What if you get out there and can't get back? School will be starting up before you know it. You're not thinking of dropping out. That'd ruin everything. It's our senior year for crying out loud. Promise me you're coming back."

"Maybe, maybe not. Just have to see. Hey, did you hear? Paul joined the Marines."

"Yeah, I did. But you're dodging. Why the maybe? If you have to, go on out West and check out the hippies, but then get on back here. In time for school. You hear? Give me your word."

"How about you give me yours?" Sonny flipped on his headset, noodled out and sat on the truck's open window edge, then shined his light into the night.

With that night's haul, his cousin talked him into fronting him twenty bucks against his share of the furs, but only after Sonny gave his word to come back in time for school.

Couldn't rightly lose, even not being sure what the cache would bring—them being summer pelts and all—but they'd still have some value. Any differences would be settled on his return.

Of course Sonny wanted to get the money the next morning, but in the end, had to agree to show up at the evening's service at the Cypress Springs Church of Christ to collect his buckage.

Since, unbeknownst to his grandfather, David would not be at his sweetheart's Methodist Church there in town that Sunday morn. No sir. He planned on squiring Hannah and her cousin to his other grandfather's Pine Bluff Holiness Church.

PawPaw would never consent to it.

He pointed at Sonny's nose again. "Don't you dare tell him. Far as you know, I'm at Hannah's church with her. Got it?"

Still a freshman, his girl wasn't allowed to car date, but having the third wheel along, reluctantly, her mother allowed the foray. So that's how on the first Sunday of his summer vacation, David found himself outside the house of his one true love.

That fact he'd known for four years, since she turned ten. Even though only fourteen himself back then, he knew it; just like he knew that the Hill County—and not Dallas—was his home.

He straightened his tie, wiped off the truck's bench seat, then hurried up her walk. PawPaw and MawMaw allowed him to attend Hannah's church one Sunday morning every even month, and an evening service on the odd ones.

That proved to be about all the old man could stand him being away from the Church of Christ, even if David could talk his grandmother into about anything. With a deep sigh, he grinned, anticipating her face.

The door opened.

"David! Good morning, dear. Don't you look yummy, all spiffed up in your suit." Hannah's mother greeted him with open arms. He kept his eye on the prize. Having Hannah snugged in tight would be worth every bit of her father's grilling.

"Yes, sir. Straight there and back. No lollygagging. We'll be here for dinner. Yes, sir. No problem, sir, but remember how my grandfather Nightingale gets long-winded sometimes. It wouldn't do for us to walk out of the service before he's done, sir. And it is a twenty-minute drive."

Took all of fifteen minutes to clear the Morrison's home, but he couldn't complain, wouldn't, not ever. Being alone with her—Jill didn't count—bouncing down the farm-to-market, he was king just like his namesake!

"Tell her, David." Hannah pointed to the spot where his grandfather's tent had once stood.

He parked the truck then looked past his love to her cousin.

"According to my Aunt Em and Uncle Travis and about thirty other folks, not counting my grandfather, this monster twister wrecked the old church and tore the tent canvas off, but nary a single soul within the poles of that tent was harmed, not even a scratch."

The girl's eyes widened. "Really?"

"Not one of the poles was uprooted, and the lamps still hung on each one, burning! Auntie said it was like being in the midst of a whirlwind, but . . ." He laughed.

"She said everyone was dancing all around, except her, then my father pulled her to her feet." He shook his head. "I'd have give about anything to see it. But . . ." He met the girls' gazes. "Everyone tells the same story."

"I told you so." Hannah took his hand and squeezed.

Curls flapping her cheeks, Jill shook her head. She looked so silly, but he wasn't about to tell her.

"Did she?"

A heartbeat or three passed. Did who what?

"Dance I mean."

Ah. He realized what she asked. "Oh yeah, Auntie took to carrying on like the rest of them. It was a miracle, and from all I heard, those who lived it did some celebrating." He looked toward the church building.

"Come on. We best get on inside. Don't want to have to sit in the back."

The Reverend Nathaniel Nightingale made a fuss, but that's what his holy rolling grandfather did. Truth be known, it's always been one of the things he loved his grandfather for—nothing like John Harris, who hardly ever showed any emotion.

But David loved them both.

Shame they didn't truck much with each other. Outside of the big Fourth of July picnic, didn't see one another at all, except at his football games—and that didn't mean they sat together either.

"David!" Gramps ushered him and girls toward the front pew. "Would you lead the singing for me, Son?"

He shook his head, but the old man only nodded, then looked to Hannah. "Hello, young lady, and welcome. We're glad to have you and your friend. You ever hear my grandson sing?"

"Yes, sir. He's great all right."

His grandfather looked around the small sanctuary. "Wynona! Come over here and say hello to David's friends."

Making her way toward them, she shook hands and gave two more hugs.

"Hello, David. It's so good to see you again. I put a roast in the oven this morning and made banana pudding last night. Hope you and your pretty girlfriends can stay for dinner after the service."

"Oh no, ma'am. Sounds great, but we're eating with her parents today. I promised to get her right back straight after church but thank you for the invite." He turned to Gramps. "I'd appreciate it if you could not go too long past noon."

"Don't talk to me about that, Son, talk to Him." He pointed upwards and faced his lady friend who'd surely been responsible for keeping him going—at least in part. "I'm trying to get this boy to agree to leading the singing."

"Oh, David. That'd be such a pleasure. I'd just love to hear you sing this morning."

"Me, too!" Hannah held her hand out to Miss Winnie. "I'm so glad to meet you, ma'am. I'm Hannah Morrison."

"You certainly are. I remember you from the picnic. Your folks came a couple of years back, didn't they? So glad you could come this morning."

"Me, too, and this is my cousin Jill—our chaperone." She

wiggled her brows, smiling that beautiful smile he loved.

"It's settled then." Gramps patted David's shoulder. "We outvoted you."

"You don't have hymnals. I don't know the songs. How can I lead?"

The reverend grinned. "Oh, just sing whatever the Lord lays on your heart, Son. It'll be fine."

Too soon it got started. An opening prayer followed by announcements, followed by a testimonial. Why didn't the Church of Christ have those? He so enjoyed hearing the great things God did in peoples' lives. Seemed like a grand idea.

"This morning the Lord has blessed us! My grandson and two of his friends are here, and David agreed to lead praise and worship. Come on, boy."

A hardy round of amens pushed him toward the platform. He'd have to tell Gramps he'd quit coming if he did that to him again . . . of course, he'd been meaning to since he first started getting David to lead the music two years prior.

Before it was always only one song—like their special music or something. But this . . . He climbed the two steps onto the platform.

Leading music at the Church of Christ was different. They never asked him to except on Sunday evenings and chose all the songs for him ahead of time.

"Morning, folks."

A hearty response in kind followed.

"Well, my Gramps threw me a curve this morning." They all laughed.

A guy in the back hollered, "Doesn't he always?" A new wave of chuckles rolled over the congregation.

"Yes, sir. That's about right, but I don't rightly know what I'm doing."

The faces blurred. They faded into a mist of golden hues with sparkling stars everywhere. How amazing. He wiped his eyes, but still the beautiful fog held. Then a thousand or more voices sang in unison, extolling the majesty of God.

Wow. Amazing. Where could they be? Who were they? A warmth spread from his heart to his mouth.

For a moment, he held back then had no choice but to open his mouth and sing. "Blessed be, blessed be. Blessed be the name of the Lord! Holy be, holy be. Holy be the name of the Lord! There is no one."

They ladies all echoed a lovely, high pitched. "No one."

Were they hearing the voices, too?

"There is no one. There is no one like unto You." That part repeated, and he started all over, singing with the choir wherever they were. The second time through he peeked. He could see faces again, but the stars remained.

The congregation sang with him, hands waving toward Heaven all across the sanctuary. And in full voice, too.

Next thing he knew, he'd sung it through at least ten times.

After the first song trailed off, another came, then two more after that. No telling how long he led that last one, a slow, somber song of worship. If he peeked again, he'd surely see the Lord Himself walking up the aisle and among the people.

At some point, he had to drop to his knees then press his forehead to the floorboards. Like, like he bowed before the very throne of God. That song continued three more times though, then a hush fell over the room.

At first, a few sniffs here and there broke the silence. Then a throaty sob burst from the left side, maybe halfway back. Then another closer. He raised up. Jill stood beside his grandfather, crying her eyes out. He looked around the room.

Others wiped their cheeks. Some held their hands out toward Jill. He'd seen them do that before. They were praying for her.

A realization came. She was getting saved! The Holy Ghost had convicted her while he sang. How cool was that? He studied Hannah. Head bowed, she appeared to be praying, too.

His left foot took to tapping. He bounced up on his toes a couple of times. A river of life welled up inside him, then he had to dance, He couldn't help it. He twirled.

John David's Calling

Was that how they'd been after the twister? He never could understand it before. The Church of Christ taught him no dancing. Period. So, to do it in church seemed so ludicrous.

From multiple twirls, arms flung out to his sides, he leaped off the platform. Probably making a complete fool of himself. He didn't know how to dance! But he didn't care. Cousin Jill had escaped hell's fire.

Heaven was surely rejoicing, the angels and the great cloud of witnesses! Why shouldn't he? Plus, he'd . . . no. Only the Lord could save someone.

Had to remember that; pride went before destruction and a haughty spirit before a fall. How many times had his other grandfather pounded that proverb into him? He was blessed that God used him as a part of the process.

"Hallelujah!" Psalm says shout to the Lord all the earth. Gramps made sure David knew a lot of Scriptures, too.

"Bless the Lord!"

The shouting caught and praises around the sanctuary filled the atmosphere with a glorious joy.

"Glory! Glory to the Lord!"

Maybe half or better of the folks had either joined in the dancing at the front of the church or been carrying on in place.

Guess the others didn't like making fools of themselves, but many of them stood with arms outstretched to Heaven and tears streaming down their faces. He loved these people and Gramps' church and being in the presence of the Lord.

The jubilation played out, and the Reverend said a few words. He introduced the newest Christian to his congregation. He bent down and whispered in Jill's ear.

"Yes, sir." She nodded with a grin that stretched almost ear to ear. "I'm saved!" Joyful tears ran down her cheeks. "Jesus saved me! I . . . oh . . ." She sniffed, swallowed, then scanned all the faces as though seeing them for the first time.

"I hated my parents always making me go to church every Sunday. But today . . . I thought it might be fun, I mean . . .uh, no disrespect. But I figured it'd be better than having to go to mine."

"It's all right, little sister," some fellow hollered from the back.

"It's just . . . here . . . it was so alive! The Lord . . . He's real! And He loves me, and I wanted Him, and . . ." She shot a hand into the air. "Praise Jesus! I'm saved!"

Chapter Two

Keeping secrets wasn't lying, but the practice still pained David some when Sonny's whereabouts were cussed or discussed.

Some of his teammates thought his missing the so-called voluntary summer workouts bordered on being sacrilegious, but not David. He loved playing football well enough, but the game didn't compare with his love for the Lord.

If only he could figure out how to go to Pine Grove more than twice a month.

Good thing his grandfathers didn't talk. Or that Hannah's mother and his grandmother didn't travel in the same circles. While his folks were mostly okay thinking he attended her Methodist church on those off Sundays, they would have put their foot down square about him holy-rolling.

Made him proud his Hannah loved Gramps' church almost as much as he did. And her cousin Jill would be on his side, too.

He didn't much care for the derogatory holy-roller term, but it did kind of fit.

When the Spirit moved, how could a body be expected to sit still? So far, all he'd done was dance before the Lord, but if he even suspected it would please God, he'd be rolling on the floor with the best of them.

Didn't figure there would be anything he wouldn't do to please Him.

Sonny showed a week before school, shaggy haired and unshaven, and at least twenty pounds lighter than when he ran off. So out of shape, the rat fink got demoted to second string.

How were the Tigers supposed to win without David's favorite target? For sure, his cousin had been the best tight end in the district last season. After the Summer of Love, he could hardly block or run a proper route.

At least the big hippie-want-to-be spilling his guts about his San Francisco adventure took David off the hook about telling what he'd been up to. Diversion was a good thing.

Then his mother, of all people, decided to attend that year's homecoming game. And to put the cherry on top the proverbial ice cream sundae, she decided to stay the weekend. Seemed the dear lady had ulterior motives. Praise the Lord!

In only a few weeks he'd celebrate his eighteenth birthday.

Then there'd be nothing she or PawPaw or MawMaw could do but complain. Oh, the women might even shed some tears, but he'd be ready with deflecting arguments on every point. He'd thought of them all.

One thing good about her coming down from Dallas though. When she helped Granny cook, there wasn't a dirty pot in sight for him to scrub. He liked that.

After the last plate got dishtowel dried and put away that Saturday night, instead of him heading out for a round of spotlight hunting with Sonny, she wanted him to join her and her parents at the kitchen table.

"But Sonny's expecting me."

Nodding toward David's chair, PawPaw saw him down with his eyes. "He'll wait. Doesn't have a ride."

His mother smiled then reached across the table and took both of his hands in hers. "Son, I've made preliminary inquiries. Your grades are not exactly up to SMU standards, but I've been told that there's always room for a Prescott."

"Hmm, that so. But see? I wasn't planning on going to

college."

She jerked back like he'd punched her. "What? No! David, don't you know you'll get drafted if you don't go straight into college? I couldn't bear it if . . . if you went to Vietnam. Believe me, Son, you do not want to go there. It's a horrible war! And for what? No, sir. I won't have it."

He looked to his grandfather then back to his mother. "PawPaw went to France. Dad was at Normandy on D-Day. I figure if they call, I'll go. It's called serving your country, Mom."

"France and World War II were different. Johnson and Westmoreland have messed things up so bad over there. You trust me, don't you, boy? Listen to your mother and go on to school. Take the deferment. There's no shame in getting an education."

"But PawPaw—"

"Listen to them, David. If anything happened to you . . ." A tear trickled down MawMaw's cheek.

All three were ganging up on him, but it was his life. But how could he break their hearts? "What if Hannah and I go ahead and get married, I'd be 2A then, and—"

"Not a chance." PawPaw shook his head. "Her people will never go along with that. They won't allow it, and she'd have to have their permission. What is she now? Fifteen?"

Close to it. Her birthday was still two weeks away, so he ignored that comment. "Well, I'm sorry, but I am not going to SMU."

"Why not?" PawPaw stayed on him. "Don Meredith went there. You could walk on. Who knows? Might make the football team. You're good enough. Never seen anyone throw a pigskin with your accuracy."

"Maybe." He shrugged. "But the only school I'd consider is ORU."

"Where's that? Oregon? Ohio?" Poor Mama. She didn't have a clue.

Instead of telling her, he just smiled, savoring the moment

and the bliss ignorance offered. Soon as they knew . . . might be Normandy all over again. Right there in MawMaw's kitchen. He cleared his throat and steeled himself.

Best he get the truth of it out in the open. And while he was at it, might as well tell them what was on his heart regarding where he intended to worship all the time.

"It's in Tulsa."

"Oh, Oklahoma. Of course. But . . . is there a university in Tulsa? I can't remember one."

"There is, Mama. Oral Roberts started one there a couple of years ago." David sat a bit taller. There it was, right out on the table. He wanted to go to a Pentecostal school.

"David, no. Isn't that man the one . . . Why! If he's the one I'm thinking of, he's nothing but a . . ." MawMaw covered her mouth like she was about to say a bad word or something.

"Christian? The man loves the Lord."

His grandfather leaned back—probably still trying to figure out who Oral Roberts was—and glared.

"I been hearing you've been sneaking off to Pine Bluff of a Sunday. Didn't want to believe it. You know what's right, boy, and them fools are nothing but dead wrong."

Practically biting the blood out of his tongue, he held his peace. He knew better than argue with the most stubborn, hardheaded man in three counties. Maybe the whole state.

How many times had he heard about how Aunt Emma was lost to the one true church, doomed to burn if she didn't turn back? PawPaw obviously couldn't stand the thought of his grandest grandson beating that same drum.

And David loved the old man.

So much that hurting him like that almost made him want to confess his sins and promise to never set foot in any other church, but he couldn't. He knew the Truth.

He'd experienced the wonderful presence of God and could never go back to those dead traditions the Harrises had practiced for generations.

No way. He was bona fide full Gospel in his heart . . . just like his father and his father before him, and he might as well tell them the whole of it.

"Since you're here, Mother, and you called this meeting, there's one more thing I've been meaning to tell y'all. I've decided to change my name."

From the ladies' gasps, a person would think someone was hyperventilating. He filled his lungs.

"After my birthday, I'm going to court and officially become John David Nightingale."

No one said anything. Silence reigned.

So far so good. Not bad at all. He'd expected more protest.

"What's wrong with David John?" Did that mean his mother understood why he no longer wanted to be a Prescott? She definitely should.

"Nothing, Mama. It's just always sounded backwards to me. Plus I figured—hoped anyway—it'd honor PawPaw some. Lessen him hating it so much me being a Nightingale." He searched his grandfather's eyes for any sign.

"You're the one who taught me how important the Truth is."

MawMaw wouldn't even look up at him. "What about Emma Lee and Travis' John?"

"Everyone calls him Bucky or Buck, anyway. No one calls him John, and besides, I'm not planning on anyone calling me John either. I like my given name fine, so I'll still be David. I'll just go by my middle name." He glanced at PawPaw again, hoping above hope . . .

"I hoped you be proud."

"Always been proud you carried my name, boy, but . . ." He closed his eyes and shook his head.

"Buddy's my father, PawPaw. I should have his name. I'm not a Prescott."

"Well, I am. And you're mine."

"True, Mama. I am your son, but Harry was never my father. Broderick Eversole Nightingale is."

Everything in him wanted to say more, but the pain in her eyes hushed every word. For years he'd thought it was remembering her sins that hurt her so bad, but of late, he'd been leaning toward the fact that he was Buddy's and she wasn't.

He liked Mom A well enough but knew better than to talk about her or his father after a spell in Georgia or when they'd traveled to Texas for a visit.

Two longs and a short sounded on the phone.

MawMaw threw a nod toward the living room. "That's our ring. Get it, David, would you please?"

"Sure." He gladly jumped to his feet. Figured it'd be Sonny anyway. Probably walked on up to the store. That dimwit never had any patience. Was him. David gave him the Reader's Digest version of what had transpired then promised to hurry.

He stopped in the doorway, except the door was behind the freezer and had not ever been closed in his memory.

"Sonny walked to the store. You know Miss Ethel don't allow loitering, so can I be excused? Don't figure there's much else to say anyway."

"I can't imagine why you'd figure such a thing, David. Nothing's settled. Not one thing."

Had his mother been crying?

PawPaw waved him off. "Go on, then. We can talk some more tomorrow."

"You remember this is Hannah's Sunday."

"Go on, git. Don't want Ethel to have a cow over Sonny hanging around."

From his earliest memory, David had hunted, fished, and played most every sport in its season with his cousin; closest thing he had to a brother. When it came to church, Sonny was staunch in the traditional beliefs of the Church of Christ.

Except of late, most would have to pronounce him more backslidden than anything. If he'd done all the things he claimed while in San Francisco, the boy might actually need deliverance.

Not that his grandfather had totally convinced him a Christian could be demon possessed, but soon and very soon, David intended to do some studying on the subject. Gramps had given him a whole page of Scriptures to look up.

From the store to where he planned on starting the hunt, David relayed the conversation he'd had with his folks. Other than a grunt here or there, his cousin didn't offer many comments, seeming distant and troubled. He eased the truck to a stop.

"What's eating you, Sonny?"

Pulling out a home-rolled cigarette, Cuz struck a match with his thumbnail, held the burning stick to the tip, then inhaled. He didn't blow the smoke back out though.

"Man, that stuff smells weird." He reached inside his boot and pulled out a pack of Camels, same one he'd been working on for a week. "Here. Throw that thing away."

Sonny shook his head then held the poorly rolled cig out toward him. He spoke with an air-starved tone. "Try this."

"No thanks, it stinks."

He finally blew out the smoke. "No really. Here. Take a toke."

Realization dawned. "A toke? Sonny Harris, is that a reefer? Are you a crazy man?"

"Don't knock it until you try it, J. David. Come on. It's way cool."

"No, thank you. That stuff will make you do all kinds of horrible things. Is that what's wrong with you?"

With a shrug, he took another long drag, held the smoke in, then put the thing out by dripping spit on it. "Nothing's wrong." He barely managed the denial, letting very little smoke out then held his breath until what seemed to be the verge of passing out before he finally exhaled.

"Weed's nothing like that stupid film they played in Health." He chuckled. "You need to loosen up, Jaybird son of Buddy."

"Don't you dare call me that, especially not in front of anyone. You hear me?"

"Why not? Said yourself you're going to court and getting it legally changed. What's the big deal?" He snickered. "Might even work. The wheels of government grind, but on the slow side."

"What are you talking about?"

"Registering for the draft. Your name change might throw them off for a while—maybe long enough. My old man says if Humphrey wins, he'll end the war. You might buy yourself a year, who knows what Nixon's going to do if he wins?"

"I registered under Prescott, but if my mother will pay for it, I'm going to ORU."

"O. R. Who?"

"Oral Roberts University, Bozo. It's a Christian school of higher learning in Tulsa."

"What? You didn't tell me that part! What's wrong with SMU? I mean besides them never winning a football game."

With his cousin it was all about football. Forget any other sport or going to a university to actually learn anything. "They win now and again."

"Might beat TCU on a good year, but never Texas, A&M, Baylor, or Arkansas."

"Anyway, that's not why I'm not going there."

"Then why?"

"I've made my decision. What I believe for the Truth. I'm Full Gospel, Sonny, like my father and grandfather before me."

"Does Uncle John know about this?"

"All do now." David nodded. "Told them tonight."

"Man, you ought to go with me. Sissy's back in town. We're heading out again next week."

"No way. You can't. What about the team? And basketball? We need you. I need you."

"Yeah right, and Uncle Sam needs me, too. He's running out of cannon fodder, and I'm about to flunk out anyway. Not much keeping me here."

"Where you going?"

"A bunch of guys I met at Haight-Ashbury are going to Canada. I'm joining up with them."

"Oh man, you're going to dodge the draft?"

John David's Calling

"Sure am. Just like you, Cuz. 'Cept I don't have a rich mama to tote the note. Had to get creative, you know?"

Had him there. But getting an education deferment only put off his responsibility for four years. If the war was still going on then, he and Hannah could get married.

"Still, if I do go for more school, I won't be draft dodging. I'll just be deferring for four years."

"Or six. Or eight. Or however long it takes. Rich boys don't get drafted. Hadn't you figured that out, my man?"

"Why don't you join the Navy?"

"No thanks. I get sick on the Colorado River. I'd spend every day and night hanging my head over the rail barfing."

The rest of the night's hunting, bagging two fat coons and three ringtails, David never could put even a shallow dent in Sonny's armor.

Apparently, marijuana didn't affect his aim or ability with a skinning knife though. A time or two, he got a little silly, but that could come on when he was cold stone sober. Often did, too. He said weed got you high.

Though David almost tried it, in the end, he decided it fell into the same category as alcohol, and he'd promised Gramps he'd never take his first drink.

"Hard to be a drunk like me if you never smell a cork."

Even though the Reverend Nathaniel Nightingale hadn't taken a drink since the big twister that took his tent and put him behind the pulpit of Pine Bluff Holiness Church, he still called himself a drunk and warned anyone who'd listen about taking that first drink.

Sonny wouldn't listen to anyone though. The summer of Love had not served his cousin well.

Once David laid his head on his pillow, sleep came easy. He'd told them his plans and made up his mind. He wasn't bluffing.

If his mama wouldn't go for ORU, he'd join up. For sure and for certain as Gramps said a lot, he would not be dodging the draft. Besides, he'd rather be a Marine than an Army grunt.

His mother stretched her visit to Monday, but no argument she countered with made any difference. She ought to know he'd inherited PawPaw's stubbornness.

The great God of Heaven had revealed Truth to him. He knew it, and just like the Scripture said, the Truth had set him free. He'd been saved by grace and not works.

Traditions of men would never move him again, not away from the Truth.

For the remainder of nineteen hundred and sixty-seven—wow, almost nineteen seventy—she and her parents took turns coming at him from every conceivable direction, but he never wavered.

Oral Roberts University or the Marines.

As the new year dawned, he reminded them all that, like Mama's favorite soap opera, the sands of time waited on no man. Or was that Shakespeare? Didn't really matter, he didn't care much for either.

Then mid-February, the whole of his mother's life—and his, too, somewhat—turned upside down. Two longs and a short, the Harris' ring, pulled him from that evening's dishes. He glanced at his grandparents.

"It isn't Hannah. She never calls this early."

PawPaw nodded toward the living room. "Quit speculating and see who it is, boy."

"Yes, sir." He flung the dishtowel over his shoulder and hurried to the living room. "Hello."

A high-pitched squeal followed by some clicks and a bit of static caused him to hold the phone out from his ear.

One fine day, Cypress Springs would have a real phone system. He had to admit that was one of the few things he liked about his mother's mansion in the affluent Turtle Creek area of Dallas.

"David? That you?"

"Hey, Gramps. Yes, sir, it's me. Something wrong?"

"I'm afraid so, Son. Your father and Abigail have been in a wreck, a car accident. She's gone on to glory, David, and your dad . . . he's . . ."

"He's what? Was Mandy with them?"

"No, praise God, but Buddy's barely hanging on. Can you come get us? I need you, Son."

"Of course! I'll pack a bag and be right there."

"No, no. We can catch a train if you'll drive us to Austin."

"Forget the train. I'm going. I'll be there in an hour or less and drive us to Dalton."

"Bless you, Son. We'll be ready."

The cab stopped in front of Braniff's main door at Love Field. The driver jumped out and hurried to the back of the car.

Sandy took a quick nip from her silver flask. Shouldn't have brought schnapps; the tastier stuff hadn't touched the growing rock in her gut. She dropped her friend into its pocket in her purse.

Did she even know anyone bootlegging white lightning? That's what she needed.

The cabby opened her door and extended his hand. She took it, palming him a folded twenty in the exchange, and exited. "Keep the change."

"Thank you, Mis'ess Prescott. Have a good flight, ma'am."

She exhaled but kept from screaming and cursing as she was so tempted to do. Oh, how she hated flying! With a passion! Was there a word stronger than hate? Detest maybe, or abhorred?

Strolling right up to the first-class counter, she paid for her ticket as if she flew everywhere every day, three times on Sunday.

Then she sauntered across the rotunda's huge open area to the concourse as if any danger of falling out of the sky simply didn't exist.

Nothing to it.

As much as she despised boarding an airplane, she had little choice. She had to get to Dalton—and quick.

Figured she should short-stop the ladies' room where she also made good the opportunity to imbibe a bit more in the privacy of the stall. She emptied the flask, but that growing gut rock still mocked her and her useless rotgut.

But she had the cure.

Bless that pilot. What was his name? Randy? No. Ricky? Whoever. Her un-named hero convinced her he had just what she needed to overcome her fear. Plus, she really wanted to tour Europe on his arm.

Too bad he hadn't racked up enough seniority to have enough leave to sail. Still, he'd taught her how to fly, and her physician had no problem writing her a prescription.

Half an hour before departure, she slipped the first little darling into her mouth. Still didn't want to board and hesitated, debating with herself. Seeing Buddy won the day, and she made it onto the deathtrap.

The window seat helped, but . . .

The pain she would inflict on David when she saw him diverted her attention as the other passengers boarded. Why he hadn't called her before he got to Georgia, she would never understand.

If only he had, then she could have met them and made the trip by car with them instead of risking life and limb, getting hurled through the sky in their fancy Lockheed Electra.

Everybody still talked about Flight 352 that crashed in Dawson, didn't even make it to the border. Eighty-four souls perished in the little East Texas town.

Her heart beat like a machine gun that never ran out of ammunition. She glanced at the gentleman beside her on the aisle. He already had his eyes closed, cuddled to a pillow with a lap blanket.

The cabin door closed. She popped another pill and shut her eyes, picturing her son's father. Had she ever loved anyone other than Buddy? Must be coming up on thirty years—a

lifetime.
From the stories she'd heard, she loved him even before seeing him that first time in his father's tent. Loved the mere thought of him way back then.

How long had she loved him?

If only she could remember the evening her father took her to the Nightingale's meeting in Marble. That time he heard the angels sing—did she believe that?

However, it happened, he definitely led the whole service singing one song after another. Old timers still talked about that night. Even her father had admitted to being impressed with the boy.

Of course, that was before.

Before she started stepping out with him in his haunted Cadillac. Oh, how she loved him picking her up from school, and everyone seeing who she left with.

The engines rumbled and so did the pit of her being.

The plane began rolling backwards.

Not too bad, a little like a big car, maybe a tall truck. The man next to her leaned forward, looked out her window, then settled back again, closing his eyes. "Good day for it. You fly much?"

Swallowing, she hoped her voice worked. "Nuh-uh." She cleared her throat. "No, sir. As little as possible." A little nip might help, but she'd drained her flask. How long would it be before the stewardesses started serving?

The big bird stopped rolling backward, caught its breath, then taxied away from the terminal.

The dye was cast. She fished out her flask and upended it. A few drops wet her tongue. Her back pressed into the padded seat. Her fingers worried the arm rests' leather. Not kid, but nice enough.

Oh, God. She couldn't get out now. Her fate was in His hands.

The jet's rumble increased, whining so loud. Why had she done this to herself? Gravity pushed her back even more.

Help me, God. She squeezed her eyes shut.

"Come on. Jump up, baby. You can do it."

She bumped the man's arm. "Are you calling this death trap baby?"

He laughed at her. "Sure, that's what she is."

Faster the hunk of metal raced up the runway. A big bounce took her breath away, then a sudden jerk followed. She was going to die, she grabbed the man's forearm, digging her nails into his suit. "We're going to die!"

"No, we're not. Flying is the safest way to travel, lady."

"Liar!" She squealed, squeezing harder. Refusing to open her eyes, she shook her head back and forth against the seat. Her lungs screamed for more air. She inhaled again then again, gasping for a breath.

"Easy, lady. Calm down. We're airborne now, see? We'll be there in Atlanta in a couple of hours. Relax." He eased her hand off his arm.

"Oh." She opened her eyes and swallowed. "I'm sorry." The engines were quieter. "We're in the air?" She glanced out the window. Downtown Dallas' skyscrapers looked like a child's building blocks, and cars like ants on tiny dark ribbons. She smoothed the man's sleeve. "I'm sorry, really. Did I hurt you?"

"Not at all. Want a drink?"

"I was thinking about that, but maybe I . . . best not . . . I took a Valium . . . or two, and . . ." She melted into her chair. Everything swam around a time or two then melted into sweet nothingness.

She woke to the realization she was an evil, horrible person.

Why did she do it?

Chapter Three

Sandy stared out the tiny oval window.
Nothing but puffy white clouds, shadowed with blues and grays as though a sea beneath as far as the eye could see.

Not the way she ever thought she'd go to Heaven. She filled her lungs. "I'm a wicked, horrible person."

"Now why would you say that? You are not."

She turned toward her seat mate. Buddy smiled.

"My darling! You're alive! You're okay!" She turned and placed both hands around his bicep, still firm and bulging. "I'm so sorry about Abigail."

He laughed. "No, you are not! Why do you keep lying? You've been praying for the Lord to take her out of your way for years. How many has it been now? Since you found out I was married?"

"Over twenty."

"Twenty-four to be exact."

"Mis'ess Prescott." Someone shook her arm. "Ma'am? Wake up."

Sandy opened her eyes. The stewardess stood in the aisle. The seat next to her was empty. She glanced out the window. The plane had landed. "We're on the ground?"

"Yes, ma'am."

"Oh, thank you." The lady grinned. "We didn't die. I'm so

glad."

Her hostess offered an even bigger smile. "So am I, ma'am." She held out a business card. "The man sitting next to you asked me to give you this."

Why she accepted the pasteboard, she couldn't say. The guy wasn't even her type. Would she ever have a type again? Anyway, even if he had been, Buddy was free. "Aren't you glad you don't have to wear those silly little hats anymore?"

"Oh, they weren't so bad, but yeah. It's nice not to have to pin them on; really messed up the do, you know?"

"Actually, I've never been a hat person."

"Well, you have a good day in Atlanta, ma'am."

While she gathered her things and strode out of the emptied plane—as though it had been nothing to fly across the county—she pondered how her life would change, now that the love of her life was free. How wonderful it would be!

Mis'ess Broderick Eversole Nightingale. Sandy Nightingale. Sandra Louise Harris Nightingale. She loved it.

How long had it been since she tested out his name? Oh, how she loved him and had forever. And while she'd never hated petite Abigail, so many times she'd meditated on bad things happening to her.

It had come to pass.

Had she killed Abigail, wishing her away?

As sure as her feet trod solid ground.

Try as she may, she couldn't work up any sorrow. She was so bad, so wicked.

At the first trash receptacle inside the terminal, she stopped to toss the stranger's card, but for some reason, glanced at it first. Reverend Israel Josephs. She turned it over. Written on the back was 'You're not evil, Sandy.'

"Oh dear Lord." Was He speaking to her? Could He ever forgive her?

No, she'd gone too far, sinned too much, been away from His church too long. She raised her hand but couldn't toss the pasteboard. Instead, she dropped it in her purse then headed

toward baggage claim.
Might have time to rent a car before they came down.

Voices murmured in hushed, soft-spoken tones. So many Buddy didn't recognize. His eyes seemed to be glued shut. He tried but couldn't force them open.
Where was he?
What happened?
His left arm and leg wouldn't move. Were they stuck or something? Trapped? He raised his right arm though not off the sheet. It worked fine. He tried again, and his eyes opened enough to see through his lashes.
A tube ran from his wrist to a jar hanging over his head.
Was he in a hospital?
"What." The word barely sounded. He cleared his throat and attempted again. "What happened?"
No one answered. He tested his head, but only managed an inch, maybe two, then laid it back down. Was that Sandy? Mercy. Why was she there? Abigail was going to be so mad.
"Sandy?" His voice sounded so weak. No response.
"Sandra Louise." Though it didn't seem much stronger, she moved toward him.
"Buddy! You're awake. Thank God."
"Where's Abigail?"
"Oh, sweetheart. Don't you remember?"
No matter how much effort he put into sitting up, he could not even get his shoulders off the mattress. "Remember what? Where's my wife?"
Tears brimmed in Sandy's eyes. Why would she cry?
"A drunk driver in a truck ran the red light, Buddy. It hit on her side. She was driving. She . . . uh, she . . ." A sob escaped. "I'm so sorry."
Salty tears stung his own eyes. "Is . . . is she dead?"

"Yes, my love. Her funeral was five days ago. Mandy and the Baxters decided it was for the best. The doctors said you couldn't have gone, even if you'd been awake."

"What's wrong with me? Why have I been sleeping so long?"

"Well, you've been in a coma, sweetheart. We didn't know for sure if . . ." She wiped her cheeks and cleared her throat. "Um, your left arm and leg are broken. You shattered your hip, and three ribs broke, puncturing you lungs."

"Dear God. Oh Lord, help me. She's gone."

"Yes, dear."

"Where's Mandy? Is David with you?"

"I sent him home with your father."

"Mercy. Dad was here?"

"Yes, he was, and worried sick. He didn't want to leave, but . . . We didn't know if you'd . . ." She wiped her cheeks again then smiled, though a bit weak, it appeared genuine.

"I just can't believe how good he's doing. At ninety-eight, he doesn't look a day over eighty, but staying was wearing on him, honey."

"Where's my daughter?"

"Well, she'll be here in a couple of hours. She and I have been taking turns staying with you. Poor little thing, she's such a precious girl. She's been so sweet. We've been . . ." She smiled then the water works turned on in earnest.

"Oh, Buddy." She leaned over him, her cheek to his and whispered in his ear. "I was so scared." A sob choked her. "Buddy . . . they said you might never wake up. That if you did, you might never be the same."

Bits and pieces of the wreck overwhelmed him. Tires screeching. Impact. Metal on metal. She screamed. He'd heard her scream.

Spinning, rolling, not knowing which side was up . . . then nothing. Until he woke up just then. Praise God he woke up.

"Abigail . . . did she make it to the hospital?"

"No, darling. She was pronounced dead at the scene. The

John David's Calling

coroner said it was instantaneous."

He rested his eyes. Abigail gone to live with Jesus. Rubber sole shoes squeaking opened his eyes. "Well good morning, Mister Nightingale. You're awake. That's just wonderful. How are you feeling, sir?"

Sandy stepped back but stayed where he could see her.

The nurse came right up to his bedside.

"Not too bad, I guess. My side is all numb, and like it's..." He tried to move his left arm again. It barked. "It hurts pretty bad. Does that mean it isn't paralyzed?"

"Well, it's a good sign, but the doctor will talk to you about it. It's time for a pain shot. Where do you want it? Shoulder or hip? The last one was in your thigh."

"What is it?"

"Morphine. It'll help get you a little more comfortable."

He lifted his elbow, but it never left the bed. Would it ever work right again? Barely felt any prick, but he sure could feel the drug spread. The barking quieted. Good stuff.

Maybe he'd sleep. He closed his eyes.

Someone mopped his forehead, but he didn't open his eyes to see who. He was so tired. Why had he picked that day to get his wisdom teeth cut out?

Why hadn't he died, too?

Oh Lord. Am I reaping the whirlwind?

That answer didn't come, only pain—and more pain. While the drugs temporarily eased his broken body, only the Lord knew how to mend a broken heart.

Worse, for years he'd been a dry place—a famine not of bread or water, but one like Amos prophesied, a famine of hearing the Words of the Lord. And it left him so very thirsty.

Father God.

In the calm hours before the hospital came alive—the worst part of every day—he empathized with David's troubled soul as his newborn son fought for life. Except... no one gave Buddy a week to fast and pray for his Abigail, try to change God's mind.

He had no options.

She was gone.

He'd killed her same as if he'd been driving the truck that rammed into his car.

When Mandy came, her being so much like her mother stirred so many memories. Then when Sandy took her turn, he could hardly look at her for the guilt of loving her. Being unfaithful to his dead wife.

So long ago, the beauty had captured such a large chunk of his heart . . . but like the tree in the middle of the garden, she was forbidden fruit.

Five weeks after the wreck, no one came. Had to push a button and wait on a nurse if he needed anything. He hated being alone. Almost wished the old man hadn't insisted on paying the extra charge for a private room.

Everyone had their lives to live. Then as if solitary incarceration didn't prove depressing enough, they made him get out of bed and walk.

Mercy, Lord. Did they not know his body wasn't ready? He wasn't ready.

Mandy waltzed into his room, carrying his lunch tray. "Hey, Daddy, how'd it go?"

"So, you were in on my torture. That why you didn't show this morning?"

"Never did like seeing a grown man cry." She grinned."

"Praise God, it didn't come to that, but . . ." He returned her smile then lifted the lid off his plate. Meat loaf, ugh. He replaced it then started pouring the sugar in his iced tea. "You and Robert get the twin's school straightened out?"

She blew her bangs—that settled right back in her eyes—then shrugged. "No, sir. I convinced him not to go."

"Maybe for the best. So, are they going to split them up?"

"No, sir. Actually, it happened just like JR said. The other boy was picking on Sally. The little brat admitted it. Her brother was only defending her."

"That's great. Little girls need their big brothers close."

John David's Calling   31

"Mercy, Daddy. He's only five minutes older."

"He'll still always be her protector."

While he choked down as much of his lunch as he could stomach—sure would enjoy some of Abigail's home cooking—he persuaded his daughter into giving him a blow-by-blow of her meeting with the school principal.

He saw so much of her mother in her, some of her grandmother, too. "Shame you never knew Mama. You're a lot like her."

"You've told me about Grandmother Evelyn, Daddy. One fine day, I'll get to meet her." A tear popped up to run down her cheek. She sniffed and swiped at it. "I'm sure she and Mama are having a grand time catching up."

Allowing himself to dwell on the past a bit, he kept running up on turning points that only kept him going down too many paths of regret—for the thousandth time. He steered the discussion to the mill and feed store.

For a while, she elaborated on the day-to-day of the business, how so many of the employees were stepping up in his absence, and who her husband was considering letting go.

"You think Robert's ready to run the whole kit and caboodle?"

"Well, he's doing fine, but why would he do that? Long as you do what the doctors say, you'll be back to work in another month or two at most."

"Maybe, but I've been doing a lot of praying, Amanda. About my future."

With a glance at the wall clock, she changed the topic as smooth as Lake Allatoona on a windless day. "I can't stay too much longer, Daddy. Sandy said she was coming this afternoon." She shrugged. "There's something I've been praying about, too."

Humph. Was she about to pile on more guilt about his past? Didn't really matter. No way could his girl beat him up any worse than the self-flagellation he'd been enduring. "What about, honey? You stopped talking."

"I know, but mercy." She wiped away more tears and tried to chuckle, but it came out sad, not joyful. "To quote my father."

Coming to his bedside, she covered his hand. "I'm so conflicted, Daddy. But . . . I know Sandy loves you. It's so obvious, and . . . you probably still love her, too, and, well . . ." Tears ran to fast too catch them all.

"I confess I hated her at first . . . and for a long time."

"Sweetheart, you don't have to—"

"No, wait, Daddy." She sniffed, popped out a couple of Kleenex and wiped her cheeks again. "I mean, it was so much fun having David when we got him, but . . ." She blew her nose into the dampened tissue then tossed it into his trash can.

"Anyway, Mom and I had a long talk about you and Sandy."

"When?"

"Oh, a couple of years ago . . . but anyway . . . Please let me get this out. Okay?" She cleared her throat then swallowed.

"Mama told me if anything ever happened to her, she wanted you to be happy. Daddy, she made me promise to tell you. But I didn't want to after . . . after . . ."

"Oh, my precious, sweet girl. It had to be so hard on you. I'm so sorry. I'm sorry I wasn't there for you."

"You do not have any reason to be sorry, Daddy. It was not your fault. How many times do I have to tell you that?" She stared at him for a long minute and drew in a long, deep breath.

"So here's what I think. I think you and Sandy should get married. As soon as possible. I don't see any reason for you to wait. Mama's gone, and it's what she'd want."

He closed his eyes. What a gift his treasured Mandy was. But still. "I don't know, baby. Have you talked with Grandma about all this?"

"No. I know she won't like it coming so soon and everything, but . . . I can handle her. She'll still love you no matter what." She hiked her closest shoulder. "In the end though, it isn't her life." She leaned over and kissed his forehead then offered a forced giggle.

"To hear her tell it, I should be over there checking on her twice a day, and you should have cried a river of tears by now."

"Her new nurse working out okay?"

Finally, her laughter carried some mirth, not as much as he'd loved, but close. "Well, at least she hasn't quit, so I guess that's something. Grandma gets so cantankerous sometimes."

He sure wouldn't want the job. "Thing is, darlin', I don't think Sandy would ever want to live here, and I'm for sure not moving to Dallas."

"She bought a house, Daddy. Didn't she tell you?"

"Here in Dalton?"

"Yes, sir. Said she was tired of staying in the hotel. Bought a car, too, awhile back. She must have so much money."

"Yes, ma'am. That lady always did like spending poor Harry's money."

"It's hers now. Anyway, seems to me she's willing to move."

"You discussed any of this with David?"

"I did." She sighed, a sort of resignation. "He thinks it would be wonderful."

"What about Robert?"

"Yes, he's okay with it, too. He wants you to be happy. We all do, Daddy."

Holding out his good hand, he smiled. How could she be any more precious? "I love you, baby."

"I love you, too. Of course."

Naps, even drug-induced ones, were nice. Waking up with his angel holding his hand was the best. Except, was it? The Word said to find a wife was a good thing, but it also said how can two walk together less they be in unity.

"Afternoon, my love." She beamed.

Had Mandy said something? Probably so. Why did females have the need to tell everything they knew?

"You're looking rather chipper."

Her smiled increased. "Yes, sir! I couldn't be better. You

see, my dear, I ran into Amanda in the parking lot."
Of course, she had. He raised one eyebrow.
"She told me everything she told you. Isn't it wonderful?"
Probably not everything, but . . .
"Is it?"

Chapter Four

Sandy replayed his words.
Why would he say that?
"Yes, Buddy. Of course, it is. Why would you . . ." She cleared her throat. "As soon as you're out of here, my darling, we'll find us a judge, and . . . then all my dreams will come true."

"What about Mister John?"

"Papa? What about him? He loves our son. He loves David. He's mellowed, Buddy. A lot. He won't stand in our way."

It hurt to laugh, but he couldn't help it.

"Stand in our way? Sandy, we're grown adults. He has no say about our ways—yours or mine. Mercy." He looked deep into her eyes. "I'm talking about you being a holy roller. What's he going to think about that?"

"Oh, Buddy! Don't be silly. We don't need to get into that now. You led music at our church once. And you said it with your own mouth all those years ago—I heard you with my own ears, so there's no denying it—you claimed church was church."

"Well. Truth is . . . it isn't."

"What are you saying? That all Church of Christs . . . all the Baptists and Methodists aren't going to Heaven?"

"Mercy no, baby. You know me better than that. Besides,

that sounds a whole lot more like your old-time religion, doesn't it? No, those denominations get all the important fundamentals right, preach knowing Jesus, Him crucified. Those who believe in Him, confess and repent of their sins, Word says they will be saved."

"So why would I have to be a holy roller?"

"Well, I've been praying about having meetings again."

"What? Why would you want to do that? You almost died, Buddy. But now you've been given a second chance. We've been given—"

He held up a finger. "I will do what God asks of me. Whatever He asks of me. He has forgiven me so much, Sandy. He'll forgive you, too. But my obedience . . . it's the only way I can show Him how much I love Him. And that's above all . . . you, too."

Turning her back, she walked to the window. Oh boy, how well she knew that. She'd never forgotten him walking down that hospital corridor after Harry died, and she was free.

Leaving her there, holding baby David.

She'd always thought he'd chosen Abigail over her, but deep in her heart knew it was God he'd chosen.

Would he walk away from her again?

"I know that." She turned and hurried back to his side. Took his hand. "But let's get you well, get married before anything else happens, then we'll have the rest of our lives to decide how we want to live then—together.

"There are so many places I've been that I'd love to show you. We can travel the world together." She put her cheek to his. "I love you, Buddy."

"I love you, too, baby. Have you decided about ORU?"

Why was he doing this now? Was he trying to pick a fight? He was free! And all he wanted to talk about was religion.

"No. But that has nothing to do with us getting married. Another one of those things we can decide together, after we finally get hitched. David can go to the best university in the country. I have more money than we'll ever need. There's no reason for him to go elsewhere or for you to ever have to work."

"Well, I've been thinking about that, too. He got his mind set on going to Oral Roberts, so, if you don't pay for it, I will."

"What? You don't have any money. Why . . . I gave Mandy a check for the hospital to cover what your insurance didn't. You can't afford to send him to school. Don't be ridiculous."

"If I sell the house I can. If needed, I can borrow against my share of the Mill and Feed store, too."

"Don't. Good Lord, Buddy. David doesn't need to go there! If he wants to study religion, SMU has a ministry degree program."

He closed his eyes. Was he going to sleep? Instead of . . . He opened them then shook his head awake. "I don't completely agree with Reverend Roberts on all his Abundant Life teachings, but he is Full Gospel, and the Methodists are not."

"He'll never get a good job with a degree from . . . that . . ."

"University? Was that the word you were hunting?"

She threw her hands up. "I'm, sorry. I can't do this now." She glared then retrieved her purse. "I'm going out for a pack of cigarettes. Anything I can get you?"

"New hip would be nice."

"I'll see if I can find you one." She blew him a kiss then turned.

"David's not bluffing. He'll join up if one of us doesn't come up with the tuition."

She turned back. She wanted to dispute his claim, but in her heart of hearts, knew the words were true.

"Okay, fine. You win. I'll send him. Does that make you happy? Shall I summons him to Dalton, so he can be here when his mother and father are married?" She stuck out her tongue. "We can tell him together that he can pack for ORU when he gets back home."

David hung up the phone then walked back to the kitchen and slipped into his chair. Well, it wasn't totally his. If another older couple came for supper, PawPaw insisted he relinquish his chair for eating in the living room on the card table.

At least he didn't have to wait until all the grownups to finish before he could fix his plate like the old folks claimed it was in their day.

Shame he didn't have a time machine. He'd like to see for himself how it really was in those days. But if . . .

"Something wrong, Son? What did your mama allow? Your dad take a turn for the worse?"

"No, sir. He's fine and his rehab is going good." He looked from his mother's father to about the sweetest grandmother a boy could ever have.

If only she wouldn't have converted, but then his hardheaded grandfather would never have married her either. He smiled. "Mama said she'd pay my way to ORU."

The old dear gasped then covered her mouth and looked to her husband. David followed her gaze. Not too awful bad. Only a little wisp of steam rose from his neck. Good thing he'd seen the stare before.

Story went that John Harris had stared down many a man, including one German soldier who lived to see another day in the Great War.

Offering up his sad-eyed pup dog semi-grin—the one that usually melted the man's heart—David re-situated in his seat. It didn't work, so he filled his lungs and steeled himself. But to his surprise, the diatribe didn't come. He exhaled. "Well?"

"That's a deep subject, boy."

"Yeah, it is. Any other comment?"

"Break your jaw to say sir?"

"No, sir. Sorry, PawPaw. I know you aren't glad for me choosing that school, but—"

John David's Calling

"Guess it's the Lord's way of punishing me for all those times I poked fun at the holy rollers."

"Oh, it is not." David chuckled. "God loves you, PawPaw, and He knows you love Him, too. I promise you, I am confident that leaving the Church of Christ will not damn my soul to eternal hell. God loves me, too."

The man shook his head, stood, then pulled his napkin from his collar and dropped it on his plate. He marched out the back door without another word. David wanted to follow then thought better of it. He'd come around—or not.

Only God knew that. But as much as he loved the dear old man, he loved the Lord more. Pleasing his Heavenly Father was paramount.

Couldn't be more pleased his dad convinced his mom to actually pay for it. He'd never known anyone who could talk that woman into anything. Wow, Oral Roberts University. The prospect filled his soul with exuberance. Dad had done it.

By the end of basketball season, the riff healed over some, but it remained all too clear that PawPaw's underlying disappointment still festered. The only thing to lance the wound, let it heal, would be David renouncing his belief in the Full Gospel and publicly professing it as sin and repenting.

And that wasn't happening.

Please, God, soften the man's heart.

In part to make everyone at school happy, but more about giving his grandfather more bragging rights, he ran track that spring as well as playing baseball. He even found time for the district tennis tournament. Lost in the second round, but did well enough to letter in that sport, too.

Only the second one in Marble Falls High's history to letter in five sports. From all reports, John Harris was wearing out ears three counties over, letting any and every one who'd stand still long enough hear all about it.

On the other side of the street, no one made mention regarding his choice of schools to acquire himself a higher education. Instead of coasting to the finish line, David kicked it into high gear and ended up tenth in his class.

Not bad, one might think, except only fifteen seniors comprised the class that year, what with three girls dropping out, rumor was they were expecting, and four guys getting their GED and joining the Navy to beat the draft.

But as his mother pointed out, a man didn't have to tell everything he knew.

Sure did his heart good to see both his parents there the night he got his sheepskin. And even sitting together. Mama had been so mad over him not marrying her.

Couldn't imagine them hitched. Never even considered the possibility before. She'd told him time and again his father was the one true love of her life, that PawPaw and the devil himself had kept them apart.

David hated it all the way to the moon and back that Mom A passed in the crash, but at least she lived in a better place. Not a bad way to go though. Boom! You're in Heaven with the Lord.

The big day turned out a bit anticlimactic. Receiving a fancy piece of paper that proclaimed him to be a bona fide high school graduate didn't pack any punch at all.

Nice that they put his new name on it. He liked seeing John David Nightingale spelled out in the fancy letters. It fit him well. Praise the Lord the school's secretary took his word and didn't demand to see the court order.

The next morning, a ray of sunshine on his cheek woke him. He squinted at his clock. PawPaw had let him sleep late. Cool. No dripping ice cube torture like the old Doughboy was wont to do if a body needed a few extra Zzz's of a morning.

Being a graduate did have its perks. He stopped in the kitchen's doorway.

Wow.

His father sat in his seat with his mother at the end opposite PawPaw. Dirty dishes sat in front of everyone. David gave MawMaw a little grin.

"Morning." She nodded back, with an expression of

John David's Calling   41

anticipation that tipped him off something out of the ordinary—besides Dad being there for breakfast—was going on.

"Morning, sugar."

His father stood. "Here, Son. We saved you some."

His mother jumped to her feet. "No way. Nuh-uh. Not yet. I've waited long enough. Get yourself outside, young man." She looked at her father and wiggled her eyebrows.

"Letting a grown boy sleep until nine-thirty in the morning. I swan. Never happened when me and Emma Lee were under your roof. You're getting soft."

Her lips thinned and tried to turn down, like he and PawPaw were in some sort of trouble.

But it couldn't have been more forced, and her eyes twinkled.

"Can't it wait, Mom? I'm powerful hungry."

"Go on, Son. Mind your mother." His PawPaw threw a nod toward the front of the house. "You aren't about to starve."

Resigned, he headed through the kitchen door. Didn't need to look back to know the whole clan followed. The sound of chairs scooting back and hard soles on linoleum told him he had himself a parade.

At the front door, he froze. Right there behind his mother's Caddy, sat a 1968 Camaro! Maroon with two white stripes down the hood, the Z/28 bid him come. He turned back.

His mother beamed. "Well?"

'That's a deep subject' died somewhere on his tongue before making a sound. The chrome glinted in the sun. He couldn't believe it! All he could get out was "Wow, is that mine? Wow!"

"Of course, it is! Happy graduation, David! Couldn't let you go off to the university without a nice ride. Do you like it?"

"Like it? I love it. Wow, Mom!" He kissed her cheek and hugged her tight. "Thank you, Mama."

Pushing him back, she nodded at his dad. "Thank him, too, he helped me pick it out."

"Thanks, Dad!" He stuck out his hand. "You sure did good."

With a hearty shake, he laughed. "Hannah gets an assist. She's the one told us you'd been daydreaming about a maroon Z/28 for a while."

"Oh wow! Yes, sir! Saw one last fall at the state fair." He shook his head. It was a miracle, amazing. He widened his eyes and blinked.

Was he about to cry right then and there?

Mercy! He hightailed it off the porch without benefit of either step and ran to his new car. His car! What a gift! He never would have thought . . .

Carefully, he traced the hood with three fingers. "Oh, thank you, Lord! You do give us the desires of our hearts." He spun back. "It's perfect! I love it!"

Everything about it, he adored. Would he ever get used to it being his? The color, the stripes, the four-speed manual! No one would even think about challenging him, not that he had any need for speed. Still, nice to know if he needed to get somewhere in a hurry . . .

His mother appeared at the driver's side window, dangling a set of keys. He reached for them, and she pulled them back.

"Promise me you won't ever be hot-rodding this car, David. A vehicle can be a death trap. Remember Abigail. I couldn't stand it if—"

"Oh, Mother, are you crazy? You do not need to worry about that. I'd never dream of it. I couldn't stand it if it even got a scratch! It's . . . it's my dream car! No, ma'am. I'll never mistreat her."

She drew the keys back just out of his reach. "Promise me then."

"Yes, Mother. I promise. I'll drive like . . ." He smiled. "How about I drive better than you? That be good enough for you?"

"Plenty good enough. I've never had a wreck, and you better not either."

"Yes, ma'am." He wiggled his fingers, and she dropped the keys into his palm. "I'll be back."

"Thought you were hungry."

"Food? I can eat any day. I'm off for a spin. Don't wait up."

"Don't you dare be gone that long, David! Your father wants you to take him to Pine Bluff."

With the turn of the ignition, he brought the 302 to life.

"I love you, Mama."

Slipping her into reverse, he eased backwards.

While his son test drove his graduation present, Buddy made nice with Mister John. He talked about everything under the sun except the most important stuff.

The man's normal repugnance for anything Republican seemed to soften a little when he brought up Nixon, almost like he'd give the man a chance if he beat the vice-president in the fall.

Humphrey was going to get his vote even though he didn't much like the man, but he traditionally pulled the Democratic lever.

In a shorter time than expected, he found himself headed back to his father's church.

All the way to the highway, Buddy noticed David cringing with each rock that pinged the undercarriage. He'd slowed to a crawl by the time he pulled out onto the blacktop.

The heat rose off the asphalt in waves, the temperatures already in the nineties. Praise the Lord for air conditioning and that he'd talked Sandy into getting it in the Camaro.

What a different story the need for speed told once his son left the gravel road behind! Buddy didn't say a word until the speedometer touched eighty.

"Got a real important fella riding here with you."

His son looked down then eased off the gas. "Sorry. Didn't

realize. This baby flies. I love her!"

"I'm glad, David."

From there to Pine Bluff, he held it right on sixty. A bit of conversation sprinkled the drive, but mostly his son was all about the ride.

Sure seemed to be enjoying himself immensely with his prize. He eased onto the church's parking lot, turned off the key, then faced him. "So, you going to finally make my mother an honest woman?"

Buddy laughed. "Don't mince your words, do you?"

"No, sir. But with Mom A in Heaven, don't you think it's time?"

"We've been talking about it, but the Word says how good and how pleasant it is when two dwell together in unity."

"What's that supposed to mean?"

"Well, while she isn't quite as staunch a Church of Christ member as Mister John, but close."

"Hey, worship here. Let her go with PawPaw. Isn't like they don't believe in Jesus. Right?"

"And this coming from someone heading to ORU."

"I'm not saying for you to join the Church of Christ. I'd only want for you two to be happy. And my parents to be married."

Same arguments the boy's mother made. "It isn't that simple. I've sent out a few feelers. Not sure I'll buy myself a tent, but I intend to get back to preaching the Gospel."

"Wow, that's great, Dad. I take it she doesn't want any part of that."

"And you'd be right. She's campaigning hard for us getting hitched then spending some of Prescott's money traveling the world in our golden years. Figures we can spend half your inheritance and still leave you with a nice nest egg."

"But you're not that old. What? Like fifty-two?"

"Close. Fifty-four."

David opened his door then looked back. "I'm praying you'll work it out."

"So am I, Son." Buddy got out. "Come on. Let's see what the old man is up to."

All that summer, David expected a wedding announcement, but none came. Then even though no one shared any details, apparently, they'd had a big fight, and his father went back home to Dalton.

He didn't really like the term, but if there ever were two star-crossed lovers, it had to be his parents. The Friday night before the Monday he left for Oklahoma, he got the shock of his life.

As had become his habit, he picked up Hannah and her cousin Jill then headed toward downtown.

Before he reached the square, Jill put her hand over the seat onto his shoulder. "David, drop me off at the corner, please."

He glanced at her in the rear-view mirror then at Hannah who arced both eyebrows and nodded.

"What's up?"

"I don't want to see the Planet of the Apes."

"Why not? I hear it's too cool. Charlton Heston doesn't make bad movies."

Hannah touched his arm. "Let her out, and we'll pick her back up after the movie is over. Please."

He did as told. How could he argue with both of them? At the corner, he stopped. Hannah leaned forward, and Jill climbed out then ran into the diner.

"Who's she meeting?"

"Gerald."

"Jill and Gerald? Really, that should never have been. When did this happen?"

"Oh, they're only friends. He saw the movie the other night and is going to tell her all about it." She turned sideways in the seat. "Turn the car around first chance you get."

"Where are we going?"

"Thought we might ease on up to the mountain."

"You serious?"

"Yes, sir. Of course, I am."

His pulse quickened. He'd never . . . but heard from plenty of guys who had. What was she thinking? Twice, he started to turn back around and get to the theater, but his starter kept breaking.

Before he turned off the farm-to-market, he killed his lights as he'd heard was the custom.

"What you don't see, you won't have to lie about." How many times had he heard that from the regular visitors to the mountain? Had any male his age not gotten the warning a day or two after procuring a driver's license?

Hannah didn't say a word, like she knew all about it. But he was positive that like him, she'd never been there before. He eased to an empty spot a good hundred yards from the closest car-sized shadow and rolled down the window.

His sweetheart followed suit and a breeze flowed through the Camaro. Seemed a little cooler than the air back in town. She scooted around onto her knees and took hold of the seat's top.

"Want to get in the back?"

"What has gotten into you, girl?"

"You. I love you, John David Nightingale. I can't believe you're leaving Monday."

The moon shone bright above, almost full. A bit of its light shone on her, highlighting her face with a silvery glow, but he couldn't read her eyes. He'd heard the desperation in her voice though. She leaned her head against the seat and stared at him. Being sad over him going to Tulsa was understandable, but . . .

"I love you, too, Hannah Claire. Why are we here?"

Chapter Five

David waited for an answer, but she only shook her head.

In the time lag, he tried to understand what was going on. "I'm not mad. More flattered. But . . . I don't trust myself, Hannah, and . . ."

With a hard sniff, she wiped her cheek. "I. Can't. Stand the thought of you going to Vietnam, David." A sob escaped. "I love you."

"But I'm not. I've got a deferment. You know that. I'm only going to Tulsa."

"But . . ." Her tears ran freely. "You're going to be so far away . . . and without me and Jill and Mama—all of us who helped you—you'll flunk out, then they'll draft you. And . . . and . . . but if I was pregnant . . ."

"Then our parents would have to let us get married, and I could go with you to Tulsa and help you. Don't you see?"

Breaking completely, she sobbed, laying her head on his chest. "So, don't you want to climb over to the back seat? Really, David. Will you? Please? We can get married when you come back for Thanksgiving."

Dear Hannah. If she wasn't being so serious, he might bust a gut laughing, but according to his father, that was always and forever the wrong answer. Laugh with them, Son, he'd advised.

But never at them.

"Sweetheart." He stroked her hair.

With a whimper, she quietened then wiped her nose on the underside of her skirt. Even in the pale light of the moon, he could see the sadness in her eyes.

"I love you. And yes, we will get married one of these days, but not at Thanksgiving. Hannah, you're only fourteen, and I won't turn nineteen until November. Girl, your daddy would shoot me if you were to turn up in the family way.

"Maybe Jill, too, once her part was found out. And be it known, your sins will find you out. Says so in the Bible."

"Yeah, but it also says children are a blessing from the Lord."

"It does! And I hope we'll have a bunch! But all in due season. Remember, to everything there is a season and a time—God's perfect time—for every purpose under Heaven."

"Please, John David Nightingale, do not quote The Byrds to me!"

"That's Scripture, Hannah. King Solomon, not the Byrds."

A pout marred her lips. "What about you flunking out? You yourself said if not for us, you wouldn't have graduated. I couldn't stand it if . . ."

"I know, I do. And it's true, you helped me pass, but I'm taking a light load. Just enough to qualify as a full-time student. And Mother's already lined up a whole string of tutors. I'll have all the help I need. Flunking out . . . that's not an option."

"You promise?"

"Yes, of course. Let's get you finished with school—or at least way closer to graduating—before we even think about when we're getting married." He lifted her chin and looked into her eyes.

"Rest assured, sugar. I will be standing there, waiting at the altar, when you walk the aisle. I've known that for four years now."

She grinned. "So . . ." She leaned in close. "Do you at least want to kiss me?"

That night and the almost too many kisses lingered with David all the way to Tulsa. Like he'd promised her and his mother and any and everyone else who mattered, he buckled down and threw himself into his studies.

To his surprise, he loved it all to no end. Even though the Bible had been drummed into him, his PawPaw's church wasn't perfect by a long stretch.

But he appreciated it beyond measure that they'd taught him the Word.

Of course, his professors at ORU lectured from different perspectives and way different interpretations of the Scripture, but because of attending Gramps' church, those weren't so unfamiliar. He hadn't chosen ORU to debate theology.

Then to his chagrin, midway in an early lecture on Psalms, the professor stopped and stared right at him.

Having not done anything wrong, he stared right back.

Every paper he'd turned in right on time, and he carried a solid 'B' average.

What the man's problem was, David had no idea.

The professor looked down to his lectern, tracing a paper there with his index finger. He figured maybe the seating chart ... then his pointer stopped, and he looked up again, resuming his intense staring. "John David Nightingale."

"Yes, sir. I go by David."

"Are you related to Buddy Nightingale?"

"Yes, sir. He's my father."

"Thought so. He was on the TV show last night. The apple didn't fall too far from the tree."

"Yes, sir. Gramps says I'm like having his son all over again."

"You sing?"

"Yes, sir." Where all that might be going, David had no idea. Or why he'd been singled out either.

"Come down here, son."

Go down there? He didn't want to, but exactly like being at

his grandfather's church, he saw no way out without paying a higher price than he could afford. He joined the man at the podium then turned around and faced the class.

Sure looked different gazing up instead of down.

"You got a favorite Psalm you sing?"

"Yes, sir. I do."

"Grace us with it then."

He opened his mouth and belted out, "Praise ye the Lord! Praise God in His sanctuary!" That's all it took to carry Him up into the Heavenlies before the throne of God.

The classroom, students and professor all faded away. He sang his praises to the Most High God Almighty—for His mighty acts! For His excellent greatness!

A hundred seconds—or maybe an hour later—he came to himself kneeling, his hands stretched Heavenward. He stood, nodded at the professor, then took a step toward his seat.

A hand on his shoulder stopped him. "David."

He turned around.

His teacher smiled. "Thank you, son. I believe you were aptly named."

With a thank you nod, he hurried back to his seat, taking the wide steps two at a time and avoiding the other guys' eyes.

"Men, King David was a man after God's own heart. I believe we've just witnessed an example of that."

From that day on, instead of being a nobody freshman from the sticks, he was King David. So what if some put a bit of mockery in their voice? Most didn't. And either way, he liked it—a lot.

Never introduced himself that way though; pride going before destruction and a haughty spirit before a fall and all.

The heat, much milder in Oklahoma, gave way to mid-October's soul-refreshing cool breezes, and the leaves turned their beautiful autumn hues. David loved the fall season far better than the others. He did miss football though.

Then the Friday before the week off for Thanksgiving, the man himself—Oral Roberts—led chapel. His rousing sermon

John David's Calling

followed exceptionally great praise and worship. Then in closing, Brother Roberts challenged them all with a simple request.

"While you men are surrounded by your loved ones, giving thanks to God for all His mighty blessings this next week, I want you to seek the Lord about a specific amount—a love offering if you will. Then whatever that number is, I'm going to ask you to bring it with you when you come back. See how God will stretch you. And experience Jehovah Jireh's provision."

At first, David dismissed Brother Robert's request.

As his father before him, he didn't so much buy in to the Abundant Life message. God definitely loved a cheerful giver, and even though the Word said give and it shall be given unto you, it also said whatever a man sowed he would reap.

The only crop David wanted was men's souls. Like Jesus told Peter, come follow me, and I will make you a fisher of men.

But as his Zee ate the blacktop south toward Texas, the challenge kept boiling to the top of his thoughts. Right after he crossed the Red River, he relented and asked according to the man's request. After all, he was the one who insisted on going to ORU.

What could it hurt to ask?

"Okay, Lord, what would you have me give?"

A THOUSAND DOLLARS

"What?" Well, that was crazy. Had he heard right? "A thousand dollars? Really? Is that You, Lord? Because You know I don't have a thousand bucks."

YES YOU DO

The voice of the Lord was so real within Him.

His heart pounded against his ribs and skin surely like a maniac pounding against the door of his padded cell. He actually glanced down to see if his chest moved with the beating it took. He wrestled with what God asked.

"Lord, I love this car."

Nothing.

"You gave her to me. She was a desire of my heart, and You made it happen, and I . . ."

All the way down Highway 75, he wrestled with what he should do. Could do. She would be so angry.

But . . . he didn't need her permission. She'd made a big deal out of giving him the title, and he had it stashed right along with his amended birth certificate in the false bottom of his suit case.

But even if he did sell her, why would he want to give the money to Roberts? He was already rich enough.

It'd be like giving him twenty bucks or something.

The Zee was worth way more than that to him.

Still, if God . . .

He was of age. He could sell it. Oh Lord, is it really You? Is that what You're asking me to do?

Again, no answer. But then . . . he already had his answer.

Something his father told him smacked him upside his head as he pulled up to the house on Turtle Creek.

'God only gives you one task at a time.'

If he didn't know better, and if swearing wasn't Bible-forbidden, he'd swear Buddy Nightingale stood right behind him; like he'd just heard that with his ears—his physical ears!

Once upstairs in his room, the one he hadn't spent more than a month consecutive in the whole of his life, he sank to his knees.

"Yes, Lord. I will sell my car and give a thousand dollars."

A peace settled over him. Yes, he loved his car, but he loved the Lord way more.

The next morning, he fixed himself bacon, eggs, and cream gravy, but instead of taking time for biscuits, he toasted four pieces of white bread. Two for gravy and two for jelly.

Bless his mama's heart for keeping cold milk in her ice box just for him. Or maybe he should be blessing her caretaker's heart.

If he had it right, she'd followed his father to Los Angeles to be in the congregation for his first big meeting. He'd drive on down to Cypress Springs that day, but first . . .

Showered, shaved, and determined to be obedient to what he knew the Lord was telling him, he set out with a plan and a purpose.

Took half the day, but he found the right deal and traded the Camaro for a two-year-old Chevy plus a thousand and fifty dollars. The extra cash would come in nice. Hannah had secured Jill's service for most of the week he'd be in Cypress Springs.

For a bright side to the deal, his new, used sedan had bench seats.

Or was that a bad thing?

The last note faded. For several seconds, the faithful waited for the next song, but it didn't come. Sandy eased down onto the extra-hard folding chair as Buddy headed toward her.

She loved the man with her whole heart. Had for almost as long as she could remember, but . . . she hated that he believed all that holy roller . . . stuff.

At least Sunday morning was the last of it. Only one more preacher. She'd made it through the week-long revival. Who would have thought they could fill the Los Angeles Convention Center? But they had.

The speaker took the podium and launched into a different version of the same message last night's guy had brought. She didn't have the Scriptures' addresses memorized.

So, she couldn't rightly dispute what those folks claimed as the true interpretation of God's word, but . . . so what? Did it matter? Buddy was so hardheaded; she could show him a thousand passages.

He'd never change his mind.

But how could he expect her to?

Then how could holding to her religious upbringing be worth not being with him? Could she play act? Sometimes she thought nothing in the world should be worth keeping her from being one with him.

Together forever. It was all so unfair.

Why should she be expected to turn her back on everything she knew?

Hopefully, he'd come to realize they could disagree on religion and still be happy together. After all, she'd come all the way to California, and clapped and carried on like the best of them.

Only she knew she played like being at one of David's football games instead of inside a church. How could they so disrespect God?

Sooner or later, he had to realize God had made her especially for him.

To be his one and only eternal love.

Not soon enough for her, the last poor soul who needed to have a daub of oil smudged on their forehead and to be prayed for found the exit.

Mercy, all right. How did they stand staying so long? And Buddy singing softly while all of it went on . . . To. The. End. She couldn't believe it. Foot tapping ninety to nothing, she checked her wristwatch again.

Finally, he gathered his stuff then joined her. "You hungry?"

"Well, of course I am. Good grief, Buddy. It's almost three o'clock in the afternoon."

"I know. Wasn't it awesome? By the way, there's no such thing."

"As what?"

"Good grief."

Rolling her eyes, she wagged her head and sighed heavily. "If you say so, Nightingale."

"I do."

"Want to marry me? Awesome!"

"Think your father will approve of having two holy rollers in the family?"

"Come on. I'm hungry, and I'm buying."

All that weekend, David tried to let the wad of dead presidents sleep peacefully in the false bottom of his suitcase, but his thoughts kept rounding back to the stash of cash.

Especially after church Sunday, while he filled his plate and ate his dinner-on-the-grounds meal, he wrestled with where the Lord wanted him to invest those car bucks.

A soft NO had come that morning when he asked if Pine Bluff was where it should go.

Could he really give it to Oral Roberts?

He'd heard from the Lord, and this had to be some kind of test. What if the money led directly to someone getting saved?

For one soul, he'd give it all.

No one can take it with them, but a person sure can lay up treasure in Heaven.

"What are you thinking?"

"Huh, what?" He looked across the table. Hannah frowned.

"You've been staring off. I said, what are you thinking about?"

"Oh, my car money."

"I still think it stinks that the Lord made you sell her. I loved that car. I know you did, too, and that you were willing . . . it just makes me love you all the more. Still, I'm sad though."

He nodded then smiled. "I love the Lord, and you, and my family, and the new sedan will get us there and back."

Wrinkling her nose, she winked. "Finish your plate. You promised your mama we'd be there by four."

"Airplanes are never on time."

"So? Jill and I like watching them take off and land. I wouldn't mind being early."

It was fun driving the sixty miles from Pine Bluff to Austin, except Hannah passed too much time messing with him. Like her sitting next to him with her leg pressed to his didn't provide distraction enough.

Poor Jill must hate him being there, but at least she claimed to enjoy going with them and never minded. He hoped she wasn't lying.

Yeah right, two's company and three's a crowd.

Only fifteen minutes late, not too bad. And the girls seemed to have a good time on the trip. Pleased him his parents held hands, walking the gangway. Sure would like to know what the big fight had been about.

However, those who knew kept their secrets well, no sharing, no clues.

Maybe he ought to take the girls to Llano. Aunt Lee Lee would know. At the baggage claim, he bumped Hannah's shoulder. "You ever been on a horse?"

"Of course."

He looked past her to her cousin. "What about you, Jill? Want to go riding?"

"Sure, when?"

"I don't know. I'll have to call Uncle Travis and see when it's good for him."

"Here comes mine. There! Those two green ones are mine." His mother announced with some anxiousness in her tone to no one in particular. She definitely acted as though between him and his father, her suitcases should be plucked from the conveyor, and that she had no more responsibility in securing her luggage.

David got them all to the curb then fetched the sedan.

Hannah opened the back door, and his mother grinned like he was so smart then patted his head. "Thank you for borrowing this car. Whose is it?"

"It's his. Can you believe he sold the Zee?"

She looked from Hannah to him then back and forth twice. "You did what? When? Why?"

Smiling, he wiggled one shoulder up a quarter inch as her answer.

"Why haven't I heard of this?"

Um-hmm, anger salted her tone.

"Now, Mother. Calm down. I didn't want to spoil your trip. I knew you wouldn't like it." He walked around to the driver's side. "Dad, we figured you would ride up front with me, and the ladies can have the back seat."

Climbing into the driver's seat, he grinned and whispered, "Help me, Lord. This was all Your idea."

His plan worked great until he started the engine.

"So, John David Nightingale, pray tell. Why did you sell that car?"

"Well." He glanced at her in the rear-view mirror. "Last Friday at Chapel, Brother Roberts challenged us to seek the Lord about a love offering." Another quick look told him in an instant she was appalled.

Her pretty face—normally soft and loving—anything but! "Anyway, on the way home I asked God for an amount. He said a thousand dollars."

"He said a thousand dollars! God just said that to you."

"Yes, ma'am, in answer to my question. So, I traded the Camaro for this baby and the buckage."

"Where?"

"Dallas."

"What car dealer?"

"Bucks or Rucks. Something like that. I'm not sure. A little place on Harry Hines."

"We're going to Dallas tomorrow, and get that car back."

"You can. If you want it." He shook his head. "I am not. I made the deal, and I'm sticking to it. I have no idea what he'll be asking for it."

She scooted up and poked his father's shoulder. "Tell him, Buddy. Tell him he's made a horrible decision! Tell him it's an awful deal!"

"Mercy, Sandra Louis." His father turned in his seat. "Sit

back and enjoy the ride. When you're trading, in God's economy, everyone walks away blessed. If David heard from the Lord, then it absolutely was not a bad deal."

"Well! I never!"

"Maybe that's your problem then, sweetest heart."

Chapter Six

Hannah loved David with her whole heart and then some. She had for as long as she could remember. His father and Gramps were top shelf, but mercy—to quote the old reverend—his mother was a such a contradiction.

Sweet as maple syrup one minute then harder than granite the next. The lady loved her son, that was evident, but she always wanted to control him.

The fact that his dad hadn't married his mom wasn't the least bit hard for Hannah to understand, even if her sweetheart couldn't see it.

The car weaved and darted its way out of the terrible Austin traffic with nary a word from anyone until David hit the highway to home, then like someone had flipped a switch, Sandy turned away from the window and smiled at her.

"So, what are the plans?"

"Huh?" Hannah swallowed then found her voice. "Oh. Umm, we're eating Thanksgiving dinner at MawMaw and Pawpaw's with everyone, then David and Jill and I are going to my house for supper." She smiled.

"Remember last year, we had dinner at our house and supper in Cypress Springs, at Uncle James's."

"Humph. I don't. I wonder why I have no recollection."

"You were somewhere in Mexico, Mama."

"Oh, yes, I remember. That stupid hurricane messed things up to where I couldn't get back in time."

"So, you just stayed another week."

She leaned up and patted her son's shoulder. "You're such a good rememberer."

With a glance in the rear-view mirror, he winked at Hannah.

Holding back a giggle, she winked back. Oh, how she loved him! If only he would have agreed to her plan, then instead of having her cousin tagging along all the time, she could be married with a baby on the way.

One fine day . . . if only it was sooner and not later.

Mis'ess Prescott looked past her at Jill. "Are you playing basketball this year?"

"No, ma'am."

"Oh, I thought you loved it?"

"No, ma'am. That was my mom. She played."

"That's right and, how is she?"

"Good enough I guess."

Apparently, the woman didn't know about Jill's daddy divorcing her mother. David should have told her, but most likely he knew she couldn't have cared less, truth be known. Hannah filled her lungs.

"How was California? Did you go to the beach?"

"It was fabulous, but we really didn't have much time for laying out. Saw a few of the sights, but it seemed like we were always at the church, either in a service or rehearsing for the next."

"That's a shame not to get to play in the Pacific when you were so close. Where are you going next?"

"I'm not sure." She leaned forward and tapped Buddy's shoulder. "Have you decided where you're going next?"

Reaching over, David turned the radio down and his father sat sideways in his seat.

"Tulsa sooner or later. I don't know if he wants me to come before the first of the year or not, but Brother Roberts asked me to do a couple of his TV shows. And I've gotten three offers to hold revivals. But so far, I haven't accepted any of them." He stretched his neck left then right. Need to pray about it."

For the rest of the way to Cypress Springs, the conversation never veered back to Jill. Bless her pea-picking heart. Hannah couldn't decide who her daddy's leaving hurt worse, her or her mama.

How could that no-good decide he couldn't live without his sexretary? Why could he just pick up and leave his family like that?

Her heart broke for her cousin. She ought to stop calling that homewrecker the ugly name. Wasn't like the woman wasn't going to be family as soon as the six-month waiting period was over.

Shame the no-good bum was blood kin. She'd definitely rather it be Jill's mother and not the other way around. But Jill was blood, and nothing could change that.

Hannah's daddy understood her saying so, but he said his brother was his brother, and Jill's mama wasn't blood. He insisted blood was thicker than water, no matter who did what—whatever that meant.

The drive through the Texas Hill Country was beautiful that time of year. Hannah loved that she lived in the most beautiful part of Texas. She'd been up to Northeast Texas once when her parents allowed her and Jill to make a day trip to Clarksville with Gramps, Buddy, and David. They had a funeral to go to.

The area had a few hills up there and some of the tallest trees she'd ever seen, but nothing compared with the Hill Country as far as she was concerned. She loved the Clarksville town square though.

What fun, stopping off for a soda at Blackmon's Pharmacy all by themselves while the men went to Allen's Lumber for something.

As planned, David short-stopped the Harrises, then instead of a quick getaway, MawMaw went and brought out one of her buttermilk pies, and soda all around, to keep a growing boy's feet under her table long enough for two pieces.

After refusing a third, he stood. "We best get going. I promised Hannah's mom we wouldn't be too late."

All the way from Cypress Springs to Marble Falls, she kept hoping he'd take a detour somewhere, but the big lug drove straight to her house. He eased the Ford to a stop right out front.

Jill jumped out. "See you later, David."

"Thank you, Cuz."

She smiled—a bit too much. "Anytime." Then she disappeared inside.

Hannah swallowed, forcing the jealousy down. David was hers, and everyone knew it. But she wanted him all to herself. All the time.

"You getting out?"

She pressed her leg against his. "Not just yet, don't you love these bench seats?"

He put his arm around her and tugged. She tilted her chin and licked her lips.

"Yes, I do."

David let his lips linger too long. Oh the sweetness! Praise God he kept his hands where they belonged. He leaned back onto his door. "You need to go inside."

She glanced over her shoulder then turned toward him again. "Mama hasn't started flipping the porch light yet. We've still got time." She grinned and scooted even closer, kissing his neck.

He scrunched his shoulder. "Hannah."

She leaned back with a sultry little grin plastered on her lips. He loved those lips.

"Yes?"

"Please, baby, go inside. You're driving me crazy."

"Fine." She eased over. "Don't forget to call your Uncle Travis about us coming out this week. Riding sounds fun, and I'd like Jill to meet Cody, maybe get to know him better."

"I won't. Isn't he a little old for her?"

"No more difference than there is between Travis and Emma Lee. So good, then. Now kiss me goodnight."

Did he ever, but it wasn't until her mama started flipping the porch light that she finally exited the Ford. He waited for her to blow him one last kiss then cranked Old Faithful to life. Her upstairs bedroom light flipped on, and a Jill-sized silhouette stood in the window.

Was she looking down at him? Then what had to be Hannah sidled up next to her.

Slipping the sedan into gear, he eased on home.

His girl occupied most of his thoughts as he drove, but her cousin kept circling around. A sigh escaped. Poor Jill. He needed to have a heart to heart with her, but Hannah made sure he was never alone with her older cousin.

And he wasn't about to stool her off, but the girl needed to set her bonnet for some other guy.

For a half mile, the story of Jacob and his four wives came to mind. But like the patriarch . . . he only loved one young lady, and for sure Hannah's father would never trick him.

On the other hand, her old man might shoot him dead if he caught him doing anything inappropriate with his daughter—or his niece.

To the bones, Mister Henderson was a good man. David liked him a lot.

Once off the blacktop, his ruminations turned to varmint hunting. Maybe he ought to try and work some in over his break. Some extra cash would be nice, but the thrill of it would be even nicer.

Shame Sonny had gone off to live in that stupid commune. How could he? Images of a bunch of naked folks running around flashed across his inner eye.

"Satan, I rebuke you in the name of Jesus."

For the rest of the way to PawPaw's, he wrestled with lust of the eye. Short of the driveway, he killed the lights and opened the glove box. He fingered around in the dark until he found his pack of cigarettes then lit one. He hated the habit but it sure relaxed him.

If only the Lord would have put it in a verse somewhere that clearly stated, thou shall not smoke—but then He didn't even forbid drinking, only drunkenness.

Sure couldn't get drunk off of tobacco. Well, weed, according to Sonny, but tobacco couldn't hold a candle to it. Nothing like weed—or so he'd been told.

After finishing his cigarette and field stripping it, he eased on up the drive. Mama's Caddy wasn't there. Where might she be? Man, he needed to talk with them both.

They should be abstaining from all appearances of evil, no matter how old they were or how long they'd been loving each other. His dad needed to fix things.

He couldn't wait to get Aunt Lee Lee alone and find out all the scuttlebutt. Surely if anyone knew the whole story, she would. And he had no doubt he could get her to talking.

Over the next two days, the chance to set his parents straight never presented itself. The third, the Wednesday before Thanksgiving, he drove Hannah and Jill to Llano.

On the way, Hannah went on and on about Cody Wayne Buckmeyer. So much that it about made him sick. Cody this and Cody that. Big deal. So, he'd gone to A&M and rode a few bulls.

Probably half-tamed, hand-raised bottle babies.

"And." Hannah drew out the word like she had something really important to say. "He's not married."

Her matchmaking-self had gone into overdrive with her captive audience. He couldn't believe she was touting his cousin for Jill.

"What about Amy Zimmerman?"

Hannah turned from Jill and glared. "Oh, they're not serious. He's known her since high school, and if he was

John David's Calling

serious about her, he would've given her a ring by now." She looked back to her cousin.

"I'm telling you, he's a hunk and he's available!" Then she turned again, poking his arm. "Remember the Fourth of July picnic? He brought her."

"Sure, what about it?"

"Well, she told us girls that Cody Wayne better get off the dime, or she'd be back on the market."

"So, are they like going steady or what?"

"No, that's the deal! She said that he hadn't made any kind of commitment. Your Aunt Lee Lee thinks he's still pining over Cindy Morrison."

"Who?"

"Your cousin, silly. Aunt Cora's granddaughter. Her daddy was Ambassador to Egypt then she worked in President Johnson's White House."

"How do you know all this stuff? Much less keep it straight? And when did you talk to Auntie?"

She slugged his shoulder, not too hard, but way more than a love tap. "David. Your family is going to be my family and vice-versa. A body needs to keep up with kin."

"Ow." He rubbed his shoulder. "Whatever. I'd appreciate you not whacking me."

Cody was way too old for Jill; she was a bit older than Hannah's fifteen, but not much, maybe sixteen, seventeen at most, and his cousin was pushing thirty. Then again, stranger things had happened.

And unlike Leah, Jill didn't have weak eyes.

Other than being sad over her daddy being such a cad, the girl was top shelf.

Hey, that was it.

He glanced past Hannah. "Since it appears to be a fine day for matching, I know a guy who'd be perfect for you, Cuz."

Hannah elbowed him.

"Oh, yeah? Who? I know everyone in three counties."

"Adam Churchdog. Uh, his real name's Churchill, but some

of the guys hung Churchdog on him. He likes it."

Jill leaned out. "He goes to ORU?"

"Yes, ma'am. He and I started together. We've been talking about requesting a room together next semester. We're already in a couple of study groups together. He's a great guy. Loves the Lord and doesn't pick his nose or anything stupid."

Hannah elbowed him again. "David."

"What?"

Thought he caught a bit of disappointment from the way Jill acted when Cody Wayne appeared then could barely spare a hello. So he couldn't ride with them. But before his goodbye, she peppered him with as many questions as she could get in. Maybe she was interested.

The afternoon horseback riding was awesome.

His girl showed her jealous streak a bit over his cousin. Sarah being a senior and a rodeo queen and maybe as pretty as her mama—if that was possible—made her a likely target for the green- eyed monster.

But praise the Lord, Hannah never got her claws out.

Still hadn't wormed any free time with his aunt, and the afternoon was wearing thin. To his thinking, Emma Lee Buckmeyer had always been the pick of the litter.

Not that he'd ever say that aloud to anyone—especially his mother. Then Sarah Grace invited Hannah and Jill to go feed the new bottle babies. Perfect.

As soon as he got the girls loaded and back on the road, Jill pummeled him with questions about Adam all the way home. Maybe she was interested in him, too . . . but then . . . guys were like buses—be another one along any minute.

If he could get a long-distance romance going between those two, though, maybe she'd stop mooning over him before Hannah caught her outright.

Be nice having his bud in the family . . . if it came to that.

Hannah had never been so sore in the whole of her life, but she wasn't about to sit on her duff and not help. Her mama would tan her hide if word got back she didn't help in the kitchen of a hostess after getting an invitation for Thanksgiving Dinner.

It sure seemed somewhat unfair, that the men all congregated in the living room around the television—just because of being male. But then they didn't know what they were missing.

A girl could learn a lot by asking a strategic question now and again. Her and David's age difference had been mentioned more than once, but like her daddy always claimed, she'd been born old.

Just after her thirteenth birthday, he told an uncle she was going on thirty, so for sure, she must be grown at fifteen.

"Here, dear." MawMaw handed her a bowl of green beans with bacon chunks. "Put this on the table, then go tell David to let them all know it's time to get everyone seated."

She did, he did, and once the food was blessed, the conversation ramped up with all the 'pass this' and 'I need that.' With plates all full though, it all but died for a while. She put little samples of almost everything on her plate then only picked at it.

Her tummy was about as sore as her legs. She ought to slap David for suggesting horseback riding.

Cleaning her plate seemed to ease the stiffness. Maybe a little more turkey would be okay. MawMaw made the best gravy ever!

David scooted his chair back then stood. "You need anything, Hannah?"

"Oh, no thank you!" She smiled, shaking her head. "I'm stuffed."

"Okay then." He leaned in close. "I'll be back in a minute. I need to talk with Mama."

"Sure." She nodded then scooted over into his chair.

"Mister Nightingale, sir?"

The man she hoped would be her father-in-law real soon turned toward her and smiled. "Yes, ma'am?"

Man, no way could he deny David being his son. She loved those smiling eyes her sweetheart inherited. "May I ask you a question?"

"Well, sure. I'm guessing if my son has his way, you'll be my daughter before too long."

The man definitely knew how to say all the right things, and she loved it. What had her sugar said to his dad about her? But pumping Buddy for whatever David had told him would have to come later.

She'd thought of something she figured she should know and might not get another chance to visit with the one who could enlighten her. "Well, how much do they pay you for singing on TV?"

The man turned serious. "Expenses, plus . . . a little honorarium."

Not good enough. She flashed her biggest smile—the one that always melted her daddy's heart though it did little for her pigheaded boyfriend. "What's a little?"

"Mercy, girl. Some folks consider it rude to ask how much money folks make."

"Oh really? Hmm." She slumped a smidgen and gave him her puppy dog look. "Then how am I supposed to find out what I need to know? I mean . . . I don't mean to be rude or anything, but I don't know who else I'd ask."

The man seemed to contemplate not telling her then shrugged. "Well, let's say a hundred dollars a show."

"Okay, that's good. What about singing at meetings? Like when you went to California . . . Do they pay expenses, too?"

"Yes, ma'am." He snorted a laugh. "They do."

"And how much for the honorarium?"

"Girl, where are you going with this?"

She offered a real smile. "Well, your father says my David has the gift same as you, and he knows the Word, and loves the

Lord."

"Yes, he sure does, but you haven't answered my question."

"Oh, I'm just thinking maybe he shouldn't be going to ORU. I mean, you'd hire him, wouldn't you? He said you were thinking about getting a tent and preaching like you and the reverend did before the twister ripped it all to pieces."

"That wouldn't be a good idea. He'd lose his student deferment."

"Well, Daddy says Nixon is going to end the war."

"Maybe, but we'd all hate it if he got drafted. And just because the president-elect campaigned on a thing—no matter how much he wants to do it—doesn't mean Congress will go along with him. He's dead in the water then, can't get it done without them."

She caught the sob before it got out. Hadn't told him the best part yet, and he hadn't said he wouldn't hire David. Plus even if he didn't, Pine Bluff might. That would be swell if he could live so close to home. "Thank you, sir."

"I don't know what for. I know you hate David being so far away, Hannah, but right now, that's way better than him being in the Army and across the Pacific Ocean."

"Or even worse, the Marines."

"Amen."

Chapter Seven

Fifty-two steps north, if you cut the butter on the back porch and jumped the steps, David leaned against the live oak that was older than dirt, sharing his mother's nasty Virginia Slim.

Trying hard to find the right words, he kept rewriting mentally. But that long skinny cigarette burned fast, and its cherry would soon kiss the filter. He best be about it.

"Talked with Auntie yesterday."

"Oh yeah?" She hiked an eyebrow and took the butt back. "What did she allow?"

"I asked her what you and Dad had the big fight about." Maybe she'd tell him, and he wouldn't have to stool Lee Lee off.

"And what did she say?"

"That it was round pick-your-number of the same match you two have been having forever."

She took a dainty drag then dropped the smoke and ground it out with her high dollar shoe's pointed toe. He didn't know how the ladies stood those skinny devils. Looked like they'd kill your poor toes.

"My sister talks too much sometimes."

"Well, it's my humble opinion, that the two of you should

not be traveling together or hanging out all hours until you get married."

She snickered.

"What so funny?"

"You sound just like your PawPaw."

"He's right then. And so am I. Dad should know better. You both certainly know Paul says we should abstain from all appearances of evil."

"Not that it's any of your business, Son, but we don't share a room or do anything we shouldn't."

"That's great, and I'm glad to hear it. But Mom, either get married or stop following him around like a lovesick school girl."

In his peripheral vision, a blur moved, then her hand struck his cheek. "David John Prescott! Or Nightingale—whatever you're calling yourself today—you will not talk to me like that! I'm your mother."

Though he never dreamed she'd be the one, just like he'd purposed in his heart, he turned the other cheek. "Yes. You are, Mother. Please act like it."

Her desire to slap his other cheek was perfectly clear in her eyes. She wanted to so bad, but either she thought better of it or had already hurt her hand the first time. Instead, tears welled, and she pulled another cigarette out.

"Look. I love you, David. But it isn't as easy as you make it out."

Striking a match on his jeans, he held it. "Mother, God is the same yesterday, today and forever. He's the same miracle-working God He was two thousand years ago."

She took a man-size drag then held it toward him.

Accepting, he thought of a thousand arguments, then sucked the filter, filling his lungs. He had to convince her, but the lady was every bit as hardheaded as her father. He blew the smoke out slow and steady, buying more time.

But he decided against saying more. "I love you, too, Mama." He handed the Slim back and headed inside.

Man, his cheek burned. Probably had a red hand print, too. Maybe he'd holler at Hannah and sit on the porch a while. He'd put her on the other side from his stinging cheek.

Hannah spotted the red mark right away, but didn't let on, and no one else mentioned it. Had to have been his mother. Did she slap his face regular?

The woman better never do it in front of her, or there'd be all kinds of . . . She stopped that train before it left the station. David's relationship with his mother was his.

And something she'd just have to swallow like any other bad-tasting dose of medicine. The very last thing she needed would be getting crosswise with Mis'ess Sandra Louise Harris Prescott want-to-be-Nightingale.

On the way back to Marble Falls, she mulled over exactly the best way to convince him to get on board with her plan. His reluctance frustrated her but at the same time, endeared him to her heart.

What other male would turn down the opportunity she offered? No one she knew, that was for certain. Not so much the marriage part, but the other.

Her mama made it out to be somewhat of a chore, but some of the girls whispered a different tune.

What a shame she didn't have someone to ask who would tell her the truth.

Either way, the act was like a major part of her strategy . . . and didn't the Bible say that when a person got to know another person in that sense, they were married in His sight? Plus, she and David would have the piece of paper soon enough.

Maybe the girls were right. What did her mother know about anything?

As usual, Jill chatted too much, but her cousin had been a magpie forever. Mostly, she wanted to know more about Adam

John David's Calling

Churchill, and that was a good thing. The college man could capture her romantic thoughts and get them off David.

And Hannah loved the sound of David's voice. He never leaned out to look at Jill or anything.

The conversation helped pass the time.

That evening back home, the table should have swayed under the load of food. Definitely a good thing her mother didn't cook as well as MawMaw. Though she could have totally enjoyed eating twice as much and made a pig of herself, she refrained and only ate enough so as not draw any attention.

Could've scarfed down three pieces of her great mock mincemeat pie loaded with tasty raisins, but only took one. Such self-control! She could hardly help being proud of herself. Jill had two.

Hopefully there'd be leftovers.

Dark-thirty, she eased David out to his car. Sitting in front of her house was the only place she could have him all alone—without lying or getting her cousin involved.

Jill had somewhat suspected what she'd been up to the time she had him take her to the mountain, and quizzed her a little, but never really pinned Hannah down on exactly what didn't happen.

He opened then held her door.

Waiting for him to get in, she then turned sideways and smoothed her skirt out. "I loved the Zee but these seats are so much better."

"I agree."

"Did you know they pay your father to be on TV?"

"Hadn't really thought about it."

"Expenses plus a hundred dollars a show."

"Really? Who told you that?"

"He did." She giggled. "I don't figure he much wanted to, but I asked, so he answered." She smiled and hiked her eyebrows, but maybe he couldn't even see in the dark.

"Okay. Guess that's interesting. Why'd you want to know?"

"Just curious. I mean . . . you sing as good if not better than he does. You know he's been talking about buying a tent or whatever, so he can start doing revivals like he and Gramps used to—not just leading the music at another preacher's services."

"So?"

"I was just thinking you could work with him. Be like partners. We'd have plenty of money. Have you paid any attention to how the offering plates overflow at Gramp's church? Then you could even take over for your dad when he got old or ever wanted to pastor just one church like the reverend. I think we'd really enjoy the traveling."

"What are you talking about?"

Could he be so dense? Filling her lungs, she willed her heart to beat slower. It'd be important to keep her wits and not get too emotional. Logic—not tears—would win the day.

"School, basically. There's no reason you need to go back. Why, you know more Scripture than anyone I know. You could probably teach the teachers a thing or two. And David—"

He held up one finger, shaking his head.

"Now." She ooched closer. "Just a minute. Just listen for one minute and let me finish. If we were married with a baby on the way, you'd be 2A and not likely to be drafted. Then 3A once the baby got here.

"Nixon's going to end the war." She pulled her leg back and scooted over. "I love you, and you love me. I hate you being so far away! I can't stand it."

David wrapped his arm around her shoulder and pressed his lips to hers. Way too soon for his liking though probably too long for his own good, he leaned back.

"I love you, too, sweetheart, but we've got to stay the course. You'll graduate in two years."

"Two and half. And that's like forever."

"No, it isn't. Not at all, and it's the right thing to do. You know it is. I know I've been praying about it, haven't you?"

"Oh, don't give me that." She scooted away and turned sideways, putting her bent knee between them. "I hate you being so far away, and God knows it! You're going to miss my birthday, and . . ." She sobbed.

"Daddy says we can car-date after my birthday! But you won't even be here! Oh, David! It just isn't fair! I don't want to wait!"

Brilliantly, the part of him that wanted to laugh at her theatrics kept quiet. Another part knew most of what was coming out of her mouth was more calculated than emotional. Such a sweet mixture of silk and sass.

How could he not love his sweet Hannah?

"Maybe I could skip a couple of classes and come home for your birthday."

"You could? Will you promise?"

"No, I said maybe. I'll be back in a month for the winter break, and we can talk about it then."

She stared out her window for a few seconds of silence, hugging herself like she was trying hard to come up with a new tactic. The porch light flickered.

Like she'd been shot from a cannon, she twisted around and threw her arms around his neck, smothering him with kisses. He loved her passion. The girl sure seemed to know what she wanted.

And he was blessed and highly favored to be the one.

Then too soon, she broke it off.

"Call me when you get up. Jill and I want to go fishing."

"Yes, ma'am."

The light flashing went twice as long.

Opening the door, she blew him one last kiss then jumped out.

That temptation stuff was for the birds. He hated himself, wanted her so badly, but he knew so much better than to act on his fleshly desires as his parents had. God would help him stay strong and keep on the righteous path. He could trust Him.

Next day fishing, he found out that Hannah and her cousin weren't actually all too serious about wetting a hook. Apparently, they'd decided traipsing across most of Cypress Springs, trying to find the best tank to fish was the plan.

Not that he really minded—except for the two times Jill accidentally-on-purpose tripped into his arms.

Praise the Lord, Hannah had not seen either, especially the second time when her lips came so close to his that all he would have had to do was lean forward.

That evening after Jill went in, his persistent lady tried again to convince him that getting her with child and forcing her parents into letting them marry would be the best thing to happen for all involved—especially her.

"You ever wonder why I grew up in Cypress Springs with my grandparents instead of in Dallas with my mother?"

"Not really. You've been here my whole life. Why would I?"

"You know about my parents, right?"

"Yes, you've told me the story. Your Pawpaw wouldn't let them get married because of his Church of Christ doctrine, but . . . what's that go to do with us?"

"I'm getting there. At first, Mama's husband at the time, Harry Prescott, had gone insane and she'd taken him overseas for the best doctor. Left me with MawMaw and PawPaw. Do you know why he went crazy?"

Wide-eyed, she shook her head.

"Over Dad getting her pregnant—with me."

"I didn't. I'm sorry David. I didn't know that. What happened?"

"I was only one at the time, but the short story of it is that Pawpaw had to shoot Prescott. He'd already taken one shot at Dad, but missed. PawPaw didn't have a choice. Said he liked the man well enough, he was a war hero and all, but . . ."

He didn't like that part of the story, but she needed to know.

"Wow. So, did he . . . kill him?"

"Yeah. He got shot, too, but of course, he recovered. Anyway, Mama stayed in Cypress Springs mostly for the next few years. She'd go to Dallas now and then, she has a home there. And she traveled some. I was like four when she decided I needed to move to Dallas and live there with her."

He winked. "That'd be the year you were born."

"Oh, like four years is any big deal. Mercy, David."

"Never said it was." He waited to see if she had any questions, but apparently, she was all ears. "We got to Burnett, and I figured out we're going home and started pitching a fit. I wanted my Pawpaw." He laughed.

"She says she tried to buy me off with a Coke and moon pie, but I wasn't having any part of it."

"You remember when you were four?"

"I do. I guess because it was shaping up to be the worst day of my life at the time. But she took me back home, it turned out all for the best."

"So . . . you've never . . . lived . . . with either one of your parents?"

"Not really. I'd visit some, but before I left, I always wanted to know for how long and when I'd be back home again."

"Okay. So, I repeat myself. What has this to do with us?"

"Generational curses."

"What's that?"

"The Word says that the sins of the fathers are visited upon the sons up to the fourth generation."

"Oh. But . . . I'm still not seeing where you're going. Explain more for me."

"I've never taken a drink in my life, because of Gramps . . . can't be a drunk if you don't ever drink. You've heard his testimony. I'm not uncovering him, but because of him, I'll never drink hard liquor."

"But that's a good thing. So, are you saying his father was a drunk, too? And your dad? That you're the fourth generation?"

"Well, Grandpa Charley drank, and he was a whoremonger as well. You know what that term means, right?"

"Yes, David. I am not a baby." She stared off out the windshield as though highly offended.

"Okay, wasn't calling you a baby, just wanted to be sure you're following me." How could he make her understand? He took to looking at the night sky, too, saying a silent prayer. "Anyway, my father was not a drunk, but . . . he loved the ladies."

"Really? I would never have thought it. He's such a Godly man."

"Exactly—I mean he wasn't always, but now he is. My point is that's what I want to be, Hannah—Godly. Just like I'm determined to never take a drink, I've decided I will never be intimate outside the bounds of marriage.

"It's partly for our children. Unto the fourth generation . . . I am determined to break that cycle. So, until you walk the aisle on your father's arm, and he verbally gives you to me and blesses our union . . . until you become my wife in front of God and all of our families and friends—I cannot and will not go along with your plan."

"Oh, David! That is so sweet. It is! But listen. We're in drastic times here, and it's probably going to take drastic measures. Can't you see that? If you lie with me, we'll be married according to the Bible. Isn't that right? Isn't that what it says? We only have tomorrow! You're leaving Sunday after church to go back to Tulsa."

The light started flickering.

"Oh, Mama! Why does she have to do that? We're only talking! And now all our time is wasted!"

"What if you don't get pregnant?"

Chapter Eight

Hannah heard his question, but didn't have an answer. That night, she skipped writing in her diary. She didn't want to lie to it. The part of her he rejected brooded, in no mood to chronicle her failure.

How could she not love him for being so good? And strong? And levelheaded? But how could she put that on paper without elaborating?

Might a Saturday so sweet be enough to wait another month before seeing him again? All except for needing to snatch Jill bald-headed. Grrrr . . .

Why did she have to flirt with him? She knew full well that Hannah and David planned to get married. She hated it but didn't know of anyone else who'd be willing to spend the time. At least anyone her parents would trust to chaperone.

For so long it'd been no problem, then all of a sudden . . . and her cousin! It didn't make her sad, it made her mad. Jill should know better.

But still . . . *Romeo and Juliet* would surely win best movie of the year. She'd never seen one she'd enjoyed more. She so identified with Juliet, and Olivia Hussey played the part so perfectly—her new favorite actress for certain.

If she thought she could never be with David . . . The movie had definitely been worth it.

Of course, David voted for *The Lion in the Winter,* but let her have her way and agreed to the tragic romance. If she'd have known it'd be so sad, she might have opted for his choice. She liked Peter O'Toole plenty.

The best part of the day proved the last part as always. Parking outside her house couldn't be beat—all except for that stupid front porch light.

As though fifteen years and nine months old wasn't mature enough to car date! But sixteen was. What did they think? That some light would suddenly illuminate her understanding and she'd be a woman?

Mercy, as all the Nightingales were wont to say. She liked the word, like calling on God in all instances of trouble, theirs or others', didn't matter. Soon enough, she'd be one, too.

The terrible thing about Saturday was when it ended, because it preceded Sunday—and that day brought such sorrow. As if her broken heart had been shattered, and a major piece of it stolen and carried off to Tulsa, Oklahoma.

Standing on her porch, she watched him drive off with it. She wiped her wet cheeks. Why did he have to go off so far? And her stay there without him. It so wasn't right.

The next twenty-one days passed slow as a turtle, each one like a week or worse, but they did go by. She marked them off, counting every night the little squares until he'd return home to her.

She could actually empathize with Sandy and how she had to deal with Buddy going all the way back to Dalton to live. What was wrong with those two?

Not that she was anything like David's mother though. She would follow David to the ends of the earth and do anything—whatever he asked—to be with him all the time.

Far as she was concerned, her place was by his side—always. Wherever, whenever, however . . . she couldn't care less, so long as that's where she could live.

Then finally! He came! Fun, fun, fun—until college took her sweetheart away! Again! She hated roller coasters but that's sure what she'd been riding.

Higher than the sky when with him, lower than a whale's belly when he crossed the Red River going north. At least he promised to come for her birthday!

All she did for the next two and a half months entailed devising a plan to be sure he never left without her again. Still a month before she'd be able to car date, a new one emerged and took shape.

It just might work. It presented itself in part from that question he asked that she'd never answered.

In the evenings, she started watching the news with her father. After a week, it became apparent the war would never end. She waited until Daddy's lodge night to lay out her new plan to her mother.

She made tea and carried a cup to the living room. With a whole hour before *I Love Lucy,* she should have plenty of time. Setting one cup on the table next to where her mother sat, she smiled.

"Oh, that's so sweet, Hannah. Thank you, darling." Her mother marked the place in the book she'd been reading and took a sip.

"Mama, I've been thinking."

"Ah. So, the tea is subterfuge." She blew on the brew then took another sip.

"Aww, I wouldn't say that. I knew you'd like some, but . . . Anyway, it doesn't look to me or Daddy that's Nixon's going to end this terrible war."

"Give him some time. He just got in office."

"Mother! David doesn't have time. If we wait until I graduate, it might be too late."

Her mom's brows knitted. "For what?"

"To get married, of course."

"Oh, I see. Care to explain yourself?"

"Well, a 2A classification will not guarantee he won't get drafted. And even me being pregnant doesn't get him a 3A until the baby is born. If he graduates first . . ." She let that last word hang.

"Don't be ridiculous, Hannah."

"Mother! How many times have you heard Daddy claim I was going on thirty? I know since I turned thirteen! So sixteen has got to be like grown. But listen to me, Mama, because my mind's made up.

"I'm marrying David. I love him, and he loves me. So why not sooner than later? If we get married after this summer, I could still finish and graduate in Oklahoma."

"Oh, baby, don't rush things. You've only got the rest of this year and two more. That isn't too long to wait."

"It is for me! And I can't take the chance! What if he flunks out and gets drafted? My life would be over!"

Where the conversation headed, she didn't like one bit, but at least Mama hadn't said no. Hannah couldn't afford to lose any momentum.

"I hate him being gone! I couldn't stand it, knowing he was in danger in Vietnam! I'll die if anything happens to him."

"Sweetheart, nothing is going to happen to David. Don't borrow trouble."

Her cheeks warmed. Loving the best boy she'd ever met was not borrowing trouble. She shook her head. "I'm not!"

"Just trust God. He'll keep David safe wherever he is. The Lord has plans for that young man."

"Arrrgh! If he wasn't so pigheaded, I would not be having this conversation with you!"

"What is that supposed to mean?"

Pushing her palms toward her mother, she stood. "Nothing! Forget I said anything! Why can't anyone understand?"

Her mother jumped up. "No, ma'am, I most certainly will not! I will not forget it! Have you and David done something you shouldn't have?"

"No!"

"Then what are you talking about?"

"Nothing! A big fat nothing! Didn't you hear me? You know, nada, zilch, zero!" She spat the words at her mother, glaring.

She stared at her for a long second . . . then grinned. "I see. So. You wanted to, and he refused."

Tears refused to be kept from spilling over and raced to her chin. She nodded.

"Well, bless his heart. I knew that boy had a head on his shoulders, and integrity. He's worth waiting for, Hannah. There's no need to rush anything."

"You're so stubborn! Just like him! Have you not been listening to me at all?" She spun around and marched upstairs to her room. She fell across the bed sideways and wept hot, angry, frustrated tears.

She hated missing Lucy, but she wouldn't be able to laugh at the crazy lady anyway, not the way her insides churned. The redhead's antics couldn't brighten her sour mood. Nothing would except being Mis'ess John David Nightingale.

But he was in Oklahoma.

David missed his love but kept himself busy. Then one Friday afternoon everything changed. A trio of upperclassmen cornered him in the day room. The man in the middle, the ringleader if he had it right, held out a pile of tracts toward him.

"Take 'em. We're going to Hell's Acre after supper, and you're coming with us."

Accepting the stack of thin folded papers, he studied the top one. Though not his idea of evangelism, it couldn't hurt. Besides, what choice did he have? "What time and where do you want me to be?"

"Meet us here at eight. We're taking your sedan."

"Yes, sir." The thought to stand at attention and salute passed through his head, but that would have been a bit over the top. Never hurt to have friends in high places, so why look a gift horse in the mouth? Or antagonize an upperclassman?

Praise the Lord, his mother hadn't cut off his gas card over him selling the Z though he'd half-expected it. Just like him, she was still working on being a cheerful giver.

But then . . . him putting the ten Benjamins in the offering was what he'd heard. And he wanted to be obedient. Nothing had been said about him liking it.

Jesus didn't like going to the cross, but in obedience, he went and saved the world.

Whoever wanted to scoot their boots showed up on Friday night at the Acre—not that David ever darkened the door of any such establishment. He hated all the traffic, but he'd filled his tank, and the old girl didn't mind stop-and-go.

Nothing like his Pawpaw's cantankerous old truck with its two choices. Sixty or off.

Pickups packed the place's parking lot. "There, turn in there." The ringleader pointed to the back row. "Park close to the exit, too, so we don't get blocked in."

As instructed, David obliged. He hung back while the others started passing out the tracts and telling the folks hurrying to the hideaway of immorality that Jesus loved them.

A few took the pamphlets, but most either cursed or ignored the trio. The closer he got to the sprawling metal building, the louder the music.

Whoever played sure knew what they were doing, but the singer kept going flat.

Guess it didn't matter. Seemed the folks continued coming.

He smiled and gave out a few tracts but wasn't belligerent about it. He'd heard how the trio practiced an in-your-face kind of Christianity. Hell's hot, and you're going if you don't repent and turn around.

But he just wasn't so sure about all that. MawMaw always said he'd catch more flies with honey, so he kept flashing his crooked smile.

After an hour or so, the music stopped.

"What happened?"

John David's Calling

Ringleader smiled. "Band's taking a break."

"Oh."

A chill washed over him. Then almost like he stood on the moving sidewalk at Love Field, he floated toward the front door. He paid the cover. The lady looked him over hard but, in the end, didn't ask to see his license.

The darkness froze him until his eyes adjusted. He trotted across the empty dance floor and tapped the stand-up mike. The thuds echoed.

A warmth spread from his heart to his throat. He opened his mouth and sang. A new song.

Each time through, more folks gathered. One especially caught his eye—a young lady not much older than him. The depth of sadness splashed across her face broke his heart.

Another song erupted. A banjo joined in, and someone tapped out the rhythm on the drum. He sang it through, then on the second go-round, an old man joined him, singing the harmony.

Way before he wanted it to be over, it was. He looked around and nodded his thanks to the band. When he turned back, tears streamed down the young lady's cheeks.

In an instant, like he'd lived it himself, he knew her life's story and stepped toward her. "Miss Woods?"

She faced him.

"Your father loves you. And you need to go home."

She shook her head.

A cowboy stepped in front of her. "She ain't going nowhere." The stench of alcohol traveled on the breath of each word.

"If she wants, I'll take her home. It isn't your choice, friend."

The drunk cursed him. "Sure ain't yours, pretty boy."

"You're right. It'd be hers and hers alone. Glad we agree on that." He scooted to the side and looked around the cowboy. "Della, what do you want?"

She looked from him to the cowboy then back. "How do

you know my name?"

"The Lord told me, just like he told me your father loves you."

"Well, he doesn't! He hates me."

David shook his head. The crowd had made a circle around them like they expected a fight. He held his hand out. "Come on. I'll take you home or wherever you want to go."

Cowboy slashed at David's arm. "You ain't taking her anywhere. Best you hit the trail, Cow Paddy." The drunk roared at his own dumb joke.

"Della?"

She looked first at him then behind him to his right. David whirled and faced the man. "Sir, I will not defend myself, but if Della wants to leave with me, you will not stop her."

A fat right hand zoomed toward his nose, he leaned back, and it missed its mark. Cowboy followed the ill-fated swing to the ground. David took the lady's hand and tugged. No more arguments. She went with him.

Halfway to the exit, something slammed into his back. He found his balance without knocking the lady down then turned around.

Stumbling toward him, the cocky cowboy lifted balled fists. Time slowed. David didn't see a way out. He balled his own fist and caught the guy in the gut. The blow stopped his charge, and he bent over, retching.

David eased him to the concrete floor, found the lady, put his hand on her back, then led her outside. Feet running on gravel pulled him around one more time. The trio of upperclassmen hurried toward him. The ringleader smiled.

"We best get her home. That cowboy's going be a bear once he pukes up his beer."

Nathaniel eased the phone back into its cradle. "Bless the

John David's Calling

Lord, His mercy endures forever."

"Was that Buddy?" Wynona called from the kitchen. "Is there something wrong?"

"Yes and no." He pushed himself up from his phone chair, waited a bit for his hips to stop barking, then made his way to his recliner. "Come in here and sit a spell."

"Be right there. Want more coffee?"

"No, ma'am. I'm coffeed out. Take a Coca-Cola though."

Like the good girl she'd turned out to be, his honorary daughter brought him a Coke on ice then turned her rocker a little more toward him. "Well, tell me what Buddy allowed? Has Sandy come around yet?"

He shook his head. "No, she's resisting. Followed him to California again though. He's in Burbank. Just finished taping another show of *Oral Roberts Presents* with Brother Roberts. Seems my grandson's been performing a few exploits for the Lord."

"Oh?"

"Yes, ma'am. He went with a bunch of upper classmen from the school to some honky-tonk dance hall—of all things—it's called Hell's Acre. They went to pass out tracts in the parking lot, but then all of the sudden David goes inside." He laughed.

"No one can say the boy doesn't have gumption. Sounds a lot like his daddy and his Gramps if you ask me."

"The young man who organized the excursion said the music had stopped and David asked what happened. The boy told him the band was taking a break, then the next thing he knows, my grandson is paying his way in, like he'd switched sides or something."

He couldn't keep the snicker inside.

"Okay, what's so funny?"

"Oh, the guy didn't know how he got to the stage, but when he and the two other boys who went with him got to the door, David was already up there with the mic, singing a song they'd never heard before extolling the beauty of the Lord's Holiness.

"Said the dance floor was filled, but no one was dancing. They were all listening instead. The band joins in, and some old wild-haired dude started singing a harmony."

A chill washed over Nathaniel. "Oh, mercy. You think that could be?"

"Could be what?"

"Remember the story Buddy tells about when he was five and woke up early wanting a grape soda?"

"Sure, an old man saved him then the same fellow showed up when the little girl in the wagon got healed, right?"

"Yes, ma'am. That's the guy. We always thought he had to be an angel. Might be the same one that sang that harmony with my boy."

"Oh, I see. Then yes, surely could be. What happened next?"

"After he finished singing, he and this cowboy got into a fight over a young lady who's telling David she needs to go home."

"No! Don't tell me he got into a brawl! Not our David."

"Not really a brawl. But he called the girl by her name—even though he'd never seen her before—and told her that her daddy loved her. He didn't know the young lady had a fight with her father. Or that she really didn't really want to be there, but . . ."

"But what?"

"Well, he did hit the guy once in the gut then took the girl home."

The giggles returned, but he got control of himself.

"Here's the best part. She and her father made up and invited David to go to church with them that next Sunday. Twelve folks who'd been at the honky-tonk showed up, too. Three got saved, and the others rededicated their lives to the Lord."

"Bless God in Heaven! That's a wonderful story!"

"Amen. They asked him back that night to lead the singing."

"Awesome." She smiled so big, and that always blessed Nathaniel. He'd come to love her, as though God gave her to him to replace his daughters who would have been with him in those golden years if they hadn't gone to Heaven to live as babies.

Having Winnie there . . . well . . . he was blessed.

"Yes, ma'am, it sure is. An answer to an old man's prayer, too."

The all-around best helper girl an old man could have quizzed him for more details, but other than mentioning that it'd been Brother Roberts himself who passed the story on, Nathaniel already told her all.

Except . . . he'd not mentioned that he'd seen bits and pieces of his grandson in the dance hall for years in vision snippets.

Relief to know the boy was ministering, and not there to drink. He had no idea when or where David would be in such a place—or what he'd be doing there.

Bless God, he'd been praying for the boy's deliverance when he should have been asking the Lord for his protection.

The devil hated David for sure and certain then. Praise God though. He that was in his grandson was greater than he that was in the world.

He waited until Wynona went back to the kitchen before he slipped off the chair onto his knees. "Father, thank You for passing the torch to our David. I'll stay as long as You want, but, Lord, sure would be nice to see my sweet Evelyn again."

He sniffed then smiled, looking toward the ceiling. Oh to see his sweet wife again and be reunited for eternity . . .

"But not my will. Yours be done. Father."

Chapter Nine

Like every week, Thursday *evening* rolled around, but instead of the normal solitude during his study hour, a knock sounded on his dorm door. David stuck his finger in his book and turned in his chair. "Yeah, come in."

The same trio who'd ridden with him to the Acre the week before suddenly filled the little room. The ringleader nodded like David was a peer or something. Mike if he'd kept them straight; mercy, Mitch, Matt and Mike—of course!

"Hey, we're going back tomorrow night. You in, King?"

"I've been praying about it, but . . . I think the Lord is leading me in another direction." He nodded toward the empty far bunk. Shame Churchdog had flunked out. "Sit a spell, brothers. You up to poking a few holes in my plan?"

For the next few minutes, he laid it all out. "What do you think?"

"Why Mohawk Park?"

"It's the biggest, and folks hang around after, you know. Going to the zoo." He shrugged. "I'm open as to where we go . . . but it needs to be a public place."

One of the M's hiked his own shoulder a quarter-inch, looking left then right. The other two signaled their approval, so the guy smiled. "We're in. Who do you want?"

David put his book down, retrieved a piece of paper, wrote

out six names, then handed it over. "And anyone else you men like for your team."

"Done." The one he thought was Michael stood, soon flanked by the other two. The ringleader tipped an imaginary hat then headed out. David returned to his studies then paused. His MawMaw was so right. You really could catch more flies with honey than vinegar.

After studying until his eyes threatened to quit on him, he got onto his knees. "Lord, go before me and prepare the way. If this is not of You, show me the error of my way and guide me on the right path."

Silence echoed in the room. He waited but no answer came, so he stayed in place and continued to seek the Lord.

Too bright a light shone on the inside of his eyelids. He rolled away, bumping into something hard. He stuck his hand out . . . and found cold steel. His eyes opened. The side of his bed stared back.

What? Where was he? He sat up.

Somehow abruptly on the floor, realization dawned like the new day. He'd fallen asleep praying. Bless the Name of the Lord.

All tests are easy if you know the answers. Shame he had to guess at three or four questions, but he'd been to every class and would almost swear they'd never been covered in class. He had no idea where Professor Carey got them.

On all the others, David confidently believed he'd shine on, but then who knew whether he'd gotten them right? Guess the professor didn't want anyone to ace his test. It might make him look bad if too many scored an 'A.'

Five of the six fellows he'd requested made a point of finding him during that day to tell him they were in. The sixth plus four other guys he didn't know showed at the appointed time.

His Ford led the way with the other three cars forming a parade. Wasn't all that far, but he stopped at a gas station and filled his tank then waved the next car up and filled it, then the next until they were all full.

If his mother protested, he'd mention the Marines. She'd probably never even see the bill anyway. Some bean counter somewhere would just pay it. Besides, she supported mission work on a regular basis.

Certainly, she'd subsidize her own son's ministry. Whatever. It was all God's money anyway . . . although Mama might not see it just that way.

Dad knew.

And David definitely did not want anyone running out of gas. A workman was worth his hire. Once in the park, took a few minutes to get ready, then everyone looked to him.

The part of him that wanted more than anything to run submitted to the stronger part whose desire to be in the Lord's perfect will caused him to offer everything—his Zee, looking the fool—whatever.

Didn't matter to him. He closed his eyes, and a warmth overwhelmed him.

Oh how he loved on the Father there on the floor beside his bed that morning.

The angels sang, and David joined them.

The three musicians who'd come along and the backup singers he'd chosen bolstered the melody, then one broke off into harmony.

His rich baritone wrapped the melody like one of MawMaw's quilts on an icy night when the side porch—poorly remodeled into an extra bedroom—made him think he'd freeze before morning for sure.

The men's voices floated Heavenward.

After three times through the song, he repeated the tenor the cherubim sang.

The Spirit of the Lord led the quartet as David went off with new lyrics, and the three others sang the old. He loved it when God showed up and showed out. There was nowhere else he'd rather be.

In the presence of the Lord, his joy was made full.

John David's Calling 93

His heart might burst for the sheer delight of God's love.

A quick peek revealed a dozen or more folks gathered round. He started the new song again, and more voices joined him and his friends. But that time, he let the others take the melody and sang with the angels instead.

Basking in the glorious presence of the Almighty, pouring out his heart for—who but God knew how long—David lost all sense of time as he praised the Lord at Heaven's throne. When that song finished, he found another . . . then another.

What a night! He loved it and could not have been any more blessed. The guys gave out every single one of the tracts. And if their count was right, twenty-two souls accepted Christ.

Then just as the last new believer left, the devil reared his ugly head.

A beat-up truck with a bunch of rowdies in the back blocked his Ford. Cowboy. The fellow from Hell's Acre climbed out. David swallowed. Great. Just great.

Soon enough, the guy's posse flanked him. "Well, well, well! I heard tell you were out here, sonny boy. Singing in the park."

The man didn't seem quite as drunk as the week before.

With a smile, he stuck out his hand. "Hey, there. I'm David Nightingale."

"I don't care who you are, punk."

The man slapped his hand away then in one motion, landed a solid blow to his chin. David reeled with the strike, but somehow kept his feet. The angels must have held him up. How was he supposed to turn the other chin?

Pain racked his lower face. What a stupid thing to think. He righted himself.

Some of his buds hollered about calling the law, but he held his hands out, motioning them to stay back.

"Sir." He rubbed his jaw. "Like I told you last week, I'll not defend myself, so . . . if you need to hit me again . . ." He shrugged, stepped closer and held out his face.

A blow to his eye stumbled him. Stars swirled, but he'd

been hit harder. Granted, he'd had on a football helmet. He stood up right. "Jesus loves you, Cowboy, and I'm working on it."

"Right, punk." The man swung again, catching David square on his ear.

The ringing was deafening. He tottered but again kept his feet.

Maybe it'd be a favor if the angels would let him go to the ground once. Give him some kind of break. He rubbed his poor ear then managed a smile, though it hurt his chin and jaw to do so. He stepped closer.

"Your grandmother loved the Lord. Didn't she, Gage? Took you to Sunday School every chance she got."

"Don't you dare bring her into this." The man raised his fist but didn't swing.

"It's never too late, Gage. The Lord heard her prayers. He can make all things new, give you a brand-new heart. Nothing's too hard for Him. He can even restore your wife and son to you."

The cowboy's fists fell to his side, and his shoulders slumped forward. He met David's eyes and held a stare until his gaze turned to glaring. He turned and walked back to the truck. "Come on, boys. This punk ain't worth our time."

David held his ground until the truck turned out of the park, then sighed. Like butter left too near the stove, he melted. Strong hands caught him before he hit the ground.

For a time, he watched with his inner eye. The truck with Gage and one other guy in it crashed and burned. "Oh Lord, don't hold this sin against him."

The vision faded, the team surrounded him. Concern etched their faces. Jointly, they helped him into his car, but not before someone fished his keys out of his pocket. He protested but didn't want to have to fight anyone to prove he could drive.

Besides, with the ringing in his ear, might be for the best.

The guy driving parked the sedan. David opened the shotgun door, took two steps, then promptly fell on his hind end. Once the dorm building took to swimming, Michael and the other two M's wanted him to go to the hospital.

But he vetoed the idea, so instead, they helped him upstairs and into bed. The upperclassman patted his arm.

"Awesome night, King. I'm so sorry you got beat up, but that was something to watch though. No way I could've turned the other cheek like you did."

David grabbed his arm. "Pray for Gage, brother. I saw him crashing his truck and . . ."

"Okay, we will."

"Good." He touched his swollen cheek. "Is it bad?"

"Nice shade of bluish purple. Probably will blacken up tomorrow, but I've seen worse."

Mitch spoke, something he didn't do much of. "Your chin looks worse. You ought to go to the ER."

"It'll be okay." David tried to smile, but it hurt too much, so he settled for a nod. "Thanks, I needed that."

The guy grinned real big. "You're welcome."

Michael tossed his head toward the door. "Come on, guys. Let's let him go to sleep. Won't hurt so much then." He saluted, like David was a general or something, then backed up a step. "I'll check on you in the morning."

The ringing in his ear took turns with his eye and chin trying to keep him awake, but really quick his eyes overloaded with salt. Like the fool he was at times, he rolled over onto his sore ear. It jerked him upright.

Bless the Lord. His bedside clock claimed he'd slept the night through. The ringing only semi- deafened him. Sitting up on the bed's side worsened it, but the room stayed in place.

A good thing. He stood, waited a second, threw on his robe, and grabbed his shaving kit. Maybe a shower could bring out the human in him. Off to the bathroom he marched.

Wow. His eye and chin looked way worse than they felt, and his poor ear was all swollen up, too. But he'd live, and . . . the image of Gage's truck burning suddenly flooded his senses as though he stood on the side of the road by the tree it crashed into.

"Oh, Lord! Have mercy on that man's soul. Give me one more shot at him, please. Let me share Your love."

Like Michael said, he came around right after breakfast. Sitting in the day room, David spotted him heading for the stairs.

"Hey! Over here."

The guy wheeled, looked around, then grinned. "How you feeling, King? Ready for round two?"

David held both hands up. "I don't know. Maybe in a week or two."

Michael took the chair across from him. "Any more vertigo?"

"No, sir. I'm plenty sore, but fine. Been watching the news. Hadn't seen a bit of coverage on Gage crashing his truck. You heard anything?"

"Nope." The guy sat forward. "Hey, you play bridge?"

"No, my PawPaw didn't truck with cards. Played plenty of dominoes, horseshoes, washers—that sort of stuff."

"Forty-two?"

"Sure."

"Well, there you go. Bridge is forty-two super-charged."

"Why do you ask?"

"We need a fourth."

"Who's we?"

"Me, Sis and Mom. Dad's on a trip to Africa."

"Really. What's he doing there?"

"Oh, he's in charge of some missionaries in Nigeria and goes a couple of times a year at least."

"Cool."

"I guess so. But we had more salvations last night then those six guys over there have had in the last year."

"No joke."

"That's right. So . . . you ready?"

"For what?"

"I told you. We need a fourth, and Mom's dying to meet

you."

"Meet me? Why"

"Oh, I don't know. I may have bragged all over you a little. You know how mothers are."

"Yeah." David chuckled, but it hurt. "Okay then, fine." He stood and held his arms out to the sides. "Do I pass muster, or should I change? Put on my suit or something?"

"You're fine." His friend laughed. "Come on."

Touching both hip pockets, he confirmed he had his billfold, but the other side was empty. "We taking my car? Keys are upstairs."

"We'll take mine."

Mike—as the man insisted, didn't care much for getting called Mitch or Matt—drove a Corvette. No wonder he wanted to take the Ford that first night. And all along, David thought the upperclassman was short on gasoline or something.

The sprawling two-story sat on at least a dozen well-manicured acres a few miles out of town. The Bass estate confirmed the man came from money.

But then . . . so did he. Except his was by way of his mother marrying a man whom his PawPaw shot dead. What a deal.

Being bragged on and the retelling of the previous night's exploits could have gone to his head if he'd let it. But the Scripture about pride going before destruction and a haughty spirit before a fall kept worming its way into his thoughts.

Finally, the talk turned to the game. "We'll play a few practice hands before we get serious."

His sister Melissa, Missy for short, grinned then cut her eyes to her brother. "Fine dork, but then we're going to get real, and it's fixing to count."

Mercy, what had he gotten himself into? David wasn't sure exactly what was going on between the siblings, but figured if he hid and watched, all would be revealed soon enough.

Apparently, he was a natural, or so said they all. The game resembled forty-two a lot, except he definitely liked it better.

With dominoes, the variations were more limited and only allowed one round of bidding. A body either guessed or jumped out there and bid big, or never got a hand.

The card game seemed more like an auction. Kept going until all done.

The big sister and his mother were nice, but neither seemed as sold out to the Lord as Mike. Once the exploits of the previous night had been told and questioned, every time David tried to steer the conversation toward Church or the Lord, it got deflected to something along a more carnal vein.

After a couple of hours of playing, the cards were moved out of the way, and a nice spread of cold cuts, cheese, and fruit soon covered the table. To his surprise, his host uncorked a bottle of wine. Mike held it out toward his empty glass.

"No, thank you."

Mis'ess Bass cocked her head a smidgen. "So you don't drink a little wine for you stomach's sake?"

"No, ma'am. Promised my grandfather I'd never touch a drop. Can't become a drunk if you don't ever smell a cork."

"So . . . your grandfather? He drank more than he should've?"

"Yes, ma'am, one of them anyway, Gramps. You can count my other one in the teetotaler camp." He chuckled. "He'd tell you in a minute he's a drunk, but he hasn't taken a drink since the tornado back in '39." He liked having that story to pull out.

Told them a little, and the next thing he knew, they were begging for more.

Sure enough all three wanted to hear about the revival tent getting shredded without a soul being lost. Though he gave them the *Reader's Digest* version, it still took him a good five minutes to tell the tale.

"Really? You're not making all this up?"

"God's own truth. Had too many eye witnesses swearing to the same story, including my relatives. I know most of the others personally, too. Just like the Sadducees and Pharisees couldn't debunk Jesus' resurrection, no matter how much

PawPaw, my other grandfather, would like to discredit the event as a miracle, it flat out was, and no one in their right minds hearing what happened can deny it."

With the food eaten and wine drank, big sis fetched the cards, and the game resumed. He noticed no difference in Mike or his sister, but their mother's play seemed to suffer from the extra goblet she'd imbibed.

After the game, while his friend drove back to the dorm, he seemed almost giddy, but his driving wasn't impaired.

"We did good, partner. I won over a hundred from my snot-nosed sister. I love beating her."

"So, we were gambling?"

"Sure—well, you weren't—but it's all in good fun." He glanced over. "Say, Mitch and Matt play. Want a game after church tomorrow? Say three o'clock?"

"Sure, why not? They don't gamble, too, do they?"

"Yeah, but only pennies. Makes it more fun."

Chapter Ten

Church lacked luster, but then after Friday night in the park . . . Singing out of a hymnal lead by a man a sixteenth off beat who had a talent for going flat every ten or twelfth note just didn't do anything for David.

Why couldn't they trust the Hold Spirit to lead the services? From the praise and worship through the invitation?

But what could he expect?

Then to put the cherry pepper on top of his mustard milkshake, the preacher belabored his obscure point to the point of distraction. Mercy. Help them, Father. At least the organist knew how to play—quite gifted, actually.

Whatever made him think of visiting the congregation? Oh yeah, walking distance from his dorm.

Praise the Lord.

After a burger and a relaxing two-cigarette drive out of town a ways, he found himself in the upperclassman's day room, waiting for Matt to show. But hey, the afternoon hadn't ripened yet.

"Come here, King." Mike whirled a chair backwards to the table and took a seat, nodding him over. "Let's go over some things."

"Sure." David joined him.

His new friend delved into some of the game's finer points.

John David's Calling

A lot to remember, but the review also crystallized some of what he'd learned the day before.

Matt showed—right on time even though last to arrive—and the game was on.

Two hours and twenty minutes later, David found himself sixty-eight cents richer, but like Mike said, gambling really did make it more fun. Somewhat akin to how he hated football practice but loved the games.

After chapel that night, Mike invited him back to his dorm room. David needed to crack some books but figured a half hour wouldn't hurt.

"Sure, but I can't stay long."

With a wave at Mitch and Matt watching the *Ed Sullivan Show* in the day room, David followed Mike upstairs. The man's abode was at least twice as big as his and held only one bed, making it seem all the roomier.

Must be nice to have a sitting area and a regular sized desk. He slipped into the overstuffed chair across from Mike.

He grinned. "I got a question?"

Lifting his chin a little, David tilted his head. "Shoot."

"How does it work . . . the words of knowledge you get?"

Hmm. How should he answer? "I don't know exactly. Sometimes, I just know stuff. Other times, I see things. Guess the best way to describe it would be . . . well, it comes mostly like something you remember, like a name on the tip of your tongue, then it's there." He hiked both shoulders. "Does that make any sense?"

"Some. Samuel founded the school of the prophets, then during Elijah's time, there were the sons of the prophets. I mean, there are plenty of prophets in the Old Testament. Plus, Paul said above all we should desire to prophesy."

A chill danced over David. Was Mike going where he hoped? "Yes, sir. All true."

"You're the real deal King, but . . ." He smiled then turned serious. "Those folks we led to the Lord Friday . . . I've been thinking about them."

"Yeah? What about them?"

"Several asked me what they should do next."

"What did you tell them?"

His friend exhaled then shrugged. "Told them to find a church. Get involved somewhere. But that isn't how Paul did it, is it?"

"No, sir. What are you suggesting?"

"I don't know. Have you studied Azusa Street any?"

"Absolutely." David grinned. "Gramps got saved that second night when they were still on Bonnie Brae."

"Really" Your grandfather was there?"

"He, my grandmother, and his parents, too. His mama—my Great-grandmother Nightingale got healed there."

"Wow. No wonder that twister only took the tent. And you said he's still pastoring a church?"

"Sure is. And he'll be ninety-nine his next birthday, but he looks eighty and acts more like he's seventy."

"Wow again. That's cool."

"I think so, too. He and my grandmother stayed on Azusa Street, until the San Francisco earthquake. Her parents died when their home burned down around them. From there he went to the same school that William Seymour had gone to."

"Man! No wonder you're so blessed."

"There is a fly in the ointment though."

"What's that?"

Oh, man. He hated telling it, but maybe Mike needed to know. David stiffened his back. "My parents . . . they never married."

"So? That doesn't have anything to do with you."

"Some people don't see it that way."

"All I've got to say is those are the same folks I find myself having a problem with. How could anybody hang their bad choices on you?"

Although David didn't know exactly where the upperclassman was headed, sure sounded like he might want to tag along. "So, what do you have in mind with our new converts?"

"Well, there's a new move of God that's started, but it needs someone like you, King. Someone real. A man who can unify the church."

"Me? And exactly how do you figure I'm supposed to do that?"

"Who knows?" Mike shrugged one shoulder. "That's the rub. I don't know, but I'm thinking . . . maybe we should change our focus."

"To what?"

"Prayer and fasting."

"What are you talking about? Jesus went forty days, but . . ." Missing meals on purpose didn't thrill David's heart. He'd need a Word, a pretty loud one for something so drastic.

"Not that extreme. Thinking Fridays, maybe. Nothing but water, then we meet up that evening and pray."

A tingling danced from one shoulder to the other, not the strongest of witnesses, but no Voice from Heaven. Still, it wasn't like the guy proposed anything contrary to the Word.

Fasting and Prayer. He remembered Jesus telling His disciples certain demons only came out with prayer and fasting, so the practice must bring a stronger power to the ministry.

"I'm in. So like no food, just water, right? From when we get up Friday morning. So no coffee either?"

"Water only."

"Got a place in mind to meet for prayer?"

"How about that church you went to this morning? Dad's the bishop, and I know the pastor. They have a room I'm pretty sure we can use."

"How'd you know I went?"

Mike grinned. "Doesn't much happen around here I don't know about."

Though David would like to have known more, his friend didn't elaborate, and he didn't press the issue. Having a place so close would be nice.

"So Mitch and Matt for sure. Who else we going to invite?"

"Many are called, but few are chosen, my friend." He smiled. "I've got a dozen or so I'm praying about. You're welcome to do the same and invite who you want."

"Sounds good. All except the not eating part." He faked a punch, chuckling. "But hey! Jesus went to hell for me, guess I can skip a few meals for Him."

"Amen."

David stood. "Guess I better get my nose in a book."

"Sit back down. I've got another quick question."

"Sure." He eased back into the chair.

"Your grades."

"You sure you want to go there. I'm passing everything."

"King, they're barely so-so—even with the twice a week tutoring."

"You do know everything."

"I'm going to the dark continent in August." Mike eyed him hard. "I'd like for you to come with me."

"Mercy, if I didn't get eaten by cannibals while I was there, I'd probably have one of those not so nice letters from Nixon waiting on me when I got back."

"I've got that covered, Dad said he'll get you ordained, then filing as a conscientious objector is a slam dunk."

"But I'm not. Mom wanted me to go to SMU. I told her it was either ORU or the Marines."

"Nam is not where it's at, brother."

"I've got mixed emotions. Both my grandfathers served in WW1, and Dad stormed the beach on D-Day as a medic then took out a pill box with his bare hands."

"Wow, Buddy Nightingale! Brother Robert's favorite new songbird was a war hero? Who knew?"

"Yes, sir. Anyway, I figured if I did go, I'd like to be a chaplain, but if the need arose, I'd have no objection to fighting."

"Really. What about turning the other cheek?"

"Different deal. Thou shall not murder is what it really says, not kill. There's a difference. It'd be on Nixon and his bunch—not me—if they put an M16 in my hands."

"Hmm. That's one way to look at it, I guess. Sure was hoping you'd go with us, though. Two years in the mission field sure opens a lot of doors." Mike winked. "Anyway, think about it. The four of us working together could bring so many souls into the Kingdom."

"I will."

Giving his word had him thinking about it all right. Matter of fact, he didn't think about much of anything else when not concentrating on his studies. He'd hate flunking out like Churchdog.

That'd be like letting God down big time. He invited five guys the Lord pointed out and put on David's heart.

Friday rolled around, and most everything skidded to a hungry, caffeine-depraved stop. What was he thinking? He should have negotiated for black coffee to be on the list, but . . . water it was.

Wow, he could hardly keep his eyes open during the first class. He'd been drinking coffee laced with copious amounts of cream and sugar, like forever.

The headache at the base of his skull started right after when he should have eaten what all the city slickers there called lunch. Every time he referred to the noonish meal as dinner, it only confused them all.

Hey! A Coke would fix him up.

Wait. That wasn't on the list either.

Mercy, fasting was for the birds. He remembered MawMaw's table at Thanksgiving, and his parotid duct went into high gear. Turkey and dressing and all the fixings . . . her homemade rolls swimming in real butter.

Man, that would be grand. As the day wore on, his head pounded, and the sledges moved up his temples and across his forehead.

How could he even go out that night at all? He definitely did not feel stronger, instead like every ounce of strength drained from his body.

IN YOUR WEAKNESS I AM MADE STRONG
Cool, Lord.

He needed that. So, he could just trust the Father then . . . didn't have to worry about a thing.

By five forty-five that evening, he'd consumed several of his favorite meals in his mind, but his poor stomach benefited not one bit. If it protested any louder, he couldn't hear himself think.

What did it matter? All he could think about was food. But he trusted God.

Seventeen guys showed that first Friday night. The great turnout almost made David forget all about being hungry. At six sharp, Mike closed and locked the Sunday School classroom door. "Men, any of you eaten today?"

A chorus of nos greeted him. None answered in the affirmative.

"Good, for the first hour, let's seek God in our own way. Pray in the spirit or with understanding—that's totally up to you. Then we'll come together and see if the Lord has given anyone a word or song or Scripture." He nodded, turned, and knelt.

David found a spot and hit his knees.

Soon enough, the desires of his flesh faded away. He earnestly sought the Lord and could actually physically feel the difference the fasting had made.

That first hour passed so fast he could hardly believe it when Mike cleared his throat for attention. His eyes went straight to the wall clock, and sure enough, its hands pointed to seven o'clock.

Mike pulled up a chair and sat. "Gather around, brothers. Let's see what the Lord would have us do next."

Joining the circle, David kept quiet and listened for a while. After two or three said their peace, Mike looked to him. "You get a song?"

He nodded. "Several, actually."

"I thought I heard you singing under your breath. Let's hear them."

Halfway through the chorus of the first lively song, he had to stand. Then his feet took to dancing. Mercy!

If the son of Jessie danced with any wilder abandonment, bringing the Ark into Jerusalem, David didn't know how. He whirled and twirled, arms outstretched. He danced before the Lord as if none of his fellow classmates were even in the room.

Who cared what any of them thought? He heart was only to please the Lord that night. He'd never known such freedom in the dance. Never dreamed it could have been possible.

The praising got louder, and sixteen other men joined him, dancing and twirling around the room, dodging tables and chairs and praising the Lord with their whole hearts.

Exhaustion finally brought him to his knees, and he miraculously found enough breath to extol the beauty of the Lord's Holiness in a new, reverent, quiet worship song. With no inclination to know how long it went on, the last note faded.

A silent hush settled. No one said a word for the longest time. David basked in the manifest presence of the Lord.

Then Mike pressed himself up from his prostrate position on the floor into a standing position. "Does anyone have anything?" He waited but no one said anything.

"Bless the Lord! You're dismissed."

A bit disappointed that Mike didn't want to go out on the street, David lingered, but while his new friend gave a lot of leeway on spiritual matters, deferring to him, the upperclassman still called the shots.

Somewhat like the shepherd boy and Abner. Though the son of Jessie surely respected Saul, the young anointed king loved his first captain.

His fondness for Michael Bass was growing, but it bothered him that the upperclassman always wanted to control things . . . especially when it came to planning out David's future. He thought on such things, keeping one eye on the clock and the other on the bag of burgers and fries, he'd bought and carried up to his room to relish. The blessed clock said twelve.

Praise the Lord, he'd made it.
Had a burger ever tasted so good?

Chapter Eleven

Exactly five weeks later, Hannah lamented one more Friday night at home alone, sitting in her room, reading all about his wonderful life in Tulsa. She loved David's letters, and the regularity of them.

How she loved knowing that he thought about her often and cared enough to take his time to write when he was so busy.

His attention made her feel so special.

The part about him getting beat up, she didn't like one bit. Seemed to her that if her love made the choice to turn his cheek like God said, that the Almighty ought to at least keep him from getting hit the second time.

She hated thinking of him with black eyes and his jaw all swollen. If only she'd have been there . . . But the Friday night prayer meetings sounded so cool—way better than him being at that park with all those ruffians or the Devil's Acre with all the drunks.

What if that cowboy guy decided to come back? Or one of those loose cowgirls set their eyes on her fellow?

Though his good looks definitely played a part in drawing her to him, sometimes she thought a wart on his nose might not be a bad thing.

If she couldn't go there, she wanted him home!

Somehow, someway, she needed to convince him to change

schools. The University of Texas should be plenty good enough. At least then he could come home every weekend. Her pigheaded mother couldn't see the forest for the trees.

If only she'd agree to let her get married, but Hannah had tried every argument under the sun.

To no persuasion though, the woman's stubborn streak stretched a mile wide.

Even Baylor would be better. With Waco only two hours away, surely her parents would let her drive there to attend a Friday night prayer meeting with him—even if they insisted Jill tagging along.

And she could stay at her aunt and uncle's in Temple if it got too late for her to drive back then see him on Saturday, too.

A long wistful sigh escaped.

If only . . .

Mercy. She hated not seeing his face for such long stretches.

Rereading his excuses for not making the trip home to take her to prom, her stomach churned. Why couldn't he see how important it was to her? It wasn't fair!

Just because his friend flunked out, Jill got to go. Not that she wanted David to flunk, but every time she came around, her cousin went on and on and on about Adam Churchill and how much in love they were.

Ugh!

Though she shouldn't be, she couldn't help but be mad with Jill for already getting her beau to commit to taking her. David could cut one lousy day of school and make the trip. Well, she just wouldn't go.

Without her love it wouldn't be any fun anyway. But she still had spring break to work on him, too. At least since she's turned sixteen, Jill's chaperoning services weren't required.

Two more weeks. She hated having to wait that long.

Fourteen more miserable days of loneliness.

Her minutes in despair turned into hours; she slept, and the hours became a new day. That one morphed into the next until

John David's Calling

a week passed.

Only one more. She focused on making it through one day at a time, then on Thursday before the Friday he was going to leave, right after supper, the phone's bell sounded. She caught it on the second ring.

"Morrison residence. This is Hannah."

"Hey, babe. How's it going?"

"Oh, David, it's so good to hear your voice! It's going fine since tomorrow is Friday! What's up there? Is something wrong?"

"No. Everything's fine, but I've been asked to play in a Bridge Tournament. It's in Dallas this weekend, so I'll be a day late. Maybe two if I see Mom Saturday night after it's over."

"No! Come on, David. That isn't fair. I want you home."

"I know, but I'll be there Sunday, and we'll have the whole week together."

"No, we won't. We'll only have six days! And you know I have school! We don't get out until Thursday. You don't need to play cards! Come on home! I've been counting the days, and I can't wait another one! I thought you were, too."

"I have been, I am, but this tournament came up, and Mike signed us up, and—"

"He signed you up?" Ooo, she hated Michael Bass and she'd never even met him! Who did he think he was, signing David up for anything? "It's a stupid game! What about me? That means we'll only have three whole days together. It isn't fair!"

"You get Monday off, don't you?"

"So what? That doesn't matter if you're leaving Sunday!"

"Hannah. Now calm down and breathe."

"I don't want to breathe! I just want you to come home."

"I figure I can cut a couple of classes, so I won't have to go back until Tuesday. That'll give us all day Sunday and Monday, so back to five full days together. Playing cards takes away one—if we lose not even that—cutting those classes adds two, so you're coming out a whole day extra."

"Won't cutting class hurt you grades? It surely will, and if you flunked out and got drafted, I'd just die."

"Don't worry about that. Matter of fact, don't worry about anything. I'm doing way better this semester than the last. I want to teach you how to play bridge. It's a great game, lots of fun. And I'll be there Sunday."

That would be better. If it wouldn't hurt his grades too much, especially since she had the whole Monday off. Guess she shouldn't get so upset. He deserved to have some fun . . .

"What time Sunday?"

"Depends on if I go to church with Mother, but not too late. I'll come straight to your house."

"No stops?"

He laughed. "You sound like Dad now, but fine. I'll drive on through. Who needs to stretch their legs anyway?"

"I hate that stupid game Mike taught you."

"Don't say that. You'll love it. We can teach Jill, and Churchdog already knows how to play."

"Fine." Why did she say that? And why was he wanting to spend time with her cousin?

"So, we're good then? I've got to go. This call is costing a fortune."

She started to tell him to reverse the charges, but her mama would have a full-blown conniption fit.

"Yes, we're good—more than good. I love you and miss you something terrible. So . . . if you lose, you'll be here sooner?"

"Yes, ma'am."

"I hope you lose."

"I love you, too, but we're going to win. Don't be counting on any sooner."

"I'll count on whatever I want to count on, John David Buckmeyer. Bye."

"Good bye, sweetie."

The line went dead. David put the phone back in its cradle and faced Mike. "She's mad at both of us."

"I noticed you didn't tell her who you'd be playing with."

"Your sister?" David laughed. "No, sir. Nowhere is it written a body has to tell everything he knows."

"True. So, your young lady is a little jealous I take it."

"Ha! In spades, brother."

"Did you get in touch with your mom about us staying there?"

"Yes, I told you already."

"No, my friend. You said you left her a message with the housekeeper."

"Same difference. She doesn't care. Last I heard, she's in Burbank with Dad anyway, so we may have the place to ourselves."

"Get a chance, look this over." Mike pulled a thin book out of his back pocket. "Before we leave on Friday if you can. Mom and Missy play a little different then we do, so you'll want to familiarize yourself with these conventions."

David took the offering. "Okay."

"I'd feel better if your mother knew we were all coming. What if she shows up, and three strangers are in her home?"

He laughed. "It won't matter. The place is so big, and . . ." He patted his friend's shoulder. "You'll see."

And see all three of them did. David loved showing off his mother's house. As always, he saved the best for last. He swung wide the double doors leading to the back patio. "Come check this out."

His new friend's mother and sister gasped in unison. Mike seemed to get a bigger kick out of his women folk than the sprawling, immaculately manicured grounds along Turtle Creek. He loved it, too.

Who wouldn't? In the heart of the city, a respite of beauty

so peaceful. Tension drained away as all the hurry-hurry fled from every muscle.

Missy hugged herself then faced him. "Marry me, David. I don't ever want to leave."

"There's a blaring problem with that." He laughed. "I don't live here."

"So? Doesn't mean I couldn't." She grinned. "Why don't you, anyway?"

"Come south sometime. You'll understand."

With a cute little shrug, she returned to her gawking. As if on cue, a trio of ducks swam by, leaving their rippling V wakes that gradually overlaid each other.

Bright and early the next day, it started. The number of folks in attendance at the Dallas Mixed Master Duplicate Bridge Tournament surprised David—not even counting the players. He couldn't believe the onlookers.

What a shame church services didn't draw a like crowd. Made his heart sort of sad until he took his seat, then the excitement set in.

It took a bit to remember to stack each card he played, but he got the hang of it soon enough. Missy was a really good player.

By the lunch break—the city folks' name for the noonday meal tickled him—the lady had dragged him along into eighth place out of one hundred sixty-seven teams. Not bad for a beginner.

Mike and his mother garnered a distant forty-third.

After a delicious chicken salad with grapes and pecans and something else sweet, maybe apple, Missy leaned in. "You're doing good, but we've underbid two hands." She nodded toward a couple three tables over. "See that dark-haired guy over there?"

He glanced then nodded.

"That's Omar and Cate. I don't care what place we come in as long as we beat them."

"Oh yeah?" He gave them a second once-over. "Who are

they?"

Seemed she had to tear her eyes off the couple. "Long story, but I've come in behind them so many times, and I just know I'm the better player. Playing duplicate though, I can't fault the cards. Just once, I'd like bragging rights."

A little tingle danced up his spine, and he extended his hand toward her. "Let's pray about it."

"Really?" She grinned then took his hand. "You sure you want to get God involved in a card game?"

"Why not? King David asked for the head of his enemies. We're not getting that drastic."

"Fine, pray away."

"Lord, give us wisdom and have mercy on us. Let our finesses work and help us not to over or under bid."

"Amen." She grinned. "I better go powder my nose before we get going again."

Touching her arm to hold her up a second, he wiggled his pointer, urging her closer. "I'd rethink those bragging rights if I was you. Pride does go before destruction, you know."

"Oh you. You're right as usual." She winked and left him.

His attention turned to the man she'd called Omar. The guy sure looked familiar. Appeared to be too old for Cate, maybe forty, and his partner looked more Missy's age, mid to late twenties. He made a mental note to ask Mike about his sister's age.

If he had to guess, he'd say twenty-six to Mike's twenty-four. Seemed right.

By the late afternoon break, he and his partner had amazingly climbed into third place, but Omar and his little lady had moved into first. Missy was elated and distressed and giddy all at the same time then digressed as if all her emotions mixed together to undo her. She gave him a little nod toward the front door.

"I need a smoke. I'll be back before the next round starts."

Scooting his chair back, he stood then fell in beside her. "Sounds good."

She did a little double take. "You smoke?"

"Why not?"

She double-puffed hers down then took turns finishing his. "You ready?"

"You and that Omar guy have a history?"

At first, she didn't answer, then right before the hall's front door she stopped and turned toward him. "We were an item once, but he threw me over for the bimbo that he threw over for Cate."

Not exactly sure what all she meant by that, he hoped it had only to do with cards. He doubted it though, the way she seemed so bothered by the dark-skinned man, but he didn't look negro at all.

Maybe Pakistani or from somewhere over there by Arabia.

Card play began again, and he focused on his hand, putting all thoughts of Omar and Missy, the bimbo and Cate out of his mind. Only one place stood between him and them, no hill for a stepper, and no big deal for his big God.

His perfect defense, according to Missy, at least, of a three no-trump bid put her and him into second place with one round to go—against Omar and Cate. As it should be since they'd hung on to first place all evening.

The prize money involved interested him more than any revenge factor, but not his partner. Hopefully, she wasn't so keyed up that her judgment would be impaired.

The last hand rolled around. He and Missy needed help—maybe of the driving the entire length of the football field to score the winning touchdown kind of help. He'd done it before but had also fallen short.

The nature of the beast always meant a body would win some and lose some, but poor Missy. Seemed to him the lady had lost way more than she'd won.

He sorted his cards. His heart pulsed a tad quicker with the possibilities.

Omar opened with a club.

Missy doubled, and Cate passed.

Hey, hey. All right. David bid. "Two spades."
Omar folded his cards together and emptied his lungs. "I pass."
Missy sat a bit taller but betrayed no other emotion. "Four spades."
By his calculations—and he calculated it from many angels—he was two points short of Slam. Had anyone else with that same hand done better than game? He eyed the score pad.
Five spades wouldn't do it. Cate, sitting behind the dummy, had the weak hand. He recalculated. Probably missing at least one ace since Omar opened. Only had one chance. "Six spades."
His opponent grinned. "Double."
The ladies passed.
Would that be enough points to overtake them?
Shame he hadn't gotten more information from Missy, but why not?
"Redouble."
The man's grin turned into a full-blown, face-splitting smile. He pulled a card from his hand but didn't show it until Missy laid her hand down, then Omar flipped over the ace of hearts, exactly like David had hoped, and won the trick.
Next, he played the ace of clubs.
David trumped it then cashed the king and queen of clubs, sluffing his last two hearts on those tricks. He led to dummy's queen of spades, pulling in Omar's five.
Next, he played the dummy's king of hearts then laid his remaining cards down. Missy looked them over then squealed.
"You did it! You did it, David! A small slam! Doubled and redoubled. Woo Hoo!"
A smirk shot at Omar seemed to lighten the color of his skin—at least three shades paler.
She jumped to her feet, ran around the table, and pulled David to his. With the biggest smile he'd ever seen, she took his face in both hands, one on each cheek, then planted a long

wet one right on his smacker.

Flashbulbs popped and flashed.

He didn't kiss her back or wrap her in a bear hug—but he sure wanted to.

Oh Lord, have mercy on me.

Don't let me be like my father.

MISSY
Spades – Q, 10, 9, 2
Hearts – K, 9, 5, 4
Diamonds – K, 10
Clubs – K, Q, 10

OMAR
Spades – 5
Hearts – A, Q, 4, 2
Diamonds – J, 8
3 Clubs – A, J, 8, 6, 5, 4

CATE
Spades – Void
Hearts – J, 10, 8
Diamonds – Q, 9, 7, 5, 4
Clubs – 9, 7, 3, 2

DAVID
Spades – A, K, J, 8, 7, 6, 4, 3
Hearts – 7, 6, 3
Diamonds – A, 2
Clubs – Void

Chapter Twelve

The festive mood continued into the wee hours back at David's mother's mansion. Hands were replayed by the dozens, opponents hashed and bashed—some, a few, even deemed worthy—and the prize money counted and properly divvied.

The ladies finally called it a night when yarns were all spent, and yawns took over conversation.

Their departure left him and his friend sitting side by side on the patio. After a long stretch of silence, Mike turned sideways. "Thank you."

"Well sure. What for?"

"Being you."

"Okay, that's pretty easy. Can't be anything else."

"Good." His friend chuckled. "Stay that way, King."

Not exactly sure what he was talking about, David suspected in some way it had a lot to do with Missy. Shortly, after a prolonged silence, his house guest excused himself.

Alone, his thoughts wondered. Her being in a room three doors down from his . . . just no good. Not with the memory of her kiss still on his lips.

Not with the look in her eyes when she bid him goodnight.

If you don't ever take a drink, Gramps said, you can't become a drunk. How different would his father's life have been if he'd not succumbed to the temptation of that older lady in Arkansas?

Lust of the flesh, lust of the eye and pride of life.

All three wrapped up Miss Melissa Bass into one sweet, good-looking package. Why was the allure of an older woman so strong?

He loved Hannah and had definitely wanted her, but not like Missy.

Deep into the night he prayed.

A chilly breeze on his cheek woke him. He sat up.

"Good morning, you. Coffee's brewed."

From the chair to his right, Missy grinned. "Have you been out here all night long?"

"Looks that way." Stretching, he nodded then stood and held out his hand. "Need to powder my nose. You want a refill?"

"That would be perfectly marvelous. Black with one sugar, please."

He returned in short order with two steaming mugs. "You're up early after such a late night."

"Didn't sleep much." She took his offering. "Kept waking up."

"Sorry. Bed too soft?"

"No. Actually, it was plenty comfortable. Wasn't the bed that kept me awake." She took a sip then sat up and scooted her chair to face him more.

"We could make so much money playing bridge, David. You're so good now, and there's a man I know who could coach us. You know as partners. We'd rule the bridge world."

Couldn't help but smile at her exuberance though he had to admit a little disappointment her excitement hadn't been thinking about him like he thought. Bridge never came to mind. God had such a sense of humor.

"I was fourteen—in the seventh grade—and this eighth-grade boy was teasing Hannah, a pretty little girl at my school. She'd just gotten glasses, and the guy was calling her four-eyes and being all around unkind.

"I told him to stop, but he kept on taunting her all the more. Next thing you knew, we both sat in the principal's alcove, waiting to go into his office. My nose was bleeding all over my shirt, and he had two black eyes."

"Nice story, but what does that have to do with bridge?"

"Our partnership is what it affects. See? Hannah and I . . . well, we've been sweet on each other ever since, and I can't imagine her going along with me traipsing all over the world playing cards with you."

"Where is this young lady?" She accentuated the word young.

"Marble Falls."

"Still in high school then." Missy gazed toward the pond, probably watching the ducks glide by, leaving nary a ripple behind. He wanted to say what of it, only four years separated him and Hannah—no big deal when she was twenty and him twenty-four.

Nothing like robbing the cradle or anything. The older lady—seemingly older by the minute comparing her with Hannah—faced him again.

"What'd she think about us playing cards this weekend?"

The question hit him in the gut like a mule's kick. Her angry tone, resentment, and pleading with him not to flashed through his mind. He swallowed then cleared his throat. "She didn't know. I, uh, let her think I'd be playing with Mike."

"Well, you were in a way. I mean he was in the tournament playing bridge, so it wasn't a lie. So then, sounds safe to presume your little girlfriend is fine with you playing—just not with me."

"Or any female." He laughed. "If she had her druthers, we'd already be married, and I'd be going to Southwest Texas State."

"I see. Is that where she'll be going in the fall?"

"No, she's only a sophomore, so she'll still be at Marble Falls—for two more years after this one."

"Oh. She is young." Missy sat back, fished a cigarette out

then held the pack toward him. He took one, she lit them both. "So, when you saved her, she was like, nine? Isn't that a little young, David?"

"Only four years difference."

"So, she's like what? Fifteen?"

"Sixteen."

"And you're twenty, right?"

"In the fall. So only three years then." That sounded much better.

She seemed to want to say more, but Mis'ess Bass strolled out onto the patio and the conversation shifted to everyone's plans for the rest of the day.

After church and dinner, Hannah busied herself laying out her clothes for the next school week. Most of the time, she didn't worry with it, but with David coming, it would allow her a few extra minutes of sleep each morning if her wardrobe was all decided ahead.

She wanted to spend every speck of time she possibly could with her love. Still couldn't believe he'd given up a whole day with her to play stupid cards. She couldn't wait to see his face, feel his arms around her.

Time for evening services came and went, but no David. She'd planned on going to Pine Bluff with him. Why would he be lollygagging? Wasn't he as excited as she was? The hall clock struck eight. Where was he?

Oooo! She'd wasted the whole day waiting on him! Why hadn't he called or something? Or more important, why wasn't he there?

Finally, right before bedtime, lights shone through the window sheers, coming toward her house. She jumped to her feet and practically broke her neck getting to the front door. He stepped calmly to the porch rail as if his late arrival was no biggie.

The car slowed. It had to be him, sure looked like his Ford. The car stopped. The door opened. A squeal escaped. Being upset with him flew right out the window the minute she laid eyes on him.

He was finally there! And she ran to him, but he held his hands out—not to the side, opening his arms to receive her in his embrace, but palms forward . . . to stop her?

Why?

"Don't touch me. I'm covered in blood."

"What!" She stopped short. "Are you hurt? What happened?"

"I'm fine. Isn't my blood. There was a wreck right in front of me, and I got all bloody helping."

It took a full half hour to get him cleaned up and into some of her father's clothes.

"I'll soak your things, David, then wash them in cold water for you. That'll get the blood out."

"Thank you, Mis'ess Morrison."

Finally, she had him all alone, but way past her regular bedtime. She climbed into his sedan. Hopefully, her mother wouldn't go to flipping the stupid porch light for a while.

After all, it was special circumstances, and she'd so hovered, gleaning every detail of the accident. Hannah traced his hand with her finger.

The hand she so adored. "I'm so thankful you weren't in the crash. I was thinking all sorts of horrible things." She peered into his eyes, her own filling with moisture at the thought of anything actually happening to him. "I was so worried."

"I don't want worrying, sweetness. You never have to worry about me. Just trust God instead."

"I know, it doesn't help anything, but I've missed you so. I hate being apart."

"That won't be forever."

Ugh! Twenty minutes was all she gave her. It wasn't fair. Why did she have to sit on that light switch? She hadn't had nearly enough time to get caught up on all the kisses she gotten behind on the last three months.

And she hadn't even got around to asking him about his idiotic card game. She wanted him to think she was interested, but . . . Why did it have to be time to go in?

She hated it all to blue blazes!

She ought to be married with a baby on the way.

Unlike most Mondays, that one turned out to be a great day. Not too chilly, not too hot, but sunshiny. Still sweater weather. And with David's promise to pick her up after school, it couldn't be any more perfect.

Plus, he'd be there the rest of the week. She'd get out for Good Friday and then would have all day, morning to night, with him for four glorious days!

Early on that morning, in the halls a few of the girls whispered and snickered, but Hannah didn't think anything about it until right before third period.

That's when three of her so-called friends were all clutched up in the back of Algebra, glancing at what appeared to be a newspaper. How weird. They never read the paper.

One looked up, said something to the others and all of them pursued a mad scramble to hide the paper. They giggled and one shot her a smirky grin.

What was going on? She marched over to the trio. "Hey, what's so funny?"

"See for yourself." The smirker grabbed the folded newspaper and extended it toward her.

Another tried to intercept it. "No! Don't show her that!"

"She might as well see it. She will sooner or later!"

Hannah unfolded the newsprint.

Right there . . . for everyone in the whole wide world to see, a picture of her David kissing some bleached-blond floozy right on the lips splashed across the whole top half of the page. She froze.

How . . . what . . .? She tried to read the fine print, but tears blurred the words.

John David's Calling

How could he?

She backed away a step then whirled and ran out of the room. She didn't stop until she reached the nurse's office, slammed the door behind her, and fell into the nearest chair bawling.

Her life was ruined. All her dreams. They were over. He loved someone else, someone older and more beautiful. How could she live without him?

With her head in her lap, her tears wet her skirt. After a bit, she achieved some control and stared at the copper pennies in her loafers. She had to go on . . . somehow. He'd probably planned to tell her that afternoon. He could've said something last night.

Realizing where she was, she wiped her cheeks and smiled up at the lady who'd been patting her shoulder.

Never would she ever open her heart up to such a notorious flap mouth. "I'm sorry, Mis'ess Hinkle. You know how it is sometimes."

"Oh yes, dear, I certainly do. I can give you an aspirin if the cramps are too bad." The nurse gently stroked the length of Hannah's hair.

"Oh, thank you. That'd be wonderful." Let the old biddy think whatever she wanted, wasn't like she'd lied.

She steeled herself and returned to class. Winston Churchill said the Brits would never surrender, and for sure, she wasn't about to either. Let them think whatever they wanted.

The most perfect Monday turned into the hardest day of her life. Everyone must have surely heard. Same as always, she and Jill ate together.

Quite obviously from her face, she knew it all. Thank the Lord she didn't broach the subject though. She still had Adam. Hannah didn't know in her heart if she still had David. Being away so much . . . maybe he'd fallen in love with this tramp.

The day dragged along like a three-legged turtle.

But mercy of mercies, the last bell finally rang.

Clutching her books to her chest, she made herself smile

and marched outside.

Exactly like the two-timer promised, he waited out front, leaning against his stupid Ford, grinning like nothing was wrong, like he didn't have a care in the world. He must not have seen the paper.

"Hey, sweetie." He opened her door. "How was your day?" She slid in. He closed the door then ran around to his side.

"Take me home, please." She smiled and waved at a few of her classmates, certain they were talking about her riding off with her cheater boyfriend. Did she have any friends left? Jill . . . but of late, Adam Churchdog occupied most of her time.

"Oh, I thought we might—"

"I just want to go home."

"Okay, sure. Want to go to town and see a matinee later?"

She turned toward him. How could such a good-looking guy be so cruel? And all that time . . . she thought him to be a Godly man. "No. Thank you."

He shrugged and didn't say anything else until he parked in front of her house. Couldn't he tell she was upset? Why didn't he ask her? Because he didn't care, that's why.

But when did he plan to tell her? Or did he at all? Maybe the rat fink thought he could have his cake and eat it, too. Since she was such a dummy and didn't know her thumb from her big toe!

Serve him right to just jump out and not say a word, but . . . She faced him. "How could you?" Tears threatened, but she willed them to stay in place. Crying like a baby wouldn't help anything.

Nothing could help. He'd been her everything and had turned into her nothing. He'd cheated with an older woman. Never again.

"How could I what?"

"You know what! Are you denying it? Because if you're planning on lying to me, you better know I have proof!"

"Proof of what? What are you talking about, Hannah?"

How could he look so innocent? Such a liar. Good thing

she'd kept that copy instead of trashing it. "You want to see it?"

"Mercy, see what? Why don't you tell me what you're so upset about?" She opened her purse, pulled the folded section out, and slapped it on the seat.

"Try lying your way out of this one, Mister Nightingale, mister unholy man! The apple sure didn't fall far from the tree, did it? I've been so stupid, and you've been playing me for the biggest dunce of mankind!"

"Oh." He shook his head. "She kissed me, Hannah. I did not kiss her back."

"So now you're trying to say to me that some stranger wandered up after you and Mike won your stupid card game and kissed you? Like that! On the lips! You're such a liar."

"Mike wasn't my partner. He entered the tournament, but his mother played with him. It was a mixed-doubles. I was playing with his sister, Missy . . . uh, Melissa.

"It was just a game, Hannah, and we won first place out of a lot of other couples! She was excited. She threw her arms around my neck and kissed me. What was I supposed to do?"

"Oh, yeah. That explains everything, cheater! Your friend's sister, and she was so happy she just what? Accidentally kissed you! You must think I'm so stupid."

"No, I do not. I told you. I didn't kiss her back. I love you, baby, and only you. We talked about it Sunday morning. I told her—"

"You discussed me—with her! Sunday morning? So you spent the night with her! I can't believe you!"

He let go of a long, heavy sigh. "Hannah. Stop. I did not spend the night with her. They all stayed at Mother's."

"I see said the blind man. How cozy."

"Come on, calm down, baby."

"Calm down? Calm down! Well! You can just go right back to that Jezebel and tell her anything you want, John David Nightingale! Tell her you are my ex-boyfriend then go jump in Turtle Creek for all I care. We're done!" She glared.

What had she said? She didn't want to be done. She loved

him! She wanted to take it back, but her bruised pride . . . He'd broken her heart! Ruined everything!

The whole week. All those hours to spend, just her and him. Ruined!

"You do not mean that. Now stop this and let's talk about it. It's no big deal."

"No big deal? You kissing a woman splashed across every newspaper in Texas is no big deal. No, siree! I will not take it back!" She said it, and she meant it. "Goodbye, David. I don't want to ever see you again."

She jumped out and made herself stroll up her sidewalk as though just another day.

But it wasn't.

What had she done?

Chapter Thirteen

What a difference a day made.

Weather-wise, Tuesday played a repetitious encore, but that proved the end of any sameness. Even school—that she usually loved so much—metamorphosed into the last place she wanted to endure.

If not for her perfect attendance and sitting at the top of her class academically, she'd have stayed home.

Breaking up was hard to do.

Speaking only when spoken to, she smiled and made nice as necessary. In reality, all she wanted was to curl up into a ball and cry more. Her insides ached, and her skin seemed strangely wrong, a bad fit, too tight, uncomfortable.

Nothing in her world was right. Probably would never be again. No matter how hard she tried, she couldn't expel the awful image from her mind's eye.

A million narratives of David with Missy plagued her thoughts.

Then after what seemed like an eternity, the last bell echoed through the halls. She gathered her binder and books, grabbed her purse, and headed to the front doors, studying the floor as she'd done all day.

Pausing on the first step, her heart almost stopped when she looked up. She did a double take. Just like yesterday, there he stood next to his Ford.

Well, not exactly as the day before. Instead of grinning, he wore a somber expression and hugged a a big stuffed dog with its precious face turned toward her.

What was he doing?

What should she do?

Run! That's what she should do! Run right past him all the way home and lock herself in her room. Her feet hurried all right, down the stairs and across the lawn, but they refused to veer past the two-timer, and instead, carried her straight to him.

Traitors!

"What are you doing here? Are you deaf? I told you yesterday I didn't want to ever see you again."

He held out the plush pup. "You didn't mean it though. I love you, and you love me. We always have, and we always will."

"Liar."

"You're wearing your glasses, and you never do unless you've cried so much you can't get your contacts into your swollen, stinging eyes. Are you going to deny it?"

"So." She adjusted her frames. "I was only crying over what you threw away."

"You love me, Hannah. I know you do, and I love . . . Look, I'm sorry I ever agreed to play. I'm sorry I didn't tell you. I didn't really lie, but I let you believe something different than the whole truth."

"Same thing." She looked around. Where had all the kids come from? And why were they hanging around trying their best not to look like they were eavesdropping? What gave them any right? She hated them interfering in her business.

Wasn't like she might hit him or anything . . . even if he did deserve to get slapped in the face.

Would he turn his other cheek? In front of them all? What if he slapped her back?

She stepped closer. "Take me home."

"Yes, ma'am." He extended the dog to her then opened her

door once she emptied his hands. He went around front then climbed in behind the wheel. She pressed into her own door.

Once away from the prying eyes, she tossed the pup dog into the backseat and turned sideways. "I want to know the truth. Did you . . . uh . . ." Her cheeks burned at even the thought of him like that with that person. How could she say it?

"No. I absolutely did not. I never have and will not until the day we're married, Hannah."

"Swear?"

"With God as my witness, I have never nor will I ever lie with any woman except you. Please forgive me, sweetie. I love you. And that's the truth. The whole truth, and nothing but the truth."

Her insides rolled, and confusion pounded her skull. She wanted to stay mad at him, but he was being so sweet and dear and empathetic. And he was definitely right.

She did love him, had always, and couldn't imagine ever stopping—truth be known—whatever he did. But she'd never tell him that, give him license to sin.

Besides, what was he supposed to do when that brazen hussie kissed him?

"Will you promise me something, David?"

"Sure, if I can."

"The next time some woman who is not a relative comes at you with her lips all puckered up, promise me you'll run the other way."

"Yes, ma'am. I can do that. I promise."

"Okay then. Please pull this car over right now."

He did, and she scooted into his arms then let him smother her with kisses.

Exactly like the songs said, making up was so much better than breaking up, but breaking up to make up . . . a game for fools.

She never ever wanted to go through that again.

All of his bridge winnings—less his tithe he'd stuck back—he blew on Hannah.

Hey, found money, so why not? He valued her way more than silver or gold, but sure seemed like with each gift he gave, the deeper he sank into the soup . . . until he considered he might drown if the end of the visit didn't come soon.

Praise the Lord for Mom Morrison and her porch light—and his resolve—and God's help and strength. Man, it got real hard at times not to put his hands where they didn't belong.

Resurrection Sunday services proved bittersweet. His parents didn't make it back from wherever they'd traveled, and Gramps . . . he was just too weak to preach.

Though several of his professors warned against being a one-man show, he loved leading praise and worship then preaching whatever the Lord laid on his heart, so he agreed to fill in.

The pews were packed, it being the holiday and all. He even stood at the door and greeted them on their way out. He didn't want Gramps to have to beg, and Hannah stood beside him, smiling, blessing the people as they left.

Everyone seemed to like the service all right, but then, according to his grandfather, he'd always been their fair-haired boy.

His last night with Hannah, the hardest, tested him sorely, but he made it through without any major faux pas. Maybe her idea to go ahead and marry carried some merit after all.

Not like they wouldn't get hitched one day, and she could come to Tulsa to live, but . . . he just never had a peace about it.

God led him by His peace. Like he knew he needed to go to ORU.

Once he dropped her off at school Tuesday morning, he fled temptation on I-35 North.

Right after he crossed the Red River into Oklahoma, he

John David's Calling

caught a whiff of what smelled like electrical wire burning. He pulled to the side of the road, turned the motor off, and grabbed the door handle.

Like a linebacker hitting him head on, something pinned him to his seat.

The windshield vanished, replaced by a glowing, whirling wheel, and inside it, another one. The outer circle turned clockwise, and the inner in the opposite direction. He stared.

Ezekiel's vision? But there weren't any beasts . . . only people. Men, woman, and some bigger children formed up the wheels. Each shone so brightly, it almost hurt to look, yet he couldn't tear his eyes away.

Was it the Lord's glory?

The unction to sing or dance or both—something to praise the Lord God Almighty—overwhelmed him, but he couldn't move. Only watch. Then both wheels vanished as did whatever had pushed him back in the seat.

The windshield became the plain see-through glass it had been before, reflecting the blue sky and floating white clouds.

Closing his eyes, he inhaled deeply. Nothing but clean air, no burning wires, no smell whatsoever.

With a turn of the key, his ignition brought the motor to life, but David didn't put it into gear, not yet. He just sat there, pondering the vision and what it could mean.

"Bless You, Holy Father. Thank you for whatever it is You've just shown me. I'm all ears if You want to tell me what I saw . . . what it meant, something. Because I've got to tell you, I'm clueless."

Sitting there in silence, he listened hard, but heard nothing other than a bird in the distance, singing its praise to the Lord. Not wanting to hurry the Father, David waited and listened.

But no word came.

No explanation.

After a few more minutes waiting, he checked oncoming traffic, waited for an opening, then pulled back onto the interstate. Man, he wanted a smoke and to get himself to Tulsa, or more especially, back into the presence of Mike Bass.

He needed to share what he'd seen. Maybe God would show his friend something.

Shame his father wasn't handy. He'd rather ask his counsel.

His friend turned up in the upperclassmen's day room, watching *700 Club* on the tube. Only took a nod to get him headed upstairs.

"Good trip?"

"Yes and no."

"Thought so." Mike laughed. "I take it Hannah saw the picture."

The first few minutes he spent on what he prayed would be the one and only time he and Hannah ever broke up then turned serious. He let out all the air in his lungs. "You ever see a vision?"

"Nope." Mike whirled a table chair and sat in it backwards, facing him. "What did you see?"

"Maybe a little like what Ezekiel saw with the wheels, but instead of any beasts, the wheels were made up with people. Young adults mostly, but some older . . . He reached back into the recesses of his conscious and studied a bit. And a few half-grown kids, but little children, too. Best I could tell."

"What were they doing?"

"Some in the inner circle had their hands raised like they were praising, but I couldn't exactly hear if they were singing or praying . . . or what. Mostly men comprised the outer circle. They appeared a lot more determined. You could even say like marching."

"So, they were moving?"

"Yeah, in circles and going in opposite directions. All of them sort of glowed, golden . . . bright. Pretty awesome."

"I'll say. But you don't have any idea what it was all about?"

"Not a clue. I asked the Lord to show me, or tell me, but . . . so far . . . nothing. Zilch."

"Man." Mike stared at him a while then shrugged. "You

pray about going with us?"

"I did, yes. But the answer's still no." Not that he wouldn't go if God told him to, but he could hear Hannah pitching a fit about him being gone overseas.

"Want to get a game up?"

"Sure, as long as your sister isn't involved."

"Gotcha." Mike chuckled. "There's a mixed tournament in Oklahoma City this weekend."

"Not a chance."

While Sandy's son settled in to make the scholastic push to his summer vacation, all was not well with her soul. She poured herself a second cup of coffee, took a sip, then lit her third cigarette.

As the smoke curled off the cancer stick, she wondered where she was anyway? Burbank? No, that was last week. She'd flown with him to San Francisco.

Oh yeah, City of the Golden Gate. An Episcopal church had invited him to lead their music that Saturday evening—a special service.

Imagine that.

Though no one shared her hotel room, or even came visiting, she laughed out loud. What kind of fool was she anyway?

Following Buddy around as though his fame hit rock star level, and she dogged him harder than any number one fan—not that she didn't love the way he sang. And the few times he got to preach, she adored the way he wove stories in with a point as sharp as any needle.

And he always came back around to elaborate on it at the end. Brilliant and anointed.

The echo of her hollow chuckle faded, and she sobered. No never mind how much she clapped and acted best she could like a holy roller, she couldn't get him to the altar . . . or even her bed for that matter.

Wasn't like he hadn't been there before. Mercy—as he was wont to say about fifty times a day—he'd fathered her son! He'd claimed more than once she was the love of his life.

But no.

All she could do didn't measure up, failed to make her good enough for him to make an honest woman out of her. What did he expect of her? She might have to just face it. She'd never be good enough to be his wife.

Never be the sweet, submissive Abigail who believed whatever he said was truth.

To make it worse, her goody-two-shoes sister, the perfect picture of a holiness wife, excitedly expected her first grandchild with Travis by her side.

Life wasn't fair.

The view of the bay looked like a postcard, so majestic. The dawning of the new day painted the sky, reflected in the water . . . but . . . She walked through the sliding door and didn't stop until she reached the rail.

"You out there, God?"

"Why are you making it so hard?"

Of course, He didn't answer. He didn't speak to people anymore like so many of those she knew so well claimed. Her son, Buddy, his dad, her sister and Travis. They all reported things God supposedly told them.

Such good people, all of them, but God didn't speak to her, so why would He talk to them? He'd given the world the Bible, His Living Word, sure He spoke through it.

MY SHEEP SHALL KNOW MY VOICE

Her heart stopped, and her throat clogged. She knew that verse. Spinning around, her fists clinched. "Who's there? Buddy? Is that you?" Just like the idiot to play such a trick on her.

But her love was nowhere to be seen, and neither was anyone else. The room remained empty, except for her.

John David's Calling

Glancing at the door confirmed the chain still rested in place. Plus, she'd locked and bolted it.

"Okay, Jesus. If You're talking all of a sudden, trying to tell me I need . . ."

Wait. What did He say? Was He really talking to her?

She sank to her knees on the cool flagstone balcony. If it wasn't Him, then who? My sheep know my voice, but . . . she was a sheep, right? She went to church twice on Sundays and every Wednesday as a child.

Maybe she'd missed a few times since, but . . . My sheep know my voice. If the Bible said that, it had to be true, yet . . . Did she really know him?

"Am I yours, Lord?" She filled her lungs then held her breath, paralyzed, waiting for the answer, fearing it. She'd been baptized when she was twelve, but . . .

"Jesus! I want to be Your sheep! I need you! I want to hear Your voice, know it, but . . . but . . . I've been so horrible!" Tears overflowed and raced down her cheeks, dripping onto the floor.

"I repent, Father. I'm sorry. Please forgive me. Save me, Lord, and give me . . . a new heart."

Wave after wave of liquid Love poured over her and filled her heart. She stretched her legs prone and her arms out to the side prostrate before God's throne and worshiped Him. His everlasting, never-ending Love lifted her, washed away all her sins!

Clean! She'd never been so clean! Totally forgiven with a fresh slate!

All the hateful things she'd said and thought about Buddy's wife were gone, forgiven! All the men, all the booze, every ugly word she'd ever spoken . . . washed away by the precious Blood of the Lamb.

She pressed her forehead to the stone. "Thank you, Lord."

Realization dawned, she needed to be baptized again! She jumped to her feet, flung off her housecoat, and ran to her suitcase.

What was Buddy's room number?

Three loud booms coming from the hall brought Buddy from his lesson. He pushed himself up, marked his Bible, then walked toward the entryway. Before he reached it, another knock pounded even louder.

"I'm coming."

"Hurry, Buddy!"

The excitement in Sandy's voice spurred him to a half-trot. He swung the door open. "What is it? What's wrong?"

"Wrong?" He'd heard about ear-to-ear grins, but never really saw one. He'd definitely never seen her grin that big. "Nothing's wrong! Everything's right!"

What in the world?

"I need to get baptized! And you're just the man for the job."

He laughed. "Okay, right now? Will the pool do?"

"I don't know! You're the preacher, not me. But I want to get dunked before I drop dead or a meteor falls out of the sky and hits me!"

"Whoa." He took her hand and pulled her into his room. "Back up. Tell me what happened."

"Well." She hiked one shoulder and grinned even bigger though he'd have thought it impossible. "I got saved! Jesus! He saved me! And . . . and He talked to me, too! I thought it was you at first, but no one else was there! He told me His sheep know Him and hear His voice! That was before though! I just want to be baptized! For real this time!"

"Awesome. That's awesome." He held his arms out, and she practically tackled him throwing herself into his embrace. He wrapped her tight then swung her around and around.

"I know you were taught that baptism's essential for salvation—and yes, it is something we need to do—but it will definitely not keep you out of Heaven if you happen to die before you get wet."

"Really? Okay, if that's true, show me." She leaned back. "I want Scripture and verse."

Starting in Acts on the day of Pentecost, he went back to the Gospels and Jesus on the cross. How he told the thief that he would be with him in Paradise that very day. "Want more?"

"No." She shook her head. "Wasn't it you preaching on how out of the mouth of two or three witnesses truth got established? Just the other day?"

"That's right."

"You showed me two verses—can't they count as witnesses? And you're saying there's more?"

"Many more. I'm not saying baptism isn't good. We are to be baptized, Jesus was. I'm only saying it isn't essential to your salvation . . . like a work, but we're under grace now. Want me to show you?"

"No, I believe you. But can we go early this evening? I'd still like for you to baptize me."

"Of course." He kissed her forehead. "Yes, ma'am. I'll call and be sure the baptistery is full, see if they have a heater they can turn on."

"Great! And there's one more thing."

"What's that?"

"How about we fly to Vegas after church tonight?"

"Feeling lucky, are you?"

"No, sir. Blessed!" She stuck out her tongue. "I've only heard you say a hundred times there's no such thing as luck."

"True. So why do you want to go to Sin City?"

"Because there's no waiting period there."

"Oh? So, you don't want a big wedding then?"

"No, siree! I only want you! I want to be Mis'ess Broderick Eversole Nightingale more than anything in the world. And you know what the Bible says."

"Which part?"

"About Him giving me the desires of my heart." She

twirled her finger in his hair. "He's very happy with me right now. Buddy, will you marry me?"

He looked into her eyes, all along he'd thought it was only her not accepting the baptism and ministry of God's Holy Spirit that kept his spirit in check about marrying his love, but . . . she wasn't even a Christian until that morning.

"Tell me every detail. I want to hear it all. How it happened."

Beginning with her feeling so unworthy, she did, and he loved every word of it. Once finished, she turned serious.

"What about Vegas, Mister? I'm not sure about California, but Texas has a three-day waiting period. Won't you make an honest woman out of me, make me the happiest lady in the world? If you ask, I know God will say yes. And I say yes. What do you say?"

"How about we leave in the morning, since the rooms are paid up."

"I don't care about the money! I don't want to spend another night without you."

Such sweet drama, and he understood. He stifled a chuckle, didn't want to either, but she seemed way more pathetic about it. "Make the reservations. Services should be over by nine, and it's thirty minutes to the airport. See if they have a red-eye."

"Really?" She cuddled into his chest.

"Of course. There's nothing I want more in the world than for you to be my wife, Sandra Louise Harris." He stroked her hair. "I've loved you since I first laid eyes on you. I made so many mistakes. Will you forgive me?"

"Yes, yes. We both did. Will you forgive me?"

"I will." He pushed her back and went down onto one knee. "Sandy, my first love . . . and my last, will you do me the honor of becoming my wife?"

"Yes, my beloved. Yes, yes, yes!" She pulled him up and kissed his lips, soon to be hers forever! "I don't suppose we could maybe duck out early tonight?"

"Would if I could, but I'm preaching, too."

Chapter Fourteen

David hung up the phone then hugged himself.

His parents were married! He danced a little jig then had to tell someone. He ran all the way to the upperclassmen's dorm then searched the day room but didn't see Mike. He checked his friend's room, but the man wasn't there either.

"Oh well." He headed back downstairs.

"Hey! Matt said you were hunting me."

David grinned. "My parents called! They got married today."

Mike nodded and raised a hand Heavenward. "Praise the Lord. He answers prayer! His mercy endures forever."

"Amen. After all those years . . ."

The man nodded toward his room. "Hey, King, come on up. Talked to Dad this afternoon."

Turning around on the stairs, David went back up then waited on his friend before entering the dorm room. "What did the bishop allow?"

"Well, he heard from reliable resources that Nixon is pushing for a draft lottery."

"That doesn't sound any good. How's it going to affect us? Is the president talking about taking away the school deferment?"

"Not that I know of. The biggest thing is that their 'oldest called first' policy is changing."

"Are you still going to file as a conscientious objector?"

"No, Dad thinks that might be a bad move. Instead of waiting until August, we're leaving for Africa right after graduation."

"Oh, man. I was looking forward to you coming south."

"Me, too, but Dad thinks if I'm out of the country and in the mission field, they won't call me up."

"Why the change of strategy?"

He grinned. "Politics."

"How so?"

"Dad's exploring a run for the Senate and thinks it would look bad if his son tried to dodge the draft."

"Well, aren't we?"

"No, my friend. We are college men. Draft dodgers go to Canada. We're only putting off our service until after our education."

"I see." David laughed.

"Oh." Mike snapped his fingers. "I almost forgot. Dad said if at any time you decide you want to join us, he'll cover the cost. Hannah, too, if you go and get yourself hitched."

"I'll keep that in mind. It's very generous, but don't look for me until you see me walking up the road. Getting eaten by cannibals is not what God's called to do."

"Me neither." His friend stretched. "What say we get a game up? We've got time for a rubber or two before lights out. If we can find a couple of pigeons."

The elation of his parents marrying mixed with his disappointment over Mike leaving early and put him in a weird mood. The guy had become the closest thing to a big brother he'd ever had, and David would surely miss him.

Then the last week before finals, the dreams started.

Waking with a knowing that evil stalked . . . either him or his, he could never quite remember exactly what he'd seen or heard in his night vision. But they left him uneasy.

Staying in town long enough to watch Mike and the other

two M's walk the stage, he wound up eating way too much at their big send-off party.

The faithful Ford then headed south.

As he'd planned, he made it to Dallas right before midnight. Praise the Lord for his home away from home. Tickled him it sat almost exactly midway between Tulsa and Cypress Springs. Nothing like having a familiar bed to lay his weary bones in. He fluffed the pillow then flopped down.

Suddenly he stood in knee-high water with trees all around. Off in the distance, a voice called.

"Help me, David."

"Sonny? Is that you? Where are you?"

"Over here."

Tracing the call, he followed his ear until he found his cousin, wrapped in barbed wire around a big cypress tree at the edge of the water. "Oh man! How'd you get all tangled up in that stuff?"

"Being a fool of course." Sonny laughed. "Chasing after Sissy Kellogg! But then she changed into this big old dragon and turned on me. I ran for my life, but . . . here I am. You holding, my man? I need a little taste. I'm about to go crazy here."

Following different loops, David saw an end and carefully started unwrapping it. A barb dug into his hand. "Ouch! A taste of what?"

"Horse."

"What?"

"You know."

"No, Sonny. I don't. What are you talking about?"

"Heroin, man! Where you been?"

David sat up in bed. "Oh Lord, help Sonny."

GO GET HIM

David slipped off the bed onto his knees. After a good half hour of seeking the Lord, no other word came. He stood.

Where had he put Sonny's address? He looked through all this stuff, but it wasn't there, so he eased on downstairs, put the coffee on, then decided to call Cypress Springs.

His MawMaw might have it; and if not, she could run surely down for him. It took an hour, but the old dear came through. Now all he had to do was convince Hannah he had to go west instead of south.

"Thought I smelled coffee."

"Congratulations." David jumped to his feet and ran to his father.

"Thank you."

"Mama awake?"

"Somewhat; you know how she is in the mornings."

For sure he did. He fetched Dad a cup then bid him sit. "You ever have prophetic dreams?"

"A few, why?"

Over that cup then half the next, he told his father about Sonny. "I couldn't find his address, but MawMaw tracked it down."

"Where is he?"

"Oregon."

"Extra-long toll call."

"Longer drive." David shrugged. "Figured I'd leave after dinner."

"Need any cash?"

"That would be nice."

"What would be nice?"

David turned. His mother in all her splendor stood at the kitchen's doorway he stood. "Congratulations."

"Thank you." She walked into his embrace. "I'm sorry, Son. Forgive me for slapping you at Thanksgiving."

"Yes, ma'am. I forgive you."

"Good, now answer my question."

With her interrupting every three words, it took a lot longer to tell what he'd told his father about going to get his cousin.

"Okay, so you still haven't told what would be nice."

"Dad asked if I needed some cash."

"Right, how much you want."

"I don't know, with the gas card I shouldn't need a lot."

"I think I've got a couple of hundred in my purse, you can have that and . . ."

She looked to his father. "What about you?"

"That much, maybe more."

"That should be plenty to get me there and back."

"Hannah? Telephone, dear."

She'd heard the thing ring, but no way could she beat her mother to it from upstairs.

Better for her to answer anyway and find out who was calling for herself instead of grilling Hannah about the caller's identity. It better not be David telling her he wasn't coming. He couldn't. He wouldn't!

Nothing but a crying shame that her penny-pinching father wouldn't spring for a second line upstairs. She'd begged and been so persistent forever. He'd probably put one in the same month she married and left home. She loved him, but he could drive her crazy sometimes.

Bounding down the stairs, her ponytail bounced back and forth. "Coming, Mama!" She picked up the receiver. "Hello?"

"Hey, sweetheart! You having a good day?"

"Okay, I guess, so far, but I'm expecting it to get lots better before it's over. Where are you?"

"Still at Mom's, but I've got to go to Oregon."

"Oregon! Why? Oh, my goodness, David! No! You can't!"

"Sweetheart, slow down. Let me explain."

It couldn't be! Her worst imagination coming true. What was wrong with him?

Pulling the curly cord its full length to the parlor, she flopped into the overstuffed chair. "Fine! Explain!" And she hushed and listened. The more he talked, the madder she got.

"You're ruining my summer! It was bad enough you stayed

in Oklahoma three days extra to go to Mike's graduation, but now you're running off to God knows where! I don't want you to go!"

"I know that, but Sonny . . . he's my cousin, baby, and he needs me. Hannah, the Lord Himself told me to go get him."

How could she argue with God? It wasn't fair! She wanted him there with her! Not running off to some hippie commune. She'd heard all about those awful places with their drugs and wild women running around half-naked—or worse.

"David! Do you have to go?"

"Yes, baby. Sonny's like a little brother to me. If I didn't, and something happened to him, I could never live with myself. Not to mention being obedient to God. He told me to. He said three words. 'Go get him'! So how can I not?"

"Then come get me. Take me with you!" She wanted to reach through the line and shake some sense into him, make him come get her. But . . . "Sometimes . . . uh . . ." She couldn't decide if she wanted to kiss him or whack him.

Was he too good? Could someone be too Godly?

"Don't be silly. Your parents would never let you go."

"I'll run away. We can tell them we're going to Burnett—and we will, so it won't be lying—on our way to Oregon!"

"Hannah. We cannot do that, and you know it."

"But . . . but . . . Why! Why did God tell you that!"

He would never come and get her.

No matter what she said.

What else could she do but give him her blessing?

"I don't know, but He did, baby, and I've got to go. I'm sorry. I really am."

The line went silent. What was he waiting for? Turkey buzzard!

"Hannah? You there?"

"Yes, I'm here."

"You were saying?"

"Oh . . . nothing, I guess. Except I love you." She might as well eat her humble pie. He was going, and she definitely didn't want him to leave on bad terms. "You better call me every night. Promise?"

"Yes, Ma'am. Every day—or night. I'll call."

"And I want to know where you are and what you're doing."

"Sure, that's no problem."

"And you'll promise to come straight back here when you get him?"

"Of course. I'll make a beeline."

"All right then." She hated it but might as well accept it and be as nice as she could. "Oh, David. Did you hear? Your cousin Paul got killed last week."

"Oh no. How'd it happen?"

"Some delta in Vietnam. He was on a gunboat."

"The Mekong Delta?"

"Yes, I think that's the one."

"Mercy! Poor Uncle George. Losing Auntie last year and now Paul. When's the funeral?"

"I don't know, but I'll find out and tell you when you call tomorrow. Think you'll be able to get back in time for it?"

"Sure hope so. I guess they'll fly the body back to San Antonio. It'll probably take some time. Hey, did you hear my parents got married?"

"Yes, I did! Isn't it wonderful? Except I have to admit I'm jealous."

"Soon enough, darling lady. Did you get your job at the day care for the summer?"

"No, they didn't need me, but I've got some leads and put in my application to several places."

"You could haul hay with me if you want—soon as I get back."

"Yeah, right. No thank you, please. I can't toss those bales upon the truck."

"No, of course not." He laughed. "But you could drive the truck."

"Hey, there's a thought. We could be together all day."

He chuckled. "On second thought, I might not get much hay hauled with you around."

"Wrong, if we're getting paid by the bale, wouldn't be anything but work."

"Do you have a Class A license?"

"No, is it hard to get that kind?"

"Not really. Check it out. You might not even need one."

"I will."

"I best go, sweetness. I want to get on the road."

"Are you sure? All the way to Oregon? How far is it anyway?"

"Couple of thousand miles. No hill for a stepper."

"Okay then but be careful. You promise?"

"I will, and I'll be back as quick as I can."

"All right then." She didn't want to, but she let him hang up. Life wasn't fair, but the thought of spending the rest of the summer driving him around offered a little solace.

Not much though.

Nothing like having him right there where he belonged.

David watched as the attendant checked the oil, transmission fluid, and each tire for proper pressure. When the pump shut off, he handed the man his gas card with a folded dollar bill under the piece of plastic. "Thank you."

The grease monkey smiled then slipped the bill into his overalls.

Well, ready to go if not willing. By his calculations, over two thousand miles ahead. Nothing to do but get at it either. He shifted the Ford into gear and pulled out.

Made Amarillo that night. He hated to spend money on a room, but sure didn't want to sleep in the car.

Up bright and early the next morning, he called Hannah, but only had enough quarters to talk a few minutes. He drove the two hundred and eighty-eight miles to Albuquerque before dinner.

Not bad, except he'd gotten a bit of white-line fever a time or two. Such long stretches without seeing another car made him sleepy. He stopped for supper and gas at a truck stop along the highway, then pushed on to Bakersfield.

Had to slap his face three times to stay awake long enough to find a room. The next morning over coffee and a double stack of pancakes, he used his thumb as a ruler and figured out he had less than six hundred miles to go.

Got ten dollars' worth of quarters then called his love. Mom Morrison informed him—long distance no less—that Hannah had gone on a job interview.

"I'll call her later. Tell her I'm in California."

Had to push himself hard to get to Medford before dark, but he couldn't find the logging road that would take him to the camp where Sonny was supposed to be. Until sunset, he drove around in the area looking, but gave up when darkness fell and found himself a cheap motel with a pay phone.

Armed with even more quarters, he dialed Hannah's number. Before the operator came on the line, it hit him hard. He was on a fool's errand.

Had he really heard from the Lord?

Chapter Fifteen

"Hello, Morrison residence."

David let out the breath he been holding out. "Hannah. Hey, babe. It's me."

"Hey, yourself. Did you find Sonny?"

"Not yet."

"Aww. I'm praying you'll find him fast and get yourself back to Texas! What's the holdup? What's it like there?"

After confirming that Oregon—at least the part he'd seen—was beautiful, filled with rolling hills and a coastline that would make her sing a new song, but gray and rainy.

Every time she stopped long enough to take a breath—a sure sign she wanted him to say something—he kept asking her questions. He wanted her to talk.

Found out all about her latest interview, who was working where or going to summer school, what her friends were doing, and how it was going between Churchdog and her cousin. He listened to her answers half-heartedly, lamenting being so far away.

After a much too-thorough update on those goings on in Marble Falls, she paused—a rather pregnant passé at that, but he couldn't think of another question.

"What's wrong, David?"

Guess she knew him better than he thought. "Oh . . . uh . .

." How did one go about confessing one's doubts about hearing from God?

"Stop stalling and spill your guts. Now. What is it?"

The girl's spoiled bratiness sure exposed itself sometimes, but she was his, all his, and he loved her to distraction. Loved her passion and allowed her straightforwardness with him.

Guess he did his share of spoiling, too. He couldn't hang it all on her parents, or grandparents, or teachers, or most everyone who knew her.

Two more years before she would be his legally wedded wife, but he never doubted she belonged to him since junior high.

"You're not talking." She sang the declaration, emphasizing the 'talk' part. "Come on, sweetheart. I know something's wrong. What is it?"

First, she'd used concern in her voice, then tried anger, and then now her sweet cajoling. He knew her pretty well, too, and definitely liked the latter best of her efforts to extract information.

"I thought it would be different. I pushed hard to get here. Hoped we might even head back tonight, but I can't even find that commune. Much less Sonny."

"Okay, well. Maybe it was just the going that God wanted, to see if you'd hear Him then obey. And you did. I mean, Sonny could be anywhere. You tried. I'd say for you to go ahead and come home. You went, what more can the Lord ask?"

"I dunno. Maybe you're right. I'm definitely tired, but . . . since I'm here, I suppose it'd be prudent to ask around a little more—at least see if anyone knows anything."

Her longest pause ensued, and he was paying money for the silence, maybe two bits' worth before she finally spoke again.

"Okay, fine. Half a day tomorrow, but then hit the road back to me, Mister Nightingale. I'm at least a thousand kisses behind and way past ready to catch up."

Mercy. She wanted to put him right back into the soup then turn up the heat.

Lord, give me the strength only You can.

"Please deposit another dollar."

The methodical way the operator said that, so matter of fact, like she couldn't care less if he had another quarter or not. He hated it. "I'll call you tomorrow, I love you . . ."

Before she could answer the nasty dial tone blared in his ear. Pay phones were the pits. He hung the receiver back into its cradle then checked his watch again.

Hopefully, things would look better in the morning after a good night's rest. Indeed, the new day did. He loved it that God's lovingkindness rose fresh each morning. The gray blanket had been folded and put away, leaving the blue sky behind.

A bright sunshiny day! He loaded his stuff into the Ford then strolled into the motel office. The older lady looked up from her crossword puzzle. "Checking out?"

"Yes, ma'am." He placed his key on the counter. "Would you know anything about the Medford Commune, ma'am? Where it is or just anything."

"Oh darling. You don't want any part of that place. I've got a niece lives out there. Those people are a bunch of Godless weirdos, and you sure don't look the type. Hippie freaks if you ask me, they're all crazy on drugs and booze. Free love." She rolled her eyes, shaking her head, then looked him square into the windows of his soul.

"Trust me, dear, you do not want to go there."

"You're right. I have no intention of joining in the craziness. I'm trying to find a friend of mine—my cousin, actually."

"Oh, well then . . . that's a different matter." She tried to tell him how to get there but kept using local landmarks.

Pulling out his map, he unfolded and spread it on her counter. "Could you show me?"

She did, then offered him some glazed donuts. He waved her off, but she insisted, so he took one—then three more before she'd let him leave. Plus, a large to-go cup full of hot coffee.

Could she be an angel unaware? What were the chances he'd stop at that specific hotel where the lady had a relative in the same commune as Sonny?

Looking Heavenward, he whispered a thank You to God and headed out. Only took forty-five minutes. He'd been on the right road the day before but missed the turnoff. Hadn't seen the sign for the weeds.

Right inside the gate, he spotted a guy wearing psychedelic bell-bottom pants, a vest—without the benefit of a shirt—and a floppy hat. He hoed a row of beautiful, tall, straight plants heavy with tomatoes. David shut off the engine and got out.

"Excuse me, sir. Would you happen to know where Sonny Harris is?"

The man turned toward him. "Hey, dude. You don't look old enough to be the law, are you?"

"No, sir. Family."

"Ah." The guy laughed. "I ain't a sir. So who is the Sun Man to you?"

"My cousin."

"Oh, bad break, Cuz. He ain't here." The guy returned to his hoeing.

"Know where he is?"

The man looked back. "Sure. The law's got him locked up, been there a while."

"Where?"

"Medford, man."

"Okay, thanks."

"No problem, man." After a quick wave, the guy went back to hoeing. David turned the Ford around and headed back. Right away, he found the justice center.

The sergeant manning the front desk held up a finger when David approached and kept on scribbling on a pre-printed form. The guy looked up. "Can I help you?"

"Yes, sir. It's my understanding Sonny Harris is incarcerated here?"

The policeman nodded. "We've got a Reagan P. Harris Junior here. A.K.A. The Sun Man. That who you're talking about?"

"Yes, sir. That's him. May I see him?"

"Depends. You a lawyer?"

"No, sir, his cousin."

"You can do better than see him." The officer picked up a folder. "You can have him if you pay his fine and restitution."

"How much is it?"

The guy opened the folder. "Total's four hundred eighty-six dollars, and that goes up twenty-three dollars a day."

"Okay, thank you. I haven't got that much on me though. Could you direct me to the closest Western Union office?"

"Sure. That'd be the Piggly Wiggly. It's two blocks down, one over to your right. Turn at the light."

"Great. I'll be right back then. Thank you, sir. By the way, what's he in for?"

"Public intoxication, and he smashed a brick into the window at the drug store, but it only cracked, the owner said if he pays for the window, he won't press any charges."

"When does the next twenty-three bucks kick in?"

"Noon."

David glanced at the wall clock. Had all of forty-five minutes. "Thanks, sir."

It only took one quarter to make a collect call and then he got that two bits back.

"Good morning, this is the long-distance operator. I've a David Nightingale on the line calling collect, ma'am. Will you accept the charges?"

"Yes, operator. David? Are you there? Are you okay?"

"Yes, ma'am. I'm fine."

"Where are you?"

If she'd only give him a word in edgewise, he'd fill her in. He loved her though. "Medford, Oregon, Mom, and I need more money. Can you wire me six hundred? Sonny's in jail."

"Mercy, what did he do?"

"Public intoxication, and he cracked a window."

"Forget Western Union, find a United States National Bank, and I'll wire transfer the money there. I can do it over the phone."

"Do you suppose they have a branch here, I've only got until noon and the price goes up."

"I'll check, but I'm pretty certain they should. Call me back if not."

"Great. Thanks, Mom. I'll do that."

"I'll call my banker, get the ball rolling."

"Yes, ma'am, and thanks again."

"Hey, you tell Sonny he owes me, and I expect to be paid off. Tell him I'll give him a dollar credit every time he darkens the Pine Bluff Holiness church's doors."

"Wow, Mom. What about PawPaw's church?"

"Nope, your father isn't pastoring in Cypress Springs."

"He's pastoring? Really? When did all this happen?"

"Your Gramps called last night. Said the Lord told him to turn things over to your father."

"That's awesome news! I'll tell Sonny."

"Good, now get going and call me back if they don't have a branch there. Get me the name of any bank where you are if they don't."

"Yes, ma'am."

Hard to hurry a banker, so he did his best to be patient. Getting Sonny out before noon would pay for the motel room, but mostly, he wanted to get Sonny out. Finally, his cousin walked through the last metal door.

His cousin had on dirty jeans and a plaid shirt two sizes too large, frayed at the collar with cut-off sleeves. And he was barefoot. David had never in all his born days seen such a sorry sight.

Mercy. He wasn't sure if the jailbird needed a bath or a hot meal first. Didn't the place have showers?

"Mercy, man. You look horrible."

He nodded, but somehow came up with a sheepish grin.

"Thank you, brother. I'd about given up hope."

David wrapped his arm around the bony shoulder and led his cousin out. Didn't let go until he had him in the front seat. At exactly two miles per hour under the posted speed limit, he drove straightaway out of town.

No way was he going to give anyone else in Medford an excuse to keep him from getting all the way past the city limits safe and sound.

Sonny—who had been resting his head on the seat—sat up. "Got a ready roll on you, my man?" He patted his empty shirt pocket. "Appears I'm out."

"Look in the glove box."

"Great. You wouldn't have anything stronger in there would you? Maybe a little weed?"

"No, and you best forget about that stuff, Sonny Harris."

Sonny retrieved the pack of smokes, lit one, took a long drag, then handed it over and shook out another one. He fired up his own.

"I about went crazy in that jail, and the worst was the meter kept running. They could've kept me in there for years. They didn't even give me my one phone call. How'd you know I was in there?"

"The Lord told me. Four days ago, I was on my way home, and the man upstairs said go get you."

"Yeah right! I'm so sure He spoke to you." He scoffed. "God doesn't do that anymore. Really, man, how'd you know I was in jail?"

"I didn't." David glanced over then turned his attention back onto the road. "I went to the commune and one of your hippie friends told me. Good thing he knew. I would've hated to leave without you, but . . . Your bill had run up to over five hundred dollars."

"No joke?"

"Mama says you owe her. She's the one who financed this trip and paid your fine and restitution."

"Oh man, I'll never get her paid off."

"She's offering to give a dollar's worth of credit for every time you come to church."

"Oh man, take me back."

"You don't mean that."

"Nah. Coming out here was a big mistake. Should've listened to you, bro." Sonny sucked the last of smoke then put it out in the ash tray. "Still hate going to church though."

"Seems to me, after the Lord went to all the trouble of me driving half way across the country to spring you, you'd be a little more thankful. Dad's going to take over for Gramps, and guess what. They finally got married."

"What? How'd that happen? I mean that's great, David, but what about his wife. What was her name? Abigail?"

"She passed in a car accident. About killed Dad, too."

"Wow."

Silence rang in the car for who knew how many miles.

"So . . . I suppose she wants me to come to Pine Bluff then?"

"Yes, sir. You got it."

"All righty then." He laughed then lit up another smoke. "Guess that's a horse of a whole different color. Suppose there's any way you think she might bump it up to two bucks a visit?"

"Guess you can ask her. Say, speaking of horse, I dreamed you were shooting up, that true?"

David took the silence as a yes. "What about Sissy? Didn't even think to ask if she was at the Commune."

"Oh man, you know how she is. Took off with another dude long time ago." He shrugged. "Couple or three months I guess. That's when . . . well . . . she took a piece of my heart with her. Take my advice, brother. Don't ever let one of them get in so deep you can't live without them."

"How long you been clean?"

"Well, let's see now. I was arrested what? Three weeks ago?"

"Actually, twenty-five days according to the paperwork."

"Wow, lost some time in there I guess."

"They said you were drunk."

"Yeah, rot gut works, too. My bud at the farm was out, so I got the bright idea to go to the drug store." He laughed. "I mean when you need drugs, they have 'em, right?"

David had heard enough. "You hungry?"

"Sure, I could eat. But don't stop on my account. I can't wait to get back to Texas."

Eat, sleep, drive, then all over again the next day, except with home as his goal, David pushed himself harder. He stopped by a Sears and got Sonny some new threads and a pair of sneakers.

Shame they didn't take gas cards. He hated parting with his cash, but absolutely could not take him home semi-naked and barefoot.

Forty-nine and one-half hours after leaving Medford, he parked the Ford in front of Hannah's house.

Sonny sat up. "We there?"

David looked over his shoulder. "No, go back to sleep. I promised Hannah I'd come straight to her house."

The Morrison's front door flew open. He jumped out and met his love midway, caught her when she leaped on him, then swung her around.

"I missed you so much."

She kissed him hard then broke away. "I'm sure Mama's watching. Let's get in your car."

"Sonny's in there."

"Sonny? Great! Why didn't you take him home or drop him off on the side of the road?"

"You know what Scarlett said."

"So what? Tomorrow's another day! I've waited so long . . . and you're here now! And . . ."

"Well, get in. It'll be more private than the yard, and he's asleep in the backseat."

Turning toward the passenger side, she cuddled against him, semi-sitting in his lap, head lying on his left shoulder. He wrapped her shoulders with that arm, leaving his right free to push the curls away from her face.

The moonlight cast a silvery light on her. How could he ever wait two more years? Being far away, separated by a safe number of miles with the distraction of studies helped.

No way he could spend the whole summer around her. But what else was there to do?

She talked. He responded. She giggled. He planted kisses on her eyes and forehead, avoiding her lips best he could. Sonny never made a move.

The porch light flickered.

"What is wrong with her? Good grief, you just got here!"

She sat up and faced him, taking both his hands. "I love you. And you better be here no later than seven-thirty. I've got plans, mister."

"Mercy, baby, it's late now, and I've just driven over two thousand miles. I'm beat."

"Okay, fine. I'll give you to eight, but that's it."

"Um hmm, I see how you are." He laughed just as the light flickered again. He kissed her real quick then nodded toward the house. "Best go in. Don't want to get grounded the first day I'm home."

She pointed her finger as she backed toward the porch. "I'm serious, David Nightingale. Eight o'clock."

"I'll be here when you see me pulling up the drive. I'm not setting an alarm."

"Sure, I hear you. See you at eight, love birdie!"

Chapter Sixteen

The extra thirty minutes gave Hannah time to change outfits twice. She wanted to look perfect for him. He better not be late. Her dearest rolled up with five minutes to spare.

After one last look in the mirror, she ran downstairs, ready to spend the whole glorious June day with the one she loved more than anyone on the face of the earth.

And he loved her. She knew he did, and she couldn't wait to be his forever.

Resisting kissing him hello, she instead took his hand and led him to the kitchen. Her mother, still in her housecoat, sat at the kitchen table sipping coffee. "Good morning, David. Have you eaten, dear?"

"Yes, ma'am, but another cup of coffee would be good while Hannah changes."

"What? Why? Is there something wrong with what I have on?"

"Well . . . I guess not." He smiled. "I mean, if that's what you want to work in. Isn't, is it?"

"Work? Who said anything about working today? You just got home. I figured we'd go to Burnett, maybe have a nice lunch and take in a movie. Maybe even go see Emma Lee and her new little Patrick Henry the second. He's already a month old and I haven't even seen him yet. You don't need to work, not today."

"Sorry, but I told PawPaw you and me would haul hay for Uncle James today. Isn't the weekend yet or anything. I thought we'd talked about it."

Though she loved having her own money, she sulled up and stared at the floor. Her face kept getting warmer. She did not want to spend her first day with him after so long a time all hot and dirty and sweaty.

Grrrrr. Why would he promise something so terrible? And for her, too, without even asking!"

"Talked about it, my eye! We said something about hauling hay together maybe a week ago. But it's your first day home, David!" How could she talk him out of it? "Can't you call them and tell them I had other plans? I don't care if they get mad at me. Let Sonny do it. I mean . . . he owes you, doesn't he?"

"He'll be there, but there's no way he could do it alone. You'll see. He's not in great shape, Hannah. He's weak. It's going to take a while for him to get anywhere near back to normal. I just don't see—"

"That's the problem right there! You just do not see!" She looked to her mother. "Don't you think so?"

The lady looked up from staring at her coffee. "Don't get me in the middle of this, young lady. Besides, you wouldn't like what I had to say anyway."

"Arrrgh! You're all against me! Fine!" She threw her arms out to the side, shaking her head at him, rolling her eyes and grasping at straws—no pun intended. "Are you sure it's okay for me to drive the haul truck?"

"PawPaw said it was, and really, there's nothing to it. You've driven a three speed before, haven't you?"

"Of course, That's all they had in Drivers Ed. What should I wear?"

"An old dress? I don't care. Something you don't mind getting dirty. A skirt? It'll be hot, might be better if whatever it is was loose fitting. Radio said it might hit a hundred. Plus the hay flies around."

"A dress? Skirt? Would you shoot me if I wore my jeans? Seems way more appropriate to me."

"Guess not, but best get after it. I told Sonny we'd be right back."

"At least you dropped him off and I've got you all to myself all the way to Uncle James's."

"Yes ma'am, just me and little ole you." He glanced up and obviously caught Mom's eyes. "All the way straight there—no passing 'go', we will not collect two hundred dollars, and neither will we inherit one red dime. I toss, he stacks, you drive. Simple as that if we can ever get on the road."

"I'm going already."

What a day! She never dreamed hauling hay would be such a hard, hot, itchy chore, bouncing all over the pasture. Then backing the truck into a dark barn about gave her a heart attack.

Still, she fared way better than poor Sonny. David was right. His cousin wouldn't measure up as half the man he'd been before his walk on the wild side.

But he worked.

Day two—was he ever planning on doing anything fun? — proved all the worse for the wear. Muscles she didn't know she had jabbed at her and throbbed and pained her . . . so sore from the day before, but there she was, going to do it all over again.

The third day turned out not so bad. Well, still plenty sore, but her driving had gotten way smoother. Of course, like the idiot she could be at times, she volunteered to help unload.

What had she been thinking? How could a hay bale weigh so much and hurt your hand so bad even with leather gloves?

She'd shot her mouth off though, and there wasn't anything to do but keep on lugging those nasty bales to the end of the truck, so David could toss them to Sonny on top of the stack.

The poor sugar dragged two to her one then tossed those while she got a fourth. How could he work so fast for so long and still be moving? Just watching him exhausted her.

Praise the Lord, the last bale hit the top of the stack a solid three hours before sunset.

But who had any strength left to do anything fun?

Uncle James paid in cash, cold, hard train riding money. Filthy lucre! She loved it holding all those dollars! Against her and Sonny's protests, the love of her life split it three ways.

Except he didn't hand his cousin's part over like he did hers. He tucked it in a separate pocket from his own cash though. She'd ask later.

"Hey! We got time to hit the springs." Sonny hiked his brows. "Anyone want to take a quick dip?"

"Naw, I say let's call it a day."

She'd heard plenty about the spring-fed swimming hole surrounded by cypress trees—the one that gave the community its name—but had never been.

"Aww, come on, David. Let's go. It's been so hot, and I've always wanted to see the place. Did a crazy man really live there once?"

"Oh? You heard about him?" Sonny grinned. "Absolutely, ma'am."

"PawPaw don't cotton to mixed bathing."

"Oh, David, we're not going to take a bath. We can just get our feet wet. Cool off a little. I want to see the springs. Don't be such a fuddy duddy!"

Like David knew she would, Hannah loved the place and lamented more than once that she didn't have her bathing suit. Then again, who wouldn't love the property with all its natural beauty?

Had to be twenty degrees difference from up top. Stepping into the shade of the spring and making the way down was almost akin to entering another world.

The feathery cypress trees stood guard, their strange roots arching down. And the refreshing water splashed, running over the enormous rocks then falling into the pool. The spot soothed every sense.

It took much too long to get her and Sonny back in the Ford. Praise the Lord she hadn't remembered her swimsuit. It'd been hard enough when she tied her shirttails around her waist and pulled up her pants legs to wade into the pool, showing off her figure.

Should have just told her no to the jeans, but it was 1969, and all the girls were wearing them, even the older women. Mercy, he'd even heard some of the schools had started allowing pants. What was the world coming to? Didn't they know . . .

Exactly like he figured, she started on him that night to take her back to the springs. Sonny and his big mouth, telling tales of childhood swimming in the spring-fed pool, jumping off the cliff, sunning on the rocks until their clothes dried.

Some people had way bigger mouths than brains. Soon as he got him alone, he'd have to tell him to keep it shut more.

Man, he needed a cigarette, but she hated him smoking, so he refrained around her.

She scooted across the seat next to her door out of easy reach, like punishing him or something. "How about I wear one of Dad's old shirts over my very modest swimsuit? Will that work?" She'd put extra emphases on the 'modest' and made an exaggerated face.

"You just don't know how beautiful you are or how crazy you're driving me. I'm sorry, but . . . you running around half naked . . ." He shook his head.

"The Bible talks about even looking on a woman with lust is as bad as the act. Just your face, your eyes, your hair . . . I love you so much. Why do you want to tempt me to sin when I'm trying my best to be good?"

"So, you're saying it's my fault you're attracted to me?"

"No, no. I mean . . . it isn't your fault. Not at all. It's just, I'd appreciate a little help here."

"Oh, that's just your Pawpaw talking. All the important parts will be totally covered up, and I won't even be one-quarter naked."

"And what if someone else comes up? The whole family uses the pool, not to mention all our friends that might show. I mean a Harris has owned it forever."

"What if they do? I'll be covered up! Everyone goes swimming, dork."

"Which is why I don't! They won't be covered up, and don't think for one minute every male won't be gawking at you, even with your dad's shirt on. It'll be wet and clingy. I'd rather not put myself in that position. Why can't you see that?"

"Ooo, you're so goody-two-shoes! What's wrong with you? If someone comes, and you want to leave, just say the word, and we'll be out of there." She smiled then inched back over toward him, leaning closer like she wanted to seal the deal with a kiss. "Come on. It's so hot."

Man, he wanted to seal the deal all right, but . . . "We could go to Austin, spend some of your hay money at that new mall."

Sitting up straight again, she leaned back, locked her fingers and put them in her lap then looked forward. "I'm saving my money."

"Oh really? What for?"

"None of your business."

At least he'd successfully changed the subject. He stifled a laugh. Such a brat. "Then how about Burnett? Movie and supper?"

"If that's what you want to do. Guess I don't have a choice. Does Sonny have a car?"

"No, why?"

"You can loan him yours then. I bet he'd take me."

"Mercy, girl. If you really want to go that bad, I'll take you."

Her whole countenance changed. He loved her smiles so much more than her frowns. How could he help but make her happy? She scooted close and snuggled in. "Kiss me, you big old teddy bear."

Finally, mercifully, he escaped one more time.

Thank you, Mom Morrison.

On the drive home and then while he waited for sleep, he contemplated his lot. He loved her so much, but lust of her flesh definitely mingled in there somewhere.

Once upon a time it had only been love, young and pure, but for the last few years . . . seemed it'd gotten worse and worse. The temptation to knock on Missy's door that night after the bridge game had been strong.

She'd practically offered her pleasures straight up.

But that temptation was nothing compared to what he experienced with Hannah. And it seemed like she taunted him.

She's going to be your wife. Why wait?

He sat up in bed. That thought had not come from God.

"Satan, I bind you and yours off me in the name of the Lord. You're already defeated by the Blood of the Lamb and the Word of my testimony. I will not love my own life either, even unto death, so beat it."

That was it. He hadn't been out on the street preaching Jesus for months.

Why Mike had not wanted to keep the weekly evangelizing going on, he couldn't figure out. Things had gotten so busy with his preparations for the trip to Africa and finals and bridge and everything else.

Man, he missed his friend.

That sweet peace that passes all understanding settled over him. Then a strong hand shook him.

"David, wake up."

He pried one eye open. His grandfather stood beside his bed. "Your dad's on the phone."

David glanced at the clock, was that a four and two threes? "Is that time, right?"

"Yes, Son. Best get dressed."

He threw on his pants and a tee then hurried to the living room. His MawMaw sat, holding the phone to her ear. "Here he is, honey. We love you." She handed the receiver over.

"Dad? What's wrong?"

"The reverend went home tonight."

"Aww." Tears welled. "What happened?"

"Not sure. He woke Wynona up shouting, but by the time she got to him, he was gone."

"Where are you?"

"We're in Marble at the rent house. I called Brown's, and they went to get him."

"I'm coming there."

Hannah had mixed emotions about funerals—not that she'd ever lost anyone really close. Seemed to her though that going to Heaven had to be a good thing.

So all the folks who loved the deceased should be happy for them . . . yet . . . they're bound to miss them. Still, she liked the idea of celebrating Gramp's life.

Why, pray tell, did it have to happen right when it did and mess up all her plans? She'd worked so hard to get David to agree to take her swimming, but of course, everything was on hold.

Mercy, couldn't he do both? They'd scheduled the services for Monday morning. Why did he have to sit around with a bunch of old folks instead of being off with her having fun?

It didn't make a lick of sense and definitely wasn't fair.

Going to the springs had become a matter of principle. Matter, her eye! She huffed. Fact of it was, she couldn't do anything about it.

So, she offered polite little smiles and helped in the kitchen. At least she got to be in the same house with him—morning till night with her parents' approval.

The waiting for Monday to arrive proved almost as bad as waiting for her birthday, but it finally arrived. Maybe that afternoon, her summer vacation could finally get started for real.

David showed on the minute of when he'd said and looked marvelous in his suit.

Mercy—she sure liked using her sweetheart's word—if only her pigheaded parents would get on board and quit making them wait to get married. He put so much stock in having their blessing.

Mister Integrity.

How could she really fault him for that? She'd marry him in a red dog minute, with or without their consent—and legally she could, too. But no . . .

As he walked through the door toward her, she let herself dream a little dream of him walking the aisle to be hers forever. Well, she'd be walking toward him, but hey, a girl could dream, couldn't she?

"Ready?"

"Oh yeah, past ready."

"David. Don't you look nice, dear."

Hannah glanced over her shoulder. Her mother really did look great in black, even if she was so old at forty-two. "You do too, Mother. We'll see you there."

She turned back and took David's hand then didn't let go until he opened the Ford's passenger door. Him being such a gentleman made her feel so special and cared for.

And she'd grown to love the car, so much more practical than the Zee, though not near as much fun. She never regretted his trade. Scooting over to the middle, she tried to sit half and half on each seat.

Not so easy, but no matter how much she didn't love it, sitting right up against her sugar man was worth it all. She loved touching him, being next to him more than anything—so far anyway. She figured being up next to him in the water at the springs would be tons better with so much skin touching instead of only clothes.

Soon and very soon . . .

He snuggled in tight next to her then turned the key. "We've got more hay to haul."

"Okay, when do we start?"

"Tomorrow."

"Wait. I thought we were going swimming tomorrow."

"Work first, play later."

"Aww!" She bumped her shoulder hard against his. "How many bales?"

He laughed. "Two hundred acres' worth."

"Mercy! How long is that going to take? Didn't Uncle James have only sixty-five?"

"Sixty-eight, but he fertilizes, and it had been cut once already . . . I'm thinking maybe we can get done in a week."

No fun! He was being no fun at all! Summer vacation would be over before it ever got started at that rate. "Can we go to the spring on Saturday then?"

"I don't think we can finish that quick."

"Shoot!" With one shove, she flopped over to her door. It felt way more comfortable anyway, plus he was being so . . . so. . .

"That isn't very nice to say."

"What's wrong with shoot? You shoot guns all the time."

"And that's an exaggeration." He glances over and grinned. "Shoot is another word for a worse one. Think about it. And darn or dang . . . and geeze. That's the worse right alongside golly or gah. It's why I stick with mercy."

"Huh, I never thought of that." She giggled. "Do you have to be so grownup and levelheaded all the time?"

Oh, man, could David love her any more? Such a contrast.

Sometimes it seemed she'd not grown up at all, yet at others, like when she worked so hard in the kitchen helping out or how she took his suggestions so to heart. He appreciated that. She might not have thought of it, but as soon as he brought a thing to light, she'd abide by it without him ever having to ask.

Showed him great respect that way, like what he thought really mattered.

"Uncle Travis asked me to come help him some next week when were done with the Baylor's hay. He said you could come, too. Said he'd talk to your mother about it today after the services."

"Grrrr. You are going to take me swimming before the summer's over, John David Nightingale. Promise me the week after the Buckmeyers!"

"What about 'take no thought for tomorrow'?"

"Unless you're thinking about work? Trying to hang your hat on that verse is being a little hypocritical, isn't it?"

"Maybe."

"So why would Uncle Travis need to talk with Mama?"

"On account he figures we'll need to stay two nights."

"Ooo! That'll be fun!" She grinned then scooched back over. "Sharing a room and all."

"You're so funny! Best not be talking like that around your mother."

"Okay, fine, if you insist. What does Travis need help with?"

"The four-year-olds need to be worked."

"And what does that mean? How do you work a four-year-old?"

"Ride them."

"Cool. So we're busting broncs?"

"No, they got broke as long-twos then turned out. Uncle wants to get them ready for the big sale in Fort Worth."

"Fun, I love riding. Horses are such magnificent creatures! Are we getting paid?"

"Yes."

"Good." She leaned her head against his shoulder and snuggled in even tighter. "I still want to go swimming."

A part of him wanted that, too, but he still wasn't sure it was a good idea.

Have mercy on me, Lord.

Chapter Seventeen

David thought he'd cried out all his tears, but seeing his grandfather, looking so frail and pasty—lifeless—lying in his coffin brought on more.

Even though he knew full well he should be dancing for joy far as Gramps was concerned, but he'd so miss his wise advice and how he always made over him. The dear old man definitely loved him.

Blessed him so much that he'd taken his name, too. If he told David once, he'd said so a thousand times. Sure was glad he'd done it while Gramps was still there to enjoy it.

Hannah wrapped her arm around him when he took his seat after carrying the coffin in. Her own tears streamed down her cheeks.

Not that he'd been to that many funerals—two as a matter of fact, a great uncle and the cousin of one of his friends at college—but this one progressed about like he expected right up until after the choir sang.

The pastor from Marble's First Baptist officiated, and they sang as soon as he finished telling what a long and wonderful life the reverend had lived.

That's when things started surprising him. Miss Wynona stood and walked toward the front of the church. She clutched an old, cloth-covered book. He knew well as most everyone that she'd given birth to Cody Buckmeyer.

The man sat across the aisle in the family section beside Uncle Travis. That was all under the Blood though. God forgave her—and Travis—and gave the lady a new lease on life.

Pretty admirable, as far as he was concerned, what she chose to do with it. Serving the Lord's servant, she'd taken such good care of Gramps for the last eighteen years. She's probably a big part of the reason he lived to be almost a hundred.

Kind of like all's well that ends well, he guessed.

Standing in front of the pulpit, she turned and faced those gathered. The little church was packed, with even the standing wall-leaning space filled.

"Folks, most everyone here knows me and my sordid history, but for those who don't . . ." She wiped her cheeks then seemed to stiffen her back. "I was a drunk. I suffered so bad with the DTs, I surely would've died if not for this dear man."

Could've heard a pin drop.

"I tried to quit, and . . ." She smiled. "First time I saw Nathaniel Nightingale was when I opened my eyes—coming back to conscious—in the Llano hospital. He'd stayed the whole night, sitting with me and praying for me. He knew exactly what I needed. He prayed, and the Lord delivered me right then and there." She held a hand up high. "Praise the Lord for His deliverance."

A hearty round of amens sounded with a few muffled 'praise the Lord's mixed in.

"Travis and Emma Lee had taken me in, but when I got out of that hospital, I just couldn't stand the thought of being anywhere but where Nathaniel was. I told him I'd sleep in the church or on his floor, that I'd camp out on the grounds." She grinned. "The dear man wanted no part of any appearance of evil, but I convinced him I needed him close."

"That was eighteen years ago, and I sure have grown to love him. It's like losing my daddy." She nodded at a man in

John David's Calling 175

the front row. "Hank and I are getting married next month, thanks to this wonderful, Godly man . . . his influence and counseling."

More subdued approval rippled through the church.

"Anyway, he asked me to do something when this day got here." She patted the book. "That's the reason I'm up here. It's this." She looked right at David. "He read some of what's in here to me from time to time. Told me only a week ago what he wanted me to do with it. Much as he talked to God, I suppose he knew he'd be going home soon."

Hugging the frayed book once more, she held it out toward him. "David, he wanted you to have it. He said that you're a revivalist just like he was, and—" She laughed. "He called it The Revivalist Handbook and declared with about as much gusto as I'd heard in months, that you'd need it when you got back from Africa."

What?

She stepped toward him. He jumped up and received the journal out of her hands.

Shouldn't it go to his father? He looked to Dad who hiked one shoulder a smidgen. David never knew his grandfather considered himself such, but the word sure fit the old man to a tee.

But was he? Why would Gramps think so?

He thumbed through it, written in his grandfather's own hand. Wow.

Thank You, Father.

Miss Wynona sat down next to the man she was going to marry. Their story and his grandfather's part would be an interesting tale to hear. Someone said a closing prayer, then the funeral home's men started the process of the viewing.

From the church, the mourners paraded to the cemetery on the north side of the building. Another song caused the birds to hush their singing.

They tweeted a background to the next speaker who uttered even more nice words, then the time came to lower the casket.

As a pallbearer, he helped getting Gramps in the ground.

Such a finality to it.

Sure, David would see him again, but in what? Seventy years, eighty if he lived as long.

Maybe Jesus would come back by then.

But wow! He'd given David his book.

As much as he loved covered dish dinners on the ground, he almost wanted to skip the spread the ladies had already laid out in the fellowship hall. He couldn't wait to read his grandfather's words. But his stomach wouldn't hear of it.

Hannah sat him down with a kiss on his cheek. "I'll get your plate, sugar. I know what you like."

"Thank you."

"My pleasure." She gave him another peck. "Don't be reading that book without me."

Such was his love. He grinned. "Yes, ma'am."

She loaded his plate exactly like he would have. Well, maybe he'd have gotten three rolls instead of two, but wasn't like he was barred from seconds.

Halfway through, she leaned in close. "What did Miss Wynona mean about you going to Africa?"

"Don't know. News to me. Evidently Gramps thought I was. Mike and his dad have already left I think, and he'd invited me, but I told him no."

"He did? But . . . you wouldn't dare go without taking me, would you? Oklahoma's bad enough."

After seconds and two trips to the dessert table, he found a quiet corner and went to flipping pages in his new book, Hannah by his side. So many of the stories he'd heard, but right off, one thing struck him. His grandfather spent a lot of time praying.

Starting tomorrow, he'd get up an hour earlier.

John David's Calling

Hannah loved being David's better half. If only everyone would get on board and make it official, but still, that's what she was. His whole family and hers, too, knew it was only a matter of time.

So she couldn't figure out why they all wanted her to wait.

Reading the handbook with her love, she enjoyed enough, but more an old man's diary, excitement proved short.

More often, men probably would call it a journal. She expected some kind of how-to book, not stories from when he was in the war and doing tent meetings with Buddy's mother before she passed.

Bet the reverend enjoyed being reunited, having a great time with his wife in Heaven.

Next day back at work, she and David and Sonny started at the crack of dawn, but the temperatures already sweltered. Nothing to driving the hay truck.

Well, she still didn't like backing into the barn. She couldn't believe the guys were fine cutting her in on an even split. Almost made her feel guilty . . . but not quite.

They both gave her directions to back in straight, one on each side. But not being able to see, moving on their say so, made her paranoid.

Not being able to see good until her eyes adjusted—kind of like walking into a dark theater—she proceeded with great caution.

All in all, a good first day ensued. She'd admit to being a little sore, but her love said with her helping unload, they might finish in four days and have a whole Saturday off. Bring on the pain. She'd love to go to the springs Saturday!

Second and third days went well, too. In front of Sonny's house, David stopped the Ford and looked around. "What do you say we start an hour earlier tomorrow?"

"You some kind of slave driver? Seven is bad enough in my book."

"I figured if we start at six, we can finish tomorrow. Think about it, man. A whole day off."

"Do I get my money?"

"No, that's not the deal. So, what do you say?"

"Fine, but you're still a slave driver."

David laughed then his cousin jumped out. He faced her. "Can you be ready at five-thirty?"

"We going swimming Saturday if I am?"

"Isn't that what you said you wanted to do since forever ago? I knew I never should have taken you down there."

"Aww, give that sad story a break. But yes, yes, yes, sir!"

"So, should I come early to throw rocks on your window?"

"No, I'll be ready."

"Good."

In exactly twenty-two minutes the best part of her day started. She loved parking in front of her house with him. So romantic, yet so safe, and of course, her mother loved flipping the porch light after like only fifty kisses. She scooted away.

"I ought to take that bulb out."

"She'd ground you."

"Maybe, but wouldn't that be a fun night?"

"No, she'd figure it out and come get you."

She leaned in and kissed him one last time. "One fine day."

"Yes, ma'am, but until then, get on inside."

"You are a slave driver."

"Go on. Five-thirty comes early."

Did it ever! She set her alarm for five but got nowhere near ready by the time he showed though she went anyway, dozing on his shoulder all the way to Sonny's where she helped himself to his third cup of coffee.

It took until dark-thirty, but mostly David got it done; two hundred acres of seventy-pound hay bales in the barn. Poor Sonny, about wore him smooth out, but they'd done it.

Best part came then, getting wages. Again, poor Sonny only went home with a fresh carton of smokes and a six pack of canned cokes.

It about broke her heart for the guy, but he'd made the deal. She, on the other hand, was better than halfway to having enough to buy David's birthday present.

Just like he promised, he showed the next morning at eight sharp, dressed in cut offs that went to his knees and an old football jersey. "Morning, sunshine."

She smiled, but while she wore her very modest bathing suit and one of her father's extra-long shirts, she'd fully expected him to be decked out in a bathing suit. Didn't he want to get some sun? Surely, he would.

Maybe folks wouldn't call Mom Morrison a short-order cook, but compared to his grandmother's breakfasts, David found his love's mother's cooking wanting.

A tall stack of five flapjacks filled him up all right, but nothing like MawMaw's high-rise biscuits, cream gravy, grits, bacon and eggs-to-order with fresh cantaloupe and tomatoes on the side . . . all washed down with a tall glass of milk.

She'd spoiled him to be sure.

But there he sat with his feet under the dear lady's kitchen table.

Then as planned, he got Hannah to the springs a bit after ten, beating all the rest as he'd also figured. She spread his blanket on the biggest flattest guard rock, and he promptly laid back on it.

"You're not even getting wet? Come on! Get in with me! I thought we came to swim."

"Mercy." He grinned. "Go ahead, lying right here, watching you have all the fun suits me fine."

"Stick in the mud! Fine. I came to swim." She tossed him her towel then stepped off the rock into the shallows. "Oooo!" She jumped back. "Why is it so cold?"

"Because it's spring fed; never warms up. You just have to get used to it, and you will. We usually bite the bullet and jump in."

"Yeah right." She glared. "It wasn't this cold the other day."

"Surely was, but the temperature was over a hundred, and we were hot from working."

Her eyes went to slits, and she added a clinched fist to her glare. "You tricked me."

"Are you going swimming?" He held his mirth to a grin. "Or what?"

She wrinkled her nose then launched herself out into the deep waters. Her head popped up. He snapped a mental shot of her great expression of wide-eyed shock; one he'd never forget. He could hardly believe she'd done it.

"Mercy, it's so cold." Her teeth chattered. "Get in here and warm me up."

"You were the one who wanted to go swimming."

"Okay, meanie." She splashed water at him. "How do you like that, Mister Nightingale?"

"It's cold, but don't be getting me wet, or you'll be sorry."

"Oh, I'll be sorry, will I?" She splashed more water the second time.

"Hannah . . . Yes, you will." He pulled off his jersey and jumped in close enough to splash her.

"Ha! You're in! You're in!"

"I warned you."

"No, you warmed me! Come here and hold me."

"Won't do you a bit of good, silly. I'm as cold as you are!" He took off swimming to the other side of the pool. Hold her his eye! Danger, danger, Will Robbins!

After an hour of splashing around—she wouldn't even consider jumping off the cliff—then another half hour laying out in the sun, he'd had enough. "You ready? We still got time to get to Burnett and catch a matinee. *True Grit*'s with John Wayne's showing."

"And Kim Darby. She's so cute." She rolled over and smiled. "I love you."

"I love you, too."

"David . . . Let's get married. Raising babies doesn't take a

John David's Calling

high school degree."

Mercy, Lord. He wanted her like he'd never wanted anything in his life, but it had to be right. In the sight of God and her father, too. "Baby, we need to stay the course. I need to be back in school come fall with no distractions. If I'm going to get my degree, I need to be able to focus."

"So, you're saying I'd be a distraction."

"Of course, you would!"

"But I could help you study and edit your papers."

"The Bible says after you take a wife, you're not supposed to go off to war for a year, and I totally understand why."

"Hey." Her grin turned into a huge smile. "A year off with you would be fantastic." She scooted closer and kissed him, then pushed him back and eased onto his chest. She took to kissing his neck.

Gently, he eased her away, and pushed himself to his feet as soon as he had enough room. "Come on, you. We best go."

"Why?"

"Because we aren't married yet, and . . ." He nodded toward the creek. "Folks will be getting here pretty soon. They always do on a hot Saturday, and . . . mercy, girl, don't look at me like that."

"Not. Fair." She grabbed her towel and stood. "You're a slave driver."

"No, love. I'm only trying to be God's man, honor you, and . . ." He didn't finish. Praise the Lord for the extra hour on his knees that morning. He grabbed his jersey, but before he could get it over his head, she'd wrapped him in a bear hug. "Please don't."

"Put your arms around me, you big lug. I want to remember this moment forever."

He did but kept his hands where they belonged.

Praise the Lord for His mercy and grace.

Hannah loved him so much but harbored such mixed emotions.

Most of all, she loved what a gentleman he was. Since that first time when she offered to let him get her in the family way and he took the high road, she knew she could trust him in any situation.

On the other hand, she saw no reason in the world for her to finish high school when all she planned to do when she grew up was have babies and take care of her husband and home.

For the life of her, she could not understand why no one could see the truth of the matter and be on her side. Her mother married at seventeen, so what was the big deal?

Kind of mean of her to take advantage of his goodness though, then again, so much fun watching him squirm. One fine day, he'd finally give in and marry her.

The very first Sunday service that Buddy Nightingale stepped behind the pulpit of Pine Bluff Holiness Church, her sweetheart could barely contain his excitement.

And to put the icing on the cake, his daddy had asked David to sing a special, and he'd asked her to sing a duet with him. She loved harmonizing to his baritone.

If history held, one day it would be her love, standing in the same spot.

Being a pastor's wife in a church so close to home would be a dream come true, but she also had bigger plans for her David, too.

The service turned out to be one of the best she'd ever attended. The presence of the Lord came down so strong that she thought if she opened one eye to peek, she might see Him walking up the aisle.

On the way to Llano that next morning with him, she was puredee giddy.

An overnight adventure and riding horses to boot with her love would be so much fun. Though she never thought her parents would agree, there she was going off for two nights and three days with him—so very awesome!

Chapter Eighteen

Almost sweaty, Sandy kicked a foot out from beneath the chenille bedspread. She laid there a minute then rolled onto her side and stared at her husband.

Her husband . . . after all those years. She certainly didn't deserve God's blessing her with the love of her life. She adored watching him sleep. All the good filling her life was only by God's sweet mercy and grace.

Nature called, and better than watching him sleep, she loved drinking coffee with the man.

A quick smoke on the porch before he got up would be nice, too.

The rising sun splashed the sky with so many colors and shades that if an artist painted it exactly as it was, viewers would claim it didn't look real.

Enjoying the coolness of the early morning, she leaned back and took a long drag on her Salem. She really liked those menthols. No doubt that she ought to quit the nasty things.

Pastors' wives had no business smoking, but . . . what could she say? His did. After all, the congregation called him, not her. Wow. She had to admit that the service the day before was . . . just wow.

Absolutely something else! Nothing like she'd ever experienced in her life. If that happened every Sunday, she might want to move in and live in the church building.

So amazing and so special, she couldn't imagine it ever getting better. God's manifest presence literally flooded the place. She could stand that lots more. She loved it. Poor Mama and Daddy and their church that never experienced such.

Mercy, they had no idea what they were missing.

"Hey, there you are." Buddy walked through the kitchen door, holding two cups of coffee.

She snubbed out her smoke then accepted the steaming cup. "Good morning, my love. You slept well."

"It is and I did. He took the seat upwind. "Did Emma Lee say anything to you?"

She reached out and traced his cheek to his chin with her finger. "About what?"

"Why Travis wanted both David and Hannah to come to the ranch."

"No, she didn't mention anything about it. It sure surprised me that Mis'ess Morrison would agree to let Hannah come. From what I know of the lady, she's usually overly protective."

"Yeah, but she knows our son well enough by now. Plus, Travis assured her they would be properly chaperoned. Anyway, that aside, your brother-in-law had his ulterior motives."

"He did?" Why was she just now hearing about this? Maybe she needed to ease on over to Llano and see for herself what her sister and her husband were plotting. "Pray tell, what did Travis tell you?"

"That he's going to offer David a job."

"Doing what?"

"They're wanting him to be a youth pastor at the new Assembly of God they've started."

"Youth Pastor?"

"The concept is relatively new. It's a position where the pastor specifically ministers to the needs of the youth in the congregation—the teens."

"No. I don't want him doing that. He needs to stay in

school."

"Nixon is going to get us out of the war, Sandy. They already started that youngest first program, and if he and Hannah were married . . ."

"No! Stop. Do not even go there! The girl's still in high school! And Nixon hasn't done any of that yet. It's all still nothing more than rumor! That boy from Oatmeal . . . What is his name? He got drafted. David has to stay in school."

"Are you talking about Jacob Russet? He joined the Navy."

"Only because he got his notice."

"Anyway, as I was saying before you interrupted . . . if they were to get married."

She held her tongue but bore into him with both eyes.

"He'd be 2A, and from what I've heard, they aren't taking any of those now."

"Yeah right. You can hear a lot in a long day."

"Maybe, but according to my source, his information came straight from the draft board."

"Well, I don't agree to those two getting married. Not yet. So please don't even bring it up. I know for certain that if David stays in school, he won't get drafted, and that's good enough reason for him to stay put at ORU."

"You have a point."

"Can you believe that boy blackmailed me to pay tuition there? I'm so proud of him and his relationship with God."

"He'd make a great youth pastor."

"Of course, he would. But he'd also make a great soldier. The young man is just like his daddy--good at whatever he puts his mind to."

"So . . ." Buddy smiled. "You noticed."

She matched his smile, even though he infuriated her at times. "Say, did you quiz Wynona about the reverend thinking our boy was going to Africa?"

"I didn't. Meant to, but never really had a chance to speak with her. Too many glad-handers."

"Tell me about it." Could she be any happier? "Are we

going to Burnett today?"

"What for?"

"I thought we were going to give them a chance to bid on our lumber. I want to check out their fixtures and see if they have any we like better than the ones in Marble."

"We can, but I have three shut-ins we need to go by and visit a bit. Dad hadn't been able the last few months, so it's important we do that."

"I agree." She stood and took his cup. "Want another one before we get busy?"

"Please. With a little milk and sugar in this one."

"I know, my love. First cup's black, then the next one comes sweet and creamy."

David kept his own counsel until he crossed the Buckmeyers' front cattle guard and pulled onto the blacktop. He glanced at Hannah then gave her a little squeeze. "What do you think?"

"I love it." She laughed. "But no one mentioned what would have to happen first . . . or it's a big fat 'no' far as I'm concerned."

Exactly as he figured. Her response was no surprise, of course she'd see it that way.

"So, if we get married, you're fine with me working at the ranch and corralling a bunch of kids."

"Honey bunny, sugar pie, make me your wife, and I'd be fine with just about anything you wanted to do." She bumped her shoulder into his chest.

"Anything?"

"That's what I said, isn't it? I mean, being Mis'ess John David Nightingale is all I've wanted for so long." She whirled and stayed on her knees, facing him with wide eyes.

"Are you kidding me, David? Because you should not be

saying such things if you aren't salt of the earth serious. I'm not joking either!"

"I've just never considered working with kids."

"You did not answer my question, mister." Her finger wagged in front of him. "And you wouldn't have to corral anyone.

Not all church kids are wild Indians; besides Uncle Travis was talking about the teenagers. You know . . . like me! And like you until November . . . They'll be nigh onto full grown."

"The ones I went to church with weren't."

"Forget the kids, Nightingale. I want to talk more about wedding plans—yours and mine."

"You're so funny."

Kicking her feet out, she whirled in the seat again and that time ended up hugging the passenger door.

"Whatever you think, turkey buzzard. But I'll tell you one thing. Church of Christ children may have been off smoking behind the trees, but we Methodists were way better. There was not one trouble maker in our Sunday School Class. Not one!"

She stared out the window.

"What about Sissy?"

"What about her? She didn't come that much, but when she did, she behaved. Are you judging her? What about Sonny? She didn't do anything he didn't. Or are you excusing him?"

"No, of course not. Do you know much about the Assemblies? What they believe?"

"I don't guess so." She shrugged the shoulder closest to him. "But didn't you tell me they came out of the Azusa Street Revival?"

"Yeah, that's right, but—"

"But what?"

"Oh . . . I've been hearing about this new move of God. It's non-denominational. Some of the main stream churches are moving in that direction, breaking away from their parent organizations."

"Can they do that?"

"Apparently so. It's been happening all over, coast to coast. Some are calling themselves Charismatic."

"What? As in you have to be good looking and smooth talking to join? I mean, what does that mean?"

"I don't know about that." He chuckled. "They believe in the gifts of the Spirit. They're Full Gospel with a heavy dose of grace."

"Okay, I can be charismatic if we get married—or assembly—and the sooner the better." She scooted back over and laid her head on his chest. "After that, I don't care where you preach or lead music or work on a ranch, just as long as we're together."

"So, you don't have any convictions and you don't care about anything?"

"Of course, I care, David. I'd like for us to stay in Marble or Cypress Springs . . . somewhere in the Hill Country. Llano, Austin, or anywhere close, but wherever the Lord leads you, I'm happy as long as I'm right there with you. By. Your. Side."

He loved her saying it, but would that really be how things would work out?

Mom Morrison's apron strings so entangled his love, he couldn't imagine her not wanting to live up the street. Plus, they were all so intertwined in the community, Mister Morrison even organized the farmers market and ran the thing every week.

Folks came from miles around.

Could Hannah really be happy if the Lord sent him somewhere far away?

"Mom wanted us to come for supper."

"I know. She asked me to remind you."

"She did?"

"Yes, sir."

"Did you tell your mother?"

"I did. It's all covered."

He liked it when his womenfolk took care of the details.

That June proved profitable, except Sonny's constant

whining about money wore on him. On the other hand, his love hoarded her cash like a miser, but he didn't have a clue what for.

Every time he suggested shopping though, she never took the bait. She'd let him spend all he had, but never offered any of her hay-hauling money.

Not that he expected or wanted her to pay for anything.

The Fourth of July picnic was better than ever. He even beat his PawPaw at horseshoes. Something he'd only done once before.

Mid-August, right after the carpenters got his parents' new house dried in, the money vultures dropped a bomb on his mother. Maybe him, too. But then all things worked together for the good of those who love the Lord and are called according to His purpose.

The evening of that most awful day, he and his love sat in his parents' rent house's living room.

His mother talked on the phone, except she mostly only listened.

"Thank you, Officer. If you learn anymore, please contact me or my lawyer." She eased the phone into its cradle and leaned back. "It's even worse than I thought. He took out a mortgage on the Turtle Creek House."

"No! How could he?"

Tears streamed down her cheeks; she only shook her head.

"Apparently." His father hiked both shoulders. "She gave the man power of attorney. Years ago."

David wasn't sure what all that entailed, but it didn't sound good. "We can get my tuition money back."

"No!" His mother sat ramrod straight and slapped at her tears. "You are going to school. Period. I'll call a realtor. Even with that stupid mortgage, I should have some equity."

"What about the new house?"

"You don't worry about us." She threw her hands up. "We've been giving back your dad's salary from the church. We can start keeping that and have income. And that, that . . . crook

... didn't steal everything. We'll be fine. You will stay in college."

"But it doesn't have to be ORU, Mom. I can go somewhere close and take enough hours to keep my deferment. The difference would be considerable, and—"

"If you did do that." Hannah suddenly looked rather gleeful about the prospect. She turned to his mother. "I could help him with his studies."

"And I'd work part time. Stay here or in Cypress Springs. We could save on gasoline and room and board and the spending money you sent. And I know those tutors weren't cheap. Do you even know who much all that was costing you?"

"No, but it doesn't matter. We'll cover it."

"No, ma'am. I'm not going back. Mike and the M's are off in Africa. It wouldn't be the same anyway. I'm staying here, so you best call and get your money refunded." He looked his mother in the eye. She surely knew by then she couldn't win a war of wills with him. He had too much of his PawPaw's stubborn blood flowing through his veins.

Hannah could hardly believe her ears or that he was staying. How absolutely wonderful! "I can start calling tomorrow! Where do you want me to start?"

The lady she hoped would soon be her mother-in-law turned a steely gaze from David to her. "You're enjoying this, aren't you?"

With an almost apologetic scrunch of her shoulders, she offered her best little girl what-did-I-do look. That usually got her out of most predicaments, but of late it hadn't been doing much for her own mother—or even daddy.

But why should she apologize? Why shouldn't she enjoy the conversation that was so going her way? Sitting up more erect than before, she swooned in David's direction for courage before facing his mother.

"Only the part about him moving back. I hated him being so far away. Didn't you? I never meant to offend you, ma'am."

Mis'ess Nightingale glanced at her husband then again to David. "If you flunk out and get yourself drafted, I'm taking you to Canada."

"Mother, please. Don't be so dramatic. I'm not going to flunk out, and . . ." He grinned. "Hey, the Marines are always looking for a few good men."

How could anyone stay mad at her love? He was such a big ol' teddy bear. But apparently, his mother wasn't buying what he was selling.

"David, I don't think you're funny. I want you to promise me that you'll keep your grades up."

"Public school can't possibly be harder than what they put us through at ORU."

"Whatever you say, but I'm serious. Really. I couldn't stand it if you went to Vietnam. Have you seen what's going on over there? The carnage? It's horrible."

"I don't watch much television."

"Well, you need to. It might light a fire under you, young man."

Keeping quiet, Hannah sat back and let David and his parents talk. He'd made his decision, and he'd be staying, and she couldn't be more ecstatic about it—well, unless he would marry her as soon as a license could be valid.

Just as she'd promised, the next morning—beautiful and glorious if she did say so herself, never mind the hundred-eight degrees the weatherman predicted for its high—she headed straightaway to the library to research schools.

Right off, she narrowed it down to really only one choice: The University of Texas.

Everything else was too far, and she didn't want him living on campus. From there, in a little more than half an hour, he could drive home to Cypress Springs. And in another twenty minutes, be with her in Marble Falls.

With him being less that one hour away, she could even drive there!

Oh, what bliss! She could see him every weekend!

Armed with the registrar's phone number and address, she hurried back home and called her love who'd spent the night with his parents.

A body might think he sat beside the phone, waiting for it to ring. He answered on the first one. "Hey, babe. Good morning. What'd you find out?"

"Everything I needed to. How you feel about being a Longhorn?"

"Sure, but isn't there something closer?"

"No, not really. The closest two-year college is way over in East Texas. Well, there was one in Waxahachie, but if your mother is selling the Turtle Creek mansion . . . Anyway, want me to call UT? I've got the number."

"Mom's fixing dinner. Come on over, and we'll call from here. No need putting a long distance call on your phone."

"Can you come get me, so I can stay longer? Mom's playing bridge this afternoon, she's dibsed the car."

"I'll be right there."

Bless the Lord that they had found out about all that money stuff in time to transfer him from ORU to Texas. Her love was staying home.

Could she be more elated? And with him there, she would definitely concentrate on getting everyone on board her wedding train. She could not understand why they all put so much store in her being older.

She would never change her mind. Mercy, she'd been in love with David since she was ten and nothing was ever going to change that.

Plus, she was as mature as she would ever get.

Hannah closed her eyes and twirled in her wedding dress.

Chapter Nineteen

Three classes each on Tuesdays and Thursdays suited David fine. Might even find somewhere to stay over some Wednesday nights, but either way, he'd get his twelve hours in to keep him a full-time student and still have four days a week to work.

Well, three and a half if you took off half of Saturday to take his sweetie out of an evening.

Sundays, he preferred being at church, but if he needed to . . . not that he didn't want to attend services, but it looked like there might be one last cutting. As much as he hated tossing hay bales around, it sure beat working for wages.

Hannah loved being with him, and Sonny . . . he just hadn't been the same since that dumb trip to California. He'd find something to gripe and complain about no matter what.

Never would be right again until he got over wanting to put that poison in his veins. Never should have let him just go without a fight.

He's cut from the same cloth, but mercy. Much as David loved his cousin, he sure wanted to shoot the idiot dead sometimes.

Did all families have a black sheep?

Hannah's had her uncle who'd just remarried. But according to his love, the newlyweds were having trouble over the old goat not giving up his sinful ways.

The woman definitely should have known better. If he'd have cheated on his wife, well then . . .

His second week at school, after his last class on Tuesday, a notice on the bulletin board caught his eye. A bridge club met that very afternoon. Instead of rushing home, he decided to wander on over to the student union building. Might be fun.

After filling out a form, it only cost him two-bits to get a chair. Played twelve hands then when the others broke for supper, he headed on to Cypress Springs.

Wednesday, he hauled hay until time to get Hannah from school then tore the highway up getting to Marble Falls High before she strolled down the steps.

Leaning against the Ford, he drank in her beauty as she waltzed toward him.

Oh, man. One fine day . . .

"What are you grinning at?"

He opened her door. As much as he wanted her, he kept to a hard and fast self-imposed rule—no PDA on school grounds.

"You. How you look. How you walk. And loving every step. For a split second, I imagined you coming down the aisle all decked out in white. I can hardly wait to make you mine."

She smiled as she slid in, then waited for him with both barrels loaded when he got in. "Let's elope, David. Right now. We don't need anyone's signature. Make me your wife. I want to be yours and you to be mine as much as you do . . . Really."

"We can't. Your daddy would shoot me."

"Oh, mercy!" She elbowed him. "He would not. He may act all gruff, but he loves you. And he knows we're getting married sooner or later.

"Mama claimed she was seventeen when they got married, but I found their marriage license a while back, and she was really sixteen. What can they say? I was already on the way. They fudged on their anniversary."

"But that wasn't the right way. I want to have a righteous start. To do it right. We can wait."

"But getting married would be doing it right. We waited until we were married. Think of how much money it'd save Daddy! He'd probably be relieved." She reached up and held his face. "I love you more than life. Marry me."

"Not now. I'm sorry I said anything."

"But you did."

"Well, I shouldn't have . . . as we both can see."

"Fine." She scooted to her side, put both hands in her lap, and stared straight ahead. "If that's how you feel about it, if that's the way you want it, we'll wait."

"Thank you." He loved her so much, and it showed her respect for his judgment to the point of agreeing when everything in her wanted to do the opposite.

Her response blessed him deep down inside. She was growing up, maturing in the Lord. Still had a way to go, but God was definitely moving in her heart and answering his prayers.

"Hey, I've got a paper I need to write. Have time to help me?"

She glanced over, shrugged, then exhaled. "You're such a slave driver. A mean old slave driver who won't even marry me today!" A stifled grin played on her full lips, and he loved her all the more. "Did you and Sonny haul hay today?"

"Yes, ma'am. Sure missed having our driver there."

She spun sideways. "See? Right there! If we were married, I could have been helping instead of sitting in those boring classrooms all day, dreaming about you. I'm thinking I'd like to have two boys then a girl. Is that fine with you?"

"Whatever."

"Don't you dare whatever me! I want to know what you want. Just don't say a girl first. You know how I've hated not having a big brother."

"But." He grinned at her. "You had me."

"I was ten before you showed up. A big brother is there from the start."

He parked the Ford in front of her house. "I thought you

liked being the only child."

"Sometimes." She opened her door then nodded toward the house. "Come on in. When is that paper due?"

"Tomorrow."

"Then we best get going on it. You can stay for dinner. What are we writing this paper on? Anything fun?"

As always, October with its cool winds and beautiful autumn colors, blanketing the Hill Country with its glory, followed the less impressive September.

The only thing the ninth month had going for it was football. He still enjoyed Friday night football in his old stadium where he led the purple and gold to district. He loved throwing the pigskin for the Mustangs.

And he loved supporting Hannah's cheerleading. The girl had no limits.

Then like President Nixon campaigned for, Congress passed the Lottery Law on November twenty-sixth, with the drawing on the evening of Monday, December first.

That fateful day found David on the Morrison sofa, holding Hannah's hand as CBS News pre-empted Mayberry RFD. In shades of gray, Roger Mudd's face filled the screen of the idiot box.

"The first number will be drawn shortly."

"Even if they draw your birthday, it doesn't matter, right? Because you'll still have your deferment. Isn't that right?"

"I don't know how it works, sugar." He shook his head side to side. "Some guys are saying that isn't so."

"We should have gotten married." She squeezed his hand. "They're not taking married men, are they? I mean, we still can, can't we? Or is it too late?"

"I don't how it works. But I know we don't have to worry. God is on the throne and in control. He is completely trustworthy and happens to love me even more than I love you."

What a blessing to be able to talk about how much he loved her, to be comfortable to say such in front of her parents. They had to know already anyway.

After the first hour, Mom K set up the TV trays. She and Hannah carried in loaded plates with a big glass of iced tea, sweetened of course. "What number are they on?"

"One forty-two." He scooted to the edge on the sofa. "Thank you, ma'am. Mighty obliged."

"Oh yeah?" She bent over with her lips beside his ear. "Then marry me. Tonight. Tomorrow." On her way out the door, she hollered a sing-songy you're welcome. Back momentarily with her plate and tea, she sat next to him.

After a quick muffled prayer with his eyes closed, he took a bite. He never faulted them for not saying a prayer while the television blared. MawMaw and PawPaw never ate in front of it, they always sat at the table. He offered a thread of hope.

"I heard any number over two hundred is safe."

"You've told us."

"Okay, good."

The supposedly safe birthdays after the two hundredth went by without his being called.

"Thank the Lord. I can breathe again." Hannah rubbed his thigh.

By the time they called number three hundred, she'd worn his jeans thin. He stood and extended his hand. "Come on. Let's go get a milkshake."

His sweetheart smiled then let him pull her to her feet. "Yes, sir." She grabbed her sweater off the hall tree. "Mom, we're going for ice cream."

The older lady walked into the room. "Did they draw your number?"

"No, ma'am. And it's already over three hundred, so . . ." David held his hands out. "Looks like I'm home free."

"Thank the Lord1 Be back pretty quick. You both have school tomorrow."

"Yes, ma'am."

David didn't spill his guts until he returned with the creamy goodness in hand—his vanilla, hers chocolate. He parked the

Ford in front of her house, moved the shake from his right hand to his left, then hugged her to him.

"I'm not going back to UT next semester, baby."

"Why not?" She scooted out enough to look him in the face. "What have you got up your sleeve, mister?"

"I'm not sure. Uncle Travis said he could get me ordained through the Assemblies. PawPaw needs help. That man is so stubborn. He's planning on planting corn in the spring, and you know he'd rather eat nails than not have a big garden."

"Well. Okay. Just as long as you're not planning on going off anywhere without me."

Totally understanding exactly what bothered her, he squeezed her shoulders. The dark continent had been nagging him from time to time, too. "Africa without you would not be any fun at all."

"Good." She stared deep into his eyes, the windows of her soul fully open to him. "I'm glad you feel that way. So now, if we're going to have a June wedding . . ."

"Whoa, easy now. Who said anything about getting married next summer?"

With perpendicular thumbs, nails touching, she framed her face. "Me! Why do I have to keep telling you that it does not take a sheepskin to raise babies."

She had a point. Sure would make his life simpler. "What about your mother? Think you can talk her into it?"

"Yes! Maybe. Are you saying . . . if I do . . . Oh, David!" Her arms wrapped his neck, and she kissed his face all over. "Are you?"

"I guess so. Yes. Okay. June it is, providing you can acquire your parents' blessing."

Although an overwhelming urge to leap and twirl suddenly filled every part of her being, Hannah didn't want to get out of

John David's Calling

the car, and everyone knew no one could dance in the front seat of a Ford sedan.

"How many bridesmaids do you think I should have?"

"What? Wait. Let's get your mom on board before we talk about all that stuff."

"It's never too early to start planning." She kissed his cheek. "Are you forgetting that I found their real marriage certificate?"

"No, but just because your mother was seventeen doesn't mean—"

"Sure it does!" She waved him off. "It absolutely does, dork! Now back to my question. How many bridesmaids should I have?"

Neither that number nor any other of the thousand important matters that piled high in her brain got settled before her mother went to flipping that stupid porch light. She got in one long last kiss then scooted over toward her door and looked back.

"Hey, if you're not going back, are you even going to bother taking your finals?"

"Thought I would, best remain a student until the end of the year. The lottery goes into effect next year."

"Can you believe it's almost 1970? Wow. I'm getting married in June 1970. I can't believe it! Ooo!" She stretched her hands to the sky. "I'm so happy! Praise the Lord!"

When her hands came down, she slid them over her ecstatic face and left a serious expression for her sweetest heart. "Okay. I'm calm. We can study this weekend."

"Sure." He chuckled. "I've been invited to two study groups, too. Some of the bridge players are getting together. Thought I'd sit in on them."

She eyed him hard. Did she need to quiz him about the genders represented in this group? He didn't look guilty, and he was the most Christ-like person she knew. The light flickered again.

"Okay." She looked toward the house; her mother hadn't

come out yet. She leaned over, planted a wet one on his kisser, then got out. "I love you! See you Wednesday?"

"Yes, ma'am."

Her parents sat in the living room right where she left them, sitting in front of the TV, except the lottery had ended, and they watched *Gunsmoke*.

"Did you see what number David was?"

"No, shush." Daddy glanced at her then back to the tube.

Mother looked up, and Hannah nodded toward the kitchen, wiggling her pointer in the come here motion. When her mother didn't get up, she took to waving both arms, calling her to the kitchen.

With a huff that could be heard across the street, she finally rose then followed her in. Hannah closed the door.

"My goodness, what is it? Is something wrong?"

"No, ma'am. Not at all, not in the least. Everything is right as rain! We've decided to get married this coming June!"

"Baby, no. Let's wait until after you finish school."

"Why? You didn't! I'll be seventeen in a few months, and I don't need a stupid high school diploma to have babies and take care of David."

Her mother exhaled until she reminded Hannah of a deflated balloon. She plopped into the nearest chair then closed her eyes. That was a good sign, a sign of defeat, and if she got Mama on her side, Daddy would be a pushover!

"Oh, daughter. Please tell me you and David haven't—"

"Mother! No. Of course not. Don't you know how goody-two-shoes he is? I mean you have eyes and ears, right? So, let's get this all settled. You and I have a wedding to plan."

"Hannah Claire. Your father and I both love David, but . . ." She turned away.

"But what? There are no buts. You've known for years we were going to get married, so there are no buts." She stepped around and kneeled in front of her mother, looking up into her eyes.

Why did she look so sad? What was she talking about? She

took her mother's hands into hers. "What are you saying?"

"Honey, everyone knows about his parents. And his grandfather, too. Gramps was a drunk before he cleaned up. You weren't around to see the destruction Buddy left in his wake that first time he came to town . . . it's why John Harris can't stand the man. He broke his baby's heart."

"Oh please, give me a break, Mother!" Hannah stood. "You're judging David by his family? And it isn't like Gramps didn't quit drinking and become the most admired preacher in four counties!

"Or like Buddy didn't finally marry Sandy! I mean, they loved each other the whole time, but everyone kept them apart!" She put her most determined face on, the one that she hoped proved she meant it.

"No one. I repeat, no one is going to keep us apart, Mother."

"But he'll break your heart, baby. He's too good looking. Everything comes so easy for him, he's never had to work a day in his life."

"Yet he hauled hay all summer, and immediately quit ORU and came back to work and help his mother pay for his own school. You're crazy. He'd die before he hurt me! He loves me, and I love him.

"What's wrong with him being handsome? Mercy! I'm proud to walk on his arm!"

"Pride goes before a fall."

"Oh, Mother! You know what I mean! And David—though he likes having me on his arm just as much—doesn't have a proud bone in his body. He always acts so much like Jesus, Mama.

"Besides, what that verse really says is pride goes before destruction, and a haughty spirit before a fall. Know who told me that? Are you going to say David Nightingale has ever been haughty?"

"Whatever, dear. The sins of the fathers are visited on the sons up to the fourth generation. It's only a matter of time."

"No! Don't say that! He's never ever taken a drink or been with a woman, even though he's had plenty of opportunities. He knows about his father and his grandfather, and he's being especially careful because he knows he'll be tempted in those areas." She wanted to scream.

Why was her mother being so ridiculous?

"Why do you think we've been so protective of you, Daughter? So strict? We kept praying you or he would find someone else. We thought when he went away to school, you'd get tired of him being gone and fall in love with a boy more your age. Please, baby, don't marry him. Your father and I just don't believe—"

"Is this all because he isn't a Methodist?" She paced the room. She never dreamed . . . "That's what it is, isn't it? I can't believe you! Hypocrite!"

"Not entirely, but somewhat. You've been to their church services. Emotions run wild. The way some of those women carry on is . . . bouncing up and down . . ." She threw her hands up. "Go to bed. We'll talk more about this later."

Hannah's heart boomed in her ears. Each breath came hard. But she wasn't about to go anywhere.

"No, ma'am. I want it settled. You know full well I don't need your permission, not legally. But David—horrible, proud, holy-roller David—insisted we have your blessing! He's the one who refused to make love, too, Mother! Not me! Him!"

"Oh, Hannah!"

"So, this is the deal. We are getting married. The question is are we going to do it at a wedding in June with your and Daddy's blessings? Or are we going to go get a license and get married at a justice of the peace as soon as possible? Because I will not live in this house another night if you say no. It's your choice because Daddy will do whatever we say if we're standing together, and you know it."

Her mother shook her head.

"Isn't that why you got pregnant? Because Granny and Papa wouldn't let you marry Daddy?"

John David's Calling

"Who told you that?"

"No one. I guessed it when I found your marriage license. Seems you've been lying to me all my life! Oh, by the way, for the record, terrible David has never told me a lie."

"All the young men were going off to Korea, and . . ."

"And nothing! I'm not pregnant! David and I love each other! We have for years! Now he wants yours and Daddy's blessings, but I'm confident that I can get him to marry me even if you two refuse to bless us." She pointed her finger at her mother.

"Don't try to stop us. Just get on board and let's all be happy and not cause any huge family split and hurt feelings. Let's get my wedding all planned out."

"What are you two fussing about?"

Hannah turned around. Her father stood in the doorway.

"Hey, Daddy. Did Marshal Dillon get it all worked out?"

"Of course. Did I hear something about a wedding?"

"Yes, sir. David and I are getting married in June."

"Oh." He looked past her to her mother. "Best go on to bed, sugar. Your mother and I need to talk."

She did as told.

The other most important man in her life was about to make her dream come true.

Chapter Twenty

"All work no play makes for a dull boy."

"Whatever." David smiled at the man. "I don't play poker."

"More the better, my friend. It's an easy game. I mean, hey! Bridge is twice as hard, and you are a master."

"Wrong. I can barely hold my own with you sharks. Anyway, I need to study."

"As some famous broad once said, tomorrow is another day. Come on. Your next test isn't until Thursday. Am I right?"

"Yeah, that's true . . . I do still have tomorrow to study." He knew better, but he'd been hearing about their game, and he did know the basics. "So how much do I have to have for a seat?"

"Ten bucks. We're not big time or anything. With another twenty behind it should work."

The studying really could wait a bit. And what if . . . He'd glean good stuff from most of the guys who played, why not donate a little cash for the recreation? Those guys were a worthy cause. "Why not?"

Turned out an easy enough game to learn, except for one little fact—didn't take the best hand to win. Figuring out who bluffed and who didn't took some time and half his money.

But by the supper break, he'd almost gotten back to even. He thought hard about calling it a night, but unlike bridge where you had to play the cards, with poker, if no one called your bluff, you won the hand.

And a strange thrill accompanied the game.

A couple of new players showed after the meal. Seemed the boys were out for blood. Slow and steady, he built his stack of dollars. Then a little after nine, one of the losers suggested raising the ante from a quarter to a dollar.

Those who voiced an opinion agreed. How could he not go along? He was ahead after all.

Midnight came and went. The game had whittled down to only five guys. With the ante at five bucks then, all the silver had disappeared from the table.

David gathered the cards. "It's twelve-twenty. Win, lose, or draw I'm out of here at one o'clock."

No one objected.

The appointed time came. He gathered his cash and headed toward the door.

"Pretty low . . . winning all the money and running out."

David turned around and faced the loudmouth. "Gave you fair warning forty minutes ago, sir. I've got studying to do."

"But you've folded every hand since. What's fair about that?"

His only friend still at the table spoke up. "Leave him be. He's been playing tight all night."

"Whatever." Loudmouth nodded toward the door. "Go on then. I'll get you next time."

The urge to sit back down and show the lug a thing or three was strong, but sometimes retreat was the better part of valor. "Good evening, gentlemen."

That night while trying to unwind enough to find some shut-eye, the octagon poker table he'd been seeing in his mind's eye turned into a giant wheel of people moving in a circle.

Inside that one, another wheel of folks moved in the opposite way. Dead center, inside both wheels, a hub of people together, some holding hands.

He sought to see more and looked harder. Folks praying composed the outer wheel—some in the Spirit and some with understanding. The middle wheel . . . mostly ladies singing praises to the Lord and then worship.

The center of both wheels seemed comprised of older folks, most on their knees praying, crying out, weeping before the Lord—intercessory prayer.

The two outer wheels moved in opposite directions. He watched, but a cloud descended, engulfing the wheels. He sat straight up in bed. The sun shone through the blinds' slits. Bless his PawPaw's heart.

The old man let him sleep late. Shouldn't have stayed so long at that game. Great wages, considering how much fun he had.

Both his grandparents worked out in the garden when David got there. He slipped in beside his PawPaw and took the handles of the tiller. The thing about jarred his teeth out, but better him then his grandfather.

Of course, instead of watching, the older man grabbed a hoe and went to working between the onion sets.

Finishing the last row, he turned the contraption off, moved it out of the way next to the tool shed, then fetched the number-three wash tub and flipped it upside down to cover its motor. "Anything else?"

"No, sir. That oughta get it." PawPaw stretched his back. "Got home late last night. Were you with Hannah?"

"No, sir. Some of the guys at school wanted to play cards."

MawMaw shook her head but didn't say anything. Everyone but his PawPaw had been treating him as grown since he'd graduated from high school. Guess the old man wouldn't ever see him as anything more than a snot-nosed kid.

"Take it you were gambling?"

"Yes, sir."

"Best be careful, Son. No money I ever won gambling did me any good."

"John Harris, hold your tongue."

David bit his lip. Wouldn't do to laugh.

"Mother, he is not a child. As much as we'd like him to still be in knee britches, he's a man now—about to be married come June." PawPaw studied him hard. "All things in moderation. That's what the Good Book teaches. Moderation. Gambling can be a cruel mistress."

"Yes, sir."

He made Marble with five whole minutes to spare. While he leaned against the Ford, waiting for his betrothed, he allowed himself a little laugh over his MawMaw chiding his PawPaw. Everyone thought it was Mister John who was the staunch and strict Church of Christ believer, but David knew different.

His grandmother had converted from the Methodist and swallowed the Church's doctrine—hook, line, and sinker. Bless her dear and most precious traditional heart.

Shame she didn't believe that God spoke to anyone anymore. He loved her so much, a true saint of the Lord if there ever was one. She served everyone around her.

He could always pray that Lord would set her straight.

"What are you smiling about?"

"Get in." He focused. "And I'll tell you."

She did. He did. Then, of course, she got mad.

"Gambling? You were out playing cards until one o'clock in the morning? And here all this time, I thought you were a Godly man. What were you playing? Strip poker with a bunch of drug-crazed coeds?"

She scooted all the way to her side of the car, folded her hands in her lap, and stared forward; her favorite disapproval position.

"Oh, Hannah. You have the most active imagination of anyone I know. Why, you should be an author. Take a breath for goodness sake."

"Just pull on over, David Nightingale, and stop this car." She grabbed the door handle. "Let me out here, I can walk the rest of the way."

He stopped all right and held out his winnings toward her. Less the tithe, of course, all wrapped nice and neat in a square held with a rubber band. "Here, honey. Thought you might need this."

She cut her eyes but didn't turn her head. "What's that?"

"The money I won last night."

She took her hand off the door handle. "How much is it?"

"Three hundred and forty dollars. I put the change in my jar. Oh, and I kept out the tithe, too, so no concerns there."

She grabbed the money then glared. "Why were you gambling? What if you had lost?"

"I didn't lose. It started real low, just ten dollars. But the more I won, the more they kept wanting to play for."

"Were any girls playing in this game of yours?"

"No, ma'am. Only men . . . well, a couple of them I'd call boys. They played like . . ." He stopped himself. Comparing them to a girl would only lead to her asking when he'd play cards with a female again, and he did not want to remind her of the mixed-pairs bridge tournament.

"Like what?" Her cheeks were still pink, but not smoking.

"I was going to say little girls, but that would have been unkind."

"Oh, so you've been playing poker with little girls?"

Praise the Lord he swallowed the laugh before it got past his lips. "No, ma'am. But you and I used to play gin rummy, and if memory serves me right, you quit playing because I wouldn't let you win."

"Well, it wasn't fair. I didn't know how to play the game." She chuckled. "That was fun . . . you coming to Vacation Bible School with me that year."

"It was. Now do you want the money or not?"

"Of course, I do. Can I spend it any way I want?"

"Well, sure. I just figured you'd put it in the wedding fund."

"Maybe. But . . . uh . . . there's a dress I saw that I have fallen deeply in love with. Would it be okay if I put this with my . . . uh . . ."? She scooted closer. "I've been saving my hay money, but then I didn't have enough for what I wanted to buy you for your birthday . . . then your mother bought you one.

"So I . . . well, Daddy said I could spend a thousand dollars on my wedding however I wanted, but with . . . There wasn't going to be enough. Your mother said she and your father would chip in five hundred, so with this money added to my hay money, I can get that dress. What do you think?"

"That you need to slow down and take a breath."

She pursed her lips and pointed her finger gun toward him. "Don't be a wise acre."

"Yes, ma'am." He grinned. "And if you want that dress, then get it. I've got some money put back, too. I can help out if needed."

"And still have enough for the apartment? And don't forget we have to put down all those deposits on the utilities. I really want to have two phones, don't you? I hate having to jump out of bed to answer the phone."

"Sure, if it doesn't cost too much."

"I'll check on it."

He keyed the Ford to life then eased on up the street to her house. "I've got my last three tests tomorrow. Suppose we can take a night off from wedding planning and crack a book or three?"

Thought he did okay on his test, though he never dreamed to do as well as he did. Making two As and four Bs might even be worthy of a little praise.

Not that it really mattered, but all the hours would be transferable if he ever decided to go back. Not a total waste of his mother's investment.

The New Year carried in a new round of badgering from his dear maternal parent regarding going back to school, but nothing she said moved him off the dime he'd parked on. After a rather heated exchange, he played his trump card.

"You didn't go, and neither did Dad. Drop it, please."

It seemed his words took her back a bit. In some apparent level of shock, she glared, her mental wheels obviously spinning ninety to nothing.

Then instead of saying anything, she grabbed her purse and

headed for the door. Even before it slammed, she'd lit a Virginia Slim. He hated those things, but hey. Better than nothing.

Following her out, he helped her with her smoke. "I love you."

"I love you, too, Son. And I know you're a young man with decisions of your own to make. I understand that you want to decide for yourself without any input from your mother. But that is who I am and will always be.

"Your mother. It's bad enough you're marrying Hannah before she even finishes high school, but now you're giving up on a degree."

"They only want to teach man's doctrine, Mom. And you don't need a high school diploma to be a wife and mother. And while we're talking about it, what good is a degree going to do me?"

"Listen to yourself. Does that sound smart? I know how intelligent you are, John David Nightingale. Mercy! Don't ruin your life!"

Sucking enough fresh air to get his lungs full, he held it a minute then let the air escape ever so slowly, giving himself time to consider his response.

"I'm not, Mom. I've already got two offers. Bishop Bass wants me for the Church of God, and Uncle Travis says he can get me ordained with the Assemblies and a position as a youth minister. Eating from the Tree of Knowledge of Good and Evil, just isn't where it's at."

"Mercy. Your father could have any church he wanted if he'd a doctorate. Instead, he's stuck—"

"Or maybe." David beat her to the punch. "Right where God wants him."

"You don't know that."

"Sure, I do. Dad doesn't lean to his own understanding anymore. You surely aren't going to try and deny that he acknowledges God in all his ways. Am I right?"

"Yes. That's true."

John David's Calling

"So then God's directing his path. Accept it. Pine Bluff is where God set Gramps. It's a growing church. I mean hey, if Dad wanted, he could easily be a big TV preacher. How many invites do you think he's already turned down, Mother? Mercy. He could start his own show, be like—"

"Really? He could?"

"Sure. And be exactly like all the others, spending the last five minutes begging for money. We'd all be rich."

"Not all of them are like that. You can't take any group of any people and call them all bad."

"So, there are some really good mafia goons?"

"You know what I mean."

"Whatever." He sat down on the edge of one of the porch rockers. "One bad apple does spoil the whole barrel. A little leaven leavens the whole loaf."

"Well, you're going to need some riches. You have no idea. You're going to have a wife to take care of, and to hear her tell it, a new baby to support nine months and one day later."

"If all else fails, we can pay the bills hauling hay."

"And what will you do when your PawPaw's truck breaks down?"

"Fix it, like always."

"You have all the answers, don't you?"

"No, but the Lord does, and He and I are on real good terms."

Later that month, the upstart AFL won the Super Bowl for the second year in a row. Far as his concern went, that game would have to go a long way to be decent, much less super.

The Chiefs demolished the Vikings twenty-three to seven. Not nearly as good as last year's game, where Broadway Joe's Jets pulled the upset of the century over the Colts . . . Now that game . . .

But David loved it anyway, especially for the dollar he won from Dad Morrison. Then even before the post-game celebrations were over, the Morrison's phone rang.

"David! It's for you."

Hmm. He wasn't expecting anyone to call. He took the receiver from Mom Morrison. "Hello."

"Hey, Cuz. I need my money."

"What's wrong, Sonny?"

"Nothing. Why does something have to be wrong? Sissy called."

"Oh, and that makes everything right?"

His cousin ignored his tone. "She's in Los Angeles and wants me to come join her."

"Brother, don't go. She's poison."

"Not to me, dude. I love her, have forever. I'm telling you, she makes my world right."

"Mercy, Sonny." What was he going to do? The guy was his own man.

"By my calculations, you're holding a hundred and twenty-six dollars for me. That right?"

"What about the money Mama spent getting you out of jail?"

"What about it? I've been going to their church every Sunday. She'll just have to trust me for the rest. I'm planning on bring Sissy back here. Get her away from that bunch of dopers on the West coast."

"Where are you?"

"Uncle John's. Should've known you'd be at Hannah's."

"Put PawPaw on the phone."

"David? That you?"

"Yes, sir. Can you get Sonny his money?"

"Sure. You still using that old cigar box in the top of your closet?"

"Yes, sir, but he's only got one hundred and twenty-six coming. The rest is mine. And go into my room by yourself."

"Right. Want to me to hogtie him instead? We could keep him in the root cellar."

David laughed. "No, sir. We'd have to let him go some time. Just give him buckage, and . . ." Tears welled. "Tell him I said goodbye and to write. Tell him that we love him."

"You got it, Son. See you later."

He eased the phone back into its cradle.

Oh Lord, don't let me be right. Bring him back home.

"Was that Sonny?"

"Yeah." David nodded then told his love the sad story of Sonny following the siren's song.

She slipped into his embrace. "You tried, but he's a grown man."

Yes, he tried, but had he tried hard enough?

Chapter Twenty-one

A few days after the big football game, David found a fat letter with strange stamps and colored marks all over it, hiding among all the junk mail in his grandparents' box.

Right there on the top left corner declared Mike Bass its sender. How cool. He resisted opening it then and there, deciding to savor the news from his long-lost buddies.

So instead, he headed home. A part of him didn't want to see it at all. He'd struggled with his friend being on the mission field while David remained safe and sound, living a fine life in the Texas Hill Country.

Normally, he considered the quarter-mile walk to the post office a treat, but with each step, his heart grew heavier. No chance whatsoever of getting eaten by cannibals in Cypress Springs.

Might get caught in a crossfire between two idiots feuding over the same gal, but that sort of thing had pretty much died out. Why couldn't he have been born a hundred years ago?

He looked skyward. "Thank you, Lord, that I outgrew that notion."

After handing MawMaw her mail, he retreated to his room.

John David's Calling

Greetings King,
    Hope this finds you well and strong in the Lord. Matt and I find ourselves in need of a fourth for bridge. You interested? Mitch went back with Dad. Hopefully, he can regain the faith he once had.

What a blessing! Number three-forty-eight in the draft lottery! Heard you transferred to the University of Texas. It's a good school, but what kind of Bible department do they have? If any.

The bishop's offer still stands. All you have to do is give him a call if that's the path you want to travel.

We could sure use you. Your options are open, my man. Did I mention bridge most nights?

I'd say we've had limited success here. Satan resisting us at every level, of course. We're trying a new tactic. Instead of handing out food and medicine, we've bought five acres, and we're digging a well.

Planning on a big garden, and goats, too. We'll continue to feed as many as possible. And by the way, we're accepting donations.

Send them to the bishop's office in Tulsa. There's a full-time nurse here from Kentucky. She's a decent player. And a doctor (a killer player) who comes once a month.

Our services are quite different. Much more emotion. You'd love it, brother. Sure could use someone who sings and dances and oh, yeah! That's you.

Hey, and most likely, you could pick up some new moves. Didn't your namesake have a wilderness experience? You could have yours here.

Pray about it, brother. Having you here would be awesome and think of all the treasure you'd be laying up in Heaven.

I love and miss you, man. As you can see, I'm enclosing some pictures and a map of our compound.

The locals are kindhearted folks, but so

> intertwined in their idolatry and superstitions, it's hard to get through to them. Their witch doctors have a strong hold over them.
>   The evil around those guys is palpable. I often can't help a shiver up my spine.
>   No fear, just gross.
> > Keep us in your prayers,
> > Blessings,
> > Mike

David relished the pictures and smiles he missed so much.

Then he gave the map a close go over. Looked plenty well thought out and well organized. He carefully folded and returned all to the envelope, then slipped off his chair onto his knees.

"Lord, not my will but Yours be done. Show me what You'd have me do." He pressed his forehead to the floor and waited, but no vision or words came. So he praised the Lord for the beauty of His Holiness then prayed for his friends.

"David."

"Yes, ma'am." He raised up. "In here, MawMaw."

"Phone, sweetheart. It's Sandra Louise."

Hurrying to the living room, he picked up the receiver and sat in MawMaw's chair. "Hey, Mom."

"Hello, sweetheart. I was calling to see if you were free this afternoon?"

"Sure. What do you need?"

"Well, the builder's wanting us to do a walk-through and give him a punch list. I was hoping you might come."

"Great, I thought they had another couple of weeks."

"They did." She laughed. "But that was two weeks ago."

The excitement in her voice made him smile. "Okay then. How about I get Hannah from school, and we meet you there."

"That works. And . . . Oh, your father got a call this morning. He can't go but thought you might be interested."

"In what? A TV gig?"

"Well, yes and no, there's a non-denominational church in

John David's Calling

Austin, and they're having a camp meeting. They invited Buddy to lead the music, but they are going to run it live on the local Christian station."

A chill washed over David. "When?"

"Starts two weeks from this Sunday and runs until the next. Would you like me to call the guy for you? Be your agent?" She giggled. "Or, I can give the number to you. Either way."

An even stronger witness moved over his heart. Not the small, still voice he'd prefer, but the timing was just like the Lord. "Sure, you go ahead and call them, Mom. If they want me, tell them I'll be there."

"Great." She laughed again. "I'll call the guy as soon as we hang up here. See you this afternoon at the new house."

Hannah loved having her own personal chauffeur, but him being so strict about no public display of affection in or around the school seemed a bit crazy.

Mercy! Everyone with half a brain knew she would become Mis'ess David Nightingale in five months. June could not get there quick enough for her. She and her mother had decided on wild flowers for the bride's bouquet and boutonnieres.

Little by little, her wedding was coming together.

A decision here and one over there; David wanted to wear jeans with a sports coat which was fine by her.

Her gallant fiancé held the Ford's door open for her. She stole a kiss on the way by. "Have a good day, my beloved."

"Yes, ma'am. Always." He ran around, got in, then retrieved an envelope from the dash. "This came today."

A letter from Mike Bass . . . in Africa . . . She read it then glanced over the map and pictures. "Very interesting. Are you thinking about us going to Africa?"

"I'm praying about it."

The car picked up speed. He'd gotten up onto the highway.

"Where are we going?"

"The new house. We're meeting Mom and Dad there. The builder wants a walk-through and a punch list."

"What's that?"

"We'll be looking for anything that still needs to be done, which we'll put on a list for him. He's getting close."

"Cool."

"Yeah, guess they'll be moving in before too long. I already called your mother and told her what we were doing and that we'd be late."

"Aww, thank you, sweetheart. That was considerate."

"You're welcome. I do my best."

The house looked great, fabulous. It pleased her that she found more stuff than anyone—not that anyone was keeping score, but Sandy seemed to genuinely appreciate Hannah's sharp eye for detail.

Then like it was nothing, right before time to leave, David's mother mentioned that she called someone, and they wanted him to come. For a camp meeting somewhere.

Why hadn't he mentioned that?

Keeping an ear peeled, she listened, more than a little upset, but she kept her cool. All the way until money was mentioned, then she couldn't help but squeal.

"Really? How awesome!" She kept looking back and forth between mother and son. "A five-hundred-dollar honorarium? Wow! That's like a month's worth of hauling hay—for the both of us."

"Yes, ma'am. I admit that I thought about asking for more, but . . ." She smiled. "He's not as well-known as his father . . . yet."

The first chance she got, she scooted in close then lowered her voice where only Sandy could hear. "Thank you! I'm so excited! Just you wait."

The lady nodded with a huge grin then slipped her hand into Hannah's and squeezed. "Hey, who's hungry? If we hurry, maybe we can beat the rush at the Blue Bonnet."

"Sounds delish, and I'm past ready."

She loved the cafe but could barely enjoy the food for being so excited over David leading the music at a camp meeting—and one the local television station would be airing.

That could be big, really big! She took a sip of sweat tea. "Sorry to be so dumb, but what exactly is a camp meeting?"

"Back when the Methodist circuit-riding preacher came to town, everyone would camp out for a week or two, having church every night."

"Oh? Like a revival?"

"Pretty much the same difference. But the Austin church is having day services, too. And a women's conference on Saturday."

"What's that?"

"It's a well-kept secret." David's father smiled. "But don't ask me any hard questions. I've never been to one—you know, since they're ladies only."

"Oh, I see." She looked to his mother who hiked a shoulder.

"I've never been to one either."

"So, are either of you planning on going any of the nights?"

"We can probably make a service or two. Would you like to ride with us when we do?"

"That'd be wonderful."

"I can come get you."

She faced David. "Not if you're doing two services a day, silly. And for what they're paying us, you need to be Johnny on the spot."

David loved her saying 'us.' But then that's pretty much how it was with him, too. He and his beloved had become a 'they.' Shame he still had five months to go.

Seemed with each day that got marked off, his desire for her grew. She completed him yet remained such a contradiction. Soft and sweet one minute, hard and harsh as nails the next.

The girl practiced such levelheadedness about so many things yet wanted to blow all her hay money on a dress she'd wear one day.

Praise the Lord, the flickering porch light saved him one more time. He loved her so much, but maybe he should hibernate until June.

Kissing her one last time, he searched her eyes, loving the depth in them. "I love you, baby."

"I know." She scooted to her door, blew him a last kiss, then got out and stuck her head back in. "I love you, too. Will you pick me up tomorrow?"

"I'll be there, unless someone wants me to work."

He didn't mind the lull. Especially with what the church offered to pay. Maybe they'd let him pass the hat for Mike. It'd be nice to help out. For sure he couldn't go to Africa until later in the summer, if then.

Wouldn't have to be like God talking to Moses out of the burning bush, but he'd need a strong witness with confirmation.

His bud didn't say anything about cannibals, but that didn't mean they weren't over there . . . lurking in the jungle.

Once Marble's lights were in his rearview mirror, he reached toward his glove box.

QUIT

He jerked his hand back. "Okay, Father. If You say so."

Though he heard nothing else, he rose and fell to the sound of his Master's voice. Plus, he'd always said if the Lord told him to quit, he would. And David had no doubts that He just had.

"Mercy, Lord. Didn't even really want one until You told me to quit."

The rest of the way home, he had himself a nice little pity party until it dawned on him. "Satan, I bind you off of me by the blood of Jesus, you are defeated by that blood, and I will not love my life even unto death. So forget it. I've already

John David's Calling

quit."

It'd be a lie to say he didn't still want a smoke, but not enough that he thought he might die without one.

As though taking tobacco away wasn't enough—with three days to go before the camp meeting started, the Lord impressed upon his heart to fast until he sang the first song.

What was he going to do? Have a hamburger stashed out in the church somewhere? Hannah could bring him something. Or his mother. Turned out to be the longest eighty hours of his life.

How had Jesus gone forty days without eating? David didn't tell anyone but Hannah. He couldn't keep anything from her anyway.

The Church at Austin held their regular Sunday morning services then that evening started the Holy Spirit on the Move Camp Meeting 1970. It officially started at six.

After an opening prayer and service times announced, the man nodded toward him.

Man, how he loved that the only instruction he'd been given was to proceed as the Lord led.

Started with an old favorite . . . the doxology. He loved it when the Lord did such, start with a song that usually finished a service. The response was pretty standard. The singers sang and harmonized; the others came along without much gusto.

When the last note faded, he closed his eyes. A new song rang in his heart. The words and music flooded his soul. He opened his mouth and sang.

A faithful few caught it right off, but the rest came in soon enough. Good thing the rafters were locked in with grade eight bolts, for the house rocked.

After eight new praise songs—or was it a hundred? —the need to worship the Almighty overcame him. "Holy . . . Holy . . . Holy . . .is . . . the . . . Lord . . . God . . . Almighty."

After not nearly long enough, a hand rested on his shoulder, yanking him out of the Spirit's flow. He looked to his side.

"Thank you, son. I'll take it from here."

Even though he wanted to slip out and find the nearest

hamburger joint, he figured Hannah would be aghast, seeing how she'd taken a seat right up front. So, he slipped in next to his love and put food out of his mind.

Though Hannah had seen him do it before, she'd never seen him in front of so many people and with the television camera rolling. Mercy! What a way to make a living!

Dollar signs drifted across her inner eye, piling higher and higher in her imagination. She'd love nothing better than being a pastor's wife and traveling with her famous husband.

Slipping her hand into his, she squeezed. He looked over and smiled.

Maybe she should move the wedding up. What if someone in California—after seeing what he could do—wanted him to be on their TV show? As a regular? Buddy had said his honorarium could be a hundred plus expenses.

And that had to be per episode, right? No telling what they'd give David. Five hundred a week? Or more! And that would leave so much time for all kinds of fun stuff.

Disney Land, Knots Berry Farm, the movie studios, and the beach! How far was it from Burbank up to the Redwood Forest? She'd always wanted to see those fabulous giant trees, and they couldn't be too far.

Touring the vineyards in the Napa Valley might be fun, except that with David being such a teetotaler, maybe not. Mercy, Paul said take a little wine for your stomach's sake, didn't he?

And Solomon put it in the proverbs to give a poor man a little wine, so he could forget his troubles for a while. It wasn't fair, but . . . it might be in his genes.

Then she'd hate it if he became a drunk, so . . . better safe than sorry.

Forget the valley with all its grapevines.

John David's Calling

The preacher's voice rose an octave, and she shook her head to come back from her daydreaming. She turned her attention to the man who'd be writing David's check.

Wouldn't want anyone to think she wasn't listening. What had he been saying? She scooted in tighter next to her love.

All in all the service proved to be a good one. Three folks came forward for salvation and dozens more wanted prayer.

It pleased her that they wanted David to come and lay hands on folks, too. He was a good pray-er, just talking to God without all the pomp and fancy words, just in the same tone he'd talk to anyone else, he sounded real.

Several of the older ladies up front intercepted any female who walked the aisle, and she liked that, too. She definitely didn't want David to be all huddled up with some stranger lady crying on his shoulder and whispering who knew what into his ear.

She needed to remember to talk to him about a no hugging rule.

Finally, the pastor dismissed the congregation, and it was over. Except she could hardly believe it when she saw the clock on the back wall that over three hours had gone by.

As always, he opened the Ford's door for her. "You hungry?"

"Well, yeah, but let's get something fast. Mama wants me home by ten."

"You ever had a Whataburger?"

"I don't guess so. Is it just a hamburger?"

"I suppose. Some of the men were talking about them, how great they were. There's a restaurant not too far from here."

"Okay, sounds great! We'll get it to go and eat on the road."

What a burger, indeed. No way could she eat all of that huge sandwich.

Of course, it wouldn't go to waste though. She had to work at not being jealous that her sweetheart could eat all of his with french fries then finish hers and never gain a pound. Her leftovers probably played their part in his original plan.

It made her giggle how he kept looking over once she started nibbling. Finally, she couldn't take another bite and handed over the last third. "Want the rest of my fries, too?"

"Please, ma'am, and thank you."

"You know, I've been thinking, and there's really not a reason in the world why we have to wait until June to get married. Not one I can come with, anyway."

With a sly crooked little grin, he glanced at her. "What are you saying?"

"I mean . . . I was just thinking about tomorrow. I hate it that you're having to drive all the way back just to take me to school. I'll be in class, you'll have this long drive again . . . all alone. That can't be any fun. I'm just saying, if we were married, we could get a room or stay with someone from the church. One trip there and one back. Think of the gas we'd save."

Bursting out laughing from the gut, he shook his head. "Saving a few dollars in gas is no reason to move up our wedding. Everything's set for June. We can't change it now, and from—"

"Why not?"

"If you'll let me finish . . . From what you told me, it took your dad two days to talk your mother into letting you miss your last year of school."

"Yeah? So what? She hated it when he was right. "Okay, but I can skip this week. What time are you leaving in the morning?"

"Slow down, my love. Let's just keep the peace. Mom and Dad are coming Tuesday and Thursday, and she wants to come Saturday for the women's conference, so you'll not miss that much."

Silence reigned for several miles while she tried to calculate a new approach, but nothing came. He stopped in front of her house.

"Kiss me." She leaned over, and he did.

"You better get inside. It's after ten."

"You're such a slave driver."

"I love you."

"I know you do." She took his hand and rubbed his thumb . . . repeatedly. "Just once, I'd like it if you took my side."

He exhaled a little too loud like he was trying to cover a laugh. "When it's just me and you, you want me to take your side?"

"What is so funny about that, David Nightingale? Tell me."

"You can figure it out. I have faith. To my way of thinking, I already give in to you way too much."

She scoffed. "Can't happen."

Putting his other hand over hers, he squeezed it. "Listen, I know you love me, and I sure love you, but baby, we just can't have what we want all the time."

Yanking her hand from his, she opened the door and slipped out then leaned back in. "Tell me about it."

"Good night." He grinned then drove off and left her standing there watching him leave . . . again. She hated watching him go, not being with him.

The two services she attended that week were basically carbon copies of Sunday night's session. Different songs and everything, but wow. How did he do it every time? Make the Lord come down like that.

One thing she knew. She loved it! Maybe a few more folks accepted the Lord, but it seemed not as many wanted prayer.

A stiff north wind greeted her Saturday morning. The temperature had dropped thirty degrees overnight, but no predicted snow or sleet, praise the Lord. Her mother wouldn't have let her out of the house otherwise.

Sandy came early and for the first time, accepted the cup of coffee her mother always offered every time his mother came by. The conversation seemed a bit strained between them, but real soon, they'd be sharing grandbabies.

A lot sooner than later, if David wasn't such a pigheaded slave driver. Mercy, they could get it all done in a month or less if she cut out some of the pomp.

She'd always wanted a big wedding . . . but she wanted way more to be his wife. Hadn't said anything to her mother, but she hadn't ordered the invitations yet either—just in case.

The wall clock's hands claimed ten minutes before eight. Sandy drained her cup and carried it to the sink. "You ready, sweetheart?"

"Yes, ma'am."

The drive progressed pleasantly enough. The lady talked mostly about the wedding and how much fun it would be if David got himself on Christian television. She arrived with minutes to spare, but not enough for Hannah to hunt David down.

It warmed her heart to see him waiting by the door to the fellowship hall where the conference was being held.

"Hey, Mom." He kissed the lady's cheek then winked at Hannah. With his cheek to hers, he hugged her and whispered, "Couldn't miss seeing you, I love you so much. Gotta go."

The men had the sanctuary for a special 'pastors and worship leaders only' meeting.

That morning actually turned out to be quite a surprise, nothing like she expected. She never did get bored at all. There was lots of sharing and fun stuff going on constantly.

The women even played some Bible games that mothers could teach their children. If only she had children to teach them to! She couldn't wait.

After a fun skit about witnessing and how to make it easy, they had a foot washing service. That surprised her the most.

An older lady washed her feet and spoke loving, encouraging words. Then while she dried them, she blessed Hannah's upcoming nuptials. But how could she know? Would Sandy have said something?

Dinner, except they called it lunch, was yummy and plentiful. She sat with some of the younger women. Two were still in high school, but seniors though. Afterwards, they broke everyone up into small groups for more sharing and prayer.

One of the young women in her group, she'd met at dinner.

Her name was Carmen, a beautiful Mexican girl. As soon as she graduated, she and her boyfriend were getting married, too! Hannah loved getting to know her and share stories.

Twenty minutes into the four o'clock session, the tone changed.

Chapter Twenty-two

The pastor's wife, who'd been leading the music, stopped after only a few songs. "Ladies, there's someone special here this afternoon that I'm going to turn over the service over to.

Please give a warm welcome to our guest speaker today. We're so blessed to have her. I'm honored to introduce you to Luauna Jenkins."

Who? Luauna Jenkins? She'd never heard of her. The lady, maybe in her early thirties, stepped up to the podium, accompanied by a polite round of muted applause; seemed as if no one else knew the name either.

The poor woman sure looked as though she'd lived a hard life . . . but something about her . . . well, she was different.

"Blessings, ladies." She smiled and made a point of slowly looking from one side of the room to the other.

Did she stop on every face as she had Hannah's?

"Angel was my last stage name—as I like to think of it. But now in my new life, it has a whole new meaning. So, you can call me either Luauna or Angel."

Stage name? Had she been an act . . .?

As if she'd herd Hannah's thoughts . . . "Oh, I was an actress all right. But not in any playhouse or on TV or any other place I'm proud of." She stepped from behind the lectern.

"Once . . ." She lowered her eyes to the floor and seemed to study it. Was she going to say something else? "Some might have referred to me as a soiled dove. A nice name for a whore, wouldn't you say?"

Swallowing, Hannah looked around. Was everyone as shocked? A prostitute right there in the church? What was going on?

"Three years ago, I met a dear old lady." She grinned. "The sweet little thing—barely a hundred pounds at best, with crippled hands . . . She shared her unconditional love. So sweet. No matter how much grief I gave her, she kept coming back. The woman literally loved me into the kingdom." She held her hand high.

"Praise Jesus! He saved me, set me free from my sin and shame."

The room erupted in cheers and shouts of praise. Hannah jumped to her feet and twirled around, she loved stories like that. She joined the shouting, though she'd never raised her voice in the church.

At football games, yeah, but . . .

"Thank you, Lord! Praise You! Your mercy endures forever!" She twirled right over and back into her seat.

What would Sandy think?

"Amen." Angel held her hands out, and the room quieted. "Now I told you that to tell you this. The Lord is holy. And ladies, He requires us to be holy, too. Just as He is. We all know the devil is out to kill, steal, and destroy." She walked out from behind the lectern and dragged a folding chair in front of it then sat down.

"I want to ask all the married women who were virgins when they married and have never strayed to come and stand behind me."

The pastor's wife and ten more ladies went forward.

"So, now . . . would all the virgins come stand with these ladies? I'd like you to mix in with them, please."

Hannah jumped to her feet, and another four young ladies

followed her into the group standing behind Angel.

"Now." The woman bowed her head. "As we agreed in the beginning, sisters, this is a private meeting. We know there's no condemnation in Christ. He wants you to be free, to live an abundant life.

"But one of the devil's favorite schemes for girls is to get them seeking love, approval. All you ladies who would like to become rededicated virgins, come join me; stand or kneel or sit in front of me."

A vise squeezed Hannah's heart. Bless all those ladies' hearts who still made up the audience . . . they'd fallen, too. All of them. Man.

"Then I'm going to ask these virtuous women, these dear ladies behind me, to encircle us and pray for us. We'll repent for our bad choices, from all those foul, unholy relationships when we were deceived—or even if we knew full well what we were walking into—and failed and disappointed our Creator.

The Lord has told me that today . . . right now as they pray . . . He's going to set you free. Just as He set me free."

All but two came forward, including her future mother-in-love. The two sadly slipped out the back. Tears streamed down Hannah's cheeks as she prayed for the ones she laid hands on.

Could there possibly be a dry eye in the room?

For how long she prayed, she had no idea, but it was wonderful. Then the pastor's wife started clapping and shouting praise to the King of Kings!

Then she took to dancing!

Jumping to her feet, Angel fell in right behind her. Hannah joined in as the women sang and danced in a circle around those still praying. She leaped and twirled before the Lord.

What a meeting! Sandy passed her then turned back and hugged her tight. Tears glistened in her eyes. The woman took Hannah's face in her hands and searched her eyes.

"It made me so proud for my son when you went forward."

Tears filled her eyes, too, then. "Bless God. But if not for David . . ." She laid her head on Sandy's shoulder. "He's so

Godly and so good. I love him so much and know how blessed I am. Thank you, Mis'ess Nightingale, er, Sandy."

"Won't you call me Mom?" She leaned back then held her hand out. "Come on. What do you say we go find the men and see if we have time to get something to eat before tonight's service?"

"That sounds perfect."

The special pastors-only assembly proved somewhat lame when compared to the meetings David had been in with Mike and the Mis'ess.

Much to his mother's regret, there wasn't enough time for a sit-down in a fancy restaurant before the evening services, so he introduced his parents to Whataburger. Dad loved the place; Mom, not so much.

Twenty minutes before the scheduled start-time, he excused himself and retreated to the quiet spot he'd been using in the choir's practice hall. There, he prostrated himself before the Lord. "Guide me Father. Fill me with Your Holy Spirit."

For a few minutes, he waited. Then in his mind's eye, he saw a young Mexican girl dancing and praising the Lord with a tambourine. An old man with wild gray hair beat a drum strapped around his neck like in a marching band.

Like a pied piper, a young boy playing a flute followed him. The whole congregation fell in behind the trio, and the lot of them went wild, extolling the beauty of the Lord's Holiness.

The vision faded, then shortly after, a hand touched his shoulder. He raised up. "Is it time?"

The pastor nodded. "Almost, but don't run off after we're finished tonight. We want to talk with you and Hannah."

"Okay." David pushed himself off the floor. "Where do you want to meet?"

"My office." The man smiled. "I had the treasurer cut you a

check. Who wants to wait on the mail for their money?"

"Thank you, sir."

The man smiled. "Thank you, son. It's been awesome." He chuckled. "Hate to admit it, but I'm sort of glad your dad couldn't make it."

In the minutes he had left, he located Hannah and told her of the meeting. Of course, she wanted to know more than he knew to tell her. What the reverend had said, what it was about, anything . . . but he refused to speculate.

After the opening prayer, announcements were made, including a big share-service the next day followed by a covered-dish dinner in the fellowship hall, then he got the nod. "Praise the Lord. David, come on up here."

A hearty round of amens echoed across the sanctuary. Seemed like the ladies out-voiced the men, greeting him. He scanned the crowd but didn't see any of the folks in his vision.

Was it true and from God? Or the devil trying to embarrass him?

I INHABIT THE PRAISES OF MY PEOPLE

Wow. He loved it when that happened. The Lord did inhabit the praises; Scripture said so. His people, not Satan's.

"Folks, just now while I was praying before services, I saw three people. Is there a young Hispanic lady here? One with a tambourine?"

The lady from his vision jumped to her feet and jangled the zils. "Right here, sir."

"Good, that's great. How about a gentleman with a drum like from a marching band?"

The old boy with wild gray hair rose from the back pew. "At your service, Brother David."

"Excellent." What did the Lord have in store? "How about a young man with a flute." Chills washed over him. "That you've never played before today—don't be shy. Come on."

A small hand shot up, holding the instrument. The boy followed. "Gramps just gave it to me this afternoon."

"Would you three please come to the front?"

They made their way as requested, and an even stronger witness engulfed him.

"Anyone with any ailment at all? Cancer? Heart problems? Toothache? It doesn't matter. The Lord wants to heal you. Please come forward." He nodded toward his trio. "Play and march. Anyone that wants to join these is free! The Lord is mighty to save."

Hannah and his parents were first in line behind the trio. The girl leading the way. Soon, the whole congregation, save those who came forward for healing.

He joined the pastor and other ministers and began anointing the sick with oil, praying the prayer of a righteous man, while the church sang and danced before the Lord.

Twenty or thirty minutes, they kept at it, then the pastor released everyone to their seat. David saddled up next to the older man. "Want me to . . ." He stopped himself. "There's a woman who didn't come forward to be healed. She has a withered arm."

"Find her. Pray for her."

"Yes, sir."

David turned around and held his arms out. "Please be seated."

Like stacked dominoes, front to back, the congregation collapsed into their pews.

"I'm looking for a sweet lady here who didn't come for prayer, but God wants to heal your withered arm." How surprising that no one jumped up. "You wear big sleeves to hide it because your whole life, you've been self-conscious over people noticing." He kept looking around, walking up the aisle.

"You've never married because of it. Please. Let me pray for you, ma'am, The Lord wants to heal you today."

Nothing,

No one stood.

Then like a ray of sunshine breaking through on a cloudy day, the Lord engulfed her in his love, and he saw her. David walked the aisle until he reached her pew. "I don't mean to embarrass you, ma'am. But please don't miss this. You're the one the Lord wants to heal."

The young lady—quite attractive and not that old—stood. Tears streamed down her cheeks. She held both arms straight down, locked at her side.

David closed his eyes. A knowing like he'd never experienced before came upon him. He held both his hands out toward her. "Take my hands."

She gasped. More tears flooded her cheeks though there was no sound. She slowly turned and faced him, shaking her head from side to side. Barely shaking her head, she mouthed no.

Palms up, he wiggled his fingers toward himself a couple of times, bidding her to come. "God wants to heal you, miss, but you have to accept it."

Suddenly, Hannah was in the pew behind the lady. Leaning closer, she reached out and touched her, laying her hand on the woman's shoulder, and began praying. David didn't know exactly what else to do, but he wasn't ready to give up.

Slipping to his knees, he kept going, pressed his forehead into the carpet, and prayed in the spirit.

A collective gasp brought him up.

The lady held out two whole arms.

His own tears overflowed. Hannah's, too. He'd missed seeing the miracle, but she hadn't. All those around her also did, and they went to shouting and praising. He jumped to his feet then raised his arms skyward.

"Bless the Lord! His mercy endures forever!"

The sanctuary went wild. All the congregants celebrated, whooping and hollering and giving God glory.

Pastor never preached that night, and that suited David just fine.

He'd rather worship anyway.

John David's Calling

Too soon, it was over. Hannah could have gone on all night . . . except her curiosity kept niggling at her every time any lull or break presented itself.

All sorts of scenarios of what the pastor wanted to talk to her and David about had played through her mind. She found her love and his parents, then after hugs and kisses all around, they left her and David alone, and he led her to the church office.

Someone had very tastefully decorated his outer office with plenty of plants and a few fantastic Scripture pictures on the wall. And the man's inner office looked even nicer, richer.

The pastor's wife sat next to him, both behind his big desk. He rose and held out his hand, shook David's, then motioned toward the two chairs in front. "Sit. Can we get you anything?"

"No, sir. But thank you." He looked to her. "You okay? Need some water?"

"Oh, no, I'm fine."

The graying man took his seat. "Awesome night! Fantastic week! I want to thank you, David." He looked to her. "You, too, Hannah." What had she done? His wife smiled at her and nodded.

"Yes, sir. It's been great this week."

He slid an envelope across his desk. "Your check and a little extra. Call it an early wedding present."

David took it but didn't open it. Almost everything inside her wanted to grab the thing out of his hand and tear it open to see how much extra there was, but exercising great self-control, she smiled instead and kept her hands in her lap.

"You've met BeeBee?"

"Yes, sir. Nice man."

"He is, but he's old school. He'd never dream of singing anything he and the choir haven't practiced, and every note was perfect."

Where was the man going with this? Was he about to offer David a job? She slipped her hand into his and squeezed.

"If you'll agree to join our church, BeeBee would still be on staff as say—oh, I don't know. We'd find him a job, but we'd love to have you be our full-time song leader."

He smiled then looked right at Hannah. "And you, young lady, if you'd be interested, there's plenty of jobs for Godly associate pastors' wives around here. We'd find something you'd love."

"I've not been ordained by any denomination."

Why was he saying that instead of asking about his salary? She looked at David.

"No problem at all. Doesn't matter in the least. I was ordained by the Baptist, but as you can see, we aren't in line with their doctrine now. We can get you licensed by the state, so you'll be legal."

"But—"

The man held up a finger. "What's so evident, David, is that God has ordained you. You have . . ." He seemed to be searching for the right word. "Such an anointing for one so young."

"Well, thank you again, sir. And I'll definitely pray about it. The wedding is in June, and I can't see how I could possibly start until after that. Hannah's still in school, and well . . ."

"I understand, but you'd fit in so well, and to tell the truth, I don't want you to get away."

Hmm. Why would he say, 'to tell the truth'? Did that mean he wasn't always truthful? "But I haven't heard yet for sure what God wants me to do. I've had a few other offers, and . . . I don't know, but I've felt a tug to serve in the mission field. I want to be sure."

"Perfectly understandable; praying about it is good, and we can wait. I'm thinking six hundred a week with say another two for your young lady. We have several nice places that have been donated to the church, so housing would be included."

"Wow." Hannah smiled at him, their combined salary

would be eight hundred a week? Plus, a house? Did that include utilities? She wanted to ask, but kept her mouth shut. They were being so good-hearted.

The wow might have been too much. She wished she hadn't let it out. Mercy, and that was only their first offer. Would they pay more?

"Very generous, sir. Thank you." David stood and extended his hand. "I'll let you know once I make a decision."

The pastor and his wife both stood. He shook David's hand again, then his wife came around and hugged her. She put her mouth close to Hannah's ear. "Convince him to come aboard. We can do wonders for the Lord together."

Giving the lady a squeeze back, Hannah didn't know how to answer so she just smiled and nodded. "Amen."

As much as she wanted to jump for joy or do a double back flip, she held his hand and strolled to the parking lot without a hint of what her insides were doing.

He opened her door as usual, and she kissed him on the way by as usual, then he closed the door and headed around front. She turned sideways facing his seat with her back against her door.

He got in and shook his head. "Why are you sitting way over there? You upset about something?"

"Oh, maybe I'm a bit miffed."

"Why?"

"That you didn't take him up on that offer right then and there."

"I know what you mean. Tempting, wasn't it? But . . ." He pulled a wad money out of his shirt pocket. "What do you make of this?"

She grabbed the money and counted it. Twenty-one-hundred-dollar bills. "Wow! Where did you get this? It wasn't in the envelope, was it? You haven't had time to open that. Have you?"

"No. It isn't from the pay and wedding present." He pulled a smaller wad out of his inside coat pocket. "Count this. And there's more."

"More? But . . . ." She grabbed that wad, five more Benjamins. "Okay. Spill your guts, Nightingale. Where did all this cash come from? What's it for?"

He keyed the Ford to life. "You hungry?"

"I was, but right now all I want is answers. Do not try to change the subject."

"So you're issuing orders, now? Think that's the way to get the information you want, do you?"

"Oh, stop it. Tell me! I am hungry, I need you to get to talking, or I'll. . . I'll . . . ."

"You need to know, huh?" He grinned and pulled the Ford out of the parking lot. "Really? You're so cute."

"Yes, need! It's essential to my well-being. I don't want to eat until I know about all the moolah, baby! Don't you see?" she scooted over next to him and rubbed her head on his shoulder and her hands on his arm like a kitten wrapping around its owner's leg.

"Hey, I can cry on cue. Want to hear?"

"Uh, no." He smiled at her and chuckled. "That old man—the one with the drum—handed me the five hundred and said to give it to Hannah for the wedding."

"Really? How cool!" She stuck that wad in her purse. "What about the two grand?"

"The man said give it to Mike when I see him."

"Oh, David! No! I don't want to go to Africa. Is Mike coming home?"

Chapter Twenty-three

David glanced at his love.

"Not that I know of, but sure would be great if he did. I'd love for Mike to stand up with me at our wedding."

"Mercy, there's cannibals in Africa."

"I know, and I've never wanted to go either, but I pray all the time, not my will but Yours, Lord. So, if that's where He wants us, are we going to kick against the pricks?"

"What's that supposed to mean?"

"It's what Jesus asked Paul on the road to Damascus. You remember when—"

"Yes, yes. The bright light, blinded. I know the story, but kicking pricks? It doesn't sound very nice."

"It basically means, are you going to fight with God?"

"Absolutely not, but I've prayed since I was a little girl in Vacation Bible School that He would not call me to the mission field. I didn't ever want to be that far away from my mother—and everyone else I love. I just don't think He'd do that to me."

"You what? Why?"

"I was so scared he'd call me, and I'd have to go. I thought it'd mean I had to leave right then, and I was only nine or ten. A little girl has no business in Africa!"

"What if she's grown up, and God calls the one she claims to love more than anything or anyone in the world? Wouldn't you go with me?"

"Waaaa, I don't want to go . . ."

He didn't respond, only looked her over again and raised his brow.

"But if you said God said . . . I guess I'd have to. It's very important to be obedient to Him. I know that. It's the way we show Him how much we love Him. But He hasn't said anything of the sort, has He? And we can do so much more here, can't we?"

"Baby, tonight was awesome. This whole week has been so, so—"

"Intoxicating?"

"That's an excellent word, even though we've never been drunk on alcohol, it's a great description."

"And Scripture even talks about being drunk on the Holy Spirit."

"True, but the only reason it was so good is because the Lord showed up. Without Him, it's . . ." He shrugged. "It'd just be a regular church gathering, and we both know how boring that is."

She scooted in close and snuggled up tight. "What about doctors?"

"What about them?"

"What if God called us and I got pregnant over there?"

"Oh. Mike said there's a nurse who lives there full time, and a doctor comes once a month."

She fell silent while he maneuvered the Ford through the streets of Austin.

"How about Chubby's? They're open late."

"Sure, whatever."

Was she crying?

"Hey, let's see how much extra the church gave us." He fished the envelope out of his coat pocket and handed it over.

Though she took it, she didn't tear into it like he expected. Instead, she tapped the check to one end then worked the other open a little tiny tear at a time.

Made him want to grab the thing and rip it, but he kept his hands on the steering wheel. She finally fished the check out and unfolded it.

"Wow! It's for seven-fifty! Plus." She looked down into the envelope, fingering something. "There's another three hundred cash in here."

"Praise the Lord! His mercy endures forever. That's awesome!"

"I can't believe we worked so hard and got so hot and sweaty all summer and didn't make this much. I like this way better! God is so good!"

He parked then came around to open her door. Like had become her really good habit, she kissed him on the way out then grabbed his hand.

After the waitress took the orders, Hannah leaned across the table. "Both our mothers would hate not being there when our babies are born. I don't want to leave Texas. Not to live."

"I know, baby, and I'm with you. I'd love staying right here, but you know the story of Naomi and Ruth, don't you?"

"Of course! Why do you do that? I am not stupid."

"Didn't mean to infer anything of the sort. Quite the opposite, you're one of the smartest women I know. Only trying to put you where I am, what I'm thinking about."

"So, what does Naomi and Ruth have to do with anything?"

"Well, it's like she told her mother-in-law. "Wherever you go, I'm going. If the Lord wants me to go to Africa or Timbuktu, then . . ." He took her hand. "I love you with my whole heart, Hannah Claire Morrison, but God has to come first."

Tears welled, but she blinked them away. "I know that, but He loves me. I know he does. And the Word says He'll give me the desires of my heart. It's my desire to stay in Texas, and no more than sixty miles from Marble Falls."

She wiped the couple of tears away that had escaped to her cheeks. "I love you, David. Please put this silly Africa notion out of your head."

Before he could respond, the waitress brought her hot fudge sundae and his burger and fries. He blessed the food then dug in.

Mercy. Your will be done, Lord.

Winter in South Texas was so much fun. A blue norther blew in, hung around for a few days, then with a warming trend, the thermometer climbed all the way to eight-five.

Only newcomers packed away summer clothes just because of the calendar. He loved the saying that if a person didn't like the weather in Texas, to stick around a day or two, and it'd change.

So true.

Not that he needed the money, but after he got all PawPaw's fields plowed for the last time before planting—David took on some day work. Some farmers ran their fields a couple or three times, not John Harris.

Each time they crusted over after a rain, he'd hitch up the cultivator and get after it again. David liked that about his grandfather. He preferred farming, but helped work cattle some, too.

On the last day of February, just as he washed up for his dash to Marble, the phone rang.

"David, it's your mother, honey." MawMaw made a great personal secretary.

"Hello, my love. Could you come by here after you get Hannah?"

"Sure, no problem. Need us to stop and get anything?"

"No, I can't think of anything. Besides, I want you to hurry. I'm about to bust a gut here."

"Why? What's wrong?"

"Nothing's wrong. Everything's right! Just pick up Hannah and get on over here as quick as you can. Love you." The line went dead.

"What did Sandra Louise want, sweetheart?"

"I don't know, MawMaw. She's being weird. Wants me to pick up Hannah and rush right over to her place but wouldn't say why."

"Something's afoot. She called three times before you came in."

"And didn't say what she wanted?"

"No, only that she needed to speak with you. Probably someone wants you to lead their singing. I keep hearing good things. I'm so proud of you, but Son, you need to get back to your roots. The Church of Christ is where you need to be."

"Well, thank you, MawMaw. I love you to pieces."

All the way to Marble, he rehashed the conversation with his mother, then after telling Hannah where he was headed and why, she acted like his mother's weirdness was no big deal. But she hadn't heard the excitement in her voice.

Something was definitely up, and every scenario he'd come up with on what it could be, didn't warrant hurrying or her giddiness.

Turning off the highway, he loved again that they'd put in a cattle guard and hung a sign with Nightingale Ranch on it. He loved the logo Aunt Lee Lee had come up with, the bird with all the swirls that formed a sort of circle around it.

The winding gravel road to the house was originally planned to be blacktopped, but that project had to go on hold once the money vultures got their hooks in his mother.

The house itself, while not a monster, presented a very respectable three-thousand-square-feet home. He loved the wide wrap-around porch—glad his dad had given in on the extra two feet, twelve-foot-wide made it seem like more of a room—and the Hill Country view it afforded.

Cedar posts held its ten-foot-high roof. He loved the mixture of native rock and brick, too. And the tin roof glistening in the sun set it off right nice.

Looked a little like an old-time way station. All it needed was a stagecoach and two or three wranglers, hanging out, smoking roll-your-owns.

Man, would he ever not want a cigarette?

His mother burst out the front door, grinning like she'd just struck oil or something.

Hannah adored what her soon-to-be in-laws had done with the place. Though brand-spanking new, they'd made it look old. But one thing puzzled her. Why had they decided to call it a ranch?

They only had a little over a hundred acres and not one cow or horse or goat or livestock of any kind. Well, they had talked Uncle Travis and Aunt Lee Lee out of a really sweet calico barn cat.

Uncle put up no argument at all, but Auntie was another story.

But one feline, a ranch did not make. The calico couldn't count.

Waiting for David to get around and open her door, she marveled at what a gentleman he was. And she loved it. And she loved kissing him every time she got in or out.

On her mental list of things she needed to do, she added thanking his PawPaw for that the next time she saw him. The old man played gruff, but he had a good heart that loved deeply.

Her sugar leaned in a bit to get his usual sugar on her way by.

Oh, how she loved him . . . so much . . . but he had to forget the Africa thing.

Sandy hugged David first then held one arm out toward Hannah. She walked into the group hug. Buddy filled the door way. "Come on in. I've got a fire going."

"Dad, its eighty degrees."

"Yes, but another norther is coming. Should be here any minute."

Everyone sat way across from the blaze. It certainly looked beautiful.

"So what was the big rush all about?"

"Well. I got a rather strange call this morning. At first, I must admit my suspicions ran rampant. I thought it might be a prank, so I called your father's agent."

"Wait. Dad has an agent? When did that happen?"

"Oh, a while back. He works on a percentage, and so far, he's done his job well, bringing in way more than he's cost us. He negotiates everything, so that's nice. Your father doesn't have to sound like such a money grubber, and the man knows his market. He manages several big-name clients."

She shot Hannah a grin. "Anyway, that is not what I want to tell you, so shush."

"Yes, ma'am." He looked at her. "Hannah, no talking now."

Surprised, she opened her mouth then shut it when she got his joke and whacked his upper arm, giggling. She loved the way the three of them talked and carried on like she was already family.

Who would have ever thought Buddy Nightingale had an agent? But then he was on TV a lot, not so much since he took over as pastor at Pine Bluff. But still, they'd already made three trips that year.

"Oh, David! Hannah's been quiet as a mouse. Now listen. I mean it! Listen to me, and do not interrupt."

"Yes, ma'am."

"So. Your dad's agent actually knew the guy who called me and offered to broker the deal. He's willing to take his usual fifteen percent and says he can even get some upfront—an advance to cover your traveling expenses!"

"Whoa. Sorry." David held his hands up. "Back up. My traveling expenses? What are you talking about, Mother?"

Grinning like she just played a scrabble word on a triple letter, triple word, racking up over a hundred points, she shivered with frivolity and squealed.

"The man who called was from a motion picture studio, David! And they want you for a movie!"

Hannah jumped up. "What? Who is they?"

Somehow, Sandy managed to widen her smile even bigger.

"Paramount! They're the 'they'! Seems somehow one of their producers in Hollywood got ahold of a tape of our David singing and dancing! The guy said you praying for that girl with the crippled arm sealed the deal for him."

Looking from Sandy to David, Hannah couldn't believe he shook his head from side to side. What was wrong with him?

"You can tell him I'm not interested."

Sandy threw her hands into the air. "No, wait now. Don't say that. You haven't even prayed about it. You can't just say no like that. This could easily be God opening the door. Think about it! You could be like Pat Boone. He's influenced millions of folks for the Lord. And there's more! Guess what!"

"I don't feel like guessing, Mom."

"What?" Hannah didn't want to guess either. She just wanted his mother to spit it all out. This had to be God answering her prayers!

"The movie they want to do is about . . ." Sandy held her arms out. "Are you ready? Your grandfather! Gramps! When he was young!"

"Are you kidding me?"

"No! Someone found your grandma's book on when they started out tent preaching. And the man even wants your father to play Nathaniel when he's older! Don't you see what a wonderful opportunity this is now? I'm so excited!"

"Wow! Out of sight! It's over the moon!" Hannah couldn't contain herself. This would definitely delay any plan to cross the Atlantic! At least California was in the United States!

Praise the Lord! He was so wonderful! "Think about it, David! This is awesome! It's perfect! It's Hollywood, for crying out loud! The movies! The money!" She faced Sandy. "Did the man mention how much?"

"They'll fly you two out and pay five thousand just for the screen test! After that . . ." She cleared her throat and turned serious. "Our agent says the five is pretty standard, and he'll make sure we're treated right."

"Me? I'll get to go, too?"

"Well, I sure don't know why not."

"Ladies." David stood and backed toward the front door, as if maybe he considered actually running away or something as stupid. "I'm going to repeat myself. Not interested. Matter of fact, I've already written Bishop Bass, asking what Hannah and I needed to do so we could go to Africa this summer."

"No." Tears welled. Hannah's heart ached. "Come on, baby!" Her voice trailed. "You can't . . ."

As much as David might want to tell her he'd stay, he couldn't.

"Please. Both of you sit down."

Hannah glared, wiped her cheeks, then put on her pouty face. Such a contradiction. And his mother's expression offered no support either. Dad remained quiet and appeared relieved.

"Come on. Please. Sit down now. I listened to you, and you can give me a turn. There's something I want to say."

Both complied, but obviously, neither relished his request or what they thought he had to announce. He didn't much expect them to be happy about it.

A chill nipped him. He moved closer to the fire. "Remember at Gramp's funeral when Miss Winnie gave me the handbook, she said he told her I'd need it when we got back from Africa."

"That doesn't mean anything. You can go after the movie's over."

"Mother." He hiked an eyebrow until she looked away and scooted back deeper into the sofa. "Then at the camp meeting, on the last night after most everyone was gone, the old man with the drum suddenly stood in front of me, holding two wads of cash. One he said to give to Hannah, the other he said to give to Mike when I saw him."

His father opened his mouth then closed it without saying anything. He smiled.

"You needing to say something, Dad?"

"Oh, just thinking about that story when I was five. You remember it?" No one seemed to, and David had no idea which story he referred to. Dad laughed. "The one about going to the store alone when I wanted a grape soda?"

"Oh yeah, that one." His mother nodded.

"Me, too. You and Gramps have told it plenty."

"Well . . . the old man I saw at the store that morning and then again when the little crippled girl in the wagon got healed . . . He's the same one—that man with the drum who gave you the cash."

"Aww, Dad." Hannah turned in her seat. "How could that be? That drummer danced all around and played for hours. The man was spry. He couldn't be over fifty . . . sixty at the most. And I've heard that story, too. Wasn't that guy already pretty old when you were five?"

"Yes, ma'am, that's correct. My mother always thought he was an angel God sent to protect me. I've wondered over the years, but when I saw him the other night. I knew it was him, beating that drum. It convinced me."

"That he's an angel? Really?"

"Sure. The Apostle Paul said we better be kind to strangers 'cause we might be entertaining angels unaware."

Considering the revelation, David waited, but no one said more.

"So, here's the deal. Three times now I've either dreamed or had a vision of seeing a wheel within a wheel—somewhat like Ezekiel's vision, but in my rendition, the wheels are people.

"The outer circle is made up mostly of men with some older boys, and they're all walking in one direction, praying . . . some in the spirit and some with understanding.

"The inner wheel is mostly women and older girls, singing praises and worshiping God. They're walking the other direction around the hub. It's made up of older men and women, and they're interceding. Some in chairs, on their knees, and others prostrate."

"Oh, David," Hannah whispered.

They all stared.

"The last time I saw the vision was on the day I wrote the bishop, but with one difference. The majority of the wheel's folks were black."

"David! No! Oh, God . . ."

Chapter Twenty-four

He had a love-hate relationship with putting seed in the ground. David loved the harvest, but the process took too long coming, plus no one could control what kind of harvest a body would have.

A farmer could do everything just right, but still . . . too little rain at the time it's needed, turns what once looked like might be a bumper crop into a bust, ending up middling at best.

To his surprise, on the Saturday he and PawPaw got the last block planted, a letter with a name he didn't recognize, and a strange Oklahoma return address waited on the kitchen table at his spot.

"That came for you today, Son." MawMaw wiped her hands on her apron then took to putting the plates out. "Is it one of your school friends from ORU?"

"No, ma'am. Don't know the guy." He tore the envelope's end off then pulled out the single sheet of notebook paper.

> Hey preacher man,
> Got your name from Judy Miller. Case you don't remember her, she's the gal I was with the first night we met. I'm the cowboy that beat you up at the park. Anyway, I wrecked my truck. The thing burnt up, but the Lord spared me. Got my eyebrows almost singed clean off, and broke my leg, but the wreck's why I got saved.

> I's laying up sober in that hospital bed, when the bishop came by—Bass, you know him, right? Anyway—he showed up to visit the guy in the next bed. For some reason, he stopped on his way out, turned smooth around, and stared at me. At first, it made me mad, but something came over me, and I asked him where his church was.
> Well, he told me, but didn't stay long. Once I got out of there, I got Judy to take me. Not at all the thing I would have ever done but for that crash. Did I tell you it totaled my truck? But hey, how's that compare with eternal life? Praise God, I got saved that very day.
> I want to ask you to forgive me for beating you up, Buddy.

That was fun. Of course, the cowboy had no idea that was David's father's nickname. He scanned the rest of the letter.

> Your new brother in Christ,
> Gage Axel
> P.S. Judy wrote this for me. I didn't get much schooling past the fifth grade.

"That's sweet of him, isn't it? But when did you get beat up, dear? I never heard anything about that."

David glanced over his shoulder.

MawMaw stood behind him.

"You sure? Didn't I tell you that story?"

"No, sir. I don't believe you did because I sure think I would definitely remember that."

Maybe he hadn't. What grandmother wanted to hear about her baby boy getting whipped? While she finished getting supper set out, he told how the incident went down.

Even added the vision he'd had about seeing the man's truck crash and burn. Someone else might think he was bragging on himself, but not MawMaw.

She kissed his cheek. "I love you."

"I love you, too, MawMaw."

"Please don't be letting folks knock you around like that again though. A body has the right to defend himself."

The Scripture on turning the other cheek came to mind, but it wasn't his place to lecture the lady who'd raised him. "I'll keep that in mind."

"Good. Get your PawPaw now, would you? Tell him supper's ready."

Between the last roll and the first scoop of ice cream on his oversized chunk of chocolate cake, the man most folks called Mister John pointed his spoon at David.

"Listen, I know you'd rather go to Pine Bluff, but could you bring Hannah to church here tomorrow? Your MawMaw and I have something we want to discuss—with the both of you."

"Yes, sir, sure. We can do that." David knew better than to question PawPaw about what he wanted to talk about. "I'll call Dad after a bit. Let him know he'll have to lead his own singing in the morning." He grinned and winked.

"Good. Not like he can't carry a tune."

Next morning, Hannah stole her kiss on the way by as her love held the door for her, then snagged another one when he slid in behind the wheel. "Still no idea what PawPaw wants to talk about?"

"No, but I'm figuring they're taking their shot at getting us to wait."

"So, it's a wasted trip, right?"

"Yes, ma'am. Lord willing and the creek don't rise, we'll tie the knot this June."

"Good." She snuggled in tight next to him and enjoyed the ride. The Church of Christ wasn't bad, but it was like all the same old songs sung and the same salvation sermon preached every time she went . . . and she'd been saved for years.

John David's Calling

Exactly like she figured, but she took the bad with the good. It only lasted an hour. Then she helped MawMaw get the roast and all its trimmings on the table. She loved the old dear, even more though, she loved her cooking.

Bless God, no one had ever put a gun to her head and made her tell her mother who was the best in the kitchen.

Like every other time her feet found themselves under Miranda Harris's table, Hannah ate too much. But how could she not?

Why, it would be downright rude not to have two dips on her cobbler. She only thought she'd been doing good . . . then the old dear brought out the steaming hot panful of peachy goodness and asked her to fetch the vanilla ice cream.

So delicious! She daubed her lips then folded her napkin, but before she could get to her feet to help with the dishes, PawPaw held his hand out and jumped up.

"Nope. Not today, young lady. Miranda and I'll clear the table. You kids stay put. There's something we want to show you."

Hannah looked to David. He appeared as shocked. As many times as she'd eaten there over the years, that certainly never happened before. But hey, it was their house.

Real quick, PawPaw retrieved a manila folder from off the top of the ice box then sat back down. "Now I had Harvey draw this up, so it's all legal. No one can say anything about it. You both need to sign on the dotted line, and it's a done deal."

He unfolded a stapled legal-sized document that looked to have at least three pages.

"This is a ten-year lease on the farmland with an option to buy it at today's price any time during the term of the lease then another option to continue the lease for another ten years. So you don't have to decide that right now."

"But PawPaw—"

He held his hand up. "Your MawMaw and I'll supply the machinery in working order, pay for the seed and fertilizer, and your part is all the work." The man who'd raised him stood straight and tall then plopped the folder and its contents on the table in front of him. "We'll split fifty-fifty."

Hannah scooted over to read the paper over David's arm. After a bit, her sweetheart folded the papers again, put them back in their folder, then slid it—pushing with one finger—toward his grandfather, remaining silent.

MawMaw smiled. "We started putting a few dollars back every month right after you were born. Did the same with Sarah. And Cody, too, once he was in the family. It's a right smart amount."

"We gave Cody his already. And you and Hannah will be getting yours on your wedding day."

Were those tears in David's eyes? She couldn't tell for sure, but hers sure were misty. How sweet they were! And surely the lease would keep him right there in Burnet County. Maybe he'd even reconsider the movie deal.

"You know the river property."

David looked to his grandfather. "Yes, sir."

"We plan on splitting that between you and your cousins. We figure we'd give you first pick."

MawMaw rose, pushing herself up from the table, and retrieved a Big Chief tablet from atop the ice box. It looked a hundred years old. She placed it in front of David, talking all along.

"When John and I married, we drew up the plans together for this house." He took her seat again. "Built our bedroom and kitchen first, then kept adding on the rest as we could over the years."

"Best of times . . . building this place." PawPaw laughed. "If you want, you're welcomed to use our plans, and you'll have enough money to get your place started. We figure you'd want to build over the grape arbor."

"It's beautiful there."

"There's a great view of the river, and . . ." He shrugged. "It's where I'd build if I was you, but you can pick any part of the land."

"The whole of it is three hundred and seven acres, but we figured with the natural breaks, it would best be split ninety-eight, a hundred and four, and a hundred and five."

For a minute, no one said anything. MawMaw rubbed her hands together. "So what do you think, Son?" She faced her. "And you, Hannah. This is your life, too, you know."

She faced her love. "What do we think?"

"Oh, MawMaw." David looked from his grandmother to his PawPaw. The look on the old man's face told it all—so proud of himself. Like he'd just played the trump card. Should he tell them his heart right out? He turned toward his intended.

"Have I ever taken you up to the river property?"

"I guess not." She stood. "How about we go see it right after we finish cleaning up?"

"Oh no, dear." MawMaw jumped to her feet. "You two go on. John will help me."

"Yes, go on. Not like I've never dried a dish. We can talk more later."

David swallowed the chuckle. Anyone who knew John Harris knew he hated KP. Claimed he got more than his share in France fighting the Great War.

"Okay." He stood and held his hand toward Hannah. "If you insist."

Though he gave her every opportunity to procure her presumed-stolen kiss on her way into the Ford, she didn't. He shrugged on his way around its front. Once he got in too, he looked over and brushed her hair back, leaving his hand on the back of her head.

Pulling her face toward his, he got his own sweet smooch, not a peck on the cheek.

"Umm, I love you, dear David." She snuggled into his shoulder. The engine roared to life. "What do you think? Are you wanting to be a farmer? Do you really think we can make a living off crops?"

"Sure. They have all these years."

She scooted away and faced him. "Seems to me, the deal they're offering—all the equipment and seed and fertilizer. It's way more than generous."

"Oh yeah, plenty fair."

"Plus, with you doing revivals, and a few television shows now and then . . . Seems to me like we could do great. Sure sounds like the Lord to me."

"Maybe."

She nudged him. "What's that supposed to mean?"

"That I'll have to pray about it."

The rest of the way, she talked like his grandparents' plan was a done deal. That he'd forget all about going to Africa. Except he couldn't. Not with the vision the Lord had been showing him.

Even without him asking, Hannah scooted over as he slowed down. She jumped out and opened the gate, waited until he pulled onto the river property, then closed it. Hopping back in, she pointed at a fat heifer.

"I didn't know PawPaw had cows."

"He doesn't, it's Uncle James's. He has the three hundred acres next to PawPaw's and moves some of his yearlings over here every year after they're weaned."

"Aww, poor babies."

"What are you talking about? They're plenty big enough, and the mamas need the time to fatten up before they deliver their next calf."

She turned, getting on her knees in the seat, then hovered there over him for a minute. Searching his eyes for more than a few breaths, she kissed him before drawing close and grinned.

"So, are you going to fatten me up between babies?"

"Mercy, Hannah Let's not be talking babies right this minute."

"Oh? Why not?"

"I'll tell you after we're married."

She poked his ribs. "You buzzard. You know I hate that. You'll wind up talking the whole night through on our honeymoon night, telling me all the things you've promised to fill me in on."

Her eyes twinkled, and she whirled back into her seat properly. "After we're married, my eye."

Oh, how he hated waiting even another day. But wait he would. The thought of displeasing the Lord trumped any fleshly desires.

Knowing his parents' story made him all the more determined to be obedient to God's Word but didn't make it any easier.

He rounded the last corner and threw a nod to his left. "Right down there's the arbor. You can see the river in a minute."

She gasped then grinned. "Wow, it's awesome. Where would we build?"

Hannah took his hand and walked up the hill with him a bit before he turned and faced the river. He spread his arms out to his sides. "Put the house right here. Set the barn back a ways." He jerked his thumb over his shoulder but didn't look.

She twirled around then hugged him. "It's wonderful! Perfectly beautiful! Do you think we could really have it ready by June? I'd definitely adore to have you carry me over the threshold here."

"Whoa! Not so fast, my love. They said we get the money at our wedding. And MawMaw's 'right smart' could be only a few thousand."

"But PawPaw said it would be enough to get started. They'd give it to us early if we asked. I say let's get started."

"Hannah, he hasn't built a house in years. Pre-war prices

and what things cost now are way different."

"So? He knows so much about so many things, he knows what he's talking about. Why are you stalling? Please do not tell me that you're still thinking about going to Africa. There's no need."

"You don't think so, huh?"

"You can support us right here, and we can build our house and start our family." She stared at the river and crossed her arms over her chest. "You aren't, are you? Tell me you're not."

He clammed up and only offered a slight shoulder hike.

"Oh David! Come on. No. I don't want to go to Africa. Have you even looked up anything about the country? It's probably ten times hotter than Texas! I hate the heat! You know that."

"Nigeria is tropical, Hannah. The temperatures stay in the seventies and eighties. February is the hottest month and rarely hits ninety. Texas is way hotter."

"Oh. Well." She put her pout on. "So that's that! It's still halfway around the world, and don't forget the cannibals!" She traced her index finger on his chest.

"Come on. Let's build our home and raise our babies where their grandparents can be a part of their lives. Isn't that important to you at all? Besides . . ."

A shrill, distant cry stopped her cold.

"What was that?" She looked around.

"What was what?" He offered a bigger shrug.

"Maaamaaa."

Turning in a complete circle then taking a step or two to the sound he evidently didn't hear, she looked back. "I think . . . it's a baby."

"Like a calf, maybe?"

"No, dork. A human baby. Don't you hear the poor thing? She's calling for her mama!"

"No, I don't. If you hear it again, close your eyes, and point the direction it's coming from."

Twice more, she heard the child, but even with David

helping her search, neither found a baby or hurt animal or anything, but it definitely bothered her a lot. Would her beloved think she was acting batty?

Hearing sounds . . . What in the world?

She joined him at the Ford. "So you think I'm crazy! Hearing things! I'm telling you, David. I know what I heard!"

"You're not crazy. I'm thinking it could be the Lord."

"Why in the world would He do that? Maybe you're the crazy one!"

"I don't know. I said could be. But I don't believe there's a kid out there."

She wanted to talk about her future but he'd promised to pray about leasing the farm land, and right now she had to be happy with that.

Oh, Lord, give me the desires of my heart.

Chapter Twenty-five

Truth be known, Hannah would rather forget school. She had a wedding to plan. Besides, when would she ever need to know what color of hair Christopher Columbus had?

Stupid test. She hated history. But her mother insisted she finish the eleventh grade. Some day she might want to go back? Was Mama bonkers? In the end, Hannah stopped arguing.

Some people were so obstinate.

Finally, the bell rang, bringing Monday's school day to an end. How many more would she be required to endure? She ought to count them, figure it out and mark them off, but then knowing might make it worse.

Gathering her things, she headed toward the bicycle rack. Shame she and her mother had to share a car. But the greater humiliation—being a junior—was the Rambler sitting in the driveway at home all day.

What a waste.

Sit at school all day long or at home? What did it matter to her mother? Wasn't like Daddy couldn't run home if Mis'ess Stubborn needed to go somewhere.

Turning the corner, she stopped in her tracks.

What happened to her Schwinn? It wasn't where she'd left

John David's Calling

it that morning. Blowing out all her breath, she fumed. The florist expected her in fifteen minutes to discuss her wedding flowers!

Then she needed to stop by the five and dime and get poster board for the project due tomorrow. "Arggh! What snot-nosed brat went joy riding now?"

To walk meant everything would take so much longer, and she had so much to get done! The day was going all wrong!

A hand touched her shoulder. "It was me, but my nose is dry."

She twirled.

David grinned.

"Why'd you steal my ride, bum?"

"I didn't steal it." He nodded toward the street. "I loaded it into the Ford's trunk. Figured you'd rather come with me."

The day suddenly looked up. "Well actually, you'll have to come with me first, and I'm so glad because you can help me decide."

"Where's that?"

"The florist. I have an appointment in fifteen minutes."

"How long will it take?"

"I don't think too long, but I don't know for sure. I've never ordered flowers for my wedding before." She laid her head on his chest. "I love you. Thank you for coming to get me." She pulled back. "How come you aren't working?"

"Finished already. Got my eight hours in about an hour ago."

"Oh." She slipped her hand into his and he walked her toward the car. "What time did you start?"

"Six."

"Mercy. Isn't it still dark then?" She loved the man beyond belief. Him getting up at the crack of dawn so he could pick her up from school. He held her door for her. She grabbed her kiss on the way in then scooted to her place in the middle.

"Want anything from the Dairy Queen?"

"That'd be great, but after. Then we can take my bike home

so, I can tell Mom. But I need to stop by Woolworth's for a second to grab a poster board. You can help me with my English project tonight?"

"Oh, yes, because that's what I graduated to do." He grinned.

A Dr Pepper frosted was her favorite, and he ordered a plain old vanilla shake, so boring, but hey! To each their own. "So, have you prayed about leasing PawPaw's farm land?"

"Some."

"Well?" She paused but he offered nothing. "What did the Lord say? I could scale the wedding way back. Daddy's giving me five hundred dollars. Nothing says we couldn't use part of that money on the house."

"No. Don't cut any corners. It's your big day."

"Our big day. But you didn't answer my question. What about the deal?"

"Nothing yet. How about you cutting class Friday?"

"Don't see why not. Mama said as long as I stay on the honor roll, I can stay out as much as I want. I don't see why she makes me go at all." She shook her head. Anyway, why do you want me to cut Friday? What's up?"

"We need to go to Austin and apply for our passports."

The first thing that popped into her mind was throwing her frosted DP on him, but she resisted. "Passports? What do we need those for?" Her back stiffened board straight. "What's your problem? I do not want to go to Africa!"

"Getting passports doesn't mean we're going. They take time though."

Scooting to her window, she stared at the town she loved. He was bent on taking her away from it, and her mother and all their friends and family. And what for?

"You just said you haven't heard anything from God about the farm land, so why are you barreling ahead with this fantasy of Mike's to get you over there?"

"I'm not barreling. Only taking measures to be prepared."

"I don't want to go halfway around the world!"

"Baby, I'm not saying we are, but if we do, we'll need passports. They take about six weeks, so—"

"So what?"

"We can't go if we aren't prepared. You can think on it. Hey, there's a movie I want to see."

"What movie?"

"*M*A*S*H*, I'm hearing it's great. It's playing in Austin."

She wrinkled her nose and turned it up with her best yuck expression. "Isn't that about the Korean War?"

"Well, in a way, but not really. I heard it's a comedy. So you want to go?"

"Okay, fine." It'd be better than sitting all day in school. "As long as nothing is settled."

What a wonderful Friday, spending the whole day and evening with her handsome and charming David. The movie was nothing like she'd imagined.

The little bit of war stuff couldn't begin to outweigh the humor. She laughed the whole way through. Poor Hot Lips. But Major Burns did get his comeuppance, and she liked that.

And so . . . she applied, and David paid for her passport. It didn't mean anything though. Maybe they'd go to Puerta Vallarta for their honeymoon. Did you need a passport for Mexico?

Or since they were good for ten years, she might talk him into a trip to England. That would be a wonderful fifth anniversary trip. Or, whatever—except not Africa—they would be good for ten years, so plenty of time to plan a nice trip.

Didn't mean a thing.

That night, snuggling down into her pillow, she dreamed of one day actually sharing her bed with her beloved. She couldn't wait.

If he took her to Africa, they'd probably be on a cot—separate cots! The passport didn't mean a thing. She still hung onto that thought, but mentally ran her wedding checklist and waited for sleep.

"Maaamaaa!!!!"

In the peripheral of her conscious, the voice sounded familiar. She rolled over, reached across to David's cot, and touched his shoulder. "It's your turn."

"What?" One eye opened a quarter.

"The baby. She wants her daddy."

"Maamaa! Daaaaa!!!!"

"See?" She pushed his cot, jostling him. "Get up."

Just as the fog rolled in, he sat then stood. She pulled the sheet up over her shoulder, turned away from him, and snuggled in tight, waiting. But after too long, David hadn't returned. Hadn't brought the baby to her. She sat up.

The fog had grown so thick, she could barely see her hand in front of her face. How strange. She grabbed her housecoat and slipped off her cot.

Instead of her sandals being where they belonged, her feet sank into a swampy mess all the way up to her waist. She squinted into the darkness, and her heart beat all the harder. There had to be huge snakes and alligators in the swamp.

"David! Help me!"

"We're over here. Follow the sound of my voice."

She sloshed toward him, each step more difficult than the last.

"That's good. I can see you now, barely."

"Mama, hurry."

The swamp's muddy bottom sucked her feet down. She couldn't move. "I'm trapped, David. Help me." Fear tightened its grip and choked her.

A splash sounded, then suddenly, he stood before her in the fog. So dark and foggy, He held a toddler. The little girl held her arms toward her. "Mama."

She reached for the baby, but David and the child disappeared. Hannah sat up in bed, then frantically patted the covers, but it was her bed . . . in her room . . . not a cot. And no one was there—but it had been so real.

A dream.

Praise the Lord. It was only a dream.

But ooo, what a nightmare!

David loved spring, but as the sprouts grew in his grandfather's fields, so did his apprehension. He'd made up his mind, knew what he had to do, but hadn't shared his decision with anyone. Hannah had to be first.

No one could accuse him of relishing that conversation. No doubt an argument would ensue. Telling his parents and grandparents loomed almost as dreadful.

Too many times to count, he'd asked the Lord to strengthen him, then after a wonderful day in Austin, capped by watching George C. Scott's *Patton*, he could delay no more.

Time to face the music. He prayed God's Holy Spirit to go before him, but he couldn't wait any longer. Hannah's mother. She'd take to flicking the porch light any minute.

For the fiftieth time, he kissed her—or was it ten times that number? —then leaned back. "Baby, look at me."

She opened her eyes. "Yes."

"I've decided about Africa."

Scooting back halfway to her door, she stared. "You've decided all by yourself? Without me?"

"Well . . . uh . . . yeah, I guess so."

"What does that mean? You guess so. I do not want to go, David. I've told you that, and now you're telling me you've decided—for both of us—like you're the king or something. It's my life, too, you know."

"I do know, baby, but—"

"But what? What part of 'I don't want to go' do you not get? So you're just going to forget about PawPaw's offer? Tell him no?"

"No, only postponing, He'll wait two years. I mean he probably won't be happy about it."

"No one is going to be happy about you going half way

around the world for two days! Much less two years!"

"I wrote Bishop Bass like a week ago. It's a done deal."

Pushing herself away from him, she opened her door. "Creep! What a creep! I can't believe you're doing this to us. Leaving me! Not marrying me!" She jumped out, still screaming hysterically. "I've already spent all that money Daddy gave me! And you're leaving me! I can't believe you!" She ran toward the house.

"Mercy." He jumped out, but she never stopped or even looked back. He waited until her bedroom light came on upstairs, but she didn't come to the window to peek out or blow him a kiss.

Well, that didn't go well.

Great! Had he ruined his life?

He looked skyward. "Oh, Lord! I know it was You, wasn't it? Are You planning on me being like Paul? Then why have You let me love her all these years? Is giving her up some kind of test?"

Tears welled, but he blinked them away. She loved him, and . . .

And what?

Why shouldn't she want to get married and go with him? Had he even told her he wouldn't leave until after the wedding she'd been working so hard on? Thinking about it, he didn't think so. He'd meant to.

Mercy, he had it all planned out down to the very word, but then . . . nothing went right. Nothing like it was supposed to.

She loved him and no other.

But did she love her parents more?

Did South Texas have such a hold on her? Couldn't she bear the thought of leaving?

Her light went off.

Mercy. Nothing to do but go home.

The die was cast, but at what price?

Could he afford to pay?

John David's Calling

When the Ford came to life, Hannah eased to the window and peeked out the curtain, just barely. She didn't want to get caught. She looked around the window frame and watched his taillights bounce out her drive.

How could he?

Was he calling off the wedding? Did he plan on leaving before it?

He wouldn't dare.

What would she do?

Oh! What a rat fink. She could cancel the flowers and the cake. Photographer, too. But all that money put out on invitations and her dress . . . and her veil. He couldn't be thinking of just chunking it away.

Like one of his nasty cigarette butts. She could tell his MawMaw that he smoked. It'd serve him right . . .

A heavy sigh hurried out in a huff. That'd only hurt a dear, sweet lady. She couldn't do that.

Hmm, come to think of it . . . of late . . . she hadn't smelled any tobacco on him. Had he quit?

Humph! Quit smoking. Quit thinking right. Quit caring about her. That was for sure.

Why was he doing this?

Never, never, never! She should never have agreed to a stupid passport.

Wait! He planned on her going, or why wouldn't he have just snuck off and gotten himself one? He thought she'd go. At least he hadn't planned to cancel the wedding . . . which meant he expected her to go. Well . . .

She threw herself across her bed. Anger turned to sorrow then morphed into tears.

"Why, Lord?" She boohooed. "Why . . ." She sniffed and swiped her cheek. "is he being so . . ." Three hard sobs racked her body. "Mean!"

She wept. There was no way she was going to Nigeria! What would he say to that?

What would she? Her parents. MawMaw and PawPaw. His parents? Sometime, she must have fallen off to sleep. Because when she opened her eyes . . . Had she really heard that? Yes. She was pretty sure.

Calling her ears to attention, she closed her eyes to listen as hard as she could, tilting her head one way then another Nothing though. She closed her eyes. Her heartrate slowed again, and she fell into the darkness again.

"Maaama."

That time, Hannah sat up in bed. Who was that? Or what?

But of course, the sound didn't repeat itself.

Great. David was leaving and taking away any chance she had of being a mother with him to Africa. She hated him. She rocked back and forth in the bed, hugging her pillow.

A lone tear rolled down her cheek. How could she bear him being gone?

Could she have a life without the big lug?

He had to be the daddy of her babies. Only him. He'd be the best daddy in the world. She wiped both cheeks.

Her head fell forward with her chin on her chest. She had to figure something out, come up with a way to make him see the light. She couldn't go to the Dark Continent. Why would anyone want to?

But she didn't hate him, not really. Oh, she hated what he was doing plenty . . . but she couldn't live without him. That was truth.

A scream died in her throat. Last thing she needed was for Daddy to come running.

Into the wee hours of morning, she plotted and planned, figured and fanned every spark that might burst into a good idea at any time. But no. Nary had a idea presented itself. She scoffed. She just couldn't decide. The last thought before she finally dozed off was . . . did she hate him or love him the most?

Chapter Twenty-six

"*Sweetheart? Wake up. David's here.*"

"What?"

"You slept late, it's past nine, and David's here. He says you two were going shopping today."

Hannah sat up. "Tell him . . ." What she thought to say died on her tongue. "Tell him I'll be down when I'm down."

Her mother sat on the bed. "Did you two have a fuss last night?"

"You could say that, but I'd call it worse than a fuss."

"I thought I heard you crying. Not to ruin his surprise, but he's got a present for you."

She wiped sleep and dried tears from her eyes then continued pushing her hair back and massaging her temples. Her head hurt, and groggy was too good a word for her condition. "What is it?"

A scoff called her to give her mother a look. She grinned. "I'm not telling you that. I probably already said too much. You'll just have to come see." Mama nodded toward the bedside table. "I brought a cup of coffee milk."

"Two sugars?"

"Of course. Now hurry up. Don't keep him waiting too long."

Though Hannah nodded, she refused to shake a leg or light

any fire under or any other stupid metaphor for hustling. She'd take her sweet time, and he could stay or not. Didn't matter to her. Except . . . it did.

No records were in jeopardy, but she definitely didn't slow walk him. What if he'd seen the light and changed his mind? That's what she hoped for—to change his mind, not run him off.

"I don't remember any plans for today." She stopped at the kitchen's doorway. "What are we shopping for?"

"You said last night we still needed some things for the wedding." He grinned. "But if you'd rather, we can go to the movies instead."

"Where's my present? Mom said you brought me something."

A glance at her mother got him a little I'm-sorry shrug, but his smile increased. "In the living room."

Strolling right past, she neither touched him nor offered a smile. At the end of the hall, she came to an abrupt halt. Sitting on the couch was a stupid, dumb teddy bear even bigger than the one he'd gotten her before.

What did he think she was going to do with the giant space-taker-upper? Grrr. He never thought about putting any thought into her gifts, just grabbed whatever.

And now she had two useless dust gatherers.

It did hold a big sign that said, 'I Love Hannah Claire.'

The idiot forest creature did nothing to spare him her wrath. She never doubted his love, well, maybe she did, but down deep, knew that truth.

Now if the sign had added, so I won't go to Africa . . . then she couldn't stay mad at him. She turned. He stood right behind her.

"Will you forgive me?"

Hope caused her heart to leap. "For what?"

"Not discussing things with you before I wrote Bishop Bass."

Mid-leap, the thumper fell flat. "Only that?"

"I can't be disobedient to God, Hannah, so . . ." He shrugged. "Afraid so. Only that. Yes. Is there something else I need forgiveness for I'm not seeing? Something that doesn't mean being disobedient to God?"

How could she dare ask him to disobey the Lord?

"I guess not."

She thought of saying something about her idea that Mike was the one pulling his heart to the far side of the world with all his stories, not God, but that'd sound like telling him he didn't know God's voice when she knew good and well, he did.

"So . . . I forgive you."

"Thank you."

"Because I have to, but . . ." She turned and headed toward the front door. "Come on, let's go somewhere. We need to talk." She hollered over her shoulder on her way out. "We're gone, Mama."

Instead of shopping, she wanted David to take her to the park. Though not much compared to any big city standards, it had an asphalt basketball court, a merry-go-round she loved as a little girl, and a pair of heavy-duty swings.

It even had a new gravel parking lot, too. All the way, she stayed on her side, staring out the window.

Silence reigned in the confined space. Once he killed the Ford's engine, she got out without waiting on him and headed to the swings.

Settling down onto the wide wooden plank, she walked it back then lifted her legs, leaning until her hair almost touched the ground. He got there in time to push her with both hands on either side of the board.

Three more times he hefted her until she soared, then walked around to the front. She swung forward toward him. "So let's talk, David. Why'd you do it?"

"Do what?"

Swinging away, she closed her eyes and shook her head until reaching the apex and coming forward again. "Come on, David. You are not dense. Why'd you agree to go to Africa?"

"Well, uh . . ." Wouldn't a cigarette be grand about now? "There was Miss Wynona saying my grandfather told her I'd need his handbook when I got back—from Africa—number one. Two, that old man giving me the money for Mike. Three, four, five, the visions, and six, the knowing in my heart that's only gotten stronger by the day."

He waited until the swing brought her close again. "I know in my knower that I've been called to the mission field."

"So what about us? Has He said anything about us lately? And how come do you suppose the Lord hasn't said one little word to me about Africa?"

"I don't know, baby. He grabbed the chain on one side and she jerked around to a halt.

"I hate the very thought of going without you, but I'll understand if you don't want to go. It's just . . . to my way of thinking, I have no choice. I must be obedient to what He's telling me."

"So that's settled." She stared at the ground. "You're going with or without me?"

"I have to."

"What about our wedding?"

"If you don't go, we'll postpone it. You already have your dress, and believe you me, it will not go to waste, Hannah. I've only committed for two years."

"Only?" She rose from the swing and headed for the Ford. "Only two years? Sounds like forever to me."

He followed. "It'll pass so quickly. Two years is nothing. You could even finish school and maybe get a year of college in."

She reached the car and opened her own door before facing him. "I don't want to finish school! And I never wanted to go to college. Are you crazy?" She fell inside and slammed her door.

Why did she have to make this so hard? With a deep, cleansing breath, he walked around and slid under the wheel.

"Sweetheart. I'm not saying you have to go to school. I thought it might help keep you busy and hurry up time's passing."

"Well, it won't, and that isn't an option. Why can't we go ahead and get married now? Can't you wait that long to leave me?"

Her sharp words cut his heart. He never wanted to hurt her. "I don't think it would be right to get married now then me run off."

A gasp sucked all the air from the Ford. He swallowed. She exhaled.

Her eyes filled with tears, but the wetness didn't put out the fire in the windows of her soul. "So you're calling off the wedding. That's a done deal, too? Another decision you're making without discussing it with me?"

"Thought that's what we're doing."

"You're saying no wedding unless I go. I want to get married now. Like we've planned. Everything's arranged. Invitations are already mailed. You're not discussing that. You're saying unless I go, it's off?"

"I . . . uh—"

"Does that sound like a discussion to you? Does it? I still want the wedding! I don't care if you go off, at least we'd be married."

"What? And you'd stay with your parents until I got back?"

"Or get my own place. What would you care? You wouldn't be here."

"That's my point, Hannah. I wouldn't be here to keep you safe, be your husband. That's exactly why I think we should wait."

Staring at her hand, she clicked her nails against each other. "I don't want to go shopping for the wedding when it's still in the air . . . So if it isn't going to happen, let's just go to the movie."

"Sounds good."

"Yeah, maybe that'll take my mind off it. I'm so angry—so upset with you. But I don't want to be. And you know good and well I would never stand in the way of you being obedient to God. How could I?"

"I do."

"I'm just skeptical it's Him and not Mike and his dad. So what's showing? Do you know?"

"Nope. We can swing by."

Airport with Robert Stack turned out to be a hoot in his humble opinion. His love thought it more in the descriptive area of idiotic; had to be her overall mood, because with all that humor going on, she never even giggled.

Maybe a Dr Pepper frosted from the DQ would sweeten her up. One way or another something had to be determined.

At the Dairy Queen, he ordered a Hunger Buster combo and she had chili cheese fries with her favorite drink.

Leading him to a back booth, she slid in so he'd facing the door—always remembered after the first time he mentioned his preference to have the view of the door and the restaurant to protect her.

"So, we have to figure out what we're going to do, David. I have to cancel everything thirty days in advance or the financial penalty is substantial. I don't understand why we can't get married before you go. Explain that to me."

"The Bible says that when a man gets married he doesn't go off to war or anything for a year. It wouldn't be right to leave you six or seven weeks after we got married. What if you were pregnant?"

"All the better, I say." She swirled her straw around in the thick drink. "So, you aren't planning on leaving until sometime in August?"

"I'm not sure exactly yet, but yes. The bishop sends a container of supplies and food toward the end of every summer."

John David's Calling

"And so you're refusing to marry me unless I agree to go." The waitress came over with a tray, and Hannah waited until she left. "Sounds like blackmail to me."

"It's your choice. I guess I never thought you wouldn't come with me. Think of what an adventure it would be."

Tears welled in her eyes again. "I can't imagine anything good coming from it. And I never wanted to go to the mission field. I already told you about every year at Vacation Bible School." She ducked her chin a bit and looked him in the eye, sucking a straw full of her frosted.

"You did."

"What is so hard to understand then? I do not want to be a missionary! I didn't then, and I don't now."

"Hannah . . . why?"

"I was scared. I was nine years old. I didn't want to leave Mama and Daddy."

"You thought you'd have to go right then?"

"If He called me."

"Well, I do understand that. But now? You aren't nine anymore. So, then what . . . you want to cancel the wedding? Not cancel, but postpone?"

"No! We're getting married in June, Buster Brown."

"Then you'll . . . you're . . . coming with me?" He'd never expected so much favor.

"Yes. I don't want to, but yes. I choose to go with you as Mis'ess David Nightingale over staying here single and sad and depressed. I've dreamed of being your wife for so long." She picked up a fry and twirled it before popping it into her mouth.

She would go.

Praise the Lord. She agreed to go.

His breath came easy for the first time since he'd posted that letter to Bishop Bass. "That's wonderful."

"Is it?"

"Listen, baby, I hate the thought of leaving Texas, too. Our families, all our friends. But I know—Hannah, I know—the

Lord wants us to go. I won't kick against the pricks anymore." He chuckled. "I love you."

"Do you know her name? Has Mike told you about her?"

"Who?"

"The little girl."

"Okay, what are you talking about?"

"Remember that baby I heard calling up at the grape arbor?"

"I do."

"Well, I've been dreaming about her, too. She cries for her mama. In my dreams, it's the same call I heard that day. She was calling me Mama and you Da, and she's black. What do you think it means?

"I so dreaded it being true—that we were going, but . . . I admit, a part of me is excited." She reached across the table and took his hand.

"You didn't tell me."

"Because I didn't want it to be true! In the dream I had last night, you and she are in trouble. And I'm separated . . . I couldn't make my way to you. I never want to be apart from you.

"Wherever you are, that's where I want to be, so . . . Mister Smarty Pants, I guess we're going on that adventure." She rolled her eyes, obviously still not thrilled. "Africa, here we come."

"Praise the Lord!"

"Ack! I'm going to be a missionary. Doesn't God have such a sense of humor?"

Good thing Mis'ess Morrison had an itchy trigger finger with that porch light. Things were about to get serious when she took to flashing.

"One fine day." Leaning in her open door, she blew him one last kiss then ran inside.

The Monday following him revealing his and Hannah's plans to all the folks, like the Lord's timing was so perfect, a letter from Mike showed.

John David's Calling

Hey King,

I'm so looking forward to you and your bride being here. The work's born some fruit, but nothing like I want. I've decided to try a different approach and bought ten acres. We're getting it ready to plant. Dad's sending seeds and as much equipment as possible.

Water is a problem, so I've asked the Missionary Board (Dad's the chairman) to send drilling equipment and a hand pump.

Only electricity is by generator, and I don't want the garden to cost extra gasoline. Figure you being a farmer's grandson, this will be right up your alley. Gave me the idea—or was the Lord? Anyway, He confirmed it in the Word.

How can you tell someone, 'Be blessed!' and not feed them if they're hungry or give them water?

Wow, next time I see you, you're going to be a married man. Sounds wonderful. I've been spending some time with a lady doctor, but she's only here a few times a month. We write some, but mercy (hope you don't mind me using your word, I find it so appropriate), we're both committed to our work and that doesn't leave much time for anything else.

Pray for Mitch, man. Seems he's lost his faith. Went back to the States. Wired his father to send him money.

So is Churchill and your Hannah's cousin still stepping out?

And how's your dad liking pastoring a church?

Does everyone there hate me for luring you Into the missionary field?

Okay, well, that's all the news and questions I can think of, and it's getting late.

                        Love you brother!
                        Mike

Chapter Twenty-seven

Hannah loved her mother, but other than her intended, she didn't know anyone as stubborn. All her teachers knew she was getting married and would never ever darken the schoolhouse doors again.

But no, Mis'ess Morrison insisted she keep going and stay on the honor roll or no more taking days off.

Arrrgh!

So instead of doing what she wanted to—plan her wedding and trip to Africa, she had to crack her books. Oh well . . . days were passing fast, and soon enough the issue would be moot.

Praise the Lord her soon-to-be mother-in-love convinced David that jeans and a starched white shirt would absolutely not do. Nosiree! Tuxedos all around for the groomsmen and best man, with her beloved's similar but extra special.

Oh, if only she could hurry the days' hours! She was so ready to be Mis'ess John David Nightingale. She closed her eyes and imagined him standing at the front with his father and special friends on the right, and her bridesmaids and Jill on the left.

It'd be so perfect and beautiful.

"Class, time's up. Pass your test papers forward, please."

Hannah shook off her ruminations. She'd finished a quarter-hour ago, but could she turn her test in and leave? No.

Miss Spanish II forced her to sit there quiet as a mouse. The bell sounded.

Woohoo! Bless the Lord! Another day done. She grabbed her things and hurried to the door. Breaking free into the sunshine, she looked, and there he stood.

Her handsome Prince Charming with his dark hair, sweet baby blues, and trusty Ford sedan. Oh, how proud she was to call him her own! God had blessed her so!

And those suspenders she'd picked out for a surprise gift were so adorable on him.

She loved him so much and liked the car—not as much as the Camaro, even with its bucket seats—but sitting next to him, touching him shoulder to knee was worth giving the Z up. Shame the Ford couldn't be snazzier looking.

He held her door, and she double kissed him on her way in.

Once behind the wheel, he faced her. "How'd your test go?"

"*Muy bueno, pero . . .*" She laid her head on his shoulder.

"But what?"

"Well, if I'd known I was going to Africa, I could have taken Swahili. What good is Spanish going to do me? I'm so sick of school."

"No worries, my love. Nigeria was a British Colony and English is the official language of the country. Are we still on for tomorrow?"

"Yes, sir! I need time away from planning our special day! A whole day of fun with you. I'm almost getting to the point of being as sick of all the wedding hullabaloo as I am of school. I just want it all to be over."

"Sounds pretty good."

"I'll be Mis'ess Nightingale! Have I ever told you how much I love your name? Thank you for giving me your name!"

He grinned. "You're welcome."

"So, what do you have in mind for tomorrow?"

"I'd like to go Austin and check on some prices, then figured we could catch a movie."

"Prices on what?"

"Fencing, farm implements for a small tractor, maybe some hand tools."

"Boo! That doesn't sound like any fun. What for? You chose to wait on farming. In two years, I'm sure prices will change." She flipped on the radio. Simon and Garfunkel crooned "Like a Bridge Over Troubled Waters." She adjusted the volume. "I thought we were going to have a day off, a day of fun!"

"There's a Sears up the street from the lumber yard where I want to start."

"Good, you can drop me off. Is it that one where there's a K-Mart down from the Sears?"

"Think so."

"Good, I'll be there. Can we go early and have breakfast at that Cisco's place?"

"Sure."

"What movie do you want to see?"

"Thought we'd see *Paint Your Wagon*." He grinned. "It's supposed to be funny and a great love story."

"Who's in it?"

"Lee Marvin and Clint Eastwood."

"Oh, yeah, I'm so sure. It's got to be a western with those two."

"No, trust me. You'll like it."

"That's what you said about *Airplane*."

"*M*A*S*H*, too, though." He shrugged. "How about *Colossus* then, it's a sci-fi computer run amuck."

"How do you know all that stuff?"

"The newspaper."

"Oh." She exhaled. Did it really matter as long as she sat next to him in the dark? "Fine, you pick."

That evening—even before her mother went to flicking the light—he insisted she go inside.

Pouting, she scooted toward her door. "Why? What's wrong?"

John David's Calling

"You. Us! I can hardly stand it."

"Oh." She smiled. "I love you, and if you really want me to, I'll go."

"No, that isn't what I want, but yes, get your gorgeous, desirable self-inside. See you at six in the morning."

"Six?"

"Thought you wanted breakfast in Austin."

"Um . . . Eight? Maybe we could have brunch."

"Seven, and that's my final offer."

Blowing him a farewell kiss, she walked backwards toward the house, then turned and hurried up the porch steps. What a guy!

So good, so levelheaded; waiting a few more weeks was, of course, best. She thought back to when she ditched Chaperon Jill and took him up on the mountain . . . What a guy, indeed.

As planned, he showed bright and early for the trip to the Capital. She netted two sacks worth of goodies at Sears and K-Mart while he did his window shopping.

What good could come of him knowing what stuff costs in Texas when he had to buy it in Africa? Oh well, not really her concern.

If he and Mike wanted to have a big garden, fine with her. She loved gardening, canning, and even better, eating fresh vegetables.

Cisco's was a hoot, but the food didn't compare with the Bluebonnet Café. *Paint Your Wagon* turned out to be hilarious. She laughed until she embarrassed him. And how could anyone not love Whataburger?

Again, that night after a fabulous day, he sent her in early.

She loved it, loved him, and loved his integrity; such an honorable man.

Lord, make the days zoom by.

David, too, wanted his betrothal to end. She was driving him crazy. However, like the few fasts he'd endured, knowing the end from the beginning helped.

Hard work lessened his burning desire for her, but not by much. Definitely not enough. Well, maybe just enough. Praise the Lord. He loved everything about the girl. Beyond her appearance, she was such a class act.

Never had she embarrassed him. Quite the opposite, almost every time in her presence, she'd do something that made him proud.

Always helping the older ladies without being asked, she showed great respect to her elders and acted like a magnet to little children, too. They all loved her.

Though willing to laugh at herself, she sparkled and wherever she went, those around ended up laughing, too. Her intelligence was off the charts, yet the beauty remained so humble—as if she didn't even know it.

Then to top it off, his love smelled awesome even after a hard day's work. He loved that she never shied away from labor and stayed up with him though her strength kept her from accomplishing as much as him.

Then after cleaning up, she was such a picture of femininity.

David sighed.

To his surprise, the sun woke him that last morning in his grandparents' house. He halfway expected PawPaw to wake him, holding a dripping ice cube over his face just for old times' sake. But then that hadn't happened in years.

After counting his blessings for such a wonderful life and his soon-to-be wife, he found the old darlings in the kitchen.

"Morning, sweetheart." MawMaw jumped to her feet. "Ready for coffee?"

Slipping into his seat, he grinned. "Yes, ma'am." Her sweet nature was to serve.

How different would his life have been if she and PawPaw hadn't been willing to take him in? He never held it against his mother for letting them because he loved it there with them. PawPaw had definitely taught by example how to be a good man.

And he'd unquestionably been taught the Word at his church.

It sort of choked him up when she sat a steaming cup in front of him. "Now there's plenty of everything left, so you just let me know when you're ready, and I'll scramble you a pile of eggs."

He cleared his throat, pushing down the lump there and opened his eyes wider to absorb the extra wetness in them. "Yes, ma'am. Thank you, MawMaw. I sure do love you and appreciate everything you do."

PawPaw pulled what looked to be a folded check from his shirt pocket then slid it toward him. "We love you, too, Son. You've been such a gift. Always wanted a son—not that I didn't love my girls—but God sure did right by me, sending you."

He took the offering and unfolded it, eighty-six hundred and forty-four dollars. Mercy. The tears welled again, and that time rolled down his cheek. He'd never imagined. He looked at her then met his eyes. "Oh, no. This is too much."

MawMaw reached across the table and took his hand. "Why, you silly. Of course, it isn't. If I had to say, I wouldn't call it enough. That's been your money since the first dollar we put into your account."

"Oh, MawMaw."

"Now you got more than Cody. We had you longer, so there's no need to mention any amounts. It's yours all right, sweetheart. The Lord has blessed our cup, filled it to overflowing."

"Don't spend it all in one place."

Swiping at his cheeks, David blinked away the oncoming tears and looked to his PawPaw. The old man grinned. "Yes, sir. Thank you for everything you've done for me. Who knows if I'd even be alive if it wasn't for you two. I sure do love you."

Were those tears in crusty John Harris's eyes? David wasn't

sure, his were blurring so bad he could barely see.

Even though surprised by the amount of his check, he'd known it was coming. What awaited him at the church floored him. He'd never been in the Presbyterian Church building in downtown Marble Falls, but if he'd known.

How nice inside! He might have visited a time or two just for the pleasure of the stained-glass windows' beauty. How the sun shone through was breathtaking.

No wonder Hannah wanted to get married there. The way his love figured it, better than half the county had RSVP'd. Numbers held no bearing for him, and he appreciated all the details she'd seen to with all her preparations.

Nothing mattered to him that day except making her his own. The honeymoon suite he'd reserved in Austin was what interested him.

Thinking of little else as the day approached, after refusing the thoughts so often before that, he'd determined to steel himself not to rush her in any way after the nuptials.

The day belonged to her . . . her big day she'd planned for so long—she'd told him from the first wedding she'd attended as a ten-year-old. He wanted her to enjoy every second of it.

"Hold still, or I'll never get this tie right."

David focused on his mother then looked past her to his reflection in the mirror. "Mercy, the thing looks so straight a body could plum a house with it."

She backed up a step then hiked a shoulder. "Whatever." She smiled. "I sold your car, Son."

"'What?" For one instant, panic flooded him. But he'd just glanced out a side window in the nursery. "No, you didn't! It's outside getting all tricked out last time I looked. Everyone I knew from school is out there working on him. You did give me a start though."

"Not the Ford, honey." A folded piece of paper materialized in her hand. "We agreed on a price for the mansion, but they wanted the Rolls." She handed him the check. "This is yours."

Wow. "Ten thousand! Oh, Mom. Wow." He'd forgotten

she'd given him her first husband's car. How many hours had he spent play-driving the beauty? "You sure you don't need this to feed the money vultures?"

"No, no. We're fine, my sweet boy. The Lord gave us way more for Harry's house than I expected."

Mercy! He filled his lungs. The Lord was so good. Hannah was going to flip out. With his own savings, he might need two containers.

At last the day had arrived. Hannah thought so many times it never would.

Her heart brimmed to overflowing with pure bliss and love—for everyone. Her lace hanky, already stained with mascara smudges that would be under her eyes if precious MawMaw hadn't gifted her the treasure earlier.

Her mother's words, whispered into her ear in the dressing room, she'd never forget.

Then the look on her father's face bolstered her confidence that all was well. He wrapped his arm under hers and draped her hand to rest atop it.

The ascribed music signaled the procession to begin. Her maid of honor handed her bouquet over, and the mother of the flower girl gave last minute instructions and sent her down the aisle.

Mandy had flown in from Dalton and her son obviously needed some encouragement to follow.

Getting to walk on the petals finally did the trick, and the ring bearer walked ahead carrying his lacy pillow. "Turn those lights off. I can't see!"

The bridesmaids all giggled and Mandy turned to her, offering a shrug. Her soon-to-be half-sister-in-love had been a huge help and support since she arrived. That morning, she'd carried her to get a recorder to record the ceremony!

The thought had never even crossed Hannah's mind.

One by one, her attendants in summer peasant dresses of pastel dotted Swiss started down the aisle. She stood back to the side so no one would get a peek before it was time. Daddy kept patting her hand then wiping his eye.

Slightly shaking, he couldn't seem to take his eyes off her. Her heart beat faster when Jill, the last one left, and the ushers closed the doors.

Her father moved her into place as practiced at the rehearsal dinner the night before. And then the organist sat on the highly recognizable first chords of the wedding march announcing, 'Here Comes the Bride.'

The double doors opened, and Hannah gasped inside but smiled her biggest, happiest smile. It was perfect! Elegant! Exactly as she'd planned.

Those gathered to celebrate rose and faced the back of the sanctuary. Her daddy's shaking increased.

Squeezing his arm, she looked up. "We can do this. I love you, Daddy."

"Everything's so beautiful, but you most by far, my darling. This day has come too soon. I'm not ready to give you away."

"Sure you are. You adore my David almost as much as I do."

"That's true. God's good. Here we go." He stepped forward into the sea of faces.

Aware with only a peripheral vision, all her guests grinned ear to ear and blessed her as she strolled down the aisle on her father's arm. Her attention focused only on the handsome face of her husband-to-be.

How she adored him! His blue eyes sparkled, almost like in a cartoon. Ooowee, and did he look great in his tux.

At the first aisle, she stopped and first gave her mother a long-stemmed red rose then turned and presented one to Sandy with a quick hug and whispered love.

Then David came down.

Her father placed her hand in his and answered the age old

John David's Calling

who-gives-this-bride question with 'her mother and I,' then her beloved helped her up the few steps to the altar.

Her future father-in-law stood under an arch covered with greenery and her favorite flowers, cheerful daisies, holding an opened Bible.

All her dreams were about to come true.

In mere minutes, she would belong to David forever, and he would belong to her.

Though his best intentions not to rush her had been predetermined, as the reception went on and on and on and on—the unending greeting line, first dances, cutting cake, the throwing of the bouquet and garter, and more dancing—his resolve wavered.

She belonged to him, and he wanted so desperately to have her all to himself.

That reception business was the pits. Let them all party hearty as long as they wanted, but he and Hannah had a drive to Austin ahead.

Then just about the time—like Popeye—he'd had all he could stand, and he couldn't stand anymore, she appeared in street clothes. All the celebrants took to lining the way to the Ford on both sides, grabbing a silly little bag from the basket full of them.

Hannah and Jill had worked for days tying on the little flowers and hearts and ribbons. Such irrelevant traditions. Where did they all come from anyway? Maybe he'd look into that someday. She took his hand.

Or maybe not. Who cared? As soon as he reached the door, the crowd pelted him and his sweet bride with the rice. He picked up the pace to a jog, opened her door, and got her inside.

Almost there! He ran around and jumped in, gave her a kiss

and he was off.

At last!

Alone with his love.

Once out of sight, he pulled over onto the shoulder, stopped the car, and grabbed the door handle.

"What's wrong?"

"Nothing, I'm taking those clanging cans off."

"No!" She pulled him back in. "Why in the world would you do such a thing? How many times do friends tie cans on your car? Once. Once in a lifetime. Nosiree, don't you dare." She batted her lashes and smiled. "Please . . . come on! Let's cruise Main Street."

Oh no. She was certifiably bonkers. But he honored her request. She'd softened her please, so he turned around and headed downtown to drive by whoever wasn't at the wedding, he guessed.

Everyone he knew would still be there partying till midnight. He wanted to get to Austin with everything in him, but, of course, he wasn't getting away so easily.

The cans beat the road twice as noisily as the Ford's regular road song. They clanged all the way

"For how long?"

"Until they fall off." She snuggled into him, both arms wrapped around his. "Thank you, husband."

Chapter Twenty-eight

For a nano-second, David wondered about the strange bed, then the reality of where he was and who slept next to him came rushing in. The first morning with his babylove by his side had dawned.

What a night. Way beyond his expectations. Hannah snuggled in tight against his chest. One eye peeked opened.

"Good morning, Mister Nightingale."

"Yes, it certainly is! And a good morning to you, Mis'ess Nightingale."

She giggled. "We did it."

"Yes, we did." He kissed her lightly.

With a deep satisfied sigh, she grinned. "I love Love LOVE you."

"Um-hmm, I love you, too. So what do you want to do today?"

"Well, uh. . ." She gave him a wink.

"After that." He laughed. "We've got the room until noon, then we could go on to Dallas, or . . . oh wait. I have a surprise!" He scooted to the bed's edge and grabbed his wallet, retrieved the two checks and held them out. "Mother sold my car."

"Why? How are we getting to Tulsa?" She unfolded the two pieces of paper. "Oh my. Guess we could take a limousine." She fingered the checks. "Wow, David! We're rich." She arced her eyebrows. "I can't believe it! I never dreamed the Ford would be worth ten grand!"

"Not the Ford. My Rolls."

"Excuse me?" She cleared her throat. "You had a Rolls Royce?"

"I did." For the next few minutes, he told her the story. "I'd forgotten she'd given me Harry's car. Isn't God good?"

"Amen!"

Hannah sat up in bed. "Do you happen to know how much interest the Marble Falls First Federal bank is paying, because we might get a better deal in Dallas with so many people, there's probably more competition for customers. Do you think?"

"I have no idea. Why?"

"Because we need to find out. This is almost twenty thousand dollars, David, and I've still got over five hundred cash, and you, my love, still have the first quarter you ever earned, according to PawPaw."

"True, and beside that two bits, I've saved over seventeen hundred." He rose and kissed her on the nose. "Wouldn't have told you until later if I'd known you get all talkative." He grinned.

"Oh, you!" She rubbed her hands together. "If we sock that money away, we can build us a right nice home once we get back from our African sojourn."

He looked away, shrugged, then sat up in the bed. "I'd like to buy some stuff to take with us."

"Okay, sure. What do you want to get? We could go shopping in Dallas."

"Well, no. I figured we'd buy it in Tulsa."

"That's weird, seems to me Dallas would have more stores,

and better ones, too."

"I don't think we can haul it around in the Ford. I'm thinking it can't carry everything with all your suitcases."

She pushed his shoulder. "Hey, we're going to be gone for two years, what did you expect?"

"I got all my stuff in one big suitcase and a bag."

"So? Quit changing the subject. What are you talking about getting?"

"Oh, you know. Stuff we're going to need. A thousand feet of hog wire, maybe a hundred and fifty tee-posts and a tee-post driver—"

"Hold it right there. None of that stuff is any fun, and we can just get it in Nigeria. I don't think they'd let you carry all of that on the plane anyway."

"No, baby." He grinned. "We aren't flying. And you can't buy all that stuff over there. It isn't available. We're riding with the container."

"Not flying? Riding what with what container?"

"A container is the back end of an eighteen-wheeler that'll be filled with food and equipment. It travels on a cargo ship. We're going to watch over ours."

"A boat! We're going on a boat? All the way across the ocean?" She grabbed her gown, slipped it over her head, then stood. With fists on hips, she faced him. "Daviiid! Oooo! I don't want to go on the ocean! Besides, how much is all of that going to cost?"

"For the fencing? From what I've found out, I'm thinking about . . . six hundred dollars, maybe less. Hopefully."

"What?" She glared. "What's it for?"

"To fence in a garden plot." He looked out the window. She'd left the curtains open to enjoy all the lights below. He glanced back to her. "I'm buying seed for planting, too. Hannah. Why are you so upset?"

Forcing herself to take deep breaths, she considered how to answer. She really didn't know. She shouldn't be so disagreeable on the first full day of marriage.

It was only six hundred . . . and mercy, she'd just said how God had blessed them so much. Her face cooled. She loved him so much. "I don't know. I'm sorry. I guess we need to eat, so a garden's good."

He waved his hand toward himself. "Come here."

No way she could get to him quick enough. Instead of being mad, she flung herself at him, and wrapped her arms around him.

Tears welled, and she sobbed. "I'm, I'm, I'm . . . sorry, David. I shouldn't be upset. I love you, and I don't want to be angry with you."

"I love you, too, and I forgive you. It's my fault. I never thought to mention we'd be going over on the ship or considered you thought we were flying. I'm sorry, baby." Combing her hair back with his finger, he messaged her scalp. "It's . . . you're on edge. You've been so absorbed and working so hard for so long on the wedding, and now it's over."

She looked up. "But I'm glad for that because now, I'm yours."

Gently he moved her head toward his and kissed her softly on her so kissable lips. "Did I tell you how beautiful the service was? How much I appreciate everything you did to make it so perfect?"

"You thought it was perfect?" She smiled. "So did I." With a finger, she traced his brow then his nose down over his lips to his chin. "I love you so much. I don't deserve you."

"Don't be silly. You're the better half of this union, my love."

How could he be so sweet and so patient? She flopped back on the pillows. "Come prove it."

"I'll be right with you. Don't move!" He scurried to the bathroom.

"Mis'ess David Nightingale." She loved being married, and all her waiting lay behind her.

What if she was pregnant?

Would he bring her home to have the baby?

Twice that afternoon, while David drove from Austin to Dallas, he thought about getting a motel room, but though he had a pocket full of cash and the two fat checks, he also had plans for that money, every bit of it.

Somewhere before Waco, she slipped off his shoulder onto his lap and dozed.

"Lord," he whispered as an eighteen-wheeler zoomed by. "Did I lie when I didn't tell her the whole truth?"

He waited, but no answer came. Her anger over the little dab of stuff he told her about might bloom into a firestorm once she heard the whole of it. But he knew his own heart and helping Mike feed and clothe the Africans proved an urge so strong, it had to be from the Lord.

The Word said He would give you the desires of your heart and did He ever!

Slowing to merge into the traffic coming out of downtown Dallas woke his love. She pushed herself up, using his leg. "We're in Dallas, right?"

"Yes, another twenty minutes or so to Highland Park."

"We've got to another town?"

"Not really. Highland Park and University Park are surrounded by Dallas."

"Oh." She scooted over, lowered her visor, and took to primping in the mirror.

Not that she could be anything but gorgeous. Didn't she know? Nothing she could do would improve on God's creation? He eased off at Lemon Avenue and cruised toward the little island where the money folks lived. Praise God that he'd never been caught up in chasing filthy lucre.

Hannah pointed. "Aww, did you see that house? It was so cute, like from Switzerland or somewhere in the Alps."

"Might have been. Its owner could have moved it over, but you haven't seen anything yet."

Hannah had no idea what lay ahead, but wow, was he ever right! He stopped at a red light where an eight-foot stone wall stood just beyond the sidewalk with a trimmed hedge growing above the wall.

Mercy! In the area between the sidewalk and the curb a metal sign announced Highland Park. The light changed, and he eased right.

Barely a few feet up, a metal gate gave her a quick view of the three-story mansion that hid back in the corner of the gorgeous estate. "Wow."

"Yes, indeed."

She couldn't keep up with all the turns he made, for gawking at the humongous homes.

A few couldn't be seen for their fences, but most of the owners seemed to want to show off their prizes and had no fence or one easily seen through like decorative metal bars spaced inches apart. He turned into a drive.

A three, maybe four-story monster built with a mixture of rock and brick towered over the Ford. She loved the ivy that half covered it. Like an old British castle or something. The whole house amazed her.

"Wow, David. You grew up here?"

"No, didn't spend more than a couple of dozen nights in it over the years. I never liked being away from Cypress Springs."

He stopped, and she jumped out, looking up, slowly twirling. "I can't believe we get to stay here! I really, truly do feel rich now! Mama wouldn't believe this place. I'd love for her to see it!" She met him at the back of the Ford. "How long can we stay?"

"It's Mom's until closing."

"Well, when's that?"

"Two weeks from last Thursday with no hitches."

"Let's stay until then, the whole time! Every single day that it's available. Can we? Can we? Can we? I love this house!"

"We'll see."

"What is that supposed to mean?"

He laughed then held his arms out. "Want me to carry you over this threshold, too?"

"Yes, of course, but first let me get the camera! I want to take some pictures of the outside before we go in."

Snapping off five or six, she didn't wait for them to develop. She loved her Polaroid Swinger because she could know right away if they were good shots. She flipped up the flash then let him pick her up.

And he lifted her so effortlessly. She loved being in his arms and him being so strong. She gasped. For the first few pounds of her heart, she forgot to take any pictures.

Her feet touched the ground about the time she remembered to breathe. "Wow, David." She took two steps of the big entry hall's staircase. "Wow and woo hoo! Where's your room? Are we staying in yours?"

"It's upstairs. I figured we could stay in Mom's, hers has a balcony that's pretty cool."

"Oooo, cool! But I want to look around first."

It appeared that the living room was to her left and dining to the right. She went left, running around from room to room, spouting exclamations of amazement back to David as she went.

The den would easily hold a hundred people . . . and the kitchen . . . she really had no words for. The natural stone chimney in there was too much!

By the time she'd made the circle back to the foyer, David had suitcases in each hand with her overnight bag under his arm.

"This place is incredible. I'm seeing it with my own eyes, and still can't believe it. Now show me upstairs!" She kissed his neck. "I'll check it out then let's go to the third floor!"

"Mercy, Mis'ess Nightingale. It's only a house. Follow me."

He led her up the winding stairs to the second story then turned left toward the master suite where he swung the double doors wide then stepped aside for her. The bedroom was probably about as big as her parents' home.

Gasping again, she gawked. "Oh, my goodness! This is a mansion . . . no a castle. I wouldn't think Queen Elizabeth has a bedroom any bigger or more extravagant!"

Crossing the room, she opened the drapes, pulled back the door to the balcony, and stepped outside. The idyllic scene took her breath once again.

Beautiful ducks glided along, barely leaving a ripple on the green waters of Turtle Creek. Weeping willows hovered over, almost touching. Other hardwoods grew, offering their lovely shade over it all.

On the far side, the steep sloping bank was covered with the greenest grass, manicured like every other place in the ritzy neighborhood she'd seen.

It appeared surreal that she could have her own iced tea, sitting out there acting like a part of the whole amazing landscape. Why in the world Sandy ever left the place for South Texas, Hannah couldn't understand.

Stepping back inside, she gave David a pout. "I wish your mother didn't have to sell it. I'd love to live here."

She ran over and threw herself backwards onto the bed. It sucked her up! Wow, the softest one she'd ever been in. But then . . . once she thought about it, she'd maybe only been in three, no four, her whole life.

Hers, her parents', that motel her family stayed in when they vacationed in Galveston, and the honeymoon suite in Austin.

Well, that was nothing but sad. But she loved Mom Nightingale's bed the best by far, to be certain! She could hardly wait for the best husband in the whole world to be in it with her. She sat up and stretched her arms toward him.

"I love it, David. Couldn't you get the rest of the bags later? I can wait to see the third floor."

John David's Calling

Praise the Lord! David loved being a married man. Good thing he'd laid in extra film and flash bulbs.

Grabbing both, he retrieved one more of her bags, hoping the three would be enough luggage for what he hoped would only be a short stay, though he didn't hold out much expectation based on her reaction to the house.

Didn't work out anything liked he planned. He took her to Six Flags; spent the whole day there, and she took two full rolls of film on her Kodak Pocket Instamatic. She didn't want to carry the bigger Swinger and keep up with all the Polaroid photos.

Another day, she wanted to see the grassy knoll where President Kennedy had been murdered, but she didn't like being there much.

The three movies, Aquarium, and two museums took a week, but then he finally convinced her to head north. Did cost him another roll of film and bulbs, but he had to admit, being footloose and fancy free with his love was a ball.

With some reservation, he took her to see a movie at the North Park Mall and endured a couple hours of her shopping at Neiman Marcus. Swimming at the mansion ended most every day, even skinny dipping after dark with the pool lights turned off.

That had to be his favorite; a refreshing way to end the busy days.

A honeymoon he'd remember forever for sure. Actually, all the places she dragged him to turned out to be pretty much fun. Plus, in the end, she'd agreed to four movies. He liked those plenty good.

He finally got her in the Ford heading north and decided the money talk could wait no longer. He'd put it off as long as possible, but the whole truth was inevitable. "Sweetheart, the container the bishop is sending is only twenty feet long."

She scooted away enough to turn sideways. "Didn't you say that's the back of an eighteen-wheeler?"

"Yep. Most are forty feet, but the pups, the little ones, are twenty."

"That's cute, calling them pups."

"Anyway, I've been thinking, and would like for us to pay the extra for a forty-footer."

"So, double the size? Has he got enough stuff to fill that up. He probably knows what size he needs, don't you think?"

"Well . . . "

"How much money would that take anyway? I mean if he could fill it up."

"Five hundred or so."

Silence filled the Ford. She finally broke it. "That's a lot of money."

"True, but remember, we have a lot."

"We won't if we start spending big chunks of it like that. Why do you think all of a sudden he needs twice as much room?"

"Well, it isn't all of a sudden. I've been thinking on this for a while. Beside the fencing and tools for the garden, I'd like to buy a tractor."

"What? A tractor? Don't those cost like thousands of dollars?"

"I'm hoping we can find a good used one, and maybe a small plow . . . and a field cultivator. I figure we could use a two-row planter, and I'd like to lay in some fertilizer. Oh, and extra seed."

"Mercy David! How much are you planning on spending all together?"

He tore his eyes off the road, smiled at her, then looked back. "After our tithe, I was thinking . . . most of it, I guess."

She scooted to the far door, crossed her arms over her chest, then stared straight ahead. After a couple of miles or so, she turned sideways. "That's why you made all those trips to Austin, checking prices, wasn't it?"

"I said this plan wasn't a spur of the moment--"

"I guess you know that's our house you're wanting to give away."

"Give and it shall be given unto you, pressed down--"

"Oh! So, we should give all our money to missions! All of it? Then what? Wait for the Lord to give us some more so we can give that away, too?"

Her tone--the look in her eyes--tickled his funny bone, but no way could he laugh at her. That'd be a big mistake. No sir, wouldn't do at all. Not from her so-serious perspective. "Baby love."

"Sure, try sweet talking me now, huh? Forget it, David Nightingale! You're talking about putting everything we have in the world on the line. You have a wife now! And pretty soon I hope, babies. Don't I have a say in this? Isn't everything half mine now?"

"How about we agree to pray about it? And I figured we'd sell the Ford, too, so we'd have that money."

"Great! Just great!" She scoffed and stared out her window. "Homeless and afoot."

More mirth threatened, but he managed to choke it back, too.

His wife definitely had passion. One of the reasons he loved her. But her depth of caring worked against him sometimes, too.

Father, give her peace that it's Your will.

Chapter Twenty-nine

Hannah's money wheels ground to a halt. Her dream home melted away into the morass of his stupidity! Or was it spirituality? Pray about it, indeed!

The Lord had blessed their marriage with so much cash, and now David wanted to give it all away! God wouldn't do that . . . would He? A ping touched her heart.

"Okay, fine. We can use the tithe money." She slid around in the seat. "Doesn't the Word say that's what it's for? So there will be bread in God's house, right? And isn't that what you're wanting to do? Grow food for the people there."

"True. So . . . we're in agreement about using the tithe?" He glanced over and smiled. "How about seventy percent of the rest?"

"No! You're just acting crazy. Ten percent is enough. That's what God asked for." Staring at him, even though he didn't say anything, she could see his own money wheels turning. She hated being at odds with him, but she'd definitely never seen that side of him. Mercy! "The word says a fool and his money are soon parted."

"Yes, it says that, but I am a fool for Christ. Aren't you? Besides, the tithe belongs to God from the start. Scripture talks about tithes and offerings. We're solid on the tithe. What about our offerings?"

She should know better than to quote Scripture to a man raised in the Church of Christ. Arrrgh! For the next few miles, she tried to come up with something—anything to get him to see the error of his thinking, but no logical tact presented itself.

"Fine! So, I think the tithe and another . . . say ten percent for an offering should be plenty."

"I love you, sweetheart." He glanced over. "Come sit by me." He held his right arm out, and she scooted over. "I never want to fight with you over money. Let's agree on that. We will promise to each other that we won't move at all on a money issue unless we are in agreement. That sound good?"

"I love you, too. But giving all our money away . . . that's just crazy. I take it you don't think a ten percent offering is plenty."

"The Bible also says we can't out give God. I can find its reference if you want. Let's pray about it and see what the Lord tells us. You good with that?"

"Sure. How could I not be? Bully." She laid her head on his chest.

"I'm a bully?"

"You said it. A Scripture bully, and it isn't fair!"

With no response from him, she did what he'd asked and started talking to God. Pretty quick, her eyes grew salty, and she eased on down onto his thigh.

"Mama! Where's Daddy?"

Nodding toward the garden where he drove the 8N, she continued shucking corn. "He's plowing. See?"

The six-year-old put her hands on her hips and stomped one foot. "He said I could help."

"Watch it, little girl. Don't you be disrespectful."

"Sorry, Mama. Why didn't he take me?"

"David."

"What, baby?"

She sat up, but instead of being in Africa, she was back in the Ford. "How much does a 8N tractor cost?"

"Oh, a good used one . . . maybe three grand or so."

"Well." She leaned over and kissed his cheek. "Guess we better buy us one."

"All right! What changed your mind?"

"Oh, I sure would like to know her name, but our beautiful black daughter asked me just now where you were. I looked around, and there you were, plowing with an 8N Tractor."

"Did you see what I was pulling?"

"No, it was low, had some round things on it."

"All right, a disc! So we need a disc to plow with, too. What about a planter? Did you see one of those?"

"No! Surely they have something over there! Why do you really think you need to send it all?"

"While you napped, I was praying. Seems to me, we need to save the money PawPaw and MawMaw gave us. That will leave plenty to get what we're going to need."

"You really think that's going to be enough to build us a house when get back home?"

"Sure it will, especially with me doing most of the work."

"Hey, I'm helping, and don't you forget . . . Ouch!" A cramp grabbed her tummy. "Oh, no."

David glanced over but forced himself to concentrate on the road. "What wrong, babe?"

"Oh, no, no, no!" She scooted to her door and hugged herself. The water works started then she took to crying in earnest.

"Hannah, what's wrong?"

Only got a side-to-side head shake and a leave-me-alone wave. So . . . evidently, she . . . wanted to cry alone a minute and would tell him what could be wrong in a bit? He chose to remain silent until something else happened. For half a mile, she pulled her knees up and hugged herself. The crying eased.

"Should I pull over?"

"No!" She glared at him with eyes so sad it almost made him cry. She sniffed once, twice, then wiped her nose with the back of her hand. "I'm. Not. Pregnant."

"Oh. Well. Mercy, babe, we just got married. It takes time doesn't it?"

"No, it doesn't! Not necessarily." Her tone changed from the original harshness. "It only took once to conceive Cody Wayne, didn't it? Isn't that what Uncle Travis told Aunt Lee Lee? That it was only a one-night stand? The only time he'd sinned? Do you think he lied?" Back to being angry and loud in the end.

"No, of course not. Guess it's always different." Could he say the right words?

She swiped her cheeks. "Where are we?"

"Almost to Sherman."

"Is that still in Texas?"

"Yes, ma'am."

"Well, stop at the first gas station. Will you?"

"Sure."

Aware of the basics surrounding the female of the species and their times of every month, he'd never understand the mood swings the older women spoke of. How could normal hormones affect someone like that?

One minute she was crying. The next she served up so much ugly meanness, he only wanted to get away from her. She acted like she wanted to bite his head off because he was trying to comfort her.

Mercy.

Praise the Lord, an exit presented itself pretty quick. While he oversaw the attendant filling his tank, checking the tire pressure, and topping off the oil, she visited the ladies room.

Once back on the road, she seemed better. The Dr Pepper and moon pie seemed to help. Crossing the Red River, she scooted next to him. "I'm sorry for being such a big ol' cry baby. Will you please forgive me?"

"Of course, I forgive you, silly woman." He wrapped his

arm around her. "But it's okay; I understand. I want a baby, too. For the time being though, it is nice just being us. Let's enjoy our aloneness while it lasts, because once we start babies . . . it's a long-term commitment."

She snugged in tight. "I do like it being just us."

Hannah loved him so much, but how could he be so blind, so insensitive? If he was upset, she'd know exactly how to cheer him up, but he had no clue. He had no idea the pain attacking her. She needed a heating pad and a bed to curl up in.

Ought to slug him really good in the tummy. Then maybe he might have a little idea of how bad she felt.

Silly woman indeed. At least he'd called her a woman instead of his usual girl.

"Oh no."

"What now?"

Tears welled again. She scooted away from him. "I've ruined our honeymoon."

"You've got to be kidding. You haven't ruined anything."

"But we've been having so much fun! And now . . ."

Glanced at her, he motioned her over with a finger wave. "Come on, babe. I love you. We've had a wonderful time so far. I'll never forget it, will you?"

"Never." She eased back into his one-armed embrace and snugged into her place. "I love you, too."

Tulsa spread way bigger than she expected. She'd figured it to be like . . . more countryish, but its downtown skyline impressed her plenty.

Driving a quick turnaround through the ORU campus, he showed her where he'd lived while away from her, but that's all that he wanted to do. He didn't want to get out or go anywhere, claimed everyone might want to see was long gone.

"We have an invitation to stay at the bishop's house, but if you'd be more comfortable, we can get a room if you want."

"Are they expecting us today? I mean, have you talked to him? I don't want to barge in."

"I called from Dallas and told them we'd decided to stay in Mom's house a few days before we drove on up here. He said we were welcome anytime."

What would a night under the same roof as Missy Bass be like? If the trollop had any plans on David, she'd best think again, because Hannah wasn't about to put up with any shenanigans.

In the mood to fight, she dared the woman to make a move. Well, since the curse visited and there'd be no loving for a few days, she wouldn't feel weird making love with strangers outside the door.

"Let's take them up on their hospitality and save the hotel money since you're going to spend all of ours!" Hadn't meant for that to sound so mean.

Turning into the driveway of a good-sized brick home—couldn't hold a candle to the Turtle Creek mansion—David announced he'd come back out for the bags.

Was she ever wrong! Mis'ess Bass and her daughter proved to be pictures of Southern grace and charm. They both made Hannah feel right at home, as if they were some long-lost relatives that they'd longed to see for years.

And unlike the mountain she'd built in her mind, she didn't detect one ounce of any desire for her husband.

Missy's intentions toward David were only in Hannah's head. Not once did her slut radar ping. How could she not like the pair and the bishop, too?

Seemed he'd been cut from the same cloth as her father and Buddy Nightingale. The seasoned man of God obviously loved the Lord with his whole heart.

And how could she not like him when he held back none of his admiration for David. He almost sounded like a proud father.

That first night, cuddling with her love in the dark, she

kissed his cheek. "Do we have any plans for tomorrow?"

"Oh, the bishop wants us to come to his office for a while to go over some things we'll need to know about shepherding the container through customs."

"Boring. Do I have to go? Missy and Mom Bass invited me to play bridge."

"Okay, but . . . you don't know how."

"I told them that, but they said they'd teach me before the fourth shows."

"Okay, sure. I can go to the meeting alone, and I'll love you learning how to play. If you think you'll have more fun . . . Want to trade?"

"No, sir. Thank you very much, sir." She started to tickle him but stopped herself knowing where that usually led. "So after breakfast, you're going to work and I'm taking care of the playing for the day."

She loved waking up in the same bed with her husband, except her gown got more tangled. A small price to pay for the pleasure of the skin-to-skin touching though.

Seemed a bit weird, him leaving her there with the ladies, and as the morning wore on, so did her uneasiness.

After breakfast coffee and dishes, Mis'ess Bass went to working on lunch, insisting Missy skedaddle on out to the back porch with Hannah for a bridge lesson.

Just more weirdness—her sitting while a meal was being prepared, but the lady of the house insisted.

After three practice hands, a light finally glittered a bit. "So it's a lot like spades, except the trumps change. A little like forty-two, too."

"Right, not that I've ever played dominoes, but I've heard bridge is a lot like that game."

"Well, there's only one round of bidding. It seems like getting a handle on the bidding is the hardest part."

Through half a dozen hands, she and Missy bid each open hand together, then Mis'ess Bass joined the lesson and took the seat next to Hannah.

"We figured you and Missy would be partners. Gladys and I play some duplicate together, and well, she's . . ."

"Mother."

Glancing over, she waved her daughter off, then looked back to Hannah. "Oh, you'll see. She's a deaconess at the church."

"Really? Your church has women deacons?"

"Yes, ma'am. The first church did so why shouldn't we? In Romans Paul mentions a Sister Phoebe, a deacon of the church in Cenchrea."

"Wow, guess I missed that. Isn't that different? I remember something about a qualification to be a deacon was to be the husband of one wife because we had sort of a hullabaloo over that once at our church."

"What church do you belong to, dear?"

"My family is Methodist, but I've been to David's grandfather's church—well, it's his dad's now since Gramps passed. It's much livelier."

"We're a part of the Church of God denomination, maybe not quite as lively as Pentecostals, but we believe in miracles and speaking in tongues, the Baptism into the Holy Spirit and His ministry."

That gibberish called tongues, she'd shied away from though she'd heard it at the Holiness Church before. Sometimes someone would stand up and talk in unknown tongues then someone else acted like they understood.

They'd stand up and interpret it into English. But she wasn't so sure. She needed to remember to ask David about it. "What about female pastors? Does your church allow that?"

"Well, yes and no, I'm technically a pastor because the bishop and I are one in Christ, but I haven't been ordained, and I'd never try to lead a church."

Hannah liked the sound of that. "Cool. That's a good way to look at it."

One day, she'd be a pastor not just a pastor's wife. But would David be ordained as a missionary or as a pastor? Was there a difference? She mulled that question over while Missy dealt the next hand.

"Let's not show our hands this time. I'll bid for me and the dummy."

Hannah decided to save her inquiries for David and concentrate on her cards.

Right on time, Gladys showed. Hannah liked the lady, even though a bit stern. Missy betrayed no emotion when Hannah made a mistake.

The deaconess would roll her eyes every time Mis'ess Bass didn't do exactly what she thought she should. But then, she was a good player and usually made all her bids.

David came to collect her at three o'clock sharp, the arranged time. While almost always in a good mood, he seemed almost giddy. She didn't quiz him until he keyed the Ford to life.

"Seems to me like you're having a really good day. Is that right?"

"Ma'am, yes, ma'am! You should've seen the bishop's face when I told him we wanted to get a forty-footer."

"I didn't know we'd decided that, David. Didn't you say that was another five hundred?"

"Yes, that's right, sweetie. But we agreed on the tractor and plow and planter, right? All that wouldn't fit in a twenty foot. The bishop had that spoken for already. So we had to get the bigger container."

"Oh, I suppose so. I hadn't thought about that. Guess he was surprised." Maybe she should have gone with him after all, except she'd loved learning to play bridge. "What'd he say?"

"Kept on praising the Lord. And when I told him all the stuff we wanted to buy to ship over, he sent me to see a man he knows who has Tulsa Tractors and Equipment. Want to go see what we bought?"

Though she'd rather do about a thousand other things, she didn't want to drizzle on his happy day and tried to sound as enthusiastic as possible. "Sure, we can do that."

John David's Calling

Besides, it gave her the chance to see if he'd gone overboard. Knowing him, he'd probably pushed the limit. She only hoped not by too much.

The whole way there, she cuddled next to him and told him all about her lessons and games. He pulled off the blacktop through a chain-link gate and right there . . . her breath caught, and goosebumps covered her arms and legs.

For a split second, she saw her black daughter again, sitting in David's lap while he drove that very 8N. She squeezed his arm then pointed.

"That's the one! That's the exact tractor I saw!"

"Really? He wanted an extra five hundred for that one. I figured we'd buy the one over there." He pointed to his right as a man strolled out to the Ford. "He'll sell us that one for twenty-five fifty."

Following his finger, her heart fell. That one wasn't right. She looked back to the other one. "No, David." She nodded to the one she'd seen first. "That's our tractor. I just know it. Want me to talk to him?"

"Oh, so you think you can get a better deal."

"Uh, yes. You're way too easy, Mister Nightingale."

The man walking out of the metal barn-looking building wiped his hands on a red rag.

"There he is. Have at him."

"What else does he have you want?"

"A three-row planter he's asking six hundred for."

"You want it?"

The man neared, stuffing the rag in his back pocket.

"Sure."

She scooted over, grabbed her door handle, then looked back. "What about a plow?"

"Got one for four-fifty."

"And what's a good price on the planter?"

David shrugged as he opened his door. "I thought six hundred was."

Hannah didn't really want to shake the man's still-greasy

hand, but she knew better than not to. "Good afternoon, sir."

"Sure is, young lady. You're as pretty as he said, all right."

Her face warmed, but it thrilled her that David had been talking about her, saying she was pretty. "Aw, thank you. I'm the one blessed though. Did he tell you we're basically still on our honeymoon?"

"Why no! Congratulations." He nodded at her sweet husband. The guy chuckled. "And he's got you out buying tractors? You must love him a lot."

"Oh, I do. Problem is, he picked the wrong one."

His belly laughs at that one earned a smile. "He did, huh?"

"Oh, yes, sir. I'm certain." She headed over to the 8N she'd seen in her vision. The man followed like a puppy, and her dearest brought up the rear, tagging along. "I'm Hannah Nightingale, by the way. And your name?"

"Bob, ma'am. Bob Hostler."

Her turn to laugh. "You ever get teased about that?"

"Oh, some, I suppose. I figure long as they buy from me, they can call me what they want." He gave her a merry wink.

Coming up beside the tractor she wanted, she stopped and put on her horse-trading face. "Are you a Christian, Mister Hostler?"

"Yes, ma'am. I surely am."

"Did my husband tell you why we're buying a tractor and where we're taking it?"

"Not really. Figured he's wanting to put in a crop."

"Well, he actually does, that's right. But not here in Oklahoma, not even in the United States. No." She warbled her 'o' in 'no' for emphasis. "My husband wants to plant in Nigeria. That's in Africa."

"You don't say."

For a few minutes, she told him about the plans to grow food to feed the folks, so they could share the Lord's love and salvation with the natives. She surprised herself when she quoted the right Scriptures right on time in her spiel. She patted

John David's Calling

the 8N she wanted to get.

"I'd like to give you twenty-two hundred fifty cash money today for this beauty and the three-row planter he looked at earlier."

"Oh, Miss Hannah." The man looked from her to David then to the sky. "I've got more in the two pieces than that."

"What would you say to a donation slip for the difference?"

The man looked back. "You sure about that? The bishop already approved such?"

"Well." David put his arm around her shoulder. "No, but we're staying at his home. I'd be glad to bring it up at supper."

The man stared at his shoes for a long minute then looked up. "You get me a donation letter for the difference, and I'll let them both go for twenty-six fifty."

"Well, I forgot we need the plow, too. Now I don't want to beat you down. I'll tell you now, I love this tractor. But how about you throw in the plow for three grand smooth even and the letter."

"You drive a hard bargain, young lady." He held his hand out toward her. "Guess it's a deal."

"Yes, sir." She took his hand then covered it with her other. "With one condition."

The man pulled his hand back and stuck both deep into his pockets. "What condition?"

"You store them here until we're ready and then deliver them to our container."

"Miss."

"It's Mis'ess David Nightingale."

"Okay, so where's the container?"

She had no idea and looked to David.

"It will be here in Tulsa shortly."

"So, you going with him all the way to Africa?"

"Yes, sir. Wherever he goes, that's where I belong."

"Guess me offering you a job till he got back would be a waste of my breath?"

She laughed then extended her hand even farther. "So it's a

deal?"

"Yes, ma'am. Figure I better shake before you see something else you want me to throw in."

her peace that it's Your will.

Chapter Thirty

David counted out the thousand in earnest money he'd agreed to give the man then smiled. "We'll find us a bank in the morning to get our checks cashed, then I'll bring the rest. Might take a day or two for them to clear."

The man counted the bills then nodded. "No problem. I won't be selling your tractor and implements out from under you. The Bishop Bass would skin me good if I tried something like that." He laughed, and David chuckled with him.

"Okay, you take care, sir. And thank you."

"Bye, Mister Holster! Thank you again! God's going to bless you with so much business!" She literally bounced back to the Ford.

Once out of the yard, David patted his bride's thigh. "You did so good, my love! Where'd you come up with a donation slip for what he took off?"

"Daddy. He takes a bunch of letters. He does a lot of work for half the churches all over the county, and he never lets them pay him unless they insist. He always just counts his service a donation, gets a slip, then takes it off his taxes."

"You don't say."

"Yes, sir, they get the best accountant in three counties for nothing but a piece of paper." She pulled down the visor mirror and checked her mascara.

"Awesome. Sounds like everyone wins."

"Everyone, but Uncle Sam." She wiped under each eye with a fingertip, then flipped the visor back in place. "It was fun dickering. I'll help you out anytime. It's like we got the plow and planter free!"

"Right." He squeezed her hand. "Beautiful, and smart, and well . . ."

"Well what? You were on a roll there, Buster. No need to stop."

"Oh, I was going to say something about how utterly desirable you are, but . . . seeing as how we're . . . uh . . . what should we call it?"

She tickled him. "I don't know, but there's nothing says you can't kiss me!"

He did, keeping one eye on the road. "So what do you want to do now?"

"Miz B is making spaghetti for dinner and asked if we could pick up a loaf of French bread and some Parmesan cheese."

"Okay, sure. What about after supper?"

"Well, I thought you might enjoy playing bridge with me as your partner against her and Missy. I can't wait to show you what I learned."

"That sounds like fun."

"I thought so."

"You do know they gamble, right?"

"Oh, just pennies to make it interesting. I figure you can cover me."

"What a deal! I got me a card playing, horse-trading, gambling beauty so desirable it's a wonder she settled for a poor old farmer like me."

She laughed then took to tickling his ribs in earnest.

"Hold on, lady. I'm trying to drive here."

She scooted away. "Okay, but just as soon as . . . it won't be too long." She snickered then eased back next to him, pressing in tight.

The evening proved good all the way around, except Hannah figured chickening out on bidding a slam cost him an extra quarter, but she still loved being his partner.

That night after the lights went off, she snuggled into her most wonderful and comfortable place in the whole world—on his arm. "Missy said this afternoon you were like a bridge alchemist, creating tricks from thin air."

He chuckled. "That so?"

"Of course. I said it, didn't I?" She giggled. "I know you know I'm not a liar. She also said that with the right teacher, you could be world class."

"What a nice thing for Miss Bass to say, but I'm not interested. I'm after one thing."

"And what's that?"

"To hear the Lord say, 'Well done, good and faithful servant' when it's all over."

Tears filled her eyes. She rolled and snuggled even tighter. "I never want you to go to Heaven."

"What?"

"I mean . . . of course, I don't mean . . . I do want you to go to Heaven, just not without me or before me. Promise me that."

Turning a bit, he eased her more onto his chest. "I promise."

Soon—having his promise—she drifted off in that most wonderful of places.

"Mama, Johnny's dirty."

"Okay, sweetie pie. I'll be right there."

Hannah tried, but couldn't sit up. Vines or ropes entangled her. She searched but couldn't find her long knife. Then, though she didn't remember finding it, the thing appeared in her hand. She slashed at whatever had her bound her.

"Mama."

"I'm trying, honey. Mama's coming, but . . . I'm caught."

A hand shook her shoulder. "Wake up, baby."

"What?" Hannah opened her eyes, all tangled in the sheet and her gown. "Oh, Praise the Lord. It was only a dream."

"Glad to hear that." He smiled. "Why'd you hit me?"

"Oh, I'm sorry. It's just I was caught, all wrapped up in vines or cords or something and I was lashing out with this big knife trying to free myself."

"A knife, huh. Guess I'm glad it was a dream, too, then."

"The little girl—our daughter because she calls me Mama—wanted me to come change Johnny."

"I see." He chuckled. "So, we've got a son now in your dreams?"

"Apparently."

"So . . . is this your way of telling me you want our first son to be named John David? And call him Johnny?"

Mirth and joy bubbled up from her belly, and she giggled. "It's a fine name, you have to admit. Sounds good to me. Really, it has a nice ring to it, don't you think?"

"Yes, sir." She hiked one eyebrow. "In another two or three days, we can get to work on making him a reality."

After breakfast and a nice time on the back porch drinking coffee with the Basses, David took her bank shopping. However, he liked the first one so much he didn't look any further.

What could she say? He didn't like shopping and was definitely easy to please. Fine with her. If memory served, the bank's CD rate paid a quarter-point higher than what her father got in Marble.

Hey, a dollar here; fifty cents there; it all added up.

From the bank, he wanted to check out a few pawn shops. Sounded tacky and like no fun, until he held the door for her and she walked into the first one.

It wasn't dirty like she expected, and they had several glass display cases filled with sparkling gold and diamonds galore. Wow, the prices were amazingly cheap, too. Maybe she should

John David's Calling

pick out a Tulsa souvenir.

Her beloved headed straight for the tool section. She never knew, but then Marble Falls didn't have a pawn shop.

Even before she'd ogled half the glitter and glitz, he saddled up next to her. "Ready?"

"Uh, no, not yet."

Putting his mouth close to her ear, he whispered, "There's three more in town; let's check them out before we make any offers."

Quickly spying over the rest of the offerings, she grabbed a kiss then nodded. "Lead on, my captain! Did you know they had so much cool stuff? And it's so cheap. Were the tools real cheap, too?"

"Oh yeah. I mean good brand names, but at very good prices."

What a day! She loved spending money, and even more, the horse-trading! Matching wits with sellers and negotiating deals David could hardly believe . . . every time. She loved his amazement!

Shame pawn brokers didn't like donation slips, but according to her sweet husband, she'd saved him over two hundred dollars on the tools he'd bought compared to what new ones would have cost.

She found a beautiful gold chain and a diamond-studded gold cross and let him talk her into getting it. She wore it out of the store, fingering the cross.

The rest of that week, he crossed all the stuff off his list, and filled the Ford's trunk three times. Sure was a good thing the bishop's home church had a storage room.

All was in place except for David's Sunday evening ordination and filling the container due to be delivered Monday. Then she and her love would be off with it heading south on Wednesday.

Still had to sell the Ford but she figured that wouldn't be too hard.

The biggest part of her could hardly wait, but the part that wanted to run home to her mother could be rather noisy at times. That little girl who'd clung to the pew in front of her, begging God not to call her to the mission field, wondered why He had.

At least He'd waited until she was grown and had David for her husband.

There was nowhere she wouldn't go to be by his side.

David would have called the morning service more on the lame side, except no one asked his opinion. The music definitely lacked anointing. Still, compared to the services he sat through growing up, it was electric.

Well, maybe not that far. And since he hadn't been personally involved, he might be considered biased. It surprised him a little they hadn't done some recruiting.

The bishop didn't mention that evening's service until the very end, then only that David would be ordained—like an ordination was no big deal. Maybe to the three hundred or so souls attending that morning, what was one more preacher?

Did it really matter?

Who poured oil on Paul's head and proclaimed him reverend?

It had been in a regular prayer meeting that the Lord called him and Barnabas out to preach the Good News.

After a big noon meal, and a round robin of bridge, the time came to go back to church.

Hannah slid in next to him while he keyed the Ford to life. "So are you nervous?"

"Some."

"Well, there probably won't be that many folks there tonight. I mean nothing like this morning. And it isn't like you're preaching or anything. You won't have to talk, will you?"

John David's Calling

Mercy. He hadn't even thought about anything to say or that they might just give him the pulpit. Oh well, wasn't like he'd never prepared a sermon before, and the Word instructed not to be concerned about what to say.

He'd always been comfortable just to speak from the heart or sing whatever song the Lord put on his heart. Why should that evening be any different?

The closer he got to the church building, the calmer he became. As if the Lord Himself had laid his hands on him and liquid love flowed through his veins.

What an awesome God he served.

It shocked him the parking lot looked about half full, and he'd left in time to be early. He took the seat on the front row where the bishop had told him and Hannah to sit. A soft murmur filled the house as latecomers found their seats.

Were all those people there to see him get ordained or . . .?

"Mercy, David. The place is packed. Look back there." Hannah's whisper was a smidgen loud.

Wow. A few men were standing in the back while the few stragglers still coming in were scooting past their neighbors. What did the Lord have planned?

The choir—when had they taken their places? —raised their voices as the organ and piano began playing. Three lively praise songs ensued, then Bishop Bass, who'd been sitting in his chair on the stage, walked to the lecture. The house hushed.

"Evening, folks." The man looked right at David. "The young man we're ordaining tonight is the son of Buddy Nightingale and the grandson of Nathaniel Nightingale, but then you good folks knew that, so without further ado."

The bishop extended his hand.

David joined him on stage.

"Tomorrow, a forty-foot container—yes, you heard right. Not twenty but a forty-footer—will be loaded for Nigeria. David and Hannah."

The bishop motioned toward the front row. "Come on up here, young lady. If you folks haven't met this lovely lady, she's

David's wife. Newlyweds, actually, still working on their first month of marriage."

Applause erupted, and wide smiles filled the congregation. She squeezed his hand.

"Anyway, these two have not only spent their own money to pay the extra for the bigger container, they've been buying all sorts of things to take to Africa." He waited until the hoots and hollers quietened then nodded.

"Due to their generosity, we'll be taking a fine 8N tractor over, along with a plow and planter." More cheers arose. "And . . . and we're sending enough seed to plant a five-acre garden."

The folks filling the pews were nothing but rowdy in their approval.

"So." The man retrieved a little bottle of oil from his coat pocket then eased David toward him. He daubed a bit of oil on his finger then traced a cross on David's forehead then did the same to Hannah.

"The State of Oklahoma has already licensed you as a minster of the Gospel, and now you've been anointed as such in the Church of God."

The bishop eased him around toward the congregation and handed him the mic. A standing ovation greeted and welcomed him. "Say a few words, David, or sing. That's why these brothers and sisters all came tonight."

A man in the back stood. "Tell 'em about the time I beat you up."

Chapter Thirty-one

Searching the back rows and those standing, David raised a hand to shade his eyes. "Gage? That you?"

The man waved. "Yes, sir."

"To tell about that time." David chuckled. "I'd need to back up to my one and only visit to a honky-tonk."

A few gasps and murmurs rippled across the pews, but David ignored them.

"Don't think too badly of me now." He thumbed back to the bishop. "His son's the one took me."

A good laughed rolled over the congregants, and he laughed with them.

Bishop Bass took his seat, and Hannah tried to pull her hand from his, but he held it.

"I will, but before I do, I want to tell you all how blessed I am that God gave me this woman. Known her since she was in the third grade, and she sure grew up into one fine lady. I'm honored that she chose to come to Africa with me."

His sweetheart leaned into the mic, "He didn't give me much of a choice. I was scared, but God's shown me it's where He wants me. We're looking forward to ministering with Mike and the others over there. Thank you all for the opportunity."

"A woman who hears from God and obeys. See what I mean?"

Wrapping his arm around her back, he proceeded to give the *Reader's Digest* version of the three M's roping him into passing out fliers on the bar's parking lot and how that progressed to preaching in the park where he encountered Gage.

She stepped back a bit.

A warmth spread over him, and he stopped his narrative mid-sentence. In his mind's eye, a young girl not more than ten limped toward him.

Taken aback, he watched until the young lady vanished then he cleared his throat.

What was that all about?

"Excuse me. Anyway, that night, Gage, I had a vision of the wreck that put you in the hospital." Tears filled his eyes. "I think the Lord showed me as a test. A part of me wanted to gloat, but He Who lives in me is much greater than the world encouraged me to pray for you. Bless God, not only did you survive, you lived to accept the Lord as Savior."

Standing, Gage shot both hands into the air. "Amen, brother! You ever need anyone beat up again, I'm your man."

Laughter ripped through the house.

"It was my honor to take that beating, brother, since it led to you embracing eternal life." David held his hands out. The congregation quieted. "Just now while I was telling that story I saw a young lady, nine, maybe ten years old, limping up the center aisle. Anyone here like that?"

An older woman about midway in the left section stood. "My granddaughter, Brother David. She's helping in the nursery."

"Would you please get her in here."

The woman scooted out then ran toward the back. In no time, she returned holding the hand of the exact little girl he'd seen in the vision, who came limping toward him. The child's grandmother helped her, but halfway David held his hands up.

"Leave her be, Grandma. The Lord wants to help her. He'll strengthen her."

John David's Calling 323

The woman froze in place, but the girl kept on coming, though going much slower.

"Once the Lord asked the Pharisees, is it easier to say your sins are forgiven or to heal a withered hand?" Tears flowed down David's cheeks. Praise be to the Almighty. Blessed be His Holy Name. Glory bumps covered his arms and legs. "I'm here tonight to confirm there is nothing too hard for our God. No thing!"

The child's next step seemed stronger, the next one she took had hardly any limp at all. Then with an ear-to-ear smile, she broke into a jog. David stepped toward her, but she raced right by him and leaped into Hannah's arms.

She twirled her around then set her down, took her hand, and the two went to skipping and dancing around the church.

Shouts of praise and hallelujahs filled the sanctuary. Grandma went to her knees in the center aisle, holding her hands toward Heaven. "Thank You, Lord! Thank You, Father!" Tears streamed down her face.

A new song filled David's heart. He opened his mouth and belted it out. The choir joined in then the rest.

Those not singing were dancing and skipping and praising the Lord with Hannah and the precious little girl, healed that day by her loving Father.

The service ended with David, the bishop, and half a dozen other men praying for those in need. Then it was over.

Even though a part of him never wanted it to end, but that would be impractical. Folks had jobs and needed sleep and . . . but wasn't all of God's doings better than all that?

Why did it have to end?

That question stuck with him, raising its head off and on in the next three days.

Filling the container with all the stuff he'd bought, and the grain sacks the missionary board always sent turned into a pretty big chore, but a fun one, too. No wasted space, and praise the Lord, the container wasn't overweight.

The bishop had been a bit concerned when the pickup man

rolled it onto the portable scales.

Whew. Had a good five hundred pounds to spare.

Hannah hated leaving Tulsa, nowhere near as much as leaving the Hill Country, but the few days she'd been there were just wonderful; so special in ways she'd never expected. On the trip to Galveston, she pondered on all the whys those days had been as extraordinary as any she'd lived.

Perhaps a part of it was that all those people—the Basses whom she loved for sure—never knew her as Hannah Morrison. All of them considered her an adult, a married woman, Mis'ess David Nightingale. She loved that!

And even though the train trip took more than twice as long as what would have been one hard day of driving, it turned into two and a half fun days.

The sleeper was a bit crowded, but she didn't mind, not in the least. She loved going through the country though when the landscape changed to rolling hills and lots of live oaks, rocks, and some cactus.

So close to home. Had he been driving, she could have talked him into detouring to Marble. Being so close and not being able to stop for another farewell saddened her. Two years was a long time. Home.

The Texas Hill Country would always be home. She glanced over at her dozing husband. No. Truth be known, he was her home now. Wherever he wandered, that's where she belonged.

With a grin, she couldn't believe she'd even gotten him to play the scrabble game Missy put in the care package along with two decks of cards and at least ten pounds of goodies to snack on. She would weigh a ton when she got to Africa.

Oh well, she guessed she'd lose weight a plenty later, eating as the natives ate. Never had seen a fat African . . . just those

John David's Calling

horrible pictures of starving babies with their little bloated bellies.

What a grand story she'd have to tell her children.

Like the bishop said, getting the container onto the cargo ship was nothing. He warned David that trouble could loom on the other end and what to watch for.

Hoping it wouldn't be looming the day she and her husband arrived, she prayed nothing would go wrong and refused to think about it. Doing so made her anxious. Could David do anything against a bunch of thugs?

Oh yes, turn his other cheek.

The berth proved nothing like she expected, no Queen Mary cruise quarters, but probably nicer than a cheap motel, not that she'd been in that many hired rooms. She looked forward to eight whole days of just him and her—the Reverend and Mis'ess Nightingale, missionaries deluxe.

That anticipation helped with the homesickness.

Shame bridge needed four players, but she beat him steady at gin rummy.

The second day out, another possible answer to her question presented itself. She toyed with it for an hour, then tried it out with David over a game of Scrabble.

She wrote down her score, retrieved her new tiles, then touched his forearm. "Hey, I've been thinking about something."

"Really?" He glanced up and grinned. "That's crazy, so have I. What am I supposed to spell with one vowel? It's no wonder you're winning." He looked at her with a rather harsh expression.

"No, not about the game. About why I hated leaving Tulsa so much."

"So, you're ready to concede?"

"Sure. Oh yeah, that's it—when I'm sitting double your score? Not likely, Bubba." A little chuckle escaped. "Back to Tulsa."

"Why are you distracting me?"

"Because! I really hated leaving there so much, and I've been wondering . . . It wasn't like we were there that long, but I think I figured it out."

"Okay. Let's talk about it." He turned the egg-timer onto its side. "But I get double time when we get back to the game."

"Sure, isn't like you could beat me if you had all afternoon." She winked then smiled.

"At first, I came up with how they all treated me like an adult. You know, at home I'm always going to be a kid to everyone who knew me back then, but in Tulsa I'm a married woman. All of our friends there never knew me before."

"Sounds logical."

"But I don't think that's all of it. I'm thinking another reason is because of you and how they all honored you. I had no idea they'd love you that much. Bishop Bass acted like you were a son."

"They're good people."

"I guess some of your honor rubs off on me since we're one now. That little girl . . . getting healed! The praise and worship when you led it—there's absolutely no comparison to that morning."

"But don't—"

"Why not? I'm the wife of the great Reverend David Nightingale. What do you think?"

"Maybe, except for the great part."

"Now you're just being silly. Don't act like that. It's obvious to anyone you're God's man, plain and simple. And that makes you great."

David wanted to tell her pride goes before destruction and a haughty spirit before a fall, but instead, he let it lay. That battle he'd been fighting from his earliest memory.

To excel in sports had come so easy for him. And at a

young age, he realized his intellect far exceeded his grandparents and mother.

He coasted through school, keeping grades good enough PawPaw would let him play baseball, basketball, and football. Even college hadn't been as hard as he figured.

Seeing true miracles—the sick healed, crippled legs made strong, blind eyes opened—served to build his faith, and taking folks to the very throne of God with the new songs the Lord gave him blessed his soul.

He didn't know why his Father favored him so, certainly not because he deserved any of it. And though he might not know all the references, Scriptures came to his tongue at the very time he needed them.

And provision. He closed his eyes.

And Hannah.

Hard to be humble, Lord, when you bless me so. Thank You that Your mercy endures forever.

The last evening at sea, anchored off the coast of Africa, the ship waited its turn to dock in Lagos Nigeria, and sleep eluded David.

Long after his love had rolled off his arm and cuddled into a ball, he prayed, asking for a harvest.

The wheel within a wheel he'd seen before floated down from Heaven and landed like a feather on the chicken yard. He watched as the folks either prayed or sang as before, then a big tent appeared over them, the human wheels, and eased down again like a feather.

David tried to go in, but his feet wouldn't take him. Something held them, as if mired in clay or . . . even concrete.

A stream of folks came, some with crutches and canes, others being helped inside or carried on stretchers.

Another line of people leaving on the opposite end, making room for others, shouted to the sky, praising the name of the Lord, twirling and making all sorts of joyful noises—none lame or maimed in any way.

Some laughed, others sang and clapped, all with a new

spring in their steps.

"Oh, Lord, let me go to that place."

He sat up in bed. Hannah remained still, all curled up. He slipped out of bed and eased to the little round portal window in his bedroom. In the distance, lights defined the dotted land, a few skyscrapers in the city, but mostly it slept.

"Where can I get a tent that big, Lord?"

BIND UP THE VISION UNTIL THE END

David fell to his knees, then stretched out, his nose on the floor.

"Yes, Lord. Your Will be done in my life."

I have a real treat for you, Readers! I am going to give you the first chapters of TWO new books, both coming in 2018.

First up is a Biblical fiction I believe to be wholly anointed. It's the story of Abishag and the Kings of Israel she cherished.

For your reading pleasure . . .

I AM
My Beloved

Chapter One

Abishag held the cups level and took small lady-like steps, careful not to slosh. She grinned then placed the wine—except water really, her mother wouldn't allow her real wine—on the stone table.

"The bread isn't quite ready, but almost. Can you stay longer?"

He shook his head. "No, my dear. Regrettably not." He leaned in close, whispered in her ear, stood, then vanished, just as he had come.

Waiting a thumbs worth on the sundial's shadow, she emptied both cups, then took them back inside; her parched throat revived.

"Sweetheart, there you are. The bread is ready. Would you want two loafs? Or will you share?" Her mother gave her the look. The one that told it all. She never believed her when he came.

All the time talking with Father in hushed tones about her make-believe friend. But he wasn't. He was real.

"He whispered in my ear just now. Right before he vanished. He couldn't stay."

"I see." Her mother wiped her hands on her apron then knelt down. "What did your he tell you?"

"That I will lie with kings but be mother of none." Abishag smiled then continued in a breathy whisper. "He said my beauty will only be exceed by my purity."

Her friend telling the future, she liked that, but not what he said about never being a mother. She wanted real babies, not her rag dolls. That's what one did, grew, got married, and had babies. That part troubled her.

Her mother's eyes opened so wide, the white showed all around her dark circles in the middle. "Abishag! Where have you heard such a thing? Little girls know not of such things."

"I told you, Mama. My friend told me."

"And again, who is this friend? What is his name? Have you asked him as I instructed?"

"Yes, Mama. He says his name is unimportant. My guardian angel sent from Heaven. He said more, you know. About a prince . . . but I'm not sure exactly what that was about, I don't like people dying." She smiled. "May I please have some honey on my bread?"

As the years crawled on and she grew, her angel still visited though less and less. Most times he appeared in the garden. But once, when twelve years old, she'd taken the herd to graze, and he'd shown himself.

Strumming her lap harp, she sang a new song of praise. "I will sing a song unto You, Lord. Sing a song unto You, Lord." A slight movement in her peripheral vision put her senses on alert, but she kept singing, following the movement.

Then she caught a glimpse of the stalking giant. A lion! How would she ever save her father's sheep from that beast?

Her song of praise turned into a prayer. "Help me, Lord. Protect the sheep. If I should die, my soul please keep." Her heart beat faster. What should she do? Abandon the flock and try to save herself?

No. Her father placed them in her care. No matter what happened, she wouldn't leave them. Her rod! She would shout and swing it.

She studied the trees on the edge of the pasture, squinting to see better into the growth, trying to see him again. That's when he appeared, her angel. He knelt beside the big cat and whispered in its ear.

The lion must have decided he didn't want any of her lambs—or her—and instead, lay at her friend's feet, while the angel scratched behind his ears.

After the animal trotted off, her friend vanished as he had always done.

He didn't wait for a thank you or even a drink.

Had her hero, King David, had an angel, too? One who

helped him when he watched his father's sheep? She loved the few psalms of his she could recite, and father promised to get her more to learn when he went to Jerusalem again.

As a boy, her king slew both a lion and a bear. She probably would never be as brave as he. But neither had she run. How she would love to ask him, know if he visited with his own angel.

But only a few—all very important people—got to see and speak with the great man. She dreamed of being in the army the day he slew the giant. Her grandfather had been, and she never tired of hearing his story about the young shepherd boy who killed Goliath and saved Israel.

That had been the last time she'd seen her friend. It troubled her that the angel hadn't come since. Now that she'd grown into a young woman, she oft daydreamed on the fellow and wondered if he'd been real at all.

Maybe he truly was only imaginary as her mother had always tried to convince her.

But time to daydream came to an abrupt end one late fall day.

A wagon full of men, with even more soldiers riding on great steeds came rolling to her father's house like a great sand storm across the desert. After a few quick peeks through the garden lattice, she hid in her room.

Virgin daughters were never so forward as to burst into the presence of strangers.

Her door opened. "Abishag?"

"Yes, Mama?"

Her mother burst into tears then found her voice. "Quickly, now, my darling. Pack a bag."

"But why, Mother? Where am we going?"

"Only you, precious one. Your King has need."

"The king? King David? He needs me? But why, Mama? I don't understand." She reached to sweep her mother's hair back, then traced her cheek, and the tears returned.

Was she dreaming? Her chest boomed, coursing wide

every vein. Had that ever happened before in a dream?

"Who are those men, and why have they come? Tell me, please, Mother."

"He's ill and can't get warm. The palace had heard of your beauty, and the men . . . they've been dispatched to take you to Jerusalem." A sob escaped. "Please, Abishag, you must go. He's our King."

It had to be a dream. But submitting to her mother, she threw some things into her bag and let Mama guide her to the courtyard where Father stood, talking to the other men.

He held his arms wide, and she rushed to him. He kissed her cheek then lifted her off her feet, holding her out. "It's a great opportunity, daughter, to serve your king and bring honor to the family. You are to be his last queen."

Her? A queen? King David's queen?

How was it possible? She only shed a few tears at the farewells, then left her home with the strangers. Surely any moment, she'd awaken in her bed with a great story to tell at breakfast.

But the road's dust stung her eyes and cramped her breath. She held her scarf over her nose and mouth and kept her gaze on her lap. Each bump and jostle of the carriage reinforced her new reality.

That day and half the next in the bumpy coach, surround by smelly men who hardly spoke, convinced her even more that her journey was indeed real.

Then at the inn where they lodged for the night, she found rest, sleeping in the best room with three soldiers in the hall at her door and two more stationed outside.

A queen.

Though all the tribe held her father in high esteem, he was far from being a prince.

She remembered her friend's words—the ones he'd whispered in her ear so long ago—and what he'd told her.

Lie with kings.

According to Mama, was that not what queens did?

5

*****

With the burning brazer on one side and the last of the day's light on the other, David found a bit of relief reclining on his balcony. He hated being old and stricken in years, but soon . . . very soon.

His life would end. His mind's eye beheld his heart's rendition of Paradise . . . His thoughts drifted to his three dead sons.

That Amnon and Absalom's lives extended into manhood consoled him, but poor Shimea only drew breath seven days. Dead and gone almost before he lived—for David's sin. As he'd said then, he would go to his son one day.

And it would not be delayed much longer. He shivered violently then the shaking subsided.

Might that very day be the one?

Suddenly, it seemed the sun shone more brightly and offered more heat. He thanked God on high for the respite and momentary relief from his coldness. While he basked in its warmth, he pondered that question.

In the end, he concluded since several matters remained unsettled, his days were not yet complete.

His chamber's door opened, and from the sound of the sandals striking the floor's stones in the adjoining room, it appeared a troop invaded his abode.

"Sire, we found her. We bring Abishag the Shunammite."

His attending servant helped him to his feet.

There she stood, her gown flowing, hair trussed with hundreds of cascading wrinklets, covering her shoulders. She smelled of lilac and roses. He found her beauty quite unbelievable and motioned for her to twirl.

As requested, the young woman slowly pivoted, her lovely hair carpeting her back to her hips.

Her beauty surpassed even Bathsheba in her youth.

In the robes and breastplate of his office, Abiathar stood as a statue next to her. The High Priest recited the words David had heard so many times before. His flesh shivered again, that time as with no intent of lessening.

Would he ever be free from the chill that invaded his bones enough to enjoy her?

"Behold your King, Abishag of the Shunammites. Sire, behold your newest queen."

"Good. Leave us."

His servant reached for his arm, but David shook him away. "Abishag will help me to my bed."

"Yes, my king." The man bowed then backed out of the room and closed the door.

"Such a jewel to look upon you are. Your beauty thrills my heart. Come close to me, my queen."

She hurried beneath his outstretched arm.

"I am in need of your warmth and support."

"Oh, yes, beloved King."

*****

A mere shadow of the shepherd boy, though her king remained quite comely for a man of so many years. Abishag loved him fiercely from the minute her eyes fell on him, even more so than as a girl who'd dreamed of being in his presence.

Certainly, she never expected the night vision to come true. Her chest swelled with her emotion.

She cherished him.

For as long as she'd been aware, David had been her king, her hero. To be his wife, Queen Abishag of Israel, God's chosen people, so honored her. She could scarce believe the Lord's blessings upon her.

His flesh felt like snow against her own. She wrapped warm arms around him and assisted him to his bed despite his shivering. He climbed in then held the covers up for her.

Between the quilts and her own body heat, his shivers finally settled. The depth of his coldness warmed enough not to pain her to the point of pulling away.

That night, her wedding night, was nothing like her mother had spoken of. So different from what she expected, but it pleased her. The king held her tightly and spread her hair over himself.

Every time he snuggled in tighter, she loved him more and thanked God her mother had been wrong. The days turned into weeks, and occasionally, he seemed to rally, able to sit awhile alone without shivering.

Those times, he could move from the bed to his couch or his chair on the balcony with her help to steady him. The servants still served, brought all that he called for, whatever she needed or wanted.

But they no longer even tried to help him do anything in her presence. As his wife, Abishag saw to his every need, and he had no need of the physical intimacy. He could not or would not give her a child. Regarding such, mixed emotions battled within.

The closeness steadily grew between the king and her. He taught her things and spoke of Israel's history, and of the time when he ruled over only Judah.

Abishag adored his stories and delighted in listening to every one, even those he repeated as though the first time told. She couldn't love him more—and not just because he was king.

Apart from being the ruler, the man proved wise and kind and compassionate.

Then one bright skied day, exactly a new moon into her marriage, she mustered the boldness to ask a question of his youth. "My king, when in the field watching your sheep, at the times you slayed the lion and the bear, did help come from Heaven?"

A little laugh cheered her heart, but then he shook his head. "No, my beauty. I think not. Perhaps the Lord fanned my anger against those that threatened. The thought of either enemy stealing one of my father's lambs sent me into a rage which filled me with might and power." He held his hand out.

"I doubt if I could even sling a stone or brandish a sword now."

"No need, my king. You have me . . . And so many mighty men who love you. Why, no enemy would even think of confronting you or your people."

"True. But it is the Lord Who has given us peace." He wrapped one of her curls around his finger. "Tell me, my beautiful queen, why would you ask such a question about help from Heaven?"

"Once, in my twelfth summer while I led my father's sheep to pasture, a lion appeared."

He seemed to sit taller. "What did you do, my love?"

"Well, after I prayed, I determined to stay and fight. I only had my rod and hoped to run him off with it, but then I didn't have to. My guardian angel arrived and whispered in the beast's ear then scratched him heartily."

"How interesting that you, too, came from the sheepcoat to be queen of the Lord's people."

She grinned. Could she love the man more? "Live forever, my king."

"I could, my love. I'm a mere youth compared to Adam and those fathers before Methuselah's flood, but alas. The end of my days draw nigh, and soon, I will be gathered to my fathers."

A tear made its way down her cheek. How could she stand his departing? She hated his words but knew them to be true.

"Don't cry, my love. It is the way of life." He brushed her hair away from her face and held her cheek in the palm of his hand. "You have been such a blessing to me, and I do love you. Have no regrets, little one."

Burying her head into his chest, her tears wet his gown. Then a commotion outside drew her attention. She ran to the balcony and looked over the banister into the city.

"What is it, Abishag?" The distance so weakened his voice, she could barely make it out, almost inaudible.

For a heartbeat, she took in the sight then hurried back to

her husband.

"Someone important is riding in a chariot with other chariots and horsemen, and a troop of soldiers running before him. The people are cheering him, my Lord. What could he want?"

The king laughed. "It is only Adonijah, my son by Haggith. He likes doing such. He means nothing by it."

Abishag's story may even be out before JOHN DAVID'S CALLING scheduled to release in May. So, check at Amazon for its availability to read the wonderful story in its completion.

And now for your sneak peek, the coming September release and Book One of my new Family Saga series . . .

GONE TO TEXAS
Book One of the new
Cross Timber Romance Family Saga series

Chapter one

Dickson County, ten miles south of Charlotte, Tennessee
August 1st, 1840

Alicia's father shook the reins over the mule's back. "Hey, now." Like the good boys they were, the matched pair leaned into their collars. Trace chains jangled, and leather creaked as the wagon's wheels turned. "Watch your brother, sweetheart!" Her mother turned and looked over her shoulder. "And help Esther with the little ones."

For what, Ma?

The tenth time she'd told her that morning?

"Yes, ma'am. I will!" She gave her an exaggerated wave from the porch. Mercy, after seventeen years, a body would think her ma could trust her to be responsible and remember what she'd asked of her.

Watching until the rig crossed the creek, she looked toward the sky and sighed. "Oh Lord, what am I going to do?"

The sound of the big hammer, banging on the anvil pulled her eyes to the shop shed. Flynn raised the sledge again then brought it down with another boom.

"Please, Father God, let us stay. Don't take him away."

A tug on her shirt pulled her around.

"Lesha, I'm powerful hungry."

"Mercy, boy! You just had eggs and cornbread. Did you drink all your milk?"

"Yep." Her brother wiped his mouth with his sleeve.

"Does it break your jaw to say ma'am, Aaron Edmond Van Zandt?"

The six-year-old grinned. "Nope."

"You better watch it."

"Yes, maaa'am." He puffed his chest up, sucked in his poor starving tummy, and grinned even bigger. "Can I eat Arlee's cornbread slab with some honey?"

"No, sir, you certainly may not. You know the rules. If she doesn't clean her plate this meal, she can the next."

"But she hates cornpone, and I love it! And I'm powerful hungry." His brows furrowed. He crossed his arms over his chest and stomped his foot. The porch's floor boards rattled.

"Hey! Do I need to cut a switch? I said no. Now that's enough. Stop badgering me." Another blow pulled her head back to the shed. "Dear Lord, have mercy on us."

"I can help Flynn. Me, him, and Rich are partners."

"Fine by me, unless he sends you away--and if he does, do not harass him like you do me! Just come on over to Aunt Esther's. That's where I'll be if you need me. And no swimming or running off! Hear me?" She pointed her finger at him and wagged it up and down. "Papa will tan both our hides if you get lost again."

"Yes, maaaa'am."

Since he used his manners, she let the sass slide. Her brother ran to help Flynn. "Lord, go before Pa and the others. Put it in that Mister Jenkins' heart to let us stay. And please don't lead Uncle Reagan and Aunt Libby move back to Chicago. I couldn't stand it." She made herself watch the ground walking passed the shed toward Aunt Esther's cabin.

Wouldn't do for Flynn to catch her staring.

Humph. Did he even care that she was alive?

If not for the trouble brewing, the light breeze would have made the sweltering morning half pleasant enough. She liked the cold so much better than the hot, and August was the worst. Perspiration trickled down her back.

Richard ran by on her way. "Where's Aaron?" The little whippersnapper didn't even stop, just kept on running.

"In the shed! And don't be pestering Flynn! You hear me?"

Walking up to the cabin, Auntie followed her three-year-old out onto the porch, smiling. "That boy is always in a hurry. How are you this morning, Alicia?"

"Good. Concerned some, I guess. Maybe a lot, truth be known." She turned to the baby girl and grinned. "Morning, Katie Kay!" She went down onto one knee and opened her arms wide.

The little girl ran to her and threw chubby little arms around her neck. "Lesha!"

"Sure appreciate you coming over. I haven't been feeling so well." She exhaled a heavy sigh and rubbed her swollen belly.

"I'm sorry. Need any help peeling those pears?"

"No, that's all done, and they're sitting in sugar. Been up since daybreak. Thought next, I'd best get some beans to soaking for supper."

"Want me to fetch some water?"

"Please. Laud filled the barrel before he left this morning, so no need to go all the way to the creek." Aunt Ester rested an arm on the top of her tummy, patting it with her hand. "Got any mending? Thought we might sit a spell and throw a stitch or two."

"Sounds good. I'll get the water, then go see."

After filling the big pot, Alicia checked on her sister and Charity--not that those two ever really did anything wrong. But of all days, that'd surely be the one they'd pick to act out, and she wanted to nip any such notion in the bud. She couldn't handle another burden heaped on her shoulders right then. Might just do her in like that last straw.

With a little digging, she came up with two of her father's shirts and one pair of her brother's britches to be mended. That'd give her some her nice time with her aunt on the porch, and she needed to talk.

While Esther sewed, Alicia rocked the baby and read her the story of Noah out of the Bible.

Before any of the young ones asked for dinner, the three-year-old got still in her lap. She pushed off the floor with less pressure a half a dozen or so more times, rocking slower and slower for good measure then carefully stood and carried Katie Kay inside. Easing the little angel down on the bed, she tiptoed out then outside again, pulled her rocker closer to her aunt's.

"Uh . . . have you said anything to Flynn?"

Both of Esther's brows rose. "No, darling, I have not. Haven't had a chance. I know you don't want me to say something in front of anyone, do you?"

"Heaven's no. But . . . what if we have to leave? What if they go back to Chicago? Pa's been talking about going west."

"Oh, from all I hear, Liberty hated Chicago; I don't think Reagan can talk her into that. She said something about Baltimore the other day though. Plenty of work there for a first class fiddler."

Though the remark made Alicia want to scream, she filled her lungs then huffed it out instead, holding her tongue. "That's way farther north, isn't it?"

"Um-hum." Her aunt pulled thread through the fabric then stabbed the button hole again. "In Maryland."

"What would you do?"

"How many times you going to ask me that question?" She grinned. "I go wherever Laud goes, honey. I know he doesn't want the family stretched out all over the country, so I figure he'll follow his big sister around." She added under her breath, "Like a lost pup."

"But being close to family isn't a bad thing." Alicia retrieved the notions from the sewing basket, threaded a needle, then arranged her pa's shirt in her lap to close a torn seam. "Auntie, when you first met Laud, did he love you right off? I mean . . . I love Flynn so much it hurts, and he acts like I'm not even alive."

"Umm, I probably loved him first, too. But it didn't take long to hook him." She glanced up with an understanding grin. "You two have known each other for so long. I'd guess there's an overabundance of . . . you know, familiarity."

Pondering on that perspective, Alicia finished the seam, tested it, then tied off her thread with a knot and bit it loose. "Well, I turned seventeen in January. You married at my age, didn't you? And time could be running out on me That's what I'm afraid of. Especially if there's no good outcome from them going to town. If that Mister Jenkins really owns our land, and we were duped . . ."

"Girl, stop borrowing trouble. Your Pa's a smart man. He'll ferret out the truth." She laughed. "And Heaven help anyone who gets in Liberty's way."

"I think I should say something to him, don't you?"

"You might have the opportunity in a bit. He's supposed to come for dinner. Speaking of which, we best get some more wood for the fire. Figured we could bake some potatoes in the coals once the beans get to boiling. Want to fetch some fatback and onion, too?" She stuck her hand out. "But first? A helping hand, please, ma'am."

Rocking forward, Alicia stood on the upswing, then stuck out her hand to poor Aunt Esther. She set the mending in her sewing box, cradled her extended tummy, and let herself be pulled up. "If you do intend to say something, best get after it before Laud gets back if you want any privacy. Flynn's going to help him shod our off mule this afternoon."

"You really think you'll make another month?"

"Who knows? The midwife said mid-September, but Richard came early, and Katie Kay was late. Guess this one will arrive when he's good and ready."

"A boy, huh?"

The girls came up talking a mile a minute, but both turned their noses up at cornbread and sweet milk. "What's for supper?"

"If Pa gets back, your left-over cornbread first and then--"

"Oh, I ate that already."

Alicia eyed the eleven-year-old hard, but her sister didn't look away or act guilty.

Her best friend in the world and near-constant companion nodded. "Yes, ma'am, she did. About an hour ago." Sounded fishy. Her sister hated cornpone. Then most likely sensing her doubt, Charity added a little good measure. "She did give me a nibble, but she ate most of it all right."

"Umm-hmm, I see. So, is that why Aaron hasn't been hanging around begging for something to eat?"

"Probably not." Arlene shrugged. "More likely because Him and Rich and Flynn are building a fort or something."

With a glance at her aunt, Alicia only shook her head. "Don't be asking for anything to eat before we call you for supper then."

"So, what are we having?"

Aunt Esther spoke up. "Beans seasoned with fatback, baked potatoes, and I figured I'd make a big pan of biscuits."

"Umm, sounds good." In unison the girls asked, "Can we eat early?" They looked at each other and then started their own little clap, clap, slap rhyme together. "Two great minds thinking just the same, playing the game, looking for fame. Now it's sure to happen if we say each other's name!" Both of them hollered the other's name then collapsed to the ground in a pile of giggles.

"Silly girls. Go on now before I find a couple of hoes and put you two to work."

Just as she figured, at the mention of work, Arlene and Charity took off.

"Don't get out of hollering range."

Her sister gave her an over the shoulder wave without looking back.

With the fire stoked, the beans seasoned up, and the big pot hung over the fire, Alicia went to greasing the potatoes. After a while, Aunt Esther pronounced the coals just right and poked the potatoes into them. But still no boys. The lady went back to the porch and her mending. Shadows put it well past midday.

"Think we should go look for Flynn and boys?"

"I say why borrow trouble. The milk and cornbread isn't going anywhere."

"And do you know when Uncle Laud plans on being back?"

The rocker stopped, but she kept on sewing. "He figured well before dark but wasn't sure. Mister Douglas said he might have more than the two that needed new iron."

"A tomato or two could have ripened. Some okra for sure. I could go check if you want me to. Both would go good in the beans."

"They would indeed, and . . . Never can tell." Esther laughed. "A lovesick girl could get a moment alone with her sweetheart on a garden."

If only Flynn was sure enough her beau, she'd be as happy as the queen bee, but she had no inclination that he wanted the position at all. She just had to say something to him before everything fell apart. "Well, should the fellows do come around, could you maybe keep those boys up here, and send him to help?"

"Sure, sweetie. I can do that."

All the way from the cabin to the two-acre garden the three families shared, she searched for any sight of Flynn or the boys. The spring plants had all but petered out, except for the late corn, a few tomatoes, and the okra. Would the clan even be there long enough to plant a fall garden? Oh, things had to work out.

Please, God.

The soft ground reminded her of how much work everyone put in getting it ready. She looked around again. Where had those boys gotten off to?

Doing her best to put them out of mind, she got busy, holding her apron up and dropping the few ripened-enough-to-pick tomatoes then went to work on the okra. The more it got picked, the more it produced, and her ma knew a hundred great ways to fix it, too. At the end of the shoulder-high rows of plants, something hit her arm.

Careful not to spill her full apron, she turned a full circle. Was one of those scalawags chunking rocks? If it was Aaron, she'd--

"Over here."

Stepping toward the sound of Flynn's voice, she held her chest, so her heart couldn't beat its way out. After about ten strides, she spotted him crouched down and hiding in the last row of corn stalks. "What are you doing?"

"Trying not to get found. We've been playing hide-and-seek." He lowered his hand. "Get down, Richard's It, and I don't want him to find me first."

She knelt beside him. Could he hear her stupid heart? Surely it would lead the boys straight to him. Cotton suddenly filled her mouth sucking every bit of moisture. She had nothing to swallow, no matter how badly she needed to, and she could barely draw breath her throat closed so tight. "Flynn . . . uh."

"Shush." He put his finger to his lips then whispered, "I hate being It."

Understandable, she did to. One more thing in common. One more reason to love him. She put her free hand beside her mouth. "It's just that . . . uh . . . Oh, mercy. Please don't go away to Baltimore. I'm so afraid."

Her confession obviously swayed him, and he rocked away from her, falling on his backside. He stared at her for what had to be an hour or more. What was he thinking? Was he mad at her? She should have kept her mouth shut. Then he smiled.

"Really? Why do you care where we go? And what's got you scared?"

"Moving." Her cheeks warmed. "I don't want . . . Uh, I mean, I'd hate it if . . ."

"So, you don't hate me?"

"Hate you? Oh, heavens no! I uh . . ." She swallowed. "I uh . . . I don't hate you. It's kind of, sort of, the opposite."

"Really? That is not how you've been acting for the last ten months." He scoffed. "Before--when we were growing up--whenever we'd come visit or you and your folks came to see us, we always had a great time, you and me. But then once we all moved here together . . . well . . . you haven't had a thing to do with me."

"Mercy, Reagan Flynn O'Neal, Junior!" She touched his cheek. "I've been . . . uh . . ." Why were the words so hard to say? He was right there, and she couldn't tell him her heart.

He took her hand and tugged. She released her apron and fell into his arms in slow motion. His lips touched hers.

"Oooo! Nasty! Why'd you do it, partner?" Her brother's face puckered as if he'd been forced to drink vinegar. "Flynn and Lesha! Kissing! Kissing! Kissing! Yuck!" The boy turned and ran toward the cabins, calling over his shoulder, "I'm telling!"

She pushed herself away and scrambled to her feet. "Aaron! Wait!" She took two steps toward her brother then turned back.

Flynn hiked both shoulders. "What can I say? I'm sorry." Then he grinned. "That we got caught--not that I kissed you."

Sharing his sentiments failed to reduce the fear in her heart. What an awful situation. Oh Lord! She had to get to her little brother! Why had Flynn kissed her?

"Are you going to take my switching?"

"I'll be happy to if Uncle Seve will let me."

Chapter Two

Though she should run, the instituter of her present troubles sitting on his rump in the corn rows and grinning up at her like a new-found pup . . . The sight nailed Alicia's feet to the ground. "You'd really take a beating for me?"

He nodded. "That and more."

"Come on!" The sound of her brother's voice approached. Good! That meant he hadn't told yet! "See, there they is, Rich! Just like I said."

She turned around. Her bratty brother and his shadow stood wide eyed, pointing and staring from the last row of okra. "Aaron! Richard!" What should she say? The desire to lie was strong, but she'd not done anything wrong. Her lips accidentally brushing against Flynn's wasn't a big sin or anything.

"You're getting it when Pa get home! I'm telling!"

Richard chimed in with a smirky little grin she'd love to slap off his face. "Me, too! I'm telling Uncle Reagan and Aunt Lib! Yous guys are going to get it!"

Flynn rose, dusting dirt and broken corn leaves from his backside, then stood beside her. "Come on, partners. We didn't do anything wrong. Let's get us some dinner. I'm powerful hungry. How about you men?"

Aaron scoffed and pursed his lips at her. "I surely am on account of Arlee's slab of cornpone and that little dab of honey is long gone. Auntie's feeding us right?"

"Yes, sir." Flynn strolled out of the garden with a boy tagging along with him, one on each hip.

"Hope the milk's cool."

Would he be able to get them to keep their mouths shut? Should he even try? Last thing she wanted was Aaron having something to hang over her head. The little booger would spill his guts sooner or later. Best to fess up her own self and let her parents know she'd not invited the kiss and tell them her heart.

Sure looked like Flynn might love her, too.

Why else would he want to kiss her? Or be willing to take a whipping to save her from one?

And more, he'd said. What exactly could that mean? That he'd be willing to die for her? She gasped and held her heart at the thought. After, taking two steps, she had to twirl. Didn't that prove he loved her? It had to! Had his heart been revealed? Mercy, she needed to know for certain, didn't she? He surely wouldn't steal a kiss if he didn't love her.

Would he? No. Flynn wasn't like that. She'd never witnessed him in any bad light.

Oh man, she needed some time alone with Aunt Esther, needed to talk with her and get her advice. But the boys were headed there, and surely Katie Kay had woken up. Soon enough, the little doll would be taking one long nap instead of two. Her feet carried her to the garden's gate, but on second thought, she returned to the scene of the kiss and gathered the tomatoes and okra she'd dropped.

Back to the gate with her apron full, she pondered which way to go from there. Did she want to face the little skunks or give Flynn time to talk some sense into them? Then there was the vegetables to add to the beans. Two running blurs from the direction of the Worley's cabin turned into Arlene and Charity and reached her before she had the time to make any decision.

Her sister won the race, skidded to a stop a few feet away, then gulped her lungs full. Holding her hands out in a very dramatic gesture, she gasped, catching a quick breath. "Did you do it? Did you really kiss . . ." The girl grabbed another breath. "Flynn?"

Charity snatched a hold of Arlene and used her to stop. "Oh Lesha! Is it true?" She gasped then swooned. "That's so romantic! Tell us! Aaron said he saw you two."

Was she ever as bad as those two? "Well, yes, I suppose. His lips accidentally grazed mine when he tugged on my hand, but . . ."

Her little sister jumped up and down, covering her nose and mouth with her hands. "Oooo! Your first kiss! You're a real woman now, Lesha!" She stopped hopping around and gazed longingly, hands clasped together over her heart. "What was it like?" Such a breathy voice. When had she gotten so dramatic? "Are you getting married now?"

Grabbing her friend's arm, Charity shook her head. "No, silly! They can't!" She looked up at Alicia. "They're cousins, and cousins can't marry. It's against the law! Isn't it?"

Leaning in, Alicia glared at the ten-year-old. "Don't be ridiculous! We aren't real cousins! Ma and Aunt Libby are best friends, closer than sisters, since, since . . . forever. But your brother and I have no blood relations at all. Your mam is only my honorary aunt. You know that."

The younger girl stepped back and raised her nose an inch. "Well, so what? She still isn't going to like it one bit, you kissing my brother, and--"

"He kissed me, Charity!"

"And you kissed him back, didn't you?" She put her fists on her hips. "Are you saying you didn't? Aaron said you and Flynn was kissing. Each. Other. Papa isn't going to like it either."

Had she? Kissed him back? She couldn't remember. Oh no! Had the sweet memory faded so soon? "Haven't you two got something to do beside pester me? I'm sure your hoes are right where we left them."

Her sister stretched to her full height. "Pa said we had today off, so there."

"He also said I was in charge, so if you want to enjoy what's left of this day." She sighed. "I suggest you best get to it and leave me alone."

"Well, Aunt Esther said to fetch you. The beans are getting close and she wants the okra to boil some. You better go. 'Sides, she knows about the spooning, too, and she wants to talk to you."

"Here, hold out your aprons." They did, and she dumped her load evenly between them. "You two take this to Auntie, and tell her I'll be there before long." The girls looked at their load then back at her like she was insane or something. "Best get, or I'm serious. You'll be hoeing till dark."

Both girls retreated, muttering. "I never . . . a meanie."
"Yeah. She . . ."

But Alicia let it slide. She needed time to think and dealing with those two immature little horrors was too much like work. Hoping to give the little boys enough time to finish their meal and get, she decided as hot as it was in her cabin, that'd probably be the only place she could be alone. Opening both doors wide helped some, but what little breeze from the morning had stilled to about nothing.

If she sat in Pa's seat at the table, she could see Esther's cabin. Just as she figured, the baby had her nap out and played with her rag doll on the porch while her mamma rocked and visited with Flynn. The little squealers were evidently still at their cornbread and sweet milk. She couldn't see the girls, but they'd probably climbed back up into their tree, telling each other how awful she was.

For sharing her heart. How could that have been so awful? The river of sweat running down her back pert near soaked her dress. Maybe a stroll down to the creek would dry her out some and give her a little more time. Auntie would understand if she didn't go right away. Her stomach was so knotted. Would she ever want to eat again? A long pull of creek water might do her some good.

Might even give her the opportunity to meet up with Flynn getting his own self a refreshing drink.

He'd surely note the direction she went.

But would Aunt Esther let him follow?

Hope you enjoyed these peaks at my two new titles! I know the Biblical-fiction might not be the genre you usually read, but I believe I AM MY BELOVED is an especially anointed story, and I so hope you'll try it. Several times when writing it, I would have to stop for my tears and worship the Mighty God of Heaven and Earth . . .

I AM MY BELOVED will most likely already be out and available before JOHN DAVID'S CALLING.

GONE TO TEXAS is coming in September!

Caryl's Titles' Five-Star Reviews Historical Texas Romances

...for Vow Unbroken

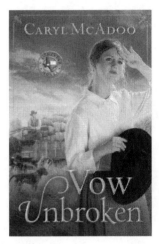

With an intriguing plot line and well-developed characters, McAdoo, who's written nonfiction and children's fiction, delivers an engaging read for her first adult historical romance.
--*Publishers Weekly*

After reading Caryl McAdoo's story of Henry and Susannah in "VOW UNBROKEN," I felt like I'd had another adventure with Tom Sawyer and Becky, this time as young adults. --Alan Daugherty: columnist *The News-Banner*

...for Hearts Stolen

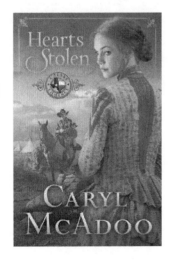

Get ready for a wild, uplifting, heart-tugging, page-turning ride. *Hearts Stolen* grabbed me at the start. Sassy's feisty, fighting spirit...I couldn't set it down. Burnt dinner, but forget eating, I ate this book up. This master storyteller weaves Texas history into a well-crafted plot with unforgettable and totally loved characters. --Holly Michael, author *Crooked Lines*

...for *Hope Reborn*

With memorable characters, Caryl's signature humor, and plenty of adventure, drama, and romance, "Hope Reborn" is anything but fluff. A strong message of salvation runs through, but well within the storyline. Enjoyed a unique twist with May writing the stories of the previous characters – clever and fun!
--Pam Morrison, Tennessee reader

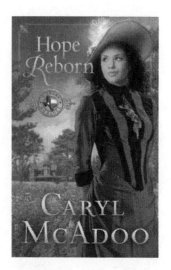

... *Sins of the Mothers*

I tell you what, folks, this girl can write! I do love this series, and maybe most especially this book. Mary Rachel Buckmeyer can out-negotiate the experts, out-guess marketing trends, and out-stubborn a mule. Trouble is, she tends to follow her heart into disaster. The guy she marries has meandering eye, lies like a braided rug, and has all the loyalty of a new-born pup. Mary hops from one frying pan to another until one man shows up who could steady her and get her out of the fixes she gets herself into. Such a great story! I know you'll love.
--Anne Baxter Campbell, author *The Truth Trilogy: The Roman's Quest, Marcus Varitor, Centurion,* and *The Truth Doesn't Die*

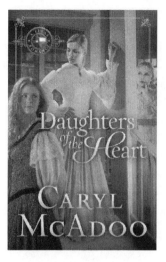

...Daughters of the Heart

A fun packed Christian romance novel with plenty of action, heartbreak, tears, deception, twists, and turns. [The three sisters] made a pact never to break their father's heart, but when suitors show up, it's hard for them to stay determined. Will they find true love? Will Dad accept a suitor for them and give his blessings?

--Joy Gibson, a Tennessee reader and pastor's wife

...for Just Kin

I have followed this historical romance series from the beginning and they just keep getting better. Lacey Rose loves Charley and is devastated when he leaves to fight for Texas with the Confederate army. Charley doesn't realize Lacey Rose is in love with him but is both surprised and pleased with the goodbye kiss she gives him. After Charley sends a hurtful letter trying to discourage her from waiting for him, Lacey Rose runs away and ends up in all kinds of

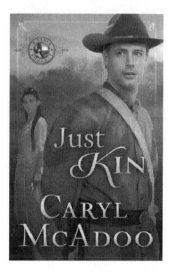

trouble. Charley also stirs up some trouble of his own when he begins looking for her. Don't miss out on this book. I loved it!

--Louise Koiner, Texas beta reader

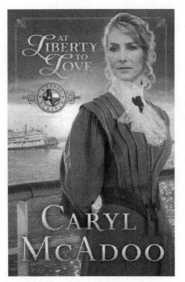

...At Liberty to Love

This was one of the best books I have ever read. The characters got so close to your heart you wish they were your family. From the beginning till the end you fell in love with each of them. The two adopted baby boys brought laughs and joy. The love story has strong Christian threads throughout. Highly recommend this book. You will love it.

--Jane Moody, reader

...Covering Love

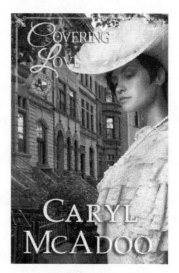

I loved reading Covering Love, an amazing story filled with all the extended Buckmeyer's family members with younger ones' love story. Great plots for each character brought laughter and tears throughout this great historical romance. Six year old little Evelyn (Evie) reading May's story about Houston and Leilani's adventure on the Gray Lady added a lovely perspective to this adventurous book filled with love, faith, determination, hard work, and romance. I look forward to reading book nine, Mighty to Save. McAdoo's books *must* be read by those who enjoy historical romance that are filled with clean, heartfelt romance and the Gospel!!

--Marilyn Ridgway, reader

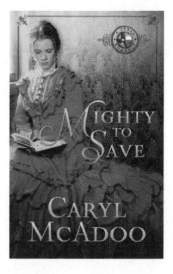

...*Mighty to Save*

Mighty to Save is one of the best books I've read, filled with characters who become friends. Emotions and all my senses were right there for the beatings, the tent revival scenes, the romance and heartache. Tears, praising, singing in the Spirit are throughout this magnificent, powerful, heartfelt, sensational story. Caryl McAdoo is one gifted author. Mighty to Save is going to be used for His glory.

– Marilyn Ridgway, a reader

...*Chief of Sinners*

I believe this one is my favorite, the most gripping and emotional. A few times I wanted to grab a couple of tissues. I just could not stop reading. So many twists and turns involved. Such a wonderful story that show the power of forgiveness, letting go, moving on and having second chances. The book is full of faith and inspiration. Christian Fiction cannot get better than this. Chief of Sinners is most definitely a must read. **100 stars**!

– Amy Campbell, reader

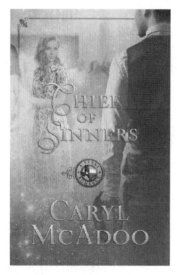

Companion and Other Historicals

...The Bedwarmer's Son

I really loved this book...didn't want to put it down. I love the way it's different than most historical romance novels, and I read many. I loved the way the author used the old man to tell Jasmine's story. I also loved both Wills' stories. Being a Christian novel just made it better. I enjoyed it so much I hated to see it end. This is the first novel I've ever read by this author, but I doubt it will be my last.

-- BJ Robinson, Author of *River Oaks Plantation*, *Siege of Azalea Plantation*, *Azalea Plantation* and others

...Son of Promise

[It] opens in Texas, early 1950's. McAdoo brings in some characters from previous books. I loved the history of Texas and especially the colloquialisms. A child born from a one-night stand when Travis Buckmeyer was just a young unmarried man is introduced. It takes the family a lot of faith in God and doing the right thing. This story shows that the love of God within can overcome all obstacles. Your past does not determine your future. Such a gentle story of faith, love, forgiveness, and yielding the sinful man to a higher power.   –Judy Schexnayder

...Silent Harmony

A sweet Christian historical romance that will warm the reader's heart. Set in the years following the American Civil War, people have lost so much, but the love of the Lord remains. McAdoo has created some delightful characters that took up residence in my soul. Grown sisters were realistically drawn with their sibling quibbles and their loyalty to each other. A perfectly delightful tale.   –Julia Wilson, UK reader

...John David's Calling

Revival, Pentecostal healing ministries as David is called from the staunch, sedate church of his grandfather who raised him to the Spirit-led ministry style of his father who wasn't in his life much as a child. He's torn between obeying God and devotion to his grandfather. In the mix is a school girl he has his heart set on marrying. There are moments of crying, both for praising the Lord and the suffering of someone as well as several laugh out loud situations. A wonderful story of obeying God.

– Cindy Nipper, an Oregon reader

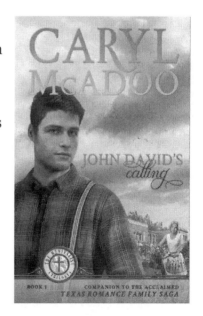

Contemporary Red River Romances

...The Preacher's Faith

This was my first book to read by Caryl McAdoo and I absolutely loved it. I will be reading more. I love the way she prays that her story gives God Glory and dedicates The Preacher's Faith to Him and His Kingdom...a good clean book to read. I was drawn into this story right from the start. I loved this book and can't wait for book two.
 --Elizabeth Dent, reader

...for Sing a New Song

Sing a New Song is a delightful breath of air. Caryl eloquently brings her audience nearer to God [with] fresh ways of viewing Christian life and all it offers. The characters are loveable and humorous. Illuminating, the story shares the Gospel beautifully. Samuel's sermons as well as the gorgeous lyrics of Mary Esther's songs fill our hearts with newfound worship. Truly an inspiring tale. Christian fiction in its best; a romantic love story that brings its readers closer to God. A treasure for sure.
 --Christine Barber, author of *Broken to Pieces*

...for *One and Done*

Faster than a major league outfielder pulling down a popup fly ball, this romance is guaranteed to snag baseball lovers and romance readers alike. Written with wit, verve and Caryl's usual flare for dialect and spicy dialogue, this is no saccharine, man-meets-woman story sanitized romantic fairytale, but so real in the mind, you can almost smell locker room sweat or mouthwatering scent of Mexican food. Identification with the hero and heroine is nearly immediate. With so much to rave about, I cannot begin to cover all the delightful surprises, so the reader simply must buy "One and Done" to see for themselves.

–Cass Wessel, multi-published author of devotions

Contemporary Apple Orchard Romance

...for *Lady Luck's a Loser*

A very unique, witty plot. I couldn't put it down. I love that my favorite characters are still active at the end of the book, only their relationships have changed. What a way for Dub to fulfill his promises to his deceased wife. Love, trust, forgiveness, and many emotions make for a well written book.

--Joy Gibson, Tennessee

The Generations Biblical fiction

... A Little Lower Than the Angels Caryl McAdoo used her research and knowledge of biblical scripture combined with an incredible imagination as a foundation to fill in the gaps of the story of Adam and Eve and their children. I was caught up in the story from page one to the ending. I particularly appreciated the "Search the Scriptures" section at the end which explains some of the Biblical clues for this work of fiction. I loved it and highly recommend it.   --Judy Levine, reader, Arizona

... Then the Deluge Comes Deluge is the second book in The Generations Series, and if the books still to follow are as good as this one and the first one in the series are it is going to be an incredible series. The author has a way of breathing life and emotions into the characters that made me feel like I was on the sidelines watching their stories unfold. This is some of the best Biblical fiction that I have read and I look forward to the rest of the series. I was furnished with an e-copy of the book in return for an honest review.   --Ann Ellison, reader, Texas

... Replenish the Earth

Caryl tells the story of the flood in such a unique way.. I like how she makes the characters so real. This Bible story just comes to life. Noah's family on the Ark taking care of the animals and then when they come to a stop, starting all over on a barren earth. I found that the family conversations, their actions and the descriptions just made this more real to me. I like that Caryl gives scripture references and her thoughts at the end of the book.

--Deanna Stevens, reader, Nebraska

... Children of Eber

So much of the tale remains faithful to the Scriptural account, but where there is silence, Caryl's author voice sings through in delicious detail. For the reader familiar with the Biblical account, she fleshes out a mere paragraph or two until the narrative vibrates with life. As if transported through a time machine, the reader reenters the world of the Ancients experiencing their lives and seeing their surroundings afresh. Those who know the Biblical account will delight in following the ancient pair into Egypt, then back to Canaan again.

--Cass Wessel, devotional author

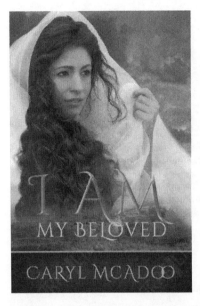

...I AM My Beloved

Caryl McAdoo makes scripture come alive in a very real, identifiable way in a fascinating account of one woman who changed history by her love for God and her choices. We can all relate to Abishag's traits which makes the story so believable. Having studied Song of Solomon over a decade, I was delighted at the story line that had such beauty and passion, intertwined with heartache and the reality of life. Full of mystery, intrigue and fervent love, I was caught up in the story, not wanting the end. --Vickie Cleveland, author of *An Invitation into His Chambers...the Power of Intimacy with God*

Mid-Grade that Grandparents love

...The King's Highway

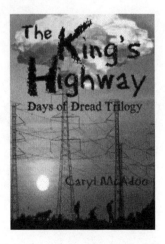

I can't remember when I have enjoyed reading a book as much as this one. If I really like a book, I can read it in a day. I read this twice in two days. I couldn't quit reading. It has to be right up there with my all-time favorites. If anyone thinks they won't read it because it's for mid-grade, I encourage you to reconsider. You'll miss a blessing. Anyone reading age from the mid grades to senior citizens (that's me) will love this book. The characters in the book are delightful.   --Louise Koiner, reader, Texas

Non-Fiction

... *Story & Style, The Craft of Writing Creative Fiction*

    This is a wonderful book for those wanting to learn more about writing. I know from experience. The content helped me tremendously!! It especially helped me gain a clear picture of POV and the use of action versus attribution to strengthen my writing and make my debut book the best it can be. Thank you, Caryl, your continued helping hands are a blessing to many of us rookie writers!
    --Andy Skrzynski, author of *The New World, A Step Backward*

Coming Soon ...

Historical

Texas Romance Companions
The RevivalistTrilogy
   Hannah's Wilderness, 1951-   book two   January, 2019
   King David's Tabernacle   book three   September, 2019

Others
   Bipartisan Love   May 15, 2019

Cross Timber Romance Family Saga
   Gone to Texas, 1840-   book one   September, 2018

Contemporary Romance

The Pitch
King of Texas, starring Patrick Henry Buckmeyer III

Mystery

Prophetic Justice

Mid-grade & Young Adult, Grandparents, too!

Days of Dread Trilogy
   The Sixth Trumpet book two
   The Kidron Valley book three

The Texas Romance Family Sagas

(Prelude) *VOW UNBROKEN*, 1832

Book #1 *HEARTS STOLEN*, 1839-1844

Book #2 *HOPE REBORN*, 1850-1851

Book #3 *SINS OF THE MOTHERS*, 1851-1852

Book #4 *DAUGHTERS OF THE HEART*, 1853-1854

Book #5 *JUST KIN*, 1861-1865

Book #6 *AT LIBERTY TO LOVE* 1865-1866

Book #7 *COVERING LOVE* 1885-1886

Book #8 *MIGHTY TO SAVE* 1850-60s &1918-1925

Book #9 *CHIEF OF SINNERS* 1926-1950

Companion books to this popular series:

THE BEDWARMER'S SON 1857 & 1928- (parallel stories)

SON OF PROMISE 1950

JOHN DAVID'S CALLING 1968-1970, The Revivalist Trilogy

All of Caryl's Books

Historical Christian
Texas Romance Family Saga series *Vow Unbroken 1832 / Hearts Stolen 1839-1844 / Hope Reborn 1850-51 / Sins of the Mothers 1851-53 / Daughters of the Heart 1853-54 / Just Kin 1861-65 / At Liberty to Love 1865-66 / Covering Love 1885-86 / Mighty to Save 1918-1924 / Chief of Sinners 1826-1951*
Texas Romance Companion Books *The Bedwarmer's Son,* 1859 & 1926 / *Son of Promise,* 1950 / The Revivalist Trilogy book one *John David's Calling,* 1968-70 /
Cross Timber Romances Family Saga *Gone to Texas, 1840 /*
Others *Silent Harmony 1867 /*

Contemporary Christian
Red River Romances *The Preacher's Faith / Sing a New Song / One and Done*
Apple Orchard Romances *Lady Luck's a Loser*

Biblical Fiction
The Generations - *A Little Lower Than the Angels / Then the Deluge Comes / Replenish the Earth / Children of Eber*
Others – *I AM My Beloved*

Mid-Grade / Young Adult River Bottom Ranch Stories - *The Adventures of Sergeant Socks: The Journey Home, bk 1 / The Bravest Heart, bk 2 / Amazing Graci, Guardian of the River Bottom Goats, bk 3 //* Days of Dread Trilogy - *The King's Highway, bk 1*

Miscellaneous Novels *The Thief of Dreams* ~ **not written for the Christian market!** / *The Price Paid (based on WWII true story) / Absolute Pi* (audio; mystery) / *Apple Orchard B&B* (re-released as Lady Luck's a Loser)

Non-fiction *Great Firehouse Cooks of Texas / Antiquing in North Texas / Story & Style, The Craft of Writing Creative Fiction*

Reach out to the author!

Website	http://www.CarylMcAdoo.com
Newsletter	http://tinyurl.com/TheCaryler
YouTube	http://bit.ly/2qGJoToBlog *(Caryl's new songs!)*
Blogs	http://www.CarylMcAdoo.blogspot.com Heart"wings" Blog
Facebook	www.facebook.com/CarylMcAdoo.author
Twitter	http://www.twitter.com/CarylMcAdoo
GoodReads	http://tinyurl.com/GoodReadsCaryl
Google+	http://tinyurl.com/CarylsGooglePlus
Pinterest	http://www.pinterest.com/CarylMcAdoo
LinkedIn	www.linkedIn.com/CarylMcAdoo

Author Pages : *(please follow)*

Amazon	http://tinyurl.com/CarylsAmazonAuthorPage
BookBub	https://www.bookbub.com/authors/caryl-mcadoo
Simon & Schuster	http://tinyurl.com/S-SCarylsPage
Email	CarylMcAdoo@gmail.com

Author reaching out to you!

Hey dear Readers!

What a blessing and gift from God you are! I'm so grateful that you've stepped out to read my novel and hope you enjoyed the story and found it gives God glory! My desire is that each one brings you closer to Him and offers scriptural principles and issues to ponder.

If you indeed enjoy the stories, I could use your help in spreading the word of these Kingdom books! To stay on top of all my book news (debuts, sales, awards) in order to share with your reading friends, I encourage you to subscribe to *The Caryler*, my quarterly newsletter. I try to make it fun with news, scripture, lyrics, including a few of my favorite things.

Speaking of lyrics, I'm so blessed that God gives me new songs! There's nothing I love more than praising and worshiping Him with music which lends to being called the Singing Pray-er. Now you can hear them at my YouTube channel! Please subscribe so you won't miss any new songs!

Reviews are so important to authors, so it'll be a big boon if you could take the time to leave a quick review (doesn't have to be long) at Amazon, Goodreads, your blog, and anywhere you enjoy reading about books. Click "Follow" while you're there, too! ☺

Of course, tell your friends—word of mouth is invaluable!

I love hearing from you and have a group of special readers who help me more than most. Let me know if you'd like to join my street team's Facebook group, Carylers Choir review crew.

Stop by my Facebook page; I just love connecting! Just search Caryl McAdoo. And last but never least, I pray that God will bless you as you have blessed me, that His favor will envelope all you do!

Love in Christ and many blessings,

Caryl

A few links Others might find helpful:

Needing help with your online presence? Go to Rocksteady Resolutions for websites, email lists, and all social media and marketing assistance. Janis McAdoo will be a God-sent blessing to you!

Have a Book you want to Promote or Publish? I highly recommend Celebrate Lit Publishing for excellent royalties, real help in marketing, and a Christian publisher of the highest integrity.

Subscribe to receive free and low-cost Christian books in your Inbox! BookBub and The Celebration Reading Room

Multi Author Collections (I'm a part of) / Lockets & Lace Thanksgiving Books & Blessings

BookFacebook groups I love: Heart"Wings" Blog and More wonderful devotionals and ministry moments
Christian Indie Books great place to find books bargains and new authors (sometimes even FREE)
Christian Indie Authors Readers Group another great place to meet new authors and book deals (FREE, too, sometimes)
5-Star Reviews of Christian Fiction: Find readers' favorites here! Join and post your own reviews of books you love!
Celebrate Lit Community Forum Keep up with Christian fiction in a fine way

Blogs I love : Heart"wings" Blog with wonderful daily devotionals that amazingly seem to be exactly what readers need to hear that very day!
The Word and the Music Personal—writing and my books
Sweet American Sweethearts Daily tidbits of history
The Bread Believer Faith, Food, Fitness and Freedom

Made in the USA
Columbia, SC
30 May 2021